My concern this night, however, as I crawled between my thin blanket and straw-stuffed pallet, was not for my disguise.

Here in the dark now, with only the soft sound of snores around me, my thoughts returned to the woman I'd discovered dead at the foot of the tower. Angry all at once, I wished I had a name to put to her. Surely by now Leonardo and the surgeon had discovered her identity, perhaps even learned the truth of what had happened to her. And, not too long ago, I might have been privy to this information, as well.

I sighed, my moment of anger fading into regret. What did I expect? Ever since the matter of the Conte di Ferrara's gruesome murder had been resolved some weeks earlier, my role as the Master's confidante had begun to diminish. It had been an eventuality that Signor Luigi, who was seemingly well acquainted with the workings of Leonardo's workshop, predicted.

"I have seen it happen many times," the tailor dolefully had warned. *"Your Signor Leonardo will chose one of his apprentices as his particular pet, to assist him with special projects or simply to amuse him. But, of course, it never lasts. Handsome and accomplished as he is, Leonardo is a glorious flame to you tiny young moths, and it is little wonder that you find yourself burned at the end of the day."*

Of course, I had not believed Luigi's words of caution. I was certain that I, above all the other apprentices, held a special place in the Master's heart. Why, he even had kept his earlier promise and taught me the rudimentary strategy of chess, a game that had played a prominent role in resolving the mystery behind the death of Il Moro's cousin.

We had sat down to the chessboard every evening for perhaps a fortnight. But then he had begged off one evening and then another. Our games dwindled to once a week for another two weeks, and then ceased altogether. It was at that point that I had noticed Tito assisting him on a regular basis.

The son of a boat builder, young Tito had some knowledge of both seamanship and woodworking. Doubtless, his had been a talent that Leonardo would have found useful as he took his most recent inventions from paper to reality. And so Tito became the new favorite, while I was again relegated to helping mix gesso and preparing plaster and tracing stencils.

"See where your misplaced vanity gets you," I muttered into the darkness.

For it had been flattering to have the Master's ear, even if it usually had not been my advice he had sought, but rather my presence to serve as a sounding board for his own ideas. And I could not deny that I had enjoyed those days of donning disguises and skulking about in the night in search of a killer . . . this despite how dangerous that role had soon proved to be. But now, my day's greatest excitement was waiting to learn if I would be one of the apprentices chosen to climb the rickety scaffolding in the antechamber we currently were painting so I could help prepare another section of the wall for fresco.

Was all of this worth the masquerade?

I had assumed when I joined the Master's workshop that my talents would be recognized from the start. I had been humbled to realize that most of the other apprentices could paint quite as well as I, some even better. And talent, I swiftly learned, was not as important as being able to imitate the Master's own style of painting. How else could he fulfill his commissions and cover wall after wall with frescoes, if he did not have an army of assistants who could paint in his same manner? Their job was to fill in backgrounds and render minor figures so that the finished work appeared painted by a single artist.

I had been forced to unlearn much of what knowledge of technique I had gained to this point. It could be months, or even years, before the Master deemed me accomplished enough to paint on my own. But would I be able to keep up my boyish masquerade for as long as that took? Even in the short time I had been at the castle, I had noticed even the younger of Leonardo's apprentices beginning to grow their way into manhood. Surely people would wonder when only I did not begin to sprout a beard or take on a deeper timbre to my voice.

Saints' blood, it was not fair! My sex should not have kept me from pursuing the painter's life. It would have been different had I wished to be a mason, or some other vocation which required physical strength. But even the Master often exclaimed that painting, unlike sculpture, was something that could be done wearing silks and velvets. Surely this meant a woman as well as a man could become a great master of that art.

I was well on my way to a bout of full-blown self-pity, when the day's exertions finally outweighed my distress. Thus, I was sleeping quite soundly when, just after midnight, I abruptly awakened to the soft sound of a footstep beside my bed. Even had I not recognized the familiar tall shadow beside me, the impatient shake of my blanketed foot would have told me who stood there.

"Dino, why are you sleeping?" the Master softly demanded, releasing my nether limb. "Come, we have work to do."

Work? I suppressed a drowsy groan. Surely after all we already had done this day, he could not want to test yet another piece of machinery.

But then again, perhaps he could.

I yawned and obediently struggled from my blanket to a sitting position. Leonardo loomed over me, distinguishable from the shadows only by the slightest flash of reddish gold where a sliver of moonlight brushed his russet mane.

"Shall I meet you in your workshop?" I whispered back, scrubbing the sleep from my eyes.

He nodded. "Do not tarry, my dear boy. I believe you will find this to be of no little interest," he replied and then vanished back through the curtain as silently as he'd come.

I must make clear that it was not odd for Leonardo to be

wandering about well after midnight. Like many men of great genius, he managed with but a few hours of slumber each night. Neither was it unusual for him to awaken one of us apprentices to join in his nocturnal forays. His reasons for searching out such companionship, however, were well beyond reproach . . . contrary to vile whispers from certain foul-minded inhabitants of the castle who hinted at more prurient motives!

The simple truth was that the Master had a habit of undertaking more commissions at one time than a single man could handle. Habitually leaving projects half-completed, he often found himself forced by irate patrons to finish a particular painting or fresco under threat of forfeiting his fee. Under such circumstances, the apprentice served as a much-needed second set of hands.

On occasion when I was the chosen apprentice, however, it seemed the Master accomplished rather less work and rather more talking. I never minded, for his lectures were fraught with odd concepts and fascinating theories that kept me wide-eyed. Too, I suspected that Leonardo sometimes suffered from the malady that could lay low even the most brilliant of men . . . in other words, loneliness.

Though he easily moved about with the highborn and could readily pass for one of their number, he was not himself of the nobility. I had learned that he was in truth the illegitimate son of prominent notary but, at the same time, he could hardly be considered on par with the castle's servants. Neither did he have much in common with the town's self-satisfied merchants and boastful guild members.

Indeed, he was a man apart, forced by both his genius and his aloof nature to exist on a rather solitary social plane. He might be consumed by his work; still, I had no doubt he required that same necessary if often banal interaction with his fellows that we all did. And so I never begrudged the lost hours of sleep when he summoned me on one of these nocturnal adventures.

I waited long enough to make sure that none of the other

apprentices had been awakened by his visit. Then, fumbling a bit in the dark, I relaced my corset beneath the tunic I wore as a nightshirt and pulled my trunk hose and shoes back on. Grabbing up my jerkin lest the night air be too chill, I quietly threaded my way through my slumbering fellows and into the night.

I had to admit to a bit of excitement as I softly knocked at Leonardo's door and then entered as he bade me. Here, again, was the breathless anticipation that I had felt as I assisted him in searching for the Cónte di Ferrara's killer. Could his summons this night perhaps have something to do with the woman whose lifeless body I had found?

Unfortunately, I would have to wait a few minutes for my answer, for the Master was engrossed in another project.

He gestured me to join him at the small round table where he was sitting, his only other illumination save the dying coals in the hearth a few candle stubs. Normally, the table was piled with perhaps a dozen books, fully half of his library! Now, however, the heavy tomes lay on the floor at his feet, the small space given over to a scrap of paper upon which he was adding a few swift chalk lines.

As I had noted when Vittorio and I left off our bundle a few hours earlier, the room had changed little in the few weeks since I'd last set foot there. The chamber held the same modest furnishing: a narrow cot, a larger rectangular table flanked by two benches, and the small table and chairs where we sat. The series of crude wooden shelves lining the wall behind me were perhaps a bit more crowded than before. Mixed among the usual crockery were items as diverse as a trio of triangular gray stones, an immense bouquet of dried yellow flowers, and what appeared to be a black leather harness.

I also counted in that jumble no fewer than four clay models of a man upon a horse. Barely bigger than a man's fist, each was a slightly different and surprisingly detailed representation of a proud equine and his noble rider.

These models, I guessed, were Leonardo's preliminary

attempts at a final design for the immense cast bronze tribute to the Duke of Milan's late father. It was this grand commission that had brought Leonardo to the city in the first place, before he had wooed the duke with promises of war machines. How long it would take him to complete the sculpture—or even if it ever would be finished—I dared not hazard a guess.

Smothering another yawn, I returned my attention to the Master. The usual bowl of fresh fruit lay at his elbow, with one plump apple missing several bites, which likely had served as his usual sparse nightly repast. He had changed his clothing, I noted, replacing his earlier brown tunic and green trunk hose with similar garments all in black as better befitted midnight forays. I wondered now if perhaps it had been his light that I had seen earlier in the darkened tower.

He finally paused in his sketching and frowned at the penciled image for a moment. Then, apparently satisfied, he leaned back in his chair and gave me a considering look.

"Tell me, my dear Dino, have you ever watched a leaf fall from a tree?"

"But, of course," I replied, puzzled by this unexpected topic of conversation. "Who has not?"

"Then explain to me how that occurs."

"It is quite simple. When the leaf dries out with the turn of the season, it loses its grip upon the branch, and then drifts to the ground, so," I replied, mimicking that familiar floating motion with my open hand.

He nodded. "Now, suppose you stood before me and held a rock shoulder high. Describe to me how that rock would fall if you released it."

"Why, it would drop straight to the ground," I said, trying to ignore the sudden sick feeling in my stomach as I guessed now where his questions were leading.

But instead of elaborating further on the topic, he slid the drawing he'd been working on toward me. "Take a look at this, Dino, and tell me what you think."

I did as instructed, studying the penciled sketch a moment. "It appears to be a picture of a man lifting a large pointed dome above his head."

Leonardo shook his head and flicked his fingers in the familiar impatient gesture. "Come now, Dino, can you not see? What I have drawn is an apparatus designed to allow a man to leap from a height and drift to the ground like a falling leaf, rather than plummet like a rock."

He took the page from me and pointed to the swiftly sketched male figure. "The idea first came to me some time ago. If you will observe, this man is holding above him a wooden framework which resembles, as you said, a pointed dome. That framework would be covered in cloth of some sort, perhaps gummed linen," he determined and paused to make a note.

That accomplished, he went on. "When the man holds this dome—or human sail, as I am calling it—above him and then jumps from some substantial height, it will catch the air, much as a leaf does. If all goes well, my invention will slow the man's descent so that he might land safely upon the earth."

"But why would someone purposely make such a leap?"

The Master gave me a mildly surprised look in return. "I can think of any number of reasons. A soldier might scale the outer wall of an enemy's fortress, perhaps to spy, or else perform some manner of sabotage. Should he be discovered, leaping safely to the ground would be a far swifter method of retreat than attempting to climb back down again."

"But wouldn't he first need to carry that sail with him up the wall before he could jump off with it?" I ventured. "I would think climbing with such a device strapped to one's back would prove difficult."

"That is not my concern."

With another flick of his fingers, Leonardo literally waved away that observation. "Another use might be escape from a tall building should a fire break out . . . not an uncommon occurrence in the city, as you know. With one of these sails in every household, think how many lives might be saved. Or, one might deliberately make the leap from a bridge or the edge of a cliff simply to experience the sensation of flight."

"Saints' blood, what a frightening thought!"

I stared at him in no little alarm, picturing the Master hanging from that fragile domed framework as he jumped from some fearsome height. "Have you actually tried this yourself?" I asked a bit breathlessly

To my relief, he shook his head. "Not as yet, though perhaps I shall try it one day soon. But I was inspired to revisit this invention by the tragic death of the woman at the tower. And that matter is what I wish to discuss with you."

He paused and favored me with a faint, ironic smile. "Once again, my dear Dino, you have brought an interesting puzzle to me. For already I suspect that there is more to this young woman's death than first meets the eye."

He rose from the table and began pacing, as was his wont when he lectured us in the workshop. "As you know, I joined our esteemed surgeon"—his aristocratic lip curled faintly at the man's mention—"in examining the unfortunate victim. Are you aware, Dino, of what happens to a human when he—or she—falls from a great height?"

Mutely, I shook my head, not particularly wishing to be edified in that particular subject but knowing I had no choice in the matter.

Not noticing my dismay, he reached for one of the clay models. A linen sack lay folded on one of those same shelves. Taking hold of that cloth bag, he slipped the figure of horse and rider inside it.

"Many factors come into play," he continued as he tied the sack shut. "Depending upon the angle of impact, the terrain, and, of course, the height of the fall, death might result from one of several causes. Often, the victim suffers a direct blow to the head, usually resulting in a broken neck. Or sometimes the person's spine and other bones are shattered. And on other occasions, the cause of death may be less obvious," he added while the sack abruptly slipped from his hand.

Barely had I time to cry a warning when I heard the muffled crack of pottery as the bundle landed upon the wooden floor. But when he merely bent and retrieved the fallen bag, I realized that what I thought was an accident had instead been a deliberate act. With a dramatic flourish, Leonardo untied the bag again and spilled broken bits of clay onto the table.

"As you can see, the sack itself remains unharmed by such treatment," he proclaimed, holding up the now-empty bag in demonstration. "Unfortunately, the model that was within it suffered damage so great that it is beyond repair. Thus it is with a person who dies as a result of a significant fall."

He shrugged. "Of course, if she had been fortunate enough to fall from the tower's other side, she might have survived. Outside the castle, the drop is straight down to the earth. Within the castle walls, there is a large portico at the tower's foot. Her fall would have been temporarily arrested as she landed upon that structure's roof, so that the remainder of her fall might have been sufficiently slowed so as to leave her only gravely injured but not dead."

Despite this belated reassurance, I swallowed uneasily, my gaze unwillingly fixed upon the clay shards that had once been a clever bit of sculpture. It was amazing how the Master could transform a linen bag and pieces of a broken statue into a grisly example of a horrific death, simply by the power of his words.

"And so this brings us back to the subject of the dead woman," he continued, tossing the sack aside.

"Her name, as it turned out, was Bellanca. She was a lady's maid to Ludovico's ward, Caterina, who is the daughter of the late Conte di Sasina. As the conte died without male issue, she assumed that title despite her youth. At any rate, it was discovered that Bellanca was missing. One of Caterina's other women identified the body in the surgery."

I had been right, then, regarding the dead woman's position within the castle. But I still sensed a mystery as to why she had met such a fate. And, for some reason, I felt compelled to know that answer.

"What happened when you and the surgeon examined her?" I anxiously asked. "Were you able to determine if she jumped from the tower or simply fell?"

Leonardo allowed himself an elegant snort. "Even our esteemed surgeon has the good sense to realize that women do not routinely fall out of tower windows without good cause. He did not bother with an autopsy but simply gave the corpse a cursory look and then opined that she took her own life."

"And do you not agree, Master?"

"I agree with the surgeon that her fall was no accident, but I am not so certain that she caused her own death."

3

The Empress

The mirror bears itself proudly, holding the queen mirrored within it . . .

—Leonardo da Vinci, *Forster III*

Leonardo's blunt words caught me by surprise. While I had suspected that the woman's fall had been deliberate, I had not guessed that something more sinister might lie behind the tragedy. I leaned forward, my earlier sleepiness banished by this revelation.

"She did not cause her own death?" I echoed. "Do you mean she was murdered?"

"It is a possibility that cannot be ignored. Tell me, Dino, did you notice anything amiss about Bellanca's clothing when you found her?"

"One sleeve of her gown had become untied and was caught upon the tower window," I promptly replied, recalling how that colorful bit of cloth had waved flaglike from on high.

The Master nodded. "Yes, but was that all?"

From his look of impatient encouragement, I realized that he expected a different answer. Shutting my eyes, I tried to re-create the ghastly scene in my mind, searching my memory for what must be a clue. Try as I might, however, I did not recall seeing anything that should not have been part of the scene.

So perhaps it was something that was not *there, instead.*

Barely had that thought flashed through my mind than I did recall something that I had not seen. With a small sound of triumph, I opened my eyes again.

"Her shoes, they were missing!"

"Very good, Dino," he congratulated me, his approving expression as great a prize as any gift Il Moro could bestow upon me. "I found that omission most unusual, as well. But I jump ahead of my tale."

He paused, his features reflecting a hint of exasperation. "I tend to forget that those who are not dedicated students of human anatomy often view death with less equanimity than do I. Women, especially, are prone to excesses of emotion at the sight of a corpse. This time, however, such histrionics proved a valuable distraction.

"The servant who made the identification—Lidia, I believe was her name—became quite distraught at the sight of her dead friend. Indeed, her distress was such that the surgeon was forced to escort her from the room and back to her quarters. Of course, while he was absent those few minutes, I took the opportunity to examine the deceased a bit more thoroughly."

As he spoke, he had resumed his earlier pacing, moving easily about the small chamber like a lithe black lion in his midnight-dark garb. Meanwhile, I listened with growing unease to this tale that was becoming increasingly unsettling with his every word.

"When examining the remains of a person who met a violent end," he explained, "it is not always easy to tell if bruises discovered upon the flesh occurred before death or as a result of the manner of death. As you might suspect, Bellanca's body showed injuries consistent with the violent impact that killed her. But upon closer inspection, I also found marks upon her arms and throat that appeared to have been inflicted while she was still alive."

He halted in midstep and fixed me with a cool look. "Faced with that evidence, I drew a new conclusion as to her probable cause of death. Indeed, I would say there is a high likelihood that the unfortunate Bellanca had been attacked by someone, perhaps even choked into submission before being tossed from the tower window."

Despite myself, I gasped. If the Master was right, then what had started as merely a tragedy had now become something far more sinister.

"But who could have done such a thing?" I wondered aloud, only to realize as I spoke the futility of asking the question.

To my relief, the Master did not dismiss my words with the disdain they deserved. Taking his seat across from me once more, he said, "I wondered much the same thing. As I told you, I had only a few minutes alone with the dead woman to conduct my examination; still, it was sufficient time for me to make a few sketches upon a bit of paper I found there. Barely had I finished when our friend the physician returned."

"He noticed nothing amiss, of course. He was far too busy complaining that he had been forced to minister to a mere servant, when he is used to attending to Ludovico, himself. He made sure to point out, however, that he preferred such menial service to his unwilling collaboration with me."

The Master gave a fastidious sneer. "You will know I was as glad to flee his surgery as he was to be quit of me. I may never get the stink of that butcher shop out of my nostrils."

I nodded, aware of Leonardo's contempt for the court physician's talents in particular and that of surgeons in general. Many of them had begun their careers as barbers, graduating from razor to scalpel with no formal training. And even those men schooled in the healing arts had little practical knowledge of anatomy, certainly not as much as the

Master did. As a result, the ill or injured ofttimes were as likely to die from any medical treatment received as they were from their illness or injury!

His momentary lapse into disdain was brief. Recovering his usual milder humor, he went on. "Given that I was not satisfied with the surgeon's conclusions, I decided that I would do a bit of investigating on my own. I waited until after dark, and then paid a visit to the same tower from which Bellanca fell."

"So that was your light I saw," I exclaimed, relieved it had been the Master's candle and not some unnatural flame that had flickered in the night. "Tell me, did you find anything?"

"If you will be patient, my dear boy, I shall tell all."

He picked up two broken pieces of the model from the tabletop and idly began fitting them together. "My initial concern was to avoid discovery by any of the soldiers there. Had I been found out, it would have been an easy matter to convince them I was there at Il Moro's behest. But letting my presence be known could well have tipped off her murderer to my suspicions, given that one of those men is the likeliest suspect for that role."

He had fitted one of the horse's clay limbs to a small piece of its shattered torso. Taking up a second delicate leg and a section of flank, he continued. "You may not know, Dino, but most of Ludovico's army consists of mercenaries, fighting men whose loyalty is bought by whichever noble will fill their purses with the most coin. To be sure, the majority of those men are professional soldiers who take pride in their skills. They may fight for the money, or the glory, or simply because it is what they do best. But for all of that, they adhere to a certain code that precludes criminal behavior."

He gave a satisfied nod as he fitted the new pieces with the old. Then, carefully balancing the partially reconstructed figure so that half a miniature equine torso stood frozen upon the table in mid-trot, he returned his leonine gaze to me.

"But know this, Dino. Among their number is inevitably

a man or two who enjoys killing strictly for killing's sake. Such a man has no conscience, no remorse, and no care what the rest of society might think of his actions. He pays homage only to Mars, the lord of war. Such a man might murder a helpless woman solely for his own amusement. It is this man who must not know what I suspect until such time as I can accuse him to his face."

Despite myself, I shivered at the thought of this unknown sycophant of the ancient battle god. Such men did exist, I had no doubt . . . and I prayed the luckless Bellanca had not been one of their victims.

Leonardo, meanwhile, had seemingly lost interest in the broken model. He let the pieces tumble apart and then shook his shaggy head.

"Ah, but you are very patient with my storytelling," he said with a small smile. "I will relate the rest of it more quickly, so that you may return to your bed before dawn. As I said, I examined the tower room, hoping to find some sign of what happened there in the minutes before Bellanca's death. That particular chamber appeared to be used primarily for storage, for I noticed as I entered that a good portion of it was filled with stacks of boxes and barrels. But my attention was for the women's shoes I spied in the center of the room."

Leonardo grabbed up the page upon which he earlier had sketched the human sail and swiftly drew two delicate slippers, poised like birds preparing for flight.

"As you see, they were not of elaborate enough material or design to belong to a noblewoman; still, they were far more graceful than the rough shoes of a common servant. In color, they were dark blue, and made of soft leather with a bit of embroidery on the toes, thusly," he said, adding to the sketch a few delicate lines resembling flowered vines. "As it was unlikely that they had been left in the tower room by accident, I could only conclude that these shoes were indeed Bellanca's."

"Certainly, you must be right," I agreed, knowing I

would happily remain awake until cock's crow to learn all that he knew of the matter. Moreover, my curiosity was stirred, so that I, myself, could not help but speculate upon the matter.

"But could it be that we are making this a greater mystery than it is?" I ventured, reflexively slipping into my former role as the eager novice as opposed to his one of coolly rational mentor.

When he gave me a querying look, I went on. "The bruises might have been inflicted another way. As for the missing shoes, is it possible that she deliberately took them off, perhaps to more easily balance upon the window ledge?"

"Well-questioned, Dino, but I fear your second argument is an unlikely one. You see, much of that floor is covered in old rushes, dry enough to splinter and which likely hide any manner of unpleasant vermin. Had she removed her slippers of her own volition, she would have done so at the window, rather than walk across that wretched floor in stocking feet.

"As for your first argument," he added almost as an afterthought, "I can assure you that those marks I saw upon her flesh were new."

I nodded my agreement. Despite the sharp pang of dismay that pierced me over the likely truth of Bellanca's violent demise, I could not deny the quiver of excitement I felt at the prospect of another mystery to be solved. Just as quickly, however, I chided myself for my foolishness. Even if Leonardo were to pursue the matter, that did not mean he would call upon me to assist him a second time.

The Master did not seem to notice my sudden lapse into silence, for his story was not yet finished.

"As little else was to be learned from those shoes, I decided to restore them to their rightful owner. But in my hurry to quit that unpleasant room, I almost missed what might be the most important clue of all. Indeed, had my candle not dripped wax upon my hand as I struggled with the tower door, I might not have paused long enough to notice the evidence lying at my feet."

He reached into his tunic, withdrawing a flat, cloth-wrapped bundle slightly smaller than his hand. Sweeping aside the remnants of the clay sculpture, he carefully he laid that slim packet upon the table.

"Observe, Dino," he said as he began unfolding the concealing scrap of wine red fabric. "Unless I am mistaken, in this bit of silk lies the key to the identity of the unlucky Bellanca's killer."

I'm not certain what I had expected to see lying upon the square of red silk. A packet of incriminating letters? Maybe a book, or even a weapon of some sort? Certainly, I was not prepared for the sight of four cards stacked one atop another. Each had been painstakingly cut from sheets of heavy paper that had been layered together, the backs of them painted bloodred.

"Why, they are tarocchi cards," I said, naming a game of strategy popular among the wealthier classes. Unable to hide my disappointment at so ordinary a find, I shook my head and confessed, "I am not certain how this can be a clue. Surely, such playing cards are common enough. They might well belong to one of Il Moro's soldiers."

"Ah, but in this you would be wrong," Leonardo replied with a small smile of satisfaction.

With one elegant hand, he spread the cards apart in a neat line and then flipped each so that they faced upward. Now I could see the individual pictures upon them that designated their places in the deck.

"These are no ordinary cards meant for casual play," he explained. "Note the excess of gilding upon them, the bright yet subtle use of color, as well as the detail of the images. These cards were specially commissioned and at no little cost. Moreover, the artist who created them was a man of some talent."

Intrigued now, I looked more closely at the four miniature works of art before me. I had played tarocchi a few times in the past, but admittedly with a deck far less elegant than these cards. The images upon them, however, were still familiar.

One was but a minor suit, the Three of Swords. The second was a court card, the boyish Knight of Coins poised upon his horse. As for the final cards, they were two of the triumphs . . . those cards whose value was greater than the common suits. One was the Devil with his lecherous glare, and the other was Fire, the image of a blazing tower.

I winced at the unfortunate imagery of that last card. The painted tower, not unlike those anchoring the surrounding walls of Castle Sforza, was depicted with a shattered dome, from which flames licked at the sky. But more disturbing were the figures of two men shown plunging from the ruined tower's heights. True, their painted features reflected no more gruesome an emotion than surprise at their predicament; still, their end was inevitable and unsettlingly reminiscent of what had happened to Bellanca.

I glanced up from that eerily prescient bit of pasteboard to meet the Master's gaze. His smile took on an ironic edge.

"An interesting coincidence, is it not? As for how I am certain the cards are somehow connected to her, I found but three of them in the tower room. This one"—he picked up the trump emblazoned with the Devil—"I discovered upon her person when I returned the shoes to the surgery."

He lifted a wry brow. "I wonder if our esteemed surgeon will even notice that his corpse, once minus her shoes, is now shod? At any rate, it was as I was replacing the slippers upon her feet that my candle reflected off the gilt adorning the card tucked into her bodice. I added that card to my collection, which you see before you."

"But surely the tarocchi deck could not belong to Bellanca, herself," I opined, knowing that so precious an item must be the possession of someone wealthy, perhaps even of the nobility. "Do you think she stole the cards?"

"I am not certain. But I do suspect that the deck's rightful owner will wish to restore this treasure to completeness. I shall safeguard these cards until such time as someone comes in search of them, and perhaps then we will also learn more about what led Bellanca to her fate."

The Master squared the painted bits of pasteboard and rewrapped them in the silk once more. Then he fixed me with a paternal gaze.

"I fear I have robbed you of too much sleep. You should return to your bed and forget this unpleasant business."

"But did you not say these cards were a clue to finding Bellanca's killer? Surely we should begin the search for this person," I blurted, and then blushed at my presumption.

He did not chide me, however, but merely shook his head. "I admire your zeal, my boy, but I doubt that our glorious duke will allow me to embark upon such a mission, even if he believed my theory of murder. Ludovico has other assignments awaiting me," he said, giving the shattered horse model a rueful look, "and I would do well not to disappoint him."

Bearing the brunt of the duke's legendary impatience was not a pleasant fate, I knew. Moreover, it was well-known that Il Moro was anxious for the grand tribute to his sire to be unveiled in the near future. Leonardo's hesitation in this matter was understandable.

Still, I could not hide my disappointment as the Master went on. "Save for the novelty it afforded earlier today, Bellanca's death will have little impact upon the court. She was but a servant, and as such is easily replaced. No one other than I will think to wonder if she perhaps did not leap from that tower of her own volition."

He rose and set the wrapped cards upon the uppermost shelf. "The physician's opinion will be the final word," he continued. "For the sake of her friends and family, perhaps he will be kind enough to label her fall an accident rather than a deliberate leap. Either way, the entire matter will be forgotten once the unfortunate woman is put into the ground."

"So perhaps a murderer will go free," I exclaimed, unable to suppress a bitter note in my words. "How can you let this happen, Master? It is not right."

"No, it is not right," he gently agreed, "but it is what will be. And you are old enough now to understand life's small cruelties such as this. Now, back to your bed; the hour is painfully late."

With those words, he pulled open the door, letting the warm night air wash through the room. I knew my place well enough not to offer further argument; thus, I silently took my leave, keeping my head bowed so that the Master would not notice the angry tears that filled my eyes. This was not the first time that he had lectured me on the futility of seeking fairness, but that did not mean I accepted the harsh lesson without protest.

I managed to contain my emotions until I reached the relative privacy of my alcove in the apprentices' sleeping quarters. Safe from view, I swiped away a few wet streaks that trailed down my face before I stripped off my jerkin and corset, and then climbed beneath my cover. The rest of my fellows slumbered still, their dreams seemingly untroubled. I wished I could join in their tranquil sleep, but my dismay kept my thoughts uncomfortably stirred.

I did not blame Leonardo, of course. He was here in Milan purely at the duke's pleasure. Should he cease currying his patron's favor, he would find himself unceremoniously tossed into the street. This would leave us apprentices without a master, and perhaps without a roof over our own heads, as well. Responsible as he was for a score of young boys—this in addition to maintaining his own livelihood— it would be more than foolhardy of him to act counter to Il Moro's wishes.

Foolhardy of him, perhaps, but what of me?

The impulsive question put an abrupt halt to my whirling thoughts. The Master was bound to follow the duke's directives, but as a mere apprentice, I fell under no such noble scrutiny. While Leonardo might not be free to investigate the matter, that did not stop me from searching out Bellanca's killer on my own!

Carefully, as if I were handling one of the Master's remaining clay models, I examined the possibility. Had I not provided him with valuable assistance when we sought out the person who murdered Il Moro's cousin? Indeed, I had survived two attempts upon my own life in order to uncover the truth. Surely I had the experience to undertake such a task on my own.

That bold realization sent an excited tremor through me so that it was all I could do not to sit up in my bed with a shout. Instead, I contented myself with beaming a triumphant grin into the surrounding darkness as I settled beneath my blanket to await sleep. Exactly how I would go about accomplishing so formidable an undertaking, I could not say. For the moment, it was enough to know that the grievous wrong of Bellanca's murder would not go unpunished, after all.

MY enthusiasm for pursuing this mystery had not waned by morning. This day's task, I determined as I climbed from my bed not long after dawn, would be to attend Bellanca's burial. Admittedly, my motivation for that act of respect was not an entirely pure one.

For I had learned from Leonardo during our previous investigation that the guilty often return to visit their victims a final time. Sometimes, such an act is spurred by remorse; other times, it is for the cruel enjoyment of reliving their last moments with the departed. By carefully observing those in attendance at the churchyard, I might well discover the identity of her murderer!

First, however, I would have to learn when the service was to be held. For that information, I would rely upon Marcella, the kitchen maid who had long since set her eye upon "Dino." It would take but a question to her at the midmorning meal, and I would surely have the information that I sought before my bowl was empty.

Trailing the other apprentices to the main workroom, I grabbed up a bundle of new brushes to finish tying and shrugged off a niggling sense of guilt at the prospect of using my masculine masquerade to my advantage. Surely the good that could be gained from Marcella's eagerness to help me would outweigh the small cruelty of my deception. Afterward, I need only plead with the Master for an hour of leave from my daily tasks in order to pay my respects to the dead.

But my grand plan almost foundered before it could be put into place when my fellow apprentices found a reason for argument before we'd even broken our fast.

"I dressed up as the woman last time. It is someone else's turn," Bernardo peevishly complained. With a snort, he tossed aside the length of linen that had been draped over his shoulders and deliberately settled his gaze on Vittorio.

Vittorio gave his blond curls a vigorous shake. "I took a turn before that," he protested. "Maybe Tito should be the one to put on the robes."

"Ha, I am far too ugly to be mistaken for a woman," that youth countered, a lopsided grin splitting his pockmarked features. "Besides, I was the one to model for Saint Anne when we were working on the stencil for the monk's hall last month. Choose someone else, not me."

It was a common argument among the apprentices whenever we prepared a stencil for one of the Master's projects. The Master would have already supplied Constantin with a sketch determining the general composition of the new work. Our job was to translate that small drawing into a full-size rendering, or stencil, of the scene. That stencil, in turn, would be transferred as a series of outlines onto the plaster surface of whichever wall the fresco was to adorn. And, of course, it was the Master who painted the greatest portion of the final work, with his genius bringing our humble drawings to glorious life.

But on any large fresco, particularly one of a religious nature, numerous background figures would be incorporated into the scene. Those minor angels, saints, and sinners usually would be drawn onto the stencil from memory by one of the senior apprentices. Usually, the life-size clay models we had in abundance in the workshop—hands, legs, feet, and even torsos—were sufficient as aids for lesser subjects. More prominent figures often required the help of a living model in order for that apprentice to better depict the twist of a torso or drape of a cloth. Hence, the occasional need for one of us to dress in women's clothing.

The argument begun by Bernardo now was going at full strength despite Constantin's attempts to restore order to the workshop. For myself, I also preferred not to act as model, but for different reasons. Given that women's clothing was second nature to me, I always feared that donning the robes might somehow give away my masquerade. Beyond that, I had joined the Master's workshop in hopes of elevating my skills as a painter. Being relegated to such a role meant an opportunity lost to prove myself and perhaps be allowed to contribute to the stencil, or even a small portion of the final fresco.

Today, however, I was willing to make such a sacrifice if it meant proceeding with our work!

"I'll do it," I called out over the hubbub, grabbing the linen as it was tossed from boy to boy, and holding it over my head like a flag of surrender. "See, you have your model. Let me take my place so we can begin our day."

"Good work, Dino," Constantin told me with a grateful nod while the others scattered to resume their usual tasks, and Paolo and Davide readied themselves to begin sketching. "As a reward, I shall ask the Master if you might be allowed to paint a small bit of the background once the fresco is begun."

"That is reward, indeed," I replied and returned his smile with one of my own.

Bundling the cloth beneath my arm, I hurried to the spot near one wall that provided the most constant light in the workshop. There, I stripped off my tunic, so that I wore only my long, white linen shirt over my trunk hose, and began draping the cloth about me to resemble a gown.

"What person am I to portray?" I asked Davide as he used a bit of gum to fasten his paper into place on his easel.

He shot me a sly look. "You are taking the role of the Magdalene, so you will want an attitude of wanton piety."

"I shall attempt to manage that," I carelessly replied.

By now, I had fashioned the cloth about me in realistic imitation of a gown, tying a complicated length of rope around my ribs to represent a laced bodice. I draped a second bit of cloth over my cropped hair. This fabric, they would depict either as a modest veil or else as flowing hair, depending upon whatever inspiration struck them.

Finally, giving in to a bit of slyness, myself, I neatly folded my discarded tunic into a small bundle. I tucked that roll into the bodice of my makeshift gown, restoring to my figure a semblance of the very breasts that I had taken such pains to bind into submission.

"There, what do you think?" I asked Davide as I hopped onto the small wooden box upon which the models normally stood and struck a pose.

By way of answer, both he and Paolo simply stared at me, openmouthed. Constantin, meanwhile, had strolled back over from where he'd left the other apprentices hard at work to join them. Even he paused for a moment before clearing his throat and commenting with obvious discomfort, "You make quite the realistic female, Dino. Your cleverness at disguise will certainly make Davide and Paolo's task that much easier."

My momentary smugness faded as I wondered if I had erred in playing this small trick upon them. But the pair promptly recovered themselves. After a few instructions to pose me so that I better resembled the figure in the Master's sketch, they diligently applied themselves to their work.

Both youths were accomplished artists, so I was patient

as they sketched. But as the other apprentices grew restless in their own tasks and were glancing our way, I soon drew no little interest from them.

"See there, Dino makes a fine girl," Bernardo called out with a snicker.

Setting down the pot of gesso he was stirring, he jumped up from his bench and began strutting about the workshop in childish imitation of a woman's walk. "Look, I am Dino, the most beautiful apprentice of all."

Vittorio promptly joined in the fun. Leaping from his own seat, he chased after the youth while the other apprentices laughingly cheered him on.

"Oh, Dino, you are so lovely," he told Bernardo. Grasping the other boy's hands, he dropped to his knees in mock awe while the other apprentices surrounded them and made kissing sounds.

"Please forgive me," he went on in a dramatic tone. "Had I known how beautiful you truly were, I never would have belched and passed wind in your glorious presence!"

By now, even Constantin was smiling, though he attempted to hide his amusement behind his hand. Davide and Paolo were grinning outright. As for myself, I tried to keep a stern mien, but when Bernardo and Vittorio began an impromptu country dance together, I gave up and burst out laughing.

And as it always seemed to happen, in the next instant my merriment was the only sound to be heard in the workshop.

I promptly clamped my mouth shut. All the other apprentices had suddenly returned to their duties, their attention firmly fixed upon the tasks before them. Even Bernardo and Vittorio were settled on a bench, studiously applying themselves to stirring the gesso pot. I gave an inward groan. Of course, such a sudden lapse into well-ordered silence could mean but one thing.

I gazed toward the workshop door to see Leonardo

standing there, framed by early-morning sunlight. His expression as he stared back at me was of unmistakable bemusement. Then, a slow smile played at his lips, and he shook his head as he started toward where Davide and Paolo stood diligently sketching me.

4

The Emperor

All people obey and are swayed by their magnates . . .

—Leonardo da Vinci, *Codex Atlanticus*

I felt a blush heat my cheeks. It was apparent that the sight of me had taken the Master by surprise. The question was, had he momentarily mistaken me for a woman in my borrowed garb? Or had he realized from the first who I was and simply thought me well suited to that feminine role? Either response could prove problematic, I knew.

To my relief, he did not immediately address me but spared all his attention for Paolo and Davide. After a cursory look at Paolo's easel, he halted before Davide's sketch and nodded.

"Excellent work, as always," he told the youth, who smiled with quiet pride at the compliment. "Your sense of proportion and your skill at depicting the movement of a limb and the flow of a garment is superior to that of many painters twice your age. But this time"—he paused and glanced over at Paolo, who was struggling not to show his disappointment at seemingly being passed over—"it shall be Paolo's rendition of the Magdalene that we will use. He has caught in his sketch a suggestion of the fierce piety one might expect from the woman known to be Jesus's closest female friend."

Paolo's eyes opened wide; then, beaming broadly, he said, "Thank you, Master. I am pleased that you approve of my vision."

As he spoke, Davide had stepped over to view his fellow's sketch. With a generous smile, he turned to his friend and said, "I agree with the Master, Paolo. This time, yours is the superior work."

Not to be outdone in munificence, Paolo shook his head. "This time, yes, but it is as the Master says. You have a great talent, Davide!"

While he and Davide continued to exchange compliments, the Master turned his attention to me. By now, I had stepped off the wooden box that had been my small stage and whipped the makeshift veil from my head. He shook his head again and lifted a wry brow.

"My dear boy, I had not realized your skill at costuming," he said with what sounded like approval. "Should you tire of painting, perhaps you might try your hand at the stage. I dare say you would be well received in any of the female roles that traditionally go to smooth-faced youths."

Blushing again, I muttered by way of excuse years as a very young boy spent in the company of numerous female cousins. Whether or not he believed that fiction, I didn't stop to worry about. Indeed, he seemed to lose interest in the matter almost immediately, taking himself off to see how Tito and Tommaso were doing with a new technique of gilding they'd been taught.

Breathing a silent prayer of relief, I hurriedly untied the makeshift gown, shaking out my tunic to resume its wear in the usual fashion. Then, taking a cue from Vittorio's earlier jesting, I managed both to belch and to break wind with considerable gusto.

The actions drew an appreciative laugh from Paolo and a smiling roll of the eyes from Davide. Certain that such uncouth behavior sufficiently supplanted any previous hint of femininity, I tossed the linen to a still-snickering Paolo and swaggered my way back to my accustomed spot at the workbench.

The remainder of the morning followed much the usual pattern. Fortunately, the amusement I'd provided in my female garb appeared to have been forgotten almost immediately in the excitement of preparing a new stencil. And knowing that I might have some small part now in painting it, I was as anxious as the rest to begin it.

In the time I had been here at the castle, we had made considerable progress in adorning the noble palace with frescoes of varying sizes and subjects. This particular fresco had been suggested by Ludovico, himself, likely because he found prurient intrigue in the story of Mary Magdalene's relationship with her Lord. In another few days, we would begin preparing the wall of a small, private hall where that scene was to be depicted. For now, however, our efforts were fixed on completing the stencil to the Master's satisfaction.

We halted as usual for our midmorning meal. As befitted our station, we apprentices—along with numerous other of the castle's servants—took our places at rough wooden tables and benches crowded beneath a narrow portico behind the kitchen. Though our dining area was sheltered from the worst of the elements, it unfortunately was situated within ready sight and smell of the kitchen's fermenting garbage dump. We'd long since grown inured to the unappetizing view, but on days when the breeze shifted in our direction, ignoring the stench was a far more difficult task.

This time, I deliberately lingered behind the others so that I would be last in line at the kitchen. My intention was to have a private word with Marcella and learn when Bellanca's burial was to be held. Knowing the kitchen maid's penchant for gossip, I had no doubt she would have the information I sought. She did not prove me wrong.

"The service will be two hours before dusk," Marcella agreeably informed me in a theatrical whisper a few minutes later, once I'd explained how I felt compelled to offer my final respects to the dead woman.

We were huddled together behind the kitchen wine barrels, which had become our unofficial meeting spot. Though I'd tried to use my full bowl as a shield against her assault, reluctantly I'd allowed the pert young woman to cling to my arm. I reminded myself at that uncomfortable clasp that my deception might be forgiven for the greater good cause.

"There is one person in particular who you must watch for," she eagerly continued in the same low tone. "He is the man who is rumored to have been her secret lover!"

A secret lover! Certainly, the fact that Bellanca had been seeing a man unbeknownst to everyone else could well explain much about her eventual fate.

"Do you know who this man is?" I asked in as careless a tone as I could muster, lest she grow suspicious at my interest.

Pleased to share more gossip, Marcella nodded and put her free hand dramatically to her heart. "He is said to be none other than the new captain of Il Moro's guard, a handsome and charming devil by the name of Gregorio."

She paused and gave me a teasing smile. "In fact, had another handsome young man not already caught my eye, I might be tempted to offer the captain some comfort in his time of loss."

I inwardly groaned at her bold words, even as I wondered if I should offer her similar banter in return. Or perhaps I might do better to play the stung suitor and pretend wounded offense at her suggestion. Seizing the opportunity, I opted for the latter course.

"Certainly, if that is how you feel, you are more than welcome to seek this man out," I replied and promptly withdrew my arm from her grip. Then, turning a wounded look upon her, I stood and added, "I thought we were friends, Marcella, but perhaps not."

Before she could sputter a protest, I had fled the kitchen and rejoined my fellows. For the remainder of the meal, however, I felt Marcella's baleful gaze upon my back. Thus, it was a relief when Constantin signaled our return to the workshop.

The Master was waiting for us. As on most days, he had indulged in his customary morning meal of bread and fresh fruit, rather than risk the servants' more uncertain fare, which consisted of the previous day's leavings from the nobles' table. While I could not fault his palate—indeed, there were mornings when I contented myself with but a chunk of bread and crumb of cheese—neither could I subsist solely on fruits, grains, and vegetables, as he was wont to do.

In our absence, he had made some modifications to the ceiling-high stencil which Paolo, Davide, and Constantin were creating. All of us moved to the far wall to see his changes, ready for another lesson in the theory of composition. Unfortunately, I was so busy wondering how best to approach the Master with the request to attend Bellanca's burial that I missed the start of his impromptu lecture.

". . . variation on the triangular composition," he was saying as I returned my attention to the stencil. "In this example, it is the figure of Christ that we intend as the focal point of the fresco. He is depicted here, standing and positioned slightly above eye level. To one side of him and a short distance away are seated two of the apostles, while at his feet kneels the Magdalene in a posture of supplication.

"The ground, of course, is the base of our three-sided equation," he explained, using his finger to draw an imaginary line along the penciled ground. Extending that line upward at an angle, he went on. "Mary Magdalene forms the second side. While previously she was depicted crouched as if awaiting a blessing, you will notice how I have modified her pose. I have raised one of her arms toward her Lord in supplication and added the countering flow of her unbound hair down her back. See how this gives us a second line."

Moving to the opposite side of the drawing, he continued. "I have made a slight change to your two apostles, as well. Originally, they sat side by side gazing upward. Now, one is positioned lower and to one side, so that a line drawn from one head to the next"—again, he traced with one finger along the paper—"gives us yet another angle. This forms the final side of the triangle, with Christ at the pinnacle."

He waited for us to take in his explanation, particularly Paolo and Davide, who were frowning and nodding in comprehension. Fixing his gaze upon the rest of us, he said, "Now, explain, Bernardo, the reason we favor this style of composition over a more linear arrangement."

"That's easy, Master," the boy eagerly replied. His words sounding an exact quote of one of Leonardo's lectures, he went on. "The triangle shape brings a sense of movement to the scene while automatically drawing the viewer's eye to the most important figure in the painting."

Leonardo gave him an approving nod. "I see you have been paying attention these past weeks. Now, does anyone have a question before we return to our work?"

"I do, Signor Leonardo," came a light, unfamiliar voice from behind us. "I would like to know what has happened to my missing tarocchi cards."

As was the habit on mild days, the workshop door stood open to let in fresh air and greater light than the room's few narrow windows afforded. The voice we'd heard had come from the elegantly dressed noblewoman unexpectedly poised now in that entry. The late-morning sun shone brightly behind her and threw her figure into shadowed relief, so that my first impression was simply of a small, slim shape draped in yards of moss green silks trimmed in gold. Then she stepped into the room, and her features came fully into view.

She was young, little more than a girl, and possessed of stunning, exotic beauty. And yet, upon second look, she should not have been beautiful at all.

Individually, her features were too strong, perhaps even mismatched. Her wide, ebony dark eyes tilted slightly at the corners, and her broad cheekbones had an unexpected sharpness. As for her nose, it was sharply defined if too strong, while her cherry dark lips were a bit too wide. Yet combined with flawless skin brushed with a hint of gold, the sum of those youthful features resulted in a face that could easily have graced one of the Master's portraits.

The only blemish I noted was the faintest expression of restless discontent that played about her lips.

And it seemed I was not alone in my assessment of her beauty. The other apprentices were staring in respectful silence at this unexpected visitor, doubtless as awed by her appearance as they were by her apparent rank. Even Leonardo appeared momentarily surprised before he recalled his manners and stepped forward.

"Welcome to my humble workshop, my lady," he swiftly greeted her and swept a low bow. "How may I be of service?"

As Leonardo spoke, Constantin recovered himself enough to snatch off his cap and prod the apprentices nearest him into a similar gesture of respect. The remainder of us quickly followed suit and made our own bows. The young woman seemed not to notice any of us, however, but strode gracefully toward the Master.

"You are my cousin the duke's master artist, Leonardo the Florentine, are you not?"

At his nod of agreement, she assumed the petulant tones of someone used to being obeyed. "As I said, I would like to know what has happened to my missing tarocchi cards."

She paused and reached into the gold silk purse tied at her waist, pulling forth a rectangular object. "They look much like this," she went on in the same haughty manner, displaying a familiar red-painted example by way of explanation. "Four of the cards are missing and were last in the possession of my servant, Bellanca. I was told that you and the surgeon attended to her after her death. Did you perhaps find those cards upon her person?"

Had I been the Master, I might have been suppressing a triumphant smile at her question. For myself, I merely shook my head in amazement. Had he not predicted not many hours earlier that the cards' owner would come in search of them?

As always, he was right, though what connection this lovely if rather ill-tempered young woman could have to so brutal a death, I could not guess. Certainly, I could not picture her overpowering Bellanca with strength sufficient to shove the larger woman from the tower! Still, I made a mental note that she seemed more concerned with the disappearance of her playing cards than she did with the loss of her servant.

Leonardo, however, appeared unsurprised at being proved correct. Assuming the faint, charming smile that I'd often seen him take with members of the nobility, he instead asked her, "As you already seem acquainted with me, my lady, may I hazard a guess as to your identity?"

At her imperious nod, he continued. "You are cousin to the duke, and mistress to the unfortunate Bellanca. Therefore, you must be Caterina, daughter of the late Conte di Sasina and his departed wife."

"I had heard you were very clever, Signor Leonardo," she replied, managing not to be charmed. "Yes, I am Caterina. And now, tell me, what do you know of those cards?"

"Unfortunately, though I did attend to your maidservant, I saw no sign of those cards that you seek," he smoothly answered.

I opened my eyes wide at this blatant lie. What motive might he have for keeping the cards from her? Given that she seemed their rightful owner, it made little sense.

Caterina's dismay mirrored my own. "You are certain, signore? I searched my quarters thoroughly. They were not there, nor were the cards in Bellanca's room. Yet I know she had them earlier that afternoon."

She stepped forward and handed the Master the one card she'd retrieved as example, her manner growing more urgent.

"This deck was painted for my mother years ago by another court artist," she explained. "Perhaps he was not as great a master as you, Signor Leonardo, but he was a talented painter, nonetheless. You can see the beauty of the gilding and the exquisiteness of the brushstrokes. It is vital that I find the missing cards and restore the deck to completeness."

The Master studied the card a moment, as if it were the first time to examine that deck; then, with a small nod, he returned it to her.

"A quite credible work," he agreed. "Tell me, did you ask the surgeon if he had seen them?"

"He claimed to have not. Indeed, it was he who suggested that I ask you. But as you are not able to help me, I do not know where else to look."

Her consternation at the cards' disappearance was apparent, and despite her earlier high-handed manner, I felt a stir of sympathy for her. It was obvious the cards represented something more to her than simply a game. Perhaps they were a connection to her dead mother, and as such were to be cherished.

For his part, the Master gave her what appeared to be a concerned look. "You have my word that I shall search out these missing cards for you. And should I be unable to find them, perhaps you will allow me to create replacements so that your deck will be whole again."

"You are most kind, though it would not be the same," she replied, sighing. And then that soft sound was abruptly echoed by a single, insistent bark from outside the workshop door.

Caterina's expression of youthful discontent dissolved into a genuine smile of indulgence. "Pio," she softly called, seemingly forgetting her distress, "you need not hide. Come, meet the great Leonardo."

At her words, a sleek black-and-white hound no taller than her knee trotted in through the open door. This was no stable dog, for tied about his elegant long neck was a broad collar of heavy, gold-embroidered green fabric that matched his mistress's garb. He gazed about him and then halted, one paw raised like a horse in mid-trot.

I smiled at the sight, recognizing in this canine the breed that was a favorite pet among the nobles. Impossibly thin, with a deep chest, long legs, and a whip of a tail, the tiny beast appeared as fragile as one of the Master's clay models. Still, I knew such dogs were sturdier than they looked; indeed, they were far more than spoiled companions, being eager hunters of small game. Moreover, their speed was greater than hounds twice their size, and their intelligence rumored to rival that of most of their owners!

After his first moment of uncertainty, Pio padded his way past us apprentices, stopping briefly before a couple of the youths for an inquisitive sniff. Grinning broadly, Vittorio managed a furtive scratch behind the dog's ears as it continued its regal way toward Caterina.

"There, Pio, you must make the acquaintance of Signor Leonardo," she told her pet once he sat obediently before her. "Perhaps if you catch his fancy, he might paint your portrait."

I smiled at that. Given that many pages of the Master's notebooks were given over to sketches of various beasts, dogs included, I would not be surprised to one day find the elegant hound had made his way into that collection.

Seeming to understand his mistress's words, Pio rose and walked over to Leonardo. Lightly, he reared up and balanced upon his long hind legs, putting one polite if insistent paw upon the Master's knee, while raising the other in the now-familiar gesture.

Leonardo stared down at the beast with a hint of an indulgent smile. Then, at a soft word from him, the dog promptly dropped down onto his haunches and stretched his long front legs before him. Obediently lowering his head, he crossed his dainty paws in what appeared to be an attitude of prayer, so that I knew why he'd been named "the pious one."

"A fine specimen, indeed," the Master agreed. "Perhaps I shall find a spot for Pio in my latest fresco. And now, can I be of any further service to you?"

Caterina shook her head, her moment of amusement fading. "Not unless you find my missing tarocchi cards. I trust you shall send me word should you find them."

Turning on her heel, she snapped a soft command to her pet and departed the workshop with the same regal air with which she had entered it, Pio prancing happily behind her.

Barely had she departed through the open doorway than an excited buzz rose from the apprentices. I caught but a few snippets of their words, given that they all seemed to be speaking at once.

". . . surely the most beautiful woman at court."

"She looked right at me, and . . ."

"I think her dog liked me."

This last came from Vittorio who, given his youth, seemed properly more impressed by the young woman's pet than by her. For myself, I was busy wondering why the Master had claimed not to have the tarocchi cards she had sought, especially since he had so accurately predicted that someone would come in search of them.

I did not have time to speculate long over that, however, for the Master gestured me toward him. "A word with you, Dino," he addressed me. Then, turning his attention to the others, he interrupted their eager gossip, saying, "The rest of you draftsmen, return to your work. The main portion of the stencil must be completed by tomorrow."

While the other apprentices reluctantly went back to their tasks, Leonardo drew me over to one side.

"I have another assignment for you, Dino," he said in a low tone. "At two hours before dusk today, the service for the unfortunate Bellanca is to be held. I would like you to join the other mourners and observe what transpires there."

Unable to believe my good fortune—had I not just been agonizing over how best to ask leave to attend this very service?—I gave an eager nod.

"Of course, as you wish," I replied, keeping my tone soft, as had he, lest the others hear. "But for what in particular would you wish me to look?"

"Why, for her killer, of course."

He flicked his fingers in the familiar impatient gesture. "As in the past, simply use your powers of observation. Take note of who is there and how they behave in the dead woman's presence. Report back anything odd or amiss to me."

"I shall do as you instruct."

It crossed my mind to ask why, after his blunt dismissal last night of the matter, he now had a sudden interest in discovering who was responsible for the young maidservant's fatal fall. I also was tempted to demand why he had lied to the Lady Caterina about the missing tarocchi cards. But, of course, I mentioned neither concern, well aware that it was not my place as apprentice to question the Master's methods. Should I need to know those answers, he would tell me in time. Until that time, I must keep my curiosity to myself.

Even so, I could not suppress an inner grin of pleasure. The Master could well have summoned another apprentice last night to debate the manner of Bellanca's death. Indeed, he could have as easily asked Tito or Davide to be his eyes and ears at the burial later this day. The fact that he had entrusted all of this to me must mean he had returned me to my past role as his assistant in bringing villains to justice!

Then I allowed myself a moment of uncertainty. It was one thing to search of my own accord for the person who, with a single push, had sent Bellanca to her death. It was quite another to do so at the Master's behest. He would expect a detailed accounting of all I learned and would doubtless show his impatience should I return no more enlightened on the matter than when I left.

Then I will just have to discover something of import, I told myself with a firm nod.

I waited impatiently for the time to pass. Finally, the clock tower struck half the hour past three. I set aside the minerals I was grinding for new batches of tempera and quietly advised Constantin I was being sent on an errand by the Master.

The senior apprentice did not question me, familiar as he

was with Leonardo's well-known habit of sending one or another of us on some mission as the fancy struck him. Moreover, we all knew far better than to lie about such a summons. No youth would willingly risk dismissal from the workshop for a furtive hour or two of idle time.

"Very well," Constantin replied, "just return as quickly as you can. We shall be carrying the stencil to the hall as soon as it is finished and will need all hands to hang it."

I gave him my promise and, stopping only to put on the cleaner of my two brown tunics, hurried from the workshop. A few minutes later, I was outside the city gates and on my way to the same churchyard where the duke's cousin had been laid to rest in the Sforza family crypt . . . that same dank crypt where I had almost met my own end a few months earlier.

I pretended the chill that swept me was but the brisk afternoon breeze that cooled the summer day and hinted at a storm to come. Not even to the Master did I admit that I still had occasional frightful dreams about those terrifying hours locked away in the dark with generations of the Sforza dead.

Stabbed and beaten into unconsciousness, I'd been bundled into a crumbling stone niche within one of the crypt walls and left there for dead by the same man I had assumed had also murdered the conte. Though in that accusation I later had been proved wrong, the man had been no less a foul villain. Indeed, if not for the timely intervention of Tommaso, I might have spent eternity among the Sforzas. And so when my ersatz jailer met his own untimely end, I'd not mourned his passing.

The short journey beyond the city was a bit longer than I had remembered, so that I quickened my pace. Even so, I still had not reached the churchyard when I heard the clock tower's distant bells ring four times. Now I was running along the narrow road, tiny puffs of dirt flying from beneath my feet with every stride as I silently berated myself for not allowing myself sufficient time. The Master had charged me with a solemn duty, and I was in danger of failing him!

With a final burst of speed that would have impressed even the contessa's swift hound, Pio, I charged past the churchyard gates. Then, panting and swiping the sweat and dust from my face with the corner of my tunic, I slipped past the chapel door and gratefully dropped into the far corner of the rear pew.

I had to squint and blink my eyes a moment before they adjusted to the chapel's dim light. Save for the pallid sunlight that softly glowed through the thick stained glass of the windows to either side of me, the only illumination came from two sputtering candles upon the altar. Thus, the shrouded figure of Bellanca, which was laid before it, seemed almost to float upon the shadows.

Unlike the funeral of the Conte di Ferrara, there was no procession of mourners passing by her simple bier; neither was the Archbishop of Milan presiding. In fact, there was no Mass being said, likely because there was no family to pay the priest. Instead, one of the brown-robed friars was muttering a few words in Latin over the dead woman as perhaps a score of mourners—all servants and apprentices, by their humble garb—knelt and made the responses.

Remembering my male disguise, I respectfully pulled off my cap and slipped to my own knees upon the rough stone floor, bowing my head and folding my hands in semblance of prayer. But through my lowered lashes, I was keenly observing those who had come to pay Bellanca their final respects. Even though I was behind them, from my angle I still had a partial view of their faces. All but two of the mourners were women, one of whom was audibly sobbing.

The kindest compliment one might have offered the plain-faced woman would have been praise for the glossy blackness of her thick braid of hair untouched by gray. Otherwise, she was unremarkable, save for her current public display of grief. Though old enough to have been Bellanca's mother, I judged her to be but a fellow servant. With her simple brown gown and head wrap, she appeared dressed for a more humble role than the dead woman had held.

Perhaps she is the same woman who first had identified Bellanca's body and then had to be helped from the surgery?

I struggled a moment to recall the name by which the Master had called her, and then it came to me: *Lidia.* I let my attention linger on her a moment longer and then focused on her three companions in that same pew.

They were wearing gowns of much the same fashion that Bellanca had worn on the day of her death, so I deduced they must be the other servants to Caterina. As I watched, they each wept a few discreet tears, their version of mourning a genteel contrast to the older servant's copious flood.

Like Bellanca, all three had flaxen hair that had been braided and stylishly wrapped in ribbons beneath close-fitting soft caps. And all had the delicate necks and slim figures of young women not much beyond childhood . . . certainly, young women no older than Caterina, herself. Surrounded by such pale beauties, the contessa's exotic dark looks would be accentuated to an advantage, rather like a sleek young panther set amid a pretty tumble of kittens.

Satisfied with my observations, I gave the remaining mourners equal if discreet scrutiny. The two men in attendance other than the friar sat at opposite sides of the small church. Appearing but a few years older than me, both wore similar expressions of dry-eyed, valiant grief that rivaled the painted emotions I'd seen on any number of the Master's frescoed heroes.

Admirers of Bellanca? Or rivals for her affection?

One wore a page's fine brown and yellow livery, while the other wore the porter's familiar blue and white tunic. Both men were equal enough to her station to seek out her favor. But had one or another of them forsaken love for jealousy? Could one of them have caused the telling bruises Leonardo had seen upon Bellanca's dead flesh and perhaps pushed her to her death?

Frowning, I looked for signs of guilt coloring their respective woe. Neither man gave any indication that he was struggling with remorse; even so, I was not ready to dismiss either of them as a possible suspect. But mindful of the Master's instructions to examine everyone present, I turned my attention to the other women.

They ranged in age from a swollen-eyed girl with curly brown hair who could have been no more than ten years old, to a hunched crone in nurse's garb whose involuntary nodding seemed to keep time with the rise and fall of the friar's Latin. Dutifully, I made mental notes of their various stations and their demeanor. None of them seemed out of place in paying their respects nor drew more than their share of attention.

But even as I began to wonder if this plan would come to naught, I was aware of the chapel door creaking open and someone slipping quietly into the seat beside me. Curious, I glanced over to learn the identity of this latecomer and abruptly found myself locked into the obsidian gaze of the most handsome man I had ever before seen.

5

The Hierophant

The definition of the soul I leave to the wisdom of the friars . . .

—Leonardo da Vinci, *Quaderni IV*

"Dino, my boy, listen to this letter I have drafted to Il Moro, and tell me what you think."

Following the Master's earlier instructions, I had returned from Bellanca's burial prepared to report my findings to him. I had discovered him here in his private quarters, intent upon the missive spread upon the table before him. Waving me to the opposite chair, he picked up the topmost sheet of paper and commenced reading.

"My Most Illustrious Lord," he began, "it is with great sorrow that I write to you regarding my financial situation. You have granted your patronage for almost a year now, during which time I have been honored to fulfill your every request. I regret to remind you that, to this date, I have been paid for but a few of the many commissions I have undertaken at your behest."

He paused and looked up, as if soliciting my approval. At my tentative nod, he went on. "I fear, Excellency, that my slow progress in the matter of the bronze horse has caused you to suffer indignation. And it must be that indignation that has allowed you to forget our agreements. For this, my Illustrious Lord, I regret the anger I have caused and beg your forgiveness and indulgence . . ."

He went on in the same vein for many more paragraphs, each one progressively more humble and fawning than the last. My reaction as I listened was colored first with mild surprise but then swiftly graduated to genuine dismay. How could the great Leonardo—a man of immense pride and passion and genius—so debase himself before the duke?

As the letter ran to a second page, I found myself inwardly cringing at every meek word, mortified on the Master's behalf. Why, Ludovico was but a rough and crude man! Though possessed of considerable power and cunning, he lacked brilliance of either mind or soul. He had seized his rank by means of force and duplicity, rather than earning it through acclaim and merit. Surely these self-berating ramblings addressed to a man so little worthy of regard had not been written by the same Master that I knew and admired!

"Excellency," he finally concluded as he reached for a third page, "I regret the time that I have been forced to spend with other patrons whose humble wages have allowed me to earn a living. Know that a meager sum from you, no more than one hundred ducats, should be sufficient to allow me the freedom to pursue the brass horse and your other commissions. I hold myself ever ready to obey your wishes. I leave you, Excellency, your humble and most grateful servant, Leonardo."

He set down the letter with a flourish and then eyed me expectantly. "So tell me, Dino, how do you find the tone of my letter? Pray, do not be shy," he persisted as I opened and then shut my mouth a time or two without actually speaking. "Tell me what you think."

"Very well, Master," I warily replied, "if you demand my true thoughts, I shall give them. I found the tone of the letter to be excessively unctuous and painfully self-effacing. It put me to mind of a lackey seeking to curry undeserved favor." When he did not bristle at my bold words, I ventured to add, "Indeed, to my mind such a missive is not worthy of you."

Leonardo sat silent a brief moment before breaking into a pleased smile. "Ah, very good. I feared I was not effusive enough," he replied in satisfaction and gathered up the pages. Then, seeing my look of confused disapproval, he asked, "My dear boy, surely you realized that such overblown flattery was deliberate on my part, did you not?"

When I meekly shook my head, he reached over and gave me a consoling pat upon the shoulder.

"Let this be a valuable lesson for you, Dino, should you one day be forced to seek out your patrons to earn your bread. It is but a game we play, bowing and scraping to those of the moneyed classes who would pay for the privilege of owning a work of art from our brushes."

He was folding the letter as he spoke. Now he caught up the burning candle at his elbow to let the stub drip onto the paper and then stamped the resulting small puddle of wax with a fancifully carved bit of stone.

Tucking the sealed correspondence into his tunic, he went on. "We shower the noble and wealthy with honeyed words and insincere flattery. In return, they dole out their patronage. As for the painters unwilling to bend a knee, they may pretend superiority to those of us who do, but they soon find that pride makes for an unsatisfying meal at the end of the day."

"But surely Il Moro, or any noble reading such a letter, would merely think you were making mockery of him," I protested.

The Master shrugged. "I fear not. Indeed, the more ridiculous the rhetoric, the more satisfied these nobles are . . . and the wider they open their purses. Of course, I always ask for twice the amount that I want. This way, when they magnanimously count out but half that figure, both sides leave satisfied."

"I-I see," I replied in consternation and lowered my gaze,

feeling suddenly foolish. I should have known better than to believe that Leonardo would author such a piece of frippery, save in some sort of jest. Had I paid closer attention to my father's business, might I have seen that he also was forced to pen such painfully subservient missives to his own clients?

"Come, Dino, do not despair," he reassured me with a kind smile. "Now that you understand the game and the reasons behind it, you will find it easy enough play when you are older. But let us move on to more important matters. Pray, tell me what you learned at Bellanca's funeral."

Eagerly, I left the one uncomfortable matter behind, even knowing that its replacement subject was equally unsettling. While Leonardo listened attentively, I made my way though the list of those I had seen in the chapel.

My conclusion that the trio of blond young women must be Caterina's remaining maidservants earned a nod, as did my guess that the older woman wrapped in her tragic sobs must be the same servant who had identified Bellanca's body in the surgery.

"Undoubtedly, you are describing Lidia," the Master agreed, "though we shall take the opportunity to view her together to make certain. I grant that we will do well to learn more about her relationship with Bellanca and determine what would spur her to such great mourning."

He took equal interest in my descriptions of the porter and the page, both of whom I had guessed might have had more than a passing affection for the dead woman.

"Very good, Dino . . . I see you have learned something from my lectures in composing a scene," he said in approval. "It is said that actions may speak with greater force than mere words. The fact that these two took pains to sit far apart from each other in so confined a space is telling. We shall endeavor to learn more about them, as well. Perhaps you might make me a small sketch of each man?"

I did as asked and was well pleased when he declared as he reviewed my drawings that he would know either man on sight now. That accomplished, I made quick work of describing the remaining mourners . . . that was, all save one. My only hesitation came when I prepared to describe the man who had slipped into the pew beside me.

MY first impression had been of a dangerously handsome man. I guessed him to be a year or two younger than the Master, though the hard lines of his face made such a determination difficult. He was not bearded, though it appeared a blade had not scraped his cheeks in some days. With his curly black hair sheared well above his shoulders and his mercenary's regalia, I guessed him to be one of the duke's soldiers.

I had seen many such men as he during my time in the duke's court. When not embroiled in a distant battle or in playing sentry at the castle gates, they did little more than swagger aimlessly about the grounds. Brash and crude sorts, these soldiers were, in their scandalously short tunics over parti-colored trunk hose, with swords dangling rakishly from their hips. Only the boldest of civilians, male or female, would purposely choose to confront them.

Yet there was something about this man that was startlingly different from his rougher brethren. Perhaps it was the suggestion of lazy sensuality that clung to him like a houri's scent. Maybe it was the set of his wide mouth, which managed simultaneously to suggest both sensitivity and a certain chill brutality. Or it could have been as simple as his hands, their digits well formed and oddly elegant for a man who made his living brandishing a sword.

My gaze had met his just long enough for me to register the supreme indifference reflected in his heavily lashed dark eyes as he took in my youth, position, and supposed gender. Just as swiftly, he'd apparently dismissed me as unimportant and turned his attention to the activity beyond the altar rail.

I had promptly done the same, focusing on the monk as he made the sign of the cross over the dead woman's body and sprinkled her with holy water. I suspected this man might be one of these mercenaries of which the Master had so disparagingly spoken, one of those fighting men who had given himself up to Mars. And so I should have viewed him as frightening or even repellent.

Instead, though I had exchanged but the briefest of glances with him, I suddenly found myself inexplicably fascinated with the man.

I continued to keep my gaze rigidly forward, even as I felt a hot blush creep up my neck and stain my cheeks crimson. I knew, however, that the man kneeling beside me was unaware of my sudden discomfort in his presence. Doubtless, he had already forgotten me, would take no further notice of me unless by some word or act I called undue attention to myself.

But I would never forget him, I felt certain!

By then, the monk was making his final genuflections while two stooped deacons dressed in rough garb emerged from the shadows. They lifted the pallet upon which Bellanca's body lay onto their shoulders and followed the monk down the aisle toward the chapel door. As I rose with the rest of the mourners, I ventured another glance at the man who had been sitting beside me. I saw to my dismay that he was gone, having left as quietly as he had arrived.

I had trailed the other mourners out of the chapel. Though the lowering sun still shone brightly, a few clouds had begun to gather in the distance, heralding a possible storm to come. It was a fitting sky to hang over this humble service, I decided as I crossed the few steps leading past the iron gateway and into the churchyard.

A moment of hesitation slowed my footsteps when I recalled the previous times I had traversed this same winding path. On those occasions, my destination had been the sprawling stone crypt of the Sforzas, cut into the foot of the small hill overlooking the burial ground. Each foray into that dank, cavelike sepulcher had ended most unpleasantly, giving me an unsurprising dislike for this cemetery.

Thankfully, we remained aboveground as we made our way to the corner spot where Bellanca was to be laid. Unlike the hewn crypts nearby, hers was but a hole scraped in the rocky ground and barely noticeable for the tangle of dying vines around it. Eyeing it, I soberly pondered the fact that she was destined to rest here alone, given that no family had stepped forward to claim her.

Had she truly been alone in the world, I wondered, or had she done as I and left her home in some small village for what promised to be a great adventure in Milan? Perhaps she had parents somewhere—maybe brothers and sisters, as well—who would grow concerned when months and then years passed with no further word from her. Would they ever learn her fate, or would her seeming disappearance haunt them until their own deaths?

Those questions pointed to my own situation. Thus I deliberately concentrated on the activity before me. Feeling uncomfortably out of place among these mourners—though, indeed my motives were sincere—I kept a short distance from the others. Lidia had resumed her sobs, the wrenching sound enough to bring tears to my own eyes. Blinking the dampness away, I stonily watched as the deacons set down the broad plank and lifted Bellanca's body.

The shroud had been tied tightly in several places so that her limp form was clearly discernable beneath the concealing cloth. One man at her head, the other at her feet, they unceremoniously laid her in the grave while the friar recited his final Paternoster and the mourners clung to one another.

As I looked on, a shadow at the edge of my vision caught my attention. This time, I did not bother with guile as I glanced over to see who was watching along with me.

A small shiver of excitement ran through me as I recognized the same soldier from the church leaning on the corner of a nearby crypt. He made a stark, dark figure against the crumbling tan stone, with his black tunic over particolored red and black trunk hose. He wore a black leather jerkin laced tightly over that tunic, and his white shirt puffed stylishly through the slashes in his sleeves . . . the effect managing to convey both stylishness and severity. The requisite sword dangled at his hip, its decorative scabbard gleaming in the afternoon sun. From the possessive way his hand rested upon the weapon, however, I sensed that—decorative or not—it likely was a lethal piece of steel.

I frowned. Now that I had a clearer look at him, it was obvious he was not a soldier of common rank. Could this be the captain of Il Moro's guard, the very man who Marcella had claimed was Bellanca's secret lover?

The possibility recalled me to my duty. Firmly reminding myself that I was here to learn who might have murdered Bellanca and not to moon over dangerously handsome soldiers, I swiftly settled upon a plan of action.

Taking care lest the captain was watching me as keenly as I studied him, I made a silent show of wiping my nose and eyes upon my sleeve. Then, as if I could no longer bear to hear these final prayers, I turned and started back toward the chapel. I waited until my steps took me past a crumbling crypt taller and broader than I; then, with a quick glance over my shoulder to be sure I was not observed, I ducked behind it.

Safely hidden, I eased along the crypt's narrow length and ventured a peek around its corner. Now the captain was positioned directly in front of me, his back to me as he stood but a short distance away. I could freely observe him from this spot, so long as he did not feel my gaze and turn in my direction.

I silently vowed that, this time, I would not let him slip away without my noticing. Already, I had cause to be suspicious of him, simply because of his presumed relationship with the dead woman. And, to be sure, the man's behavior now was unusual. Had he wished to keep knowledge of his relationship with Bellanca secret even after her death, then it would have made more sense for him to avoid her burial altogether. But if he wished to pay his respects with no care for what was said, why did he not join the others, rather than stand apart?

I puzzled over this for the few minutes it took the friar to give his concluding amen. With bowed heads, the mourners echoed that word and began trudging their way back down the path toward the churchyard gate. I had assumed the captain had meant to hide his presence there in the churchyard; therefore, I was surprised again when I saw that he did not bother to conceal himself as the knot of mourners passed him by. But all of them seemingly ignored his presence, save for one.

As she trudged past, leaning heavily on the curly haired little girl, Lidia looked up to meet the younger man's gaze. From my hiding place, I could not see the captain's expression, but Lidia's fleeting look of pain and grief was obvious even at a distance. Just as quickly, she averted her eyes and continued along the path.

They were approaching me now, so that I was forced to crouch on the far side of the crypt lest they remark upon my presence. I waited until the sounds of their footsteps crunching upon the graveled path grew fainter, and then allowed myself another look.

The group had passed the columned opening in the rusty iron fence and turned onto the dusty road headed toward the city gates. Looking back toward the gravesite, I could see the workmen scraping dirt into the narrow hole at their feet while the friar gazed into the distance, wrapped in his own thoughts.

Of the captain, however, there was no sign.

Feeling a bit unsettled at this turn of events, I peered back toward the departing mourners. Perhaps he had joined them without my noticing, I thought with a frown. And that was when a strong hand from behind clamped down hard upon my shoulder.

"You, boy," came a low voice in my ear, like a seductively whispering demon, "what do you think you're doing?"

Pain combined with instinctive fright was enough to bring tears to my eyes. Thinking quickly, I squeezed my eyes shut so that the moisture rolled unchecked down my face and then turned with a wide-eyed grimace to face the captain.

"Oh, woe, leave me be," I cried and snuffled—quite convincingly, I was sure—into my sleeve. "I did not wish anyone to see me w-weep!"

The grip on my shoulder eased. I gave a few more coughing sobs and a sniff; then, pretending to compose myself, I struggled to my feet. Mindful of my station, I dared not look directly at him but gazed up through wet lashes, wringing my cloth cap between my hands in fair imitation of distress that was not entirely feigned.

Up close, the dangerous air that I had sensed about him was intensified as he towered over me, tall as the Master. And he was every bit as handsome as he'd seemed earlier in the chapel. But what took me by surprise was his manner.

I had no doubt that any other of the soldiers, faced with what they would have assumed to be a sobbing young boy, would have reacted with taunts or laughter, perhaps even anger. The captain of the guard, however, merely stared down at me for a long minute. Then he gave a lazy shrug.

"It's over. Be off with you, boy."

I did not argue or wait for him to offer that invitation a second time. With a respectful duck of my head, I turned and trotted as fast as I was able along the familiar rocky path, glad to leave the churchyard behind me.

Now, as I tried to recall for the Master my impressions of the captain of the guard, it finally occurred to me what had unsettled me about the mercenary's presence.

"He seemed quite untouched by her death," I realized aloud. "I saw no sign of guilt nor of grief. In fact, I cannot guess why he was there, if it was not to mourn or to rejoice. I wonder if we were mistaken, and there is no mystery about Bellanca's death, after all."

Leonardo gave my suggestion but a moment's considera-tion before shaking his head. "I fear I am not yet ready to concede in this matter. It is rather like stumbling across a tapestry that has come unraveled. Until all the loose ends are knitted back together again, one cannot see the entire picture. And in the meantime you are left with an untidy tangle of threads."

Then, when I merely stared wide-eyed as I attempted to make sense of his metaphor, he smiled a little and shrugged.

"Indulge me, my dear Dino, at least for another day," he replied, snuffing the candle and rising from the table. "I have an idea that I intend to set into work tomorrow that may shed new light upon the situation. We will discuss the matter further then. But, in the meantime"—he paused and meaningfully patted the breast of his tunic—"I have an im-portant letter to deliver that cannot wait."

"My patience wears like a cheaply made cloak," proclaimed a threatening voice. "Tell me, Leonardo, how much longer must I wait for my horse?"

The stern question came from the Duke of Milan, Lu-dovico Sforza, himself. His appearance the following morn-ing in the main workshop had no doubt been prompted by Leonardo's melodramatic letter of supplication from the day before. Now, Il Moro's harsh visage looked even darker than usual as he glowered at the Master, waiting for a reply.

I was watching from behind a tall screen at one corner of the room, where I had prudently taken cover at the duke's unexpected appearance. It was just after the midmorning meal. While the other apprentices had returned to the pri-vate chamber in the castle where work on the latest fresco was beginning, I had made my way to the workshop at the Master's earlier behest. He had hinted that he had some-thing of interest regarding Bellanca's death to share with me, but the untimely arrival of the irate duke had temporar-ily halted any further conversation.

Leonardo calmly met his patron's outraged gaze. This morning, rather than his usual work garb, he wore a simple yet elegant short blue tunic trimmed in black braid over black trunk hose. In sharp contrast to the Master's sober appearance, the duke was dressed in a high-necked tunic of gold and white brocade. Over it he wore matching long robes, the rich garment deeply hemmed in black velvet so as to hide the inevitable grime from a day's wearing. A bejeweled pouch of the same fabric was belted at his waist, while a black velvet skullcap conveniently covered the bald spot increasingly evident in Ludovico's otherwise heavy curtain of black hair.

As always when I compared the two men, I found the Master to be the more regal of the pair, despite his humbler garb and inferior rank.

"Excellency, I understand your frustration," Leonardo replied in a conciliatory tone. "You must know from the many clay models I have shown you that this great bronze tribute is at the forefront of my thoughts. And given that its purpose is to honor your esteemed father, I dare not grant it less than my best efforts."

At the duke's grunt of concession, the Master went on. "But I beg you to understand, Excellency, that it is a difficult design, given its eventual immense size. And once I am satisfied with the final concept, I must still fashion a clay model half the size of the intended statue in order to be certain such a figure can actually be cast. Such work requires time . . . and money."

"Pah!"

With that sound of disgust, the duke began pacing the workshop floor, each footstep resulting in a sharp clatter. Yesterday's promised rain had fallen during the night, so that the castle grounds oozed mud within the grassy sections of the quadrangle, while leftover puddles lingered upon the courtyard flagstone. Thus, the duke wore over his elegant shoes a pair of pattens, those tall wooden sandals serving to keep the finely crafted black leather clear of the muck. Their sound upon the workshop's wooden floor provided the appropriate angry staccato to accompany his foul mood.

"I hear nothing but excuses from you, Leonardo . . . that, and requests for more florins," he thundered. "And where are those new inventions for my army that you promised? I have yet to see this expanding bridge you claimed you could build. And what of the underwater boat?"

Despite my uneasiness at being an unwilling witness to the duke's outrage, I could not help raising my brows in surprise. *An underwater boat!* Surely such a craft was beyond even Leonardo's great skill, I told myself.

"Fear not, Excellency, the bridge is almost complete," Leonardo hastened to assure him. "Just two days ago, my apprentices gave a final test to my prototype, which performed admirably. Even now, I have the local guild rushing to complete the full-scale model. I predict we shall be able to send it to the field with your men by month's end."

"And the underwater boat?" the duke retorted, though his scowl had somewhat lessened.

The Master gave him a small smile. "I fear it is still in the planning stage; however, I hope to have a small model built at the same time the bridge is completed."

"Harrumph. Very well, then, I will leave you to continue with that work. But I shall expect you to meet the promised dates, and I will hear no further excuses."

Reaching into the pouch at his waist, Ludovico withdrew a small leather bag, which jingled encouragingly as he hefted it in one palm. He handed the bag to the Master, saying, "As I am a fair man, I shall accede to your request for additional funds. But know that the amount is only half of what you asked for in your letter. The remainder, I shall hold until I see both the bridge and the underwater boat complete."

"That is most understandable, Excellency," Leonardo replied and smoothly tucked the pouch into his tunic. For my part, I smothered a grin, recalling the Master's lesson from the night before about asking for twice the amount needed and graciously settling for half. It was apparent that he knew of what he spoke.

Seemingly mollified, the duke summoned his own smile . . . or, at least, what passed for one for him.

"Very well, Leonardo," he went on, "now that this particular matter is settled, I have another assignment for you. If all goes as planned, I shall be announcing an agreement of marriage within the next fortnight. To celebrate the event, I will want you to organize a grand masquerade to be held here at the castle."

"It would be my honor," the Master replied with a small bow. Then, raising a quizzical brow, he added, "May I be so bold to ask, Excellency, if it is your impending nuptials we shall be celebrating?"

"Hardly." The duke's smile broadened into a feral grin. "I fear it would make my mistresses jealous should I decide to take a wife."

He began pacing the room again, raising an arm in a grand gesture. "No, I am arranging this marital alliance for the benefit of all Milan. I have determined to create a new ally from one of our more persistent enemies. You will agree with me, I am certain, that the most efficient way to turn a foe into a friend is through familial ties."

The duke turned to face Leonardo once more, pausing his words for dramatic effect. "And so the die is cast. I intend to broker a marriage agreement between my ward, the Contessa Caterina di Sasina, and the first agreeable duke with whom I can come swiftly to terms."

"It is a solution worthy of your illustrious father," Leonardo agreed with an approving nod. "Such an alliance can only benefit Milan. I shall begin preparations immediately for the festivities. Should I assume that the lady is unaware of your plans for her, and so needs not be consulted as to the arrangements?"

"Caterina will be told of her fate once the agreement has been signed. But, fear not, Leonardo, you will find a bride in attendance. Caterina is my cousin as well as my ward . . . and as such, she understands her duty."

"Of that, Excellency, I have no doubt."

From my hiding place in the corner, I found myself repressing a snort. She might well know her duty, but complying with it was a different matter. The duke should beware lest he assume too much when it came to affairs of the heart.

The Master, meanwhile, was tapping a finger to his chin as if in thought. Coolly, he added, "It occurs to me, Excellency, that whichever bridegroom you settle upon might be flattered at being presented a token of his bride-to-be's favor during the celebration. Might I humbly suggest that a portrait of the lady, herself—painted by your court artist, of course—would be favorably received?"

Ludovico's feral grin returned. "A brilliant suggestion, Leonardo, though I suspect you will charge me dearly for this so-called token. Very well, I shall advise Caterina that you shall have a daily appointment in her chambers to paint her, beginning day after next."

"I am at your service, Excellency."

"Yes, yes." The duke made a gesture of dismissal and turned to leave. "Just be certain you have both the painting and the arrangements for the festivities completed in two weeks' time, or I may reconsider my earlier generosity."

6

The Lovers

The lover is drawn by the thing loved . . .

—Leonardo da Vinci, *Quaderni II*

I waited until the clomping of Ludovico's wooden sandals signaled his departure from the workshop before cautiously slipping out from behind the screen and rejoining the Master.

"Ah, Dino, there you are," he said, his expression one of satisfaction as he jingled the duke's bag of coins in one hand. "I feared the sight of Il Moro sent you scurrying beneath your cot. But I shall assume you were somewhere nearer and were witness to all that transpired."

"I managed to overhear everything," I confessed. "Tell me, Master, did you know about the marriage arrangements?"

"I did not, though it comes as no surprise. Young women of her rank are traditionally used as fodder for the cannon of truce." Tucking the bag inside his tunic, he added, "But I wonder if Il Moro might make a better choice of bartered brides than the Lady Caterina."

"But she is young and beautiful and of noble blood," I

countered in surprise, pointing out the obvious. "Why would you think she would not make some duke a fine wife?"

"Why not, indeed? Come, my boy, join me in my quarters, and I shall reveal a few items of interest that might better explain my words. But first, do you still have that fine page's outfit that Signor Luigi made for you?"

He referred to those garments that I had worn on several occasions while we sought to unravel the mystery surrounding the Conte di Ferrara's murder. A good portion of our investigation had entailed the Master questioning various nobles of Il Moro's court regarding their knowledge of that tragic affair. To explain my presence alongside him, I had assumed the guise of his servant; thus, the court's tailor had made for me an elegant suit as befitted my page's role.

I nodded. "It is carefully stored away in my chest."

"Then don that clothing quickly, and join me in my workshop," he instructed and turned to leave.

I hurried to do as asked, a shimmer of excitement rising within me. Surely he would not have me take on the long-abandoned page's role, save that we were about to embark upon another investigation!

A few minutes later, I stood in the Master's doorway elegantly attired in a boyish tunic of blue silk trimmed in gold velvet over matching parti-colored trunk hose. Accenting Signor Luigi's creation were my red shoes and red cap, which matched the red laces tying my slashed sleeves to my tunic. In keeping with the fashion, I had allowed the white linen shirt I wore beneath to puff through those slits in the fabric, making my slim arms look twice their size.

"Ah, there you are." Gesturing me to join him, Leonardo seated himself at the long table at the far side of the room.

It was apparent that he had been recently at work, for the table's surface was littered with sheets of paper, a handful of various-size brushes and knives, and a pot of glue. In neat contrast was the line of a dozen palm-size seashells, each smooth half serving as a shallow bowl for a different hue of paint. Another, smaller shell held fine flakes of gold leaf, those pieces so thin that an unheeded whisper of breath could scatter them. Whatever the Master had been painting lay to one side, carefully covered with a cloth to keep the drying colors free of dust.

In the center of the table lay a familiar flat bundle.

"You will recall the tarocchi cards I found," he said, unwrapping the cloth and spreading the painted pasteboard pieces in an orderly row. "They belong to the duke's ward, and so I shall gladly return them to her. But as the cards appear to have some as yet unknown connection to Bellanca's death, I was loath to release them without first making a copy. Observe."

He lifted the cloth to reveal a second set of four cards. Taking up the original quartet, he swiftly laid them in a row beneath the others.

I gave an appreciative gasp. The cards the Master had painted were stunning duplicates of the ones belonging to Caterina. Each detail was re-created, from the stoic faces of the tiny figures falling from the tower to the excess of gold surrounding the representation of the Devil.

"No, do not touch them," he warned when I would have reached an admiring hand toward one card. "The paint is not yet dry. I fear I spent much of last night simply gluing paper together to make the cardstock. The painting and gilding were more readily accomplished than that one task, for the artist's simple style is readily copied."

"They are beautiful," I exclaimed, "and even seeing the two sets side by side, I would not know the difference. But what will you do with these copies?"

"I do not know, as yet, but should I need them, I will not have to create them from memory."

He rewrapped the original cards into their familiar packet and then spread the cloth back over the others once more. That accomplished, he settled back in his seat, a slight frown tugging at his lips. "Tell me, Dino," he asked, "have you heard of fortunes being told using tarocchi cards?"

I thought a moment, and then shook my head. "I know of old village women who predict marriage and children and how the crops will fare by gazing into a basin of water or tossing a handful of stones," I told him. "But I have never seen this done with playing cards."

"Nor had I, until I had a brief conversation with Lidia early this morning. From what I gathered, the pastime is of rather recent origin and popular primarily among women who are more likely to have the time to indulge in such folly. I suspect most of them view it as but another means of entertainment, something rather more exciting than a simple game of cards."

His frown deepened. "But likely there are some who believe they have tapped into the esoteric realms and that they can see what is to come. And, unfortunately, the young contessa's greater preoccupation with the loss of her cards than the death of her servant makes me suspect she is one of that number."

I stared at him in some alarm. "Are you saying she goes about telling fortunes? But aren't such dark practices forbidden by the Church?"

"They are discouraged, yes, but in this day and age, most clergy are sufficiently educated to understand that sorcery does not exist." He gave a flick of his fingers, indicating his own disdain for such nonscientific pursuits. "Thus, even should it be whispered that the duke's ward is a student of divination, I do not think she risks burning or stoning as punishment. But such rumors could harm Il Moro's chances of finding a willing suitor for her, and thus jeopardize the alliance he hopes to create."

"So what do we do, Master?"

"We do nothing."

With those flat words, he tucked the packet into his tunic and rose. "Such matters are best left to the duke's advisers, who surely will speak up should the young woman's pursuits prove imprudent. As for myself, Il Moro has tasked me with painting his ward's portrait and organizing an entertainment, both of which commitments shall consume most of my time. Thus, I fear this puts a halt to any investigation into the unfortunate Bellanca's murder."

"But we cannot let such an injustice go unanswered," I blurted in dismay. "I will gladly probe into the matter on your behalf . . . that is, if you will give me leave?"

Leonardo gave a small smile. "My dear boy, why do you think I had you dust off that elegant garb of yours? While I will not allow you to put yourself in harm's way, perhaps you might ask a question here and there, which in turn could lead us to an answer. And so the answer is yes, I give my permission."

Then, as I stood beaming happily at him, he gave me a gentle nudge on the shoulder. "If you wish to investigate, do not tarry here. Come, we are off to pay a call upon a lady."

"I cannot believe you found them," Caterina exclaimed in joyful relief, clutching the small bundle of tarocchi cards to her as if it contained the most valuable of jewels.

Moments earlier, the Master and I had presented ourselves at Caterina's private quarters. As a member of Ludovico's family, she was ensconced in the wing of Castle Sforza where the nobles lived, worked, and slept. I had some small familiarity with this portion of the castle, for I had accompanied Leonardo here weeks earlier while we sought to solve the Conte di Ferrara's murder.

In years past, the castle had served primarily as a fortress, which history was obvious in the series of dank, ill-lit rooms devoid of bright colors and fanciful carving. Il Moro, for all his brutish views of life, had sought to remedy that situation and create a luxurious palace for himself.

Thus, the duke had spent significant funds adding wings and remodeling quarters . . . including filling every available wall, it seemed, with Leonardo's frescoes. While the castle still lacked the breathtaking grandeur of any number of other European palaces, I never failed to be impressed with the sheer physical size of it.

Playing my role as page, I had advised Caterina's blond maidservants of Leonardo's request for an audience with their mistress. We'd been promptly ushered into her private quarters. While I remained several paces back as befitted my assumed station, and the three blond women twittered together in a far corner, Leonardo had stepped forward. With a gallant bow, he had reached into his tunic and presented the young contessa with the familiar cloth-wrapped packet.

It had been that simple action that had brought about her happy cry.

Momentarily ignoring our presence, Caterina now carefully examined each of the tarocchi cards as if to assure herself she had not imagined their return. Meanwhile, her sleek hound, Pio, had rushed from the bedchamber, happily barking at the prospect of visitors.

Today, the broad embroidered collar encircling his long neck was pink and gold, those colors matching the brocaded fabric of Caterina's long robes, and the twist of ribbons decorating her elaborately braided black hair. I saw with some amusement that Pio appeared equally pleased by the good news his mistress had received. Long forelegs tucked to his chest, he began bouncing up and down upon his slim hind legs like a marketplace acrobat.

Apparently satisfied that the cards had returned unscathed, Caterina tucked them into the pouch at her waist. She signaled her prancing pet to sit and then favored the Master with a grateful smile. "I must agree with those who call you genius, signore. How were you able to find them?"

"It was but a matter of pursuing the obvious," he coolly replied. "Since you were certain that Bellanca had absconded with them, I simply looked in the last place she was alive . . . the tower from which she fell."

"The tower, yes," she agreed, her smile fading. "It is well you searched there on my behalf, as I would not have found them, myself. Indeed, I shall never set foot there again . . . that is, I should never want to set foot in that place after what happened there."

Though I kept my expression carefully neutral, I could not help an inner quiver of surprise at the hasty correction to her words. The quick rise of color that momentarily reddened her golden cheeks as she'd realized her error assured me I had not misheard. But what reason would the contessa have had for ever going up into that tower, herself?

And, more to the point, was it possible she had been there when Bellanca fell—or was pushed!—to her death?

Though I was certain he'd been even quicker than I to note her verbal misstep and the possibilities it offered, the Master gave no indication he had heard anything amiss. Instead, he blandly said, "I am pleased to be of service to you. In fact, if it pleases you, I look forward to more time in your company. Has your cousin the duke advised you that he has commissioned me to paint your portrait?"

She nodded, wrinkling her nose in a gesture of girlish dismay. "He informed me this morning, though why anyone should wish for a likeness of me, I cannot guess. Besides, there are many other women at court far more beautiful than I who are more worthy of that honor."

"With that, I must respectfully disagree," Leonardo made haste to reply. "As one who has painted many a lady, I can truthfully say that your features are far more suitable to a compelling portrait than most. I assure you, Contessa, you shall be quite pleased with the result."

"Very well. I cannot oppose my cousin's wishes, no matter that they run counter to my own." She paused and then smiled. "But perhaps if you allow Pio to be included in the painting, I shall be a much more willing subject."

"An excellent idea. If you are agreeable, then I shall return tomorrow at this same time so we may begin work," he said and swept her a small bow. But barely had she turned away than he added, "If you do not mind, Contessa, may I ask you a question regarding the tarocchi cards?"

She turned back to face him, her expression suddenly wary. "What is it you wish to know, signore?"

"I have heard that the cards may be used for a purpose other than simply as an amusing game," he replied, his tone one of bland interest. "Indeed, I am told that some people use them to predict events that have not yet happened. Do you perhaps have that ability to read the cards in such a manner?"

"Are you asking, Signor Leonardo, if I can tell fortunes?"

The small laugh that accompanied her question sounded false to my ears. She did not make an immediate reply but spared a seemingly nervous look over her shoulder at her women. They, in turn, had ceased their chatter and were regarding the Master with what appeared to be sudden suspicion.

In the next moment, however, Caterina had regained her composure and met his gaze once more. "You surprise me, signore. You are known as a scientist and an engineer as well as an artist, are you not? Surely a man such as you cannot believe in predictions and foretelling the future."

"To the contrary, Contessa, as a scientist and engineer I am open to all manner of theories. And sometimes it does not matter what I believe . . . it matters only what others believe."

Caterina shrugged. "Very well, I have nothing to hide. My servant Lidia told me that my mother had once read fortunes in this way, by pulling a few cards at random and interpreting their meanings. She offered to teach me to do the same, and I thought it would be amusing to learn. My women and I sometimes pass the time in this fashion, but it is only a game."

"So it would seem," he agreed.

Then, as if in afterthought, he added, "Still, I confess to being puzzled as to why Bellanca would have taken those cards from you without your knowledge. I wonder if perhaps she truly believed they had some greater meaning. Can you tell me, Contessa, if one were to draw those four particular cards together, what would they mean?"

An expression of anger, and then of pain, flashed across her youthful features, the emotions so fleeting that I might have imagined them. Then she gave him a chill look.

"I would say the cards warn one to beware of dangerous familiarity with a man who claims to offer a partnership. One may easily become confused by emotion, with only disaster coming of such an unwise collaboration."

At that, she swirled about on her heel and swiftly retreated to her bedchamber, Pio bounding behind at her heels. The blond trio shot the Master looks of varying anger and dismay before quickly following after their mistress. The door shut on them, leaving Leonardo and me alone in the antechamber.

"I believe we have been dismissed," he murmured with a hint of a wry smile as I met his gaze. Gesturing me to silence, he led me back through the maze of rooms until we reached the door leading back into the quadrangle.

We strolled with seeming casualness toward the distant stone bench where, on other occasions, the Master and I had discussed any number of conjectures and speculations. Usually, his theories proved to be the more accurate, though I could truthfully say I had managed once or twice to see a connection that even Leonardo missed.

This time, I was all but biting my lip lest the many thoughts swirling in my mind come spilling out too soon. I had no doubt from our brief interview with her that the young contessa had some knowledge of Bellanca's death, perhaps even had played a role in it. Whether or not the Master was thinking the same thing, however, he gave no indication as he distributed pleasant bows and smiles to the various nobles we passed by.

Finally, as we reached the stone bench, he gestured me to sit. "I can see you are about to burst with questions and theories, my dear boy," he said with a wry lift of his brow, "so talk away. Just take care who might be listening in."

I gave a quick look about to confirm that no one was walking by within earshot and then softly exclaimed, "She has been to the tower before. I wonder if she could have been there when Bellanca fell? Maybe she caused the bruises you saw, perhaps from fighting with Bellanca to keep her from leaping, or maybe even from struggling to push her to her death!"

"I presume that by 'she' you mean the Lady Caterina," the Master interjected, cutting me short. "I will agree it is possible she knows more about her servant's death than she is saying, but my greater interest is in the man she mentioned in her supposed reading of the cards. I venture to say this has something to do with the man who has been an enigma to this point, the captain of Il Moro's guard."

"Perhaps the contessa knew of her servant's relationship with the captain and disapproved, and so she used her cards to deliver that message."

I offered this suggestion with a bit more hesitation. Certainly, it would be within Caterina's right to dictate with whom her maid associated. But I could not believe that being forbidden that particular relationship would be sufficient cause for Bellanca to take her own life. Or would it?

Leonardo, however, was shaking his head. "I fear we are about to make a novice's mistake, forming a theory before we have sufficient evidence. We shall first need to learn more about the various players; thus, I've already taken the liberty of making a few discreet inquiries about the captain."

Of course, I did not question the Master as to the identity of his source, knowing that person could as easily be the stableboy as it could be a member of the Sforza family. I had long since learned that Leonardo had the simple yet uncommon gift of being able to mingle with equal ease among both the common folk and the nobles. In turn, those of almost any rank often found themselves confessing their greatest fears and darkest sins to him, if only quite by accident. Thus, given my own small secret regarding my imprudent interest in the dangerously handsome captain, I did my best not to appear too eager to discover what the Master had found out.

"His name is Gregorio," Leonardo began, "and until recently he was in the field commanding a squadron against one or another of Milan's enemies. He differs from most of the mercenary soldiers in that he was not foreign born but apparently was raised here at Castle Sforza. It is said he took up soldiering at an early age, which explains his relative youth despite his position of responsibility."

He paused, and I waited to hear more. As always, the Master did not disappoint me.

"It seems Gregorio suffered some slight wound, which brought him back here to the castle a few months ago," he continued. "It was at that point he managed to obtain his promotion to captain of Il Moro's guard. He had the advantage over others who might have coveted the role, for he is as clever with words as he is with his sword."

Leonardo gave a slight frown. "More than one person described him as charmingly ruthless, which can indeed be a potent combination . . . particularly when it comes to women. And it does not hurt that he fills the soldier's uniform well."

"So you are saying it would not be out of character should he and Bellanca have been more than mere acquaintances," I delicately suggested while fighting a blush as I recalled just how well the captain *had* filled his uniform.

Fortunately, the Master did not notice my discomfiture, even though he did take my meaning.

"Certainly, the tower from which Bellanca fell would have been an ideal trysting place," he agreed. "Few people other than the guard have access to the walls surrounding the castle grounds. The four towers are even more closely watched, given their importance to the castle defense. One must be known—or be invited—by someone of the guard in order to gain entry to any of them."

"But how did you climb the tower without being noticed, then?" I curiously asked.

A flicker of a sly grin lightened his expression for a moment. "Let me just say that, as an avid student of architecture, I had a slight advantage. I was able to deduce where the original builder of these fortifications placed an alternate entrance that the casual observer would never notice."

A secret passage! At any other time, the lure of such a mystery would have readily distracted me. This day, however, the greater unknown surrounding Bellanca's untimely death more than served to hold my attention.

"So what would you have me do next, Master?" I asked instead. "Surely if there was a relationship between Bellanca and Gregorio, someone else must have had some suspicion. Perhaps I should try to find the two young men I saw in attendance yesterday at Bellanca's burial. If they were rejected swains, they might well have something to say about the captain that could be of use."

"An excellent suggestion, my boy," he replied with an approving nod that warmed me almost as much as thoughts of the handsome captain. "But fear not, despite my previous vow, I shall not leave all the work to you."

He rose from the bench, and I swiftly followed suit.

"For my part, I will have another word with the servant Lidia," he continued, starting back in the direction of the workshop. "Since she apparently has knowledge of the late Contessa di Sasina, she might well be someone in whom the contessa's daughter would confide. I would also venture that she has some insight into the activities of all the young women—including Bellanca—who surround Caterina."

He slowed his steps long enough to push back his right sleeve and view the odd mechanism strapped to his arm. A wrist clock, he called it . . . a miniature version he'd designed of the great tower clock topping the castle's main gate.

I noted the clever invention's reappearance on his forearm with pleasure. During our ultimate encounter with the Conte di Ferrara's killer, that same wrist clock had been sacrificed as a makeshift shield while protecting the Master from a potentially fatal blow from a knife. Though its case still appeared faintly battered, I could hear the whispering tick as its complicated collection of inner springs and cogs kept track of the hour.

"It is almost midday," he noted. "Return to the workshop

and don your usual tunic, Dino, for you shall be back to your role as apprentice for the remainder of the day."

Then, before I could give way to disappointment, he added, "But you shall take the very long way to that chamber where the others have begun work on the fresco. And perhaps along the way, you shall have the opportunity to discover the identities of the two young men in question. If you succeed, then attempt to find them and engage them in casual conversation; then report back to me what you learn."

"I understand, Master."

Indeed, if all else failed, I would go hat in hand to Marcella and make Dino's apologics to her. The kitchen maid would certainly know those youths' names. Whether she revealed them to me, however, was another matter . . . one no doubt dependent upon how well I could mollify her injured feelings.

"Very well," he replied, apparently satisfied to allow me to investigate on my own, "but do keep in mind that tomorrow—"

Whatever the Master was about to say was abruptly cut short by the echo of a woman's scream from the far side of the quadrangle. We exchanged swift glances of surprise before quickly gazing about for the origin of that frightened cry.

It took but an instant to spot its source.

A dozen or more people had gathered a short distance from the main gate, standing beneath the cylindrical tower that anchored the farthermost corner of the fortification's front wall. From their garb, most of the spectators appeared to be servants—some gesturing, others merely staring—though I spied a likely noble or two among them. We were not close enough to see what held their attention; still, to my mind, the gathering was unsettlingly reminiscent of the scenario that had played out a few afternoons earlier in the shadow of a different tower.

The Master apparently shared my concerns. "Come, Dino," he urged, starting toward the group at a quick pace.

"It appears someone is in need of assistance, which perhaps we can provide."

I hurried to follow after him. As we drew nearer, I could see the number of people milling beneath the tower swiftly increasing. Likely, the newcomers had been pulled from the ranks of those who, like us, had been strolling about the green and been abruptly attracted by the scream. *Like flies drawn to honey.* The thought flashed through my mind.

Or, like flies drawn to some other, more ghastly sticky substance.

With calm urgency, Leonardo pushed his way through the widening circle of spectators, with me close on his heels. Barely had he broken through that ring, however, than he halted. I narrowly avoided stumbling into him as I stopped, as well. Then, rising on tiptoe, I peered over his shoulder to learn what had brought him to a standstill.

At first glance, the middle-aged woman seated on the grass but a few feet from him appeared asleep. Her legs were stretched childlike before her, so that her feet and ankles protruded from the simple brown gown she wore over a threadbare chemise. She was leaning against the stone of the portico at the tower's base, her head drooping and her eyes peacefully closed. A closer look, however, revealed a thin stream of foam dripping from her slack lips, while her skin had taken an unnatural bluish white hue.

Horrified, I still continued to stare, for something about this woman seemed compellingly familiar. It wasn't until I noted her long black braid untouched by any threads of gray that I realized who she was.

"Lidia," I softly gasped, and was met by the Master's confirming nod.

He stepped forward and knelt beside the woman, while I stayed a prudent distance back with the other observers. After a perfunctory check of her pulse, he refrained from laying further hand upon her as he scrutinized her still figure. Then, to my surprise, he leaned even closer and—quite strangely—appeared to sniff at her lips!

"It's Lidia. She's dead, ain't she?" squeaked a frantic female voice behind us.

The speaker appeared to be a laundress, for her voluminous sleeves were rolled high enough to reveal almost the whole of her beefy, reddened arms, which cradled a bundle of fresh-smelling linens. With a swift jab of a chapped elbow, she managed to press between me and the rotund porter beside me to get a better look.

Other voices promptly began echoing the laundress's question. The crowd had doubled in the past few minutes, their number paying Lidia the attention in death that I was certain she never received in life. All remained a prudent distance from the victim, however, lest whatever caused her sudden death prove catching.

Despite myself, I was staring, too, unable to look away. The sight of Lidia lying there abruptly called to mind one of Caterina's tarocchi cards . . . the one representing Fire. The elaborate imagery showed two figures falling from a crumbling tower. *Two*. Was it merely unhappy coincidence that two women had each been found lying in the shadow of one of the castle's towers within days of each other?

Or could it be that Caterina's cards somehow had offered a glimpse of the future?

Apparently satisfied with his impromptu examination, the Master rose and brushed the grass from his knees. Catching his eye, I gave him a questioning look.

"Do you know what killed her?"

I kept my voice deliberately low as, rubbing my bruised ribs, I edged away from the intrusive laundress. She did not notice my defection, however, for she had grabbed the unwitting porter's arm and was busy expounding upon her own theories with him as her captive audience.

Leonardo shook his head. "While I cannot say with total certainty at this point, I have my suspicions."

He indicated a crude clay jug little bigger than his fist that lay on its side near the dead woman's right hand. It was half-hidden by the grass, so I'd not noticed it until then.

With a magician's skillful hands—among his other talents, Leonardo was quite a fair practitioner of mystical illusions—he stealthily snagged a cloth from the laundress's bundle without her noticing the theft. Then, careful not to touch it directly with his hands, he caught up the jug and swiftly wrapped it in the cloth.

Barely had he secured the small vessel, however, than the crowd around me began shuffling about like hens roused by a fox's unexpected appearance. Pushing their way through the gawkers were three of the duke's men . . . among them, I saw with a sudden quickening of my pulse, the darkly handsome captain of the guard, himself.

His men flanking him, Gregorio halted before Lidia's body, staring down at her with an unreadable expression. Then, turning to Leonardo, he demanded, "What has happened here?"

"I fear, Captain, that I know as little as you."

With that smooth reply, the Master handed off the wrapped jug to me in a gesture so casual that even I almost did not notice it. Gingerly accepting the bundle—by now, I was certain that he suspected it had contained a poison of some sort—I drifted back as unobtrusively as possible among the milling spectators so as not to call attention to myself.

"I arrived upon the scene only moments ago," Leonardo went on, his expression a study in concern. "Sadly, the poor woman—Lidia, I believe is her name—was long past help by then. I've not yet had the opportunity to speak with these people to learn if any of them saw anything amiss. If you would care to have your men detain them, I shall make quick work of that."

The captain's expression sharpened, and he momentarily ignored the Master's suggestion.

"You are Leonardo the Florentine, are you not? I have heard from my predecessor that Il Moro gives you free rein about the castle. In fact, it was you and not he who was charged with resolving the murder of the duke's cousin not long ago."

"Surely you must know that decision was Il Moro's alone," the Master replied with a small shrug. "He had reason to fear that the murderer was someone close to the court, perhaps even a member of the guard. As I was a relative newcomer to the castle, the duke felt he could trust me."

"So why do I feel I cannot trust you at all?" Gregorio countered with a slight baring of his teeth that might—or might not—have been considered a smile. "Fear not, my men and I shall handle this situation. You need concern yourself no further with the matter."

I waited for Leonardo's protest, but he simply gave a nod of acquiescence. "As you wish, Captain. But perhaps you would allow me to remove the poor woman to the surgery so that the physician might determine a cause of death. And, of course, any family she has here at the castle should be made aware of this sad turn of events."

"You give our esteemed physician far too much credit. I doubt he could determine any cause less obvious than a knife to the victim's heart or a rope about her neck. As for the woman's family, there is but one son to notify, and he is well aware of what has happened."

"But how can that be," the Master protested, "when the tragedy has only just occurred?"

The captain's twisted smile thinned to the faintest of sneers. "I thought you to be cleverer than that, Florentine. He knows because he is standing before you right now. You see, Lidia happens to be my mother."

7

The Chariot

Climb onto your wagon, and your path shall be clear.

—Leonardo da Vinci, *The Notebooks of Delfina della Fazia*

"Quickly, Dino! The plaster will dry while you stand there daydreaming," Constantin exclaimed, giving me a sharp slap upon the shoulder.

With an obedient nod, I scooped another trowel of plaster from the bucket and flung it onto the wall. A fine spattering of white blew back at me, freckling both my tunic and face. I did not bother to wipe off that mixture, however, for the next flung trowel's worth would simply add another ghostly layer to replace the one scrubbed away.

"Hurry, Dino," Tito echoed beside me. Rapidly, he tossed plaster from his own bucket, the mixture smacking rhythmically against the wall. "Vittorio and Bernardo are on our heels!"

Since early morning, we had been plastering this particular wall in preparation for Leonardo's next fresco. The project was less ambitious than many of the previous frescoes I had helped to prepare, for it was being placed in a private chamber rather than a public hall. Here, the walls were half as tall as in some of the grand rooms in which we had worked before. Thus, we were not forced to balance precariously upon long stretches of rickety scaffolding in order to cover the uppermost portions. Instead, we stood upon boxes and stools when a portion of the wall exceeded our reach.

The plaster—a simple mix of water and lime and sand—had been prepared the day before. All we needed to do this morning was stir in a bit more water and then spread it upon the wall. Tito and I had started at the room's far end, moving toward the wall's midpoint while applying a slowly widening layer of plaster. Bernardo and Vittorio followed behind us with a large board, using it between them as a tanner might use a scraper upon a hide to smooth each section of wall that we completed.

A second team of apprentices had started from the opposite end and was following the same method. Both our groups eventually would meet in the center, our combined labors resulting in a single smooth, white surface. Under Constantin's supervision, we already had met twice. After each coat, we used comblike metal tools to scratch a grooved pattern over the entire wall so that the next layer would better adhere to the one beneath.

I sighed and flexed my aching hands. By day's end, the original surface of the wall would have thickened by several inches and be ready for the final rough coat of plaster. But this would not be the end of our preparations. Using the large patterns that Paolo and Davide had created, our next step once we were assured that the plaster was completely dry would be to transfer onto the wall the preliminary chalk outlines of what would become the fresco.

This work was always done by us apprentices. Using a special tool, we would trace over the drawing, punching tiny holes along each inked line to create a stencil. We would then affix the drawing to the wall with bits of wax, and one or more of us would commence a technique known as pouncing. This entailed gently beating a small bag of charcoal powder along those pinpricked lines, the resulting puffs of black dust filtering through the holes to leave a perfect representation of the drawing in their wake.

Unfortunately, the apprentice charged with this task ended up similarly blackened, so that I unashamedly did my best to avoid this role whenever possible!

The remainder of the process was equally familiar to me by now. Once the stenciling was complete, the Master would appear to review the result. Frowning and muttering, he'd make any changes or corrections simply by rubbing away the offending charcoal and redrawing it to his satisfaction. When he at last gave his approval, the final pattern then would be inked over by Constantin, Paolo, and Davide to leave a permanent outline.

And then the true work of fresco would begin.

I flung another trowel of plaster onto the wall, picturing how its surface soon would look. Every morning, an apprentice would lay a smooth, thin layer of plaster over just the area the Master would paint that morning. It was a precise process, building upon the previous day's work. Every time the Master completed a section of fresco, its edges were neatly cut into straight lines. This allowed the succeeding day's plaster to be butted up beside it, so that the growing work appeared seamless though it was composed of numerous sections.

Of course, each day's new coating covered the outline beneath and necessitated reapplying that portion of the stencil to the wall. While that work was being done, other apprentices would busy themselves mixing the various hues of tempera needed that day. The combination of pigment, egg yolk, and warm water dried rapidly, so the colors had to be used within a short period of time.

And when all this was accomplished, Leonardo would begin his work.

It was a daunting task that allowed little room for error. As the fresh colors flowed onto the plaster one at a time, the tempera soaked into the smooth surface, actually becoming a permanent part of the wall as it dried. Sometimes, the

Master allowed us to watch as he painted, a score of us clus-
tering a respectful distance behind him as we marveled at
the magic of his swiftly moving brush. Other times, he
would shoo us away, preferring to work alone. And on some
occasions, when boredom or restlessness struck him, he did
not paint at all. Instead, he would allow one of the older apprentices possessing the skill to mimic his style to color the
entire day's section of the fresco!

Now, scraping up still more plaster, I sighed again. I suspected that, no matter how diligently we worked to finish
the wall and apply the stencil, it would be some time before
the Master returned to this chamber. After all, he had but a
fortnight to complete the portrait of Caterina and still plan
the festival that would mark her engagement to her yet-to-
be-decided-upon duke. And I suspected that after yesterday's strange death of the servant Lidia, his attention would
be even further divided, even though the duke had all but
forbidden him to turn his time to any other effort.

"Dino, you hurt my ears, the way you heave and groan
like an old woman," Tito spoke up, abruptly shaking me
from my thoughts. "I find this work tedious, too, but you
do not hear me lamenting."

Half a dozen clever retorts came to mind, but I contented
myself with sticking my tongue out at him and flinging
more plaster onto the wall. Unfortunately, my throw was a
bit more forceful than necessary, so that a large portion of
the plaster splashed in Tito's direction.

He leaped back and let loose with a few choice curses.
"See what you've done!" he exclaimed, staring down at his
plaster-spotted tunic in mock dismay.

I shrugged and gave a sheepish grin. "My apologies,
Tito. I swear it was not deliberate. Besides, you're already
half-covered in plaster."

"Yes, but that was by my own carelessness," he huffed in
melodramatic tones. "This is your plaster . . . and quite a
different matter."

"Now who sounds like the old woman?" I retorted with a

grin and returned to my work. Barely had I thrown another trowel's worth, however, than I felt something hit with a splat squarely upon my back.

"What's this?"

With that exclamation, I gave a quick look over my shoulder while Vittorio and Bernardo stood by snickering. I promptly frowned at the sight of a large glob of white plaster stuck between my shoulder blades. It hung there a moment and then slid off, landing with a plop onto the stone floor.

"Sorry," Tito said, smothering a grin of his own as he made a show of stirring more water into a new bucket of plaster. "I swear it was not deliberate."

"I'm sure it was not," I replied with exaggerated politeness even as I gave a quick glance about the hall.

Apparently satisfied that, with his rebuke to me, he had spurred us on sufficiently, Constantin had stepped from the room. Emboldened by his absence, I waited until Tito turned back to the wall again; then, scraping up another trowel full, I flung the plaster in his direction.

The glob landed with a satisfying smack upon his shoulder.

"Argh!" came his cry of surprise. Then, with a grin, he shoved his trowel into his bucket.

"You have declared war, Dino. Surrender now," he demanded, waving the plaster-laden trowel in mock threat, "or prepare to pay the consequences!"

"Never!"

With that gleeful retort, I loaded up my own trowel. We eyed each other for a few heartbeats, circling about like warriors prepared to unleash their swords; then, with simultaneous cries to battle, we began flinging plaster.

"Get him, Tito!"

"Good shot, Dino!"

"That's two hits . . . Dino, he is beating you!"

Vittorio and Bernardo, joined by the other group of apprentices, had abandoned their tasks. Forming a wide circle around us, they clapped and shouted encouragement to us both.

"Argh!" I heard Bernardo cry in mock pain after a shot of mine went wild. "You missed Tito and hit me!"

I had no time for apologies, for a clump of plaster smacked me squarely in the chest, making me laugh and gasp at once. Tito was not coming through the battle unscathed, however, for my next well-placed shot caught him in the back of the head as he'd turned for more munitions. He whipped about, eyes gleaming and grin broadening as he raised not one but two trowels laden with even more plaster.

"No fair," I protested with a laugh, though my eyes widened as I saw he indeed intended to fling both at one time. My bucket was empty now, leaving me no way to counter. Moreover, the time it would take for me to rush to the main tub near the doorway for more plaster would allow Tito to pelt me unchecked for several moments.

While the other apprentices laughingly urged him on, I dropped my trowel and clasped my hands to my chest in a gesture of exaggerated entreaty. "Please, spare me, good Tito, and I shall gladly call you the victor!"

My plea was not entirely in jest, for I pictured plaster dripping off my head and down my face as he made his final assault. Then I gave an inner shrug. No matter how it ended, we both still would be spending significant time at the fountain washing off the evidence of our small war. And likely his aim would be less accurate with his sinister hand.

Tito, meanwhile, was shaking his head. "You began the battle, Dino," he exclaimed above the sound of the other boys' cheers, "and I intend to finish it. Now, say your prayers and prepare for the end!"

With that cry, he hurled the contents of both trowels squarely at once. I did not hesitate but flung myself forward onto the stone floor, covering my head and hoping I'd been fast enough to avoid the bombardment. A few seconds later, when no shower of plaster landed upon me, I knew I was safe.

"Aha, the battle is over," I declared, sitting up and grinning triumphantly at Tito. "I believe we should call it a draw, and—"

I broke off abruptly as I saw Tito was not looking in my direction but was instead gazing in horror at a spot somewhere behind me. The other apprentices had fallen preternaturally silent, as well, their faces reflecting similar expressions of shock. I scrambled to my feet, slipping a bit in the wet plaster that spotted the floor around me. Sudden dread washed over me as I slowly turned, aware for the second time in but a few days that there could be only one reason for the abrupt end to the hilarity.

Leonardo stood but a few feet away, staring down with unmistakable dismay at the plaster staining the front of his fine black tunic. Constantin was peering over the Master's shoulder at us, his expression one of mingled disapproval and disbelief. For a few moments, the only sound to be heard was the faint splashing that was the sound of plaster dripping from Leonardo's garb onto the stone floor. Then Tito swept off his plaster-spotted hat and bowed his head.

"Master, please forgive me!" he exclaimed in a miserable voice, wringing the unfortunate cap between his hands. "I did not see you standing there, or else—"

"Or else you would have taken greater care in your aim?" Leonardo's tone was mild, but his gaze was stern as he turned it upon me. "And you, Dino, what have you to say for yourself?"

"Master, I beg your forgiveness, as well!" I cried, bowing my own head. "Please do not blame Tito for what happened. The fault is mine. I began tossing the plaster about; he merely followed my lead."

"No, it is my fault," Constantin staunchly spoke up. Squaring his shoulders, he went on. "It was my responsibility to make certain that the day's work proceeded smoothly. In that, I failed by leaving these miserable apprentices to their own devices for a few minutes."

"Well, it wasn't my fault," Bernardo piped up from behind the safety of a quivering Vittorio. "Master, I told them to stop, but they refused to heed me."

"Indeed?" came Leonardo's dry reply.

Turning to Constantin, he went on. "Tito and Dino shall remain here with me. Take the other apprentices back to the workshop. As their punishment for not stopping their fellows from causing such mayhem, they shall spend the next week boiling rabbit skins for gesso, hauling water and wood, and cleaning the workshop. Do not allow any of them to pick up a brush, even to repair it. As for your punishment"—he paused and gave the senior apprentice a considering look—"you shall spend the same week listening to their lamentations."

"Very well, Master." Constantin ducked his head in agreement, his relief at the mildness of his rebuke apparent. Then, gesturing to the others, he ordered, "Quickly, back to the workshop with all of you."

Leonardo waited until the other apprentices had taken their swift leave before turning back to Tito and me. "And now, my dear boys, what punishment should I inflict upon you?" he asked, glancing from us, to his sullied tunic, to the room in general.

Shamefacedly, I followed his gaze. Great globs of plaster littered the floor and clung to the otherwise smooth surface of the wall. As for the final section upon which we'd been working, the rough plaster was rapidly drying, for Vittorio and Bernardo had abandoned their post before smoothing it to match the remainder of the wall. If we did not begin immediate repair, we might have to chip away that section and begin again.

I felt embarrassment color my cheeks as I took in the disarray. How could I have stooped to such imprudent behavior? I silently chided myself.

Tito spoke up. "Certainly, Master, we should first smooth the remaining plaster, and then clean the floors and walls."

"And Tito and I can finish this layer of plaster ourselves," I hastened to add, while Tito nodded his agreement.

Leonardo lifted a wry brow. "That was to be expected. Now, how will you make amends beyond that?"

Tito and I exchanged glances. His look of misery likely reflected my own unhappy expression. "Of course, we shall have your tunic laundered, and the cost taken from our wages," I tentatively offered.

Tito nodded. "And we shall not touch a brush for a month."

"And we shall take up the boiling of skins and other tasks for the remaining three weeks once the other apprentices' punishment is at an end," I added with a hopeful look.

Leonardo considered our words and then nodded. "You will do all this; additionally, you will make an act of contrition to Constantin before the other apprentices asking his forgiveness for betraying his trust. And then we shall consider the incident at an end. Now, begin your cleaning and plastering.

"And do not worry," he added with a small smile as we hurried to obey. "I shall send over Vittorio with two bowls of food in a bit so you need not stop your work to partake of the midday meal."

"Thank you, Master," Tito replied . . . quite sincerely, I knew. The punishment we had received was quite mild, given our transgression. Another master might well have dismissed his apprentices for such foolery.

I made my own thanks as I grabbed up my trowel and began scraping plaster from the floor back into my empty bucket. I heard the Master's footsteps pause at the doorway, and I looked up. He gave me a meaningful nod.

"When you have finished here, Dino," he said, "I shall want to see you in my private quarters about another matter."

"As you wish," I calmly replied, though inwardly I felt a shiver of excitement. I had been waiting impatiently for such a summons since yesterday afternoon. Surely this matter must have something to do with the deaths of Bellanca and Lidia . . . and I had some small new information to impart.

Working quickly alongside Tito—he was as anxious as I was to finish our task—I thought back over the startling announcement the captain of the guard had made the day before.

"LIDIA happens to be my mother," he had coolly declared as the Master was attempting to arrange for the woman's body to be taken away to the surgery.

I had immediately believed him. Though there was little resemblance between the two save for their similar shocks of thick black hair, he did appear of an age to be Lidia's son. Moreover, I could not conceive of a reason why he would lie about such a thing, particularly since his claim could be checked by questioning those servants likely to have known of the connection between them.

What *had* concerned me, however, was his seeming indifference to the tragedy . . . far more unsettling than even his oddly aloof reaction to Bellanca's death. Surely a son could not be so untouched by his own mother's death!

What the Master had thought about it, I was not certain. He had made his polite condolences to the captain; then, taking me by the elbow, he had hurried us through the ring of bystanders who still continued to gape.

"This smacks of something more than coincidence," he'd muttered once we were clear of the crowd and he had retrieved the bundled jug from me. "What do you make of it, Dino?"

"It seems strange to me, as well, but beyond that I cannot say," I had truthfully answered. Here was yet another woman found unexpectedly dead beneath one of the castle towers, though it seemed her death was less a mystery than Bellanca's still was. Or was it?

"Do you still wish me to look for those two young men,

the porter and the page, so I can learn of their connection to Bellanca?" I asked instead.

The Master hesitated, and I was sure he had changed his mind. Then he nodded. "Look for them, Dino . . . and when you find them, make certain you also learn what they know of Gregorio, captain of Il Moro's guard."

The grim words had sent alarm through me. Though I had to admit the captain's behavior was odd, surely the Master could not suspect that a man of his position could have killed either of the women! More truthfully, I did not want to believe that the dashing captain could have had a hand in either tragedy. But whether the deaths were murder, suicide, or accident, I could not deny that the coincidences surrounding them were indeed odd. I ticked off the similarities on my fingers.

Both were servants to Ludovico's ward, Caterina. Both had some connection to the captain of the guard. And both deaths seemingly were suicides . . . though with clever twisting about of the circumstances, they well could be murders.

My heart heavy, I had done as the Master bade and went in search of the men I had seen in the chapel. The page was nowhere to be found. As for the porter, I'd fortuitously stumbled across the young man as he was relieving himself behind the stables.

I had learned his name was Luca, and it seemed he had the unfortunate habit of stealing the wine he was in charge of bringing up from the cellar. The fact that I had caught him holding a small jug in his free hand while he attended to business with the other had given me an immediate advantage. He had eagerly accepted my promise of silence in return for conversation.

Of Bellanca, he had hinted that he had known her in the usual Biblical sense, though I suspected that claim was little more than a wistful boast. He had been far less reticent, however, regarding the captain.

"Damned arrogant bastard he is, stealing away another man's woman," Luca had slurred with no little venom.

"You'd think he was a duke, himself, the way he swaggers about, and him but the son of a wet nurse. Oh, yes, I knew him as a boy," the porter went on, needing little urging from me. "He was a coldhearted, ambitious bastard then, though for some reason all the girls were drawn to him."

Finally, suspicion had penetrated the wine fumes that clouded his thoughts. "Why do you care, anyhow?" Luca had sputtered, eyeing me with misgiving. Then he looked around, wrinkling his nose in disgust. "Fah, it smells like something dead back here. I'm going back to the kitchen."

Thus summarily abandoned, I had gone to report my findings to the Master. He had not been in the workshop, however, nor in his quarters. Thus, I had resumed my usual chores for the remainder of the day, falling asleep only well after midnight after having waited in vain for him to summon me. This morning had brought no further instruction, so I'd accompanied the others here to the chamber to prepare its wall for the fresco.

IT was well past noon when Tito and I finally finished repairing our damage and scribing the now-completed layer of plaster. The remaining work would be completed the next day by other apprentices, not us, for I had no doubt Tito and I would be relegated to menial tasks along with Vittorio and the others.

"I hope you're satisfied," Tito had spoken up once, though his words lacked any malice. Thus, we had left the hall as friends, though I was certain Tito would take every opportunity in the coming days to remind me what my moment of folly had brought us.

Once we'd paid a visit to the fountain to scrub the plaster from ourselves, we parted at the workshop. Not bothering to change into my other, unplastered tunic, I hurried to Leonardo's quarters. His door was open, so I ventured inside.

He was not within, but it was apparent he had been hard

at work these past hours from the scattering of sketches upon his table. Tentatively—though I was sure he'd not begrudge me a look—I picked up the drawings and began leafing through them in openmouthed admiration.

He had kept his appointment with Caterina, it seemed, for the sketches were all of her. Doubtless, he had been trying to decide upon a final pose for his portrait of her, for each one caught her at a slightly different angle and with a different expression.

In one, she sat solemnly staring back at the observer, while Pio curled with elegant grace at her feet. A second sketch had her standing in profile, Pio at her heels in a scene reminiscent of depictions of the young goddess Diana, accompanied by her ever-present hound. Yet another showed the young contessa faintly smiling as if at some secret she held, while Pio sat upon her lap gazing out with a similar amused expression upon his delicate canine features. All of the drawings caught the inner spark that gave life to her slightly exotic beauty, so that any of the poses would result in a portrait that would be wonderful, indeed.

"What do you think, Dino?" came the Master's voice from behind me, causing me to drop the pages back onto the table with a guilty start.

He picked them up again and began leafing through them, his expression one of preoccupation. He had changed from his plaster-spattered black tunic into an equally elegant one of green silk trimmed in gold. I felt myself blush again. No doubt he had dressed this morning with deliberate care to pay his call upon Caterina, only to have Tito—and me, by extension—render that original garb unwearable.

Recalling that he'd asked me a question, I cleared my throat a bit uncertainly. "All of them are wonderful," I ventured with no exaggeration, "but I find myself preferring the last one, where the contessa smiles as if she knows something that we do not."

"I quite agree," he replied with an approving nod, setting aside the other two sketches to give this one a closer look. "Too many times, the subject of a portrait appears not to have a single thought in his—or her—mind. But this one shall be different."

He held the drawing at arm's length.

"I quite agree," he repeated, squinting as if picturing the finished work. "In fact, in choosing this particular approach to her portrait, I will be able to elevate it to something more interesting than a simple likeness to be presented to her intended husband. I predict that those who see the final painting will be less intrigued by her beauty than they will be with wondering what secret lies behind that small smile."

His expression now reflecting satisfaction, he set down the paper and turned to me.

"You can see from my handiwork that I was able to keep my appointment with the Contessa di Sasina, though I fear she was distraught over the loss of Lidia. She appeared genuinely grieved, unlike her reaction to Bellanca's death. And she cannot believe that Lidia took her own life."

"But what did you discover about the vessel we found beside her?" I asked, unable to contain my curiosity. "Did it contain poison, as you suspected it might?"

"There was little enough left behind to test," he said with some asperity, as if blaming the woman for that lack, "but enough remained for me to smell the odor of almonds mixed in with the wine . . . the same scent I also smelled upon her lips. Moreover, her end must have come swiftly enough that she did not have time to attract a crowd until after her death. Thus, I suspect the cause of her death likely was cyanide poisoning. Such a brew is easily made by boiling the pits and seeds of certain fruits and then pouring off the deadly liquid, which will rise like noxious cream to the top."

"But do you think she drank it deliberately, or did someone give it to her?" I persisted.

The Master shrugged. "That, my dear Dino, is the question we still must answer. Now, sit for a moment and tell me what you learned yesterday."

Settling on the bench, I recounted my conversation with

the porter, as well as my failure to locate the page. Leonardo dismissed my consternation on that last count with a flick of his fingers.

"Your exchange with the porter is telling enough," he assured me. "Indeed, I suspect that any conversation with the page would yield similar results and merely confirm what I already have learned on my own regarding Gregorio. However, this still brings us no closer to the truth of what happened to either woman."

"But it is not fair," I muttered, staring disconsolately at the sketches as I gave voice again to that familiar refrain. "Il Moro cared enough for his wastrel cousin to bar all from leaving the castle until his murderer was found. Yet he seems not to care that someone might deliberately be murdering Caterina's servants, one by one."

I looked up to meet Leonardo's gaze and was surprised to see a faint expression of satisfaction on his face.

"Ah, then you will be interested to hear that I have just come from Ludovico's chamber," he replied. "It seems the duke heard tell of the second suspicious death and was alarmed by it . . . though not for the reasons one might think. He is worried that a string of suicides connected with his ward might reflect badly on her value as a bride for a potential ally. And so he has commanded me to put a stop to the unpleasantness."

For a few moments, I wasn't sure whether I should feel outrage or relief at this news of Ludovico's change of heart. Deciding it did not matter what motivated the duke, so long as he allowed our inquiry to proceed, I straightened my shoulders and firmly met the Master's gaze.

"If we are to investigate, then tell me how I may help."

The Master nodded, rubbing his bearded chin in a thoughtful gesture. "If you truly mean this, Dino, I have concocted a plan that is dependent upon your fortitude and cleverness.

"No, hear me out first," he cut me short when I opened my mouth to readily agree with whatever idea he had in mind. "While not a dangerous mission, this plan requires far more of you than simply dressing as my page. And before I tell you anything else, let me assure you that you may refuse your role once you hear it, and I will not think the worse of you."

I frowned a little, unable to guess what he might mean by that last cryptic statement. But I knew, as well, that even the most outrageous of the Master's plans inevitably came to a satisfactory conclusion.

"I confess you have stirred my interest," I replied, "and I am eager to know what you would ask of me."

"Very well."

He paused for a long moment and eyed me in a considering manner that only heightened my curiosity. Just when I could bear the suspense no longer, he finally asked, "Tell me, Dino, to find a murderer . . . would you be willing to disguise yourself as a lady?"

8

Justice

Justice requires power, intelligence, and will.

—Leonardo da Vinci, *Manuscript H*

Would I disguise myself as a lady?

So unexpected was the question that it was all I could do not to burst out laughing. Here, I had spent a season diligently wrapping myself in male garb, only to have the Master suggest that I should now don women's clothing. Of course, he could not know how ironic his most strange question was, under the circumstances.

And neither could he know how I longed, quite suddenly, to wear the proper robes of my true gender. Reminding myself that I must react as Dino would to such an odd request, however, I managed a tone of properly humble offense.

"Master, what can you mean?" I protested. "Surely you cannot think I would wish to pass myself off as a female. To what purpose would I even attempt such a feat?"

"My dear boy, believe me that I mean you no insult," he was quick to reply. "As I said, hear me out first, and then make your decision."

"As you wish." Folding my arms over my carefully disguised chest, I feigned a grudging nod.

The Master was not to be put off by Dino's theatrics. Instead, taking my response as encouragement, he continued. "As you know, the common thread between the two dead women is that they both were servants of Caterina. Beyond that, we have no proof that either death is anything other than the suicide that it appeared to be.

"But when it comes to unexpected deaths, I am loath to believe in coincidence; thus, I must know more about the lives of Caterina and her women. This knowledge might reveal what led Bellanca and Lidia down their fatal paths and perhaps even help us prevent another woman from suffering the same fate."

He gave me a small smile. "I am sure you guessed that my offer to paint Caterina's portrait was born of something more than a wish to wring another commission from the duke. My hope is that, in the intimacy of her own chambers, I shall manage to gain her trust and discover what unsettling truths she might keep hidden."

"But what does that have to do with me?" I asked in true curiosity.

He raised a wry brow. "As you know, men and women live in different worlds, for all they inhabit the same home . . . or castle. I might gain the contessa's trust and be privy to a bit of gossip, but being a man, I will never be allowed to fully enter her world. Only another woman would be granted that access."

Understanding was beginning to dawn now, and I nodded. "So you are suggesting, Master, that I disguise myself as a girl and become a spy in the duke's household?"

"You are a clever young man, Dino," he answered with an approving look. "That is indeed my plan."

Idly, he picked up a bit of charcoal lying on the table and began sketching on the same drawing that depicted Caterina as Diana. With a few quick lines, the figure of a young woman began to emerge along one corner of the page. As I watched, the charcoal features began to take on a rather distinct resemblance to me.

"Il Moro has given me leave to resolve this unfortunate matter in any way I see fit," he went on as he continued to draw. "Of course, he would be suitably appalled if I told him one of my young apprentices was to put on women's robes and keep secret watch upon the contessa. But I daresay he would not protest if I told him I wished to place a trusted young woman of my acquaintance among Caterina's servants in hopes of learning something of use."

With a few more swift lines, he completed an image of me as I must have looked days earlier while wrapped in makeshift robes and posing for Davide and Paolo.

"You will remember the reaction, my boy, the day when you donned women's robes to serve as model for the Magdalene," he said, putting aside the drawing and returning his attention to me. "Even I was fooled for a moment. You showed the skill of an actor, the way you were able to mimic the grace and movement of a woman."

"But I did not mean—"

"Do not distress yourself," he gently cut me short as I tried to react as surely Dino would. "Recall that women's roles upon the stage are always filled by boys and young men. If you agree to my plan, you will be but playing a part, just as surely as if you were an actor. With the proper clothing—let us call it costuming—you could deceive even those who know you well. And this subterfuge would be necessary for only a day or two."

"So it would be like performing in a Christmas pageant, and people would not think that I truly wished to be a girl?" I asked, as if trying to rationalize such a role to myself. "And no one else would know about this, except for you and me?"

"Just the two of us, yes . . . and Luigi the tailor, of course," Leonardo was quick to qualify. "We will require his expert assistance to make this masquerade a success. But you know Luigi is to be trusted. He would not reveal a confidence once he gave his word to keep his peace regarding the matter."

I winced inwardly at the thought of Luigi's reaction. I had no doubt that the tailor would remain publicly silent. He would find such an ironic turn of events exceedingly amusing, however, so that chances were I would never hear the end of it from him in private, should I agree to the scheme.

Mistaking my silence for hesitation, Leonardo hastily resorted to more eloquent persuasion.

"You know that I would not ask such a thing of you, my dear boy, if I did not have the utmost confidence in your abilities. And I fear there is not another of the apprentices who could manage such a feat, nor one whom I would trust to keep his head in such an unsettling situation. Of course, as I told you from the first, I will not think the less of you should you decline the assignment."

He paused and shook his head, smiling a little. "It is unfortunate that we have no females among the apprentices who could take on the task. Perhaps I should consider allowing a girl or two to join your number."

At those unexpected words, my eyes opened wide. Only with an effort did I not blurt out the truth of my situation to him. Instead, I bit my lip as conflicting thoughts raced through my head . . . the same arguments that had nagged at me ever since I began this particular ruse.

Why not tell? Surely I had long since proven my worth, both as an apprentice and in a more trusted role as the Master's confidante. Make a clean breast of it, and the problem of finding someone to play the maidservant role was resolved. Then, afterward, I could return to my apprentice role. Leonardo could decide whether I should masquerade again as a male or rejoin the others in my true female identity.

On the other hand, what if he viewed my disguise as nothing more than a selfish deception? Rather than recalling my loyalty to him and marveling at my cleverness, he might view me with disdain. And even if he miraculously let me continue on as an apprentice, he might never trust me again.

But when else would such an opportune moment arise again for me to make my confession?

I took a deep breath and opened my mouth, steeling myself to confess all. Instead, what came out was, "If by playing such a role I might help prevent another untimely death, I shall do as you ask."

"Then it is settled."

He spent a few minutes more suggesting those mannerisms and phrases I might employ to better appear as a female. He reminded me, as well, of those things that a young woman did not do . . . blow her nose upon her sleeve, pass wind in company, and generally comport herself with undue vigor. He warned me, as well, of the precautions I must take when washing and when relieving myself lest my gender be discovered.

"But that is not all," he decreed, assuming a stern mien. "I know you to be a young man of good character; even so, I must remind you not to take advantage of your masquerade to spy upon the other female servants while they bathe and piss. You will find an excuse to make yourself scarce at such times, no matter how tempting you may find it to do otherwise."

"Certainly, I shall be respectful," I agreed, unable to help a blush. How often had I found a reason to turn my back or leave the room while in the company of my fellow apprentices, lest I see what an unmarried young woman was not meant to see!

With a satisfied nod, he rose from the table. "Come, my dear boy, time is short. We must pay a visit to the master tailor and see about your costume."

"Dress, er, him, as a woman? Signor Leonardo, I fear you have once more taken leave of your senses. That, or you are attempting to play a very odd joke."

Luigi sternly stared from me to the Master and then back at me again. We were in his small but well-appointed shop located in a respectable portion of the city not far from the castle. It was here that all manner of patrons—from the fashion-conscious wives of well-to-do merchants to relatives of the duke, himself—came to be clothed. Usually, the place held a customer or two. With a few charming words, however, Leonardo had somehow convinced the plump matron who had been browsing among the fabrics to return at a later time, leaving us alone with the tailor.

Now, Luigi's many chins were gently quivering in what appeared to be barely contained outrage, although I was certain it actually was suppressed humor. At the sight, I could not help but recall his words when he'd first discovered the truth of my male disguise many weeks earlier.

"I could be outraged by your boldness, meaning I must take some action against you for the good of all concerned," the tailor had decreed once he realized the boy he was dressing at the Master's request was actually a girl. *"Or I could be amused at your initiative, which means I would keep your secret safe, at least for the time being."*

He had paused to deliberate for a moment, while I waited in a state verging on terror for him to decide my fate.

I had been in the tailor's shop at the Master's behest, submitting to being measured for my sumptuous page's outfit. It was not the first time I had been in his shop, but my previous dealings with Luigi all had been unpleasant, to say the least.

The tailor and I had taken a mutual dislike to each other at our first meeting during the same live chess game where the duke's cousin had met his death. Hoping to delay news of the tragedy, the Master had assigned me to be costumed to take the conte's place.

Luigi, unaware of the circumstances, had complied with only the greatest reluctance. I had behaved with equal ill grace, in return. Given that history, when he later had inadvertently discovered my secret, I had thought myself doomed.

Indeed, I was sure that the sour-faced tailor would gleefully take the opportunity to reveal my secret to all and sundry, resulting in my immediate dismissal from my apprenticeship.

Thus, it had been to my great surprise and relief that he finally had proclaimed, *"I believe I shall choose to be amused."*

From that time on, Luigi had proven himself to be a trusted ally. Not only had he carefully guarded the secret of my true gender; he had quite likely saved my life, nursing me back to health following my grievous wounding at the hand of a knife-wielding murderer. Of course, he had never admitted to any motive save his own amusement when acting nobly in my behalf. I felt certain, however, that carefully hidden beneath his acerbic exterior was in truth a good heart.

I also suspected from a cryptic comment he'd once made that Luigi the tailor had secrets of his own to keep.

Now, however, the Master was meeting Luigi's condemning words with a chill look of his own.

"You may be certain, good tailor, that my senses are quite intact," he flatly stated. "Neither is this a jest. It happens that the duke, himself, has tasked me with settling a delicate matter of state. While the responsibility is mine, our young Dino will be playing a crucial role in its resolution. I can reveal no more, other than to assure you that this female disguise is necessary to his success."

"Bah! I have no patience for such subterfuge. Why burden me with such nonsense, when there are tailors aplenty in the city who would welcome even so odd a commission as this one?" he asked, flapping his hands as if to shoo us from his shop.

The Master refused to be shooed but firmly stood his ground. "I came to you, Signor Luigi, because your skill with a needle surpasses anyone's in the whole of Milan. I also know you can be trusted to keep a confidence, particularly when keeping that secret is crucial to the safety of young Dino."

"Indeed," he huffed, though I was amused to see him preen a little at the Master's compliments. He gave me a considering look, rubbing his beardless chin in thought. "And when will this transformation need to occur?"

"Immediately. Moreover, this disguise must be able to withstand close scrutiny. No one must suspect Dino is anything other than the maidservant he will claim to be."

"By Saint Michael, you ask much of me, Leonardo!"

With that declaration, Luigi stepped forward and grabbed me by the arm, dragging me to the center of the room. Leaving me there, he circled about me for a few moments, still rubbing his chin and muttering under his breath. Finally, he nodded.

"I can do as you ask," he agreed, "although it will require me to set aside several lucrative commissions that I am in a hurry to finish."

He favored Leonardo with the wry twist of his lips that, for him, passed for a smile. "I suppose I have you to thank for the business. I understand you are arranging a costume ball on the duke's behalf a fortnight from now. An interesting theme you have chosen—the game of tarocchi."

Then his bushy black brows all but vanished beneath the greasy fringe of black hair lying across his forehead. In an accusing tone, he added, "I don't suppose this upcoming bit of merriment has any connection with the matter you are attempting to resolve, does it?"

"Not at all," the Master smoothly lied, "though I daresay that Dino and I may both require costumes for that evening's festivities, as well."

"Why am I not surprised?" the tailor muttered to himself. Pursing his lips, he addressed Leonardo. "As you know, signore, my services are not cheap. Tell me, who will pay for this transformation I will be undertaking?"

By way of response, Leonardo withdrew from his tunic what appeared to be the same small sack of coins Il Moro had given him a few days earlier. "Fear not, you shall be paid well," Leonardo assured him and gave the bag a careless jingle.

I saw the faint, greedy glint in Luigi's small eyes at the promise of hard coin. That expression was promptly overlaid by one of concern, however, as he shot a look in my direction.

"And what of the, er, boy?" Luigi wanted to know. "We've heard no word from him. Has he agreed to undertake this scandalous role of his own free will?"

"I have, Signor Luigi," I promptly spoke up. "The Master can trust no one but me in this matter. Thus, I am willing to do as he asks, no matter that I must dress as a girl. I will be like an actor playing a role upon the stage, and the fact that I might be wearing women's robes would not signify anything else."

The tailor met my earnest gaze and heaved a great sigh. "Very well, it seems I have no choice. Signor Leonardo, leave young Dino here and take yourself from my shop. You may return in two hours to retrieve her, er, him."

"I am in your debt," the Master replied with a small bow as he started for the door. "Let me remind you once more that this masquerade is of the greatest import, so pray do not spare any expense for young Dino's transformation."

Luigi gave a sharp nod, his expression one of ironic satisfaction as he rubbed his fleshy hands together. "You need have no fears in that respect, my dear Leonardo. Just wait until you see my bill."

He waited until the shop door closed behind the Master and then locked it against any would-be customers unexpectedly walking in. Assured that no one would disturb us, he turned to me with a grin.

"This is too delicious," he said, seizing me by the arm once more but this time leading me toward the rear of his workshop. "I am to take a girl who disguises herself as a boy and dress her so that she appears to be a girl again. I am not certain if this will turn out to be my greatest challenge as a tailor or my easiest task ever."

With those words, he directed me toward a tall stool. I set down the sack containing a few personal items—among them, my ever-present notebook—that I'd brought with me, and which I would take to the castle. Then, clambering onto the seat, I watched with interest while the tailor started work.

He began by gathering pieces of female garments, from sleeves and bodices to skirts and slippers . . . all of which were in various stages of completeness. Time being of the essence, he was using what he already had at hand, rather than cutting them new. More important, it meant he need not press into service his young apprentices who toiled in the small shop next door, further assuring our secrecy.

I watched in great interest as he worked, fascinated as always by these surroundings. I have already described his workshop in my notebooks, so I will not linger long over detailing the room's contents a second time. Suffice to say that I would liken it to a chamber where bowls of bright tempera paint had been splashed upon the walls and left to dry.

Rolls of brocades and velvets and silks in myriad colors spilled from shelves lining one side of the room. Shelves along a second wall housed boxes and bins filled with every imaginable trim—furs, ribbons, strings of beads, lace—all destined for a neckline, hem, or sleeve. Here, amid the colorful chaos, Luigi daily fashioned magnificent clothing with almost the same genius as Leonardo created his brilliant paintings. Little wonder why he was considered a master at his craft, I reminded myself.

Once the tailor had deposited an armload of fabric upon his table, he returned his attention to me. "Indeed, I almost hate to take your dear master's coin for this priceless opportunity," he exclaimed, "though I shall accept it with all the proper eagerness. But before we begin your transformation, you must tell me what is going on here in Il Moro's court."

Given the fact that Luigi had loyally kept my own secret these many weeks, I did not hesitate to trust him in this particular situation. Thus, after first obtaining his vow of silence, I told the tailor of the Master's suspicions regarding the recent events surrounding Caterina and the two mysterious deaths of her servants. I even mentioned the contessa's seeming devotion to her tarocchi cards, for it occurred to me that Luigi might have some knowledge of that sort of divination.

I stopped short, however, at revealing Il Moro's intent to arrange a marriage between his ward and a duke from another province. This was, as the Master had said, a matter of state. Should the tailor accidently betray that particular confidence, it would be the Master who would suffer harsh blame for revealing that plan.

Luigi listened with avid interest to all I had to say. Here and there, he nodded when a particular bit of the tale seemingly confirmed his own opinions. Only when I finished did he offer his own thoughts. To my dismay, however, his words were directed at me.

"So, it appears the dashing captain of the guard has supplanted the great Leonardo in your affections," he said with a sly smile, waggling his bushy brows.

"No, do not protest," he cut me short when, blushing, I attempted to object to this assumption. "I am an expert in such matters and can hear the truth of your heart in your voice. Perhaps that is why you are so willing a participant in your master's wild scheme. I daresay once you have donned long robes again, you will manage to cross the handsome Gregorio's path a time or two."

Of course, my sputtering retort to this even more outlandish statement did nothing to quell his smug manner. Luigi merely grinned more broadly and started sorting through the various pieces draped over his table. When my attempt at a defense continued, however, he paused long enough to pull a length of fine white linen from one of the shelves.

"Here, go behind that curtain and put this on," he commanded, tossing what turned out to be a delicately sewn chemise at me.

Shooting him an offended glare, I grabbed up the garment and retired to the alcove he'd indicated. I swiftly forgot my pique at the tailor, however, as I gratefully unlaced the corset I wore to suppress my female curves and slipped the chemise over my bare flesh.

It was a far finer undergarment than any I'd ever before owned, more befitting a noblewoman than a young woman of my moderate station. I sighed in satisfaction, even as I realized that Luigi had taken the Master's instructions quite literally. I wondered how much this one piece would cost Leonardo . . . and whether, at this rate, the bag of florins would prove sufficient coin to pay for my new wardrobe!

I peeked around the curtain to see Luigi using black ribbon to lace together a pale green bodice and matching sleeves. "Pray, do not forget I am to be but a maidservant," I reminded him. "It would look odd, indeed, if I were to be more finely dressed than the contessa, herself."

"Bah, I know what I am doing," he returned with a grunt as he set aside those pieces.

After a moment's consideration, he pulled from the stack a petticoat dyed a deep green, which he also put to one side. Next came an overskirt of somber black enlivened with diagonal stripes of the same pale green shade as the bodice and sleeves. Finally, he produced from a box on a high shelf a pair of red stockings, which he gleefully waggled at me before tossing them onto the growing pile.

Scooping up the clothing, he carried the bundle over to me and unceremoniously deposited it upon a small bench next to my alcove. "Put these on," he commanded, "and I shall make whatever alterations are needed. And do not tarry. We have much work to do before your master returns."

I did as instructed, tying on stockings and petticoat and struggling into the ill-fitting overgarments. Indeed, I had been wearing boys' clothing for long enough now that the once-familiar weight of long skirts and the snug fit of sleeves and bodice felt uncomfortably foreign to me. Perhaps this transformation was going to be more difficult than any of us imagined, I thought in sudden alarm.

"Come, come, let me see how you look," Luigi called as I attempted to retie the lacings of one sleeve. Puffing my cheeks in frustration, I quickly stepped beyond the curtain again.

"Well, one would never mistake you for a contessa," Luigi dryly observed as he took in the ill-fitting garb, "but we are making progress. All we need now are a few alterations."

Dragging a short wooden box from beneath one worktable, he stood me upon it and began tucking and pinning cloth with a master's sure efficiency. Had he been any other man, I might have been embarrassed to be poked and prodded in so intimate a fashion. With Luigi, I had no such fears, for I knew that while he worked he viewed me simply as a convenient form upon which his creations were destined to hang.

"There, that is better," he proclaimed a few minutes later, offering a hand to help me down from my perch. "Now, quickly, remove these clothes so I can finish sewing."

I retreated to my alcove and disrobed again, handing the garments back to him through the slit between the curtains. Then, dressed only in my chemise, I stuck my head through that same opening, the curtains draped around me to preserve my modesty as I watched Luigi begin work.

With a grace unexpected in a man of his bulk, the tailor stitched, his swift needle flashing like a small serpent through the black and green fabric. While he toiled, he passed the time recounting his usual gossip.

As always, I listened to his tales with guilty relish. I'd long since learned that Luigi seemed to know everything about everybody at court and had no qualms about telling all. He had neither spies peering through windows nor disgruntled servants listening at doors to keep him informed. Rather, he depended solely upon his patrons.

These were the well-dressed merchants' wives and bored

noblewomen who routinely shared the most intimate secrets of their lives while being fitted for gowns . . . this in return for hearing equally fascinating stories about their peers from him. And while the tailor prudently never named the subjects of his gossip, his thinly veiled descriptions gave sufficient hints as to the identities of those unfortunates.

"Another masterpiece," he declared almost an hour later as he put in a final stitch on the skirt. "Let us try again."

This time, the clothing slipped on as if it were my own skin. I tugged and laced and tied until I was ready to step past the curtains again.

Luigi's usually sour smile held a hint of triumphant approval as he surveyed me. Still, he spent a few moments tightening my bodice so that I could barely breathe. Then he puffed the fabric of my chemise through the gap between my sleeves and bodice to give my garb a more fashionable air. Finally, he stepped back and allowed himself a satisfied nod.

"I think we have resolved the matter of your clothing. It is sober enough for your role, yet appropriate for a servant of a young noblewoman who would not have her maids appear too dowdy. No, wait," he exclaimed as I would have rushed to the mirror in the corner for a look. "You have forgotten the matter of your hair."

My hair!

I clapped my hands to my head in a reflexive gesture and then gave a small laugh. "I vow I had almost forgotten, for I've become so accustomed to wearing my hair shorn like a boy. But how can you possibly remedy that?"

The tailor gave me a conspiratorial wink and promptly trudged over to the shelves again. Now I noted the miniature cabinet, crafted of finely finished pale wood, which stood among the baskets of ribbons. Tall and narrow, the box might have reached my knee had it been set upon the floor.

With the same delicate care he might have used were he toting a crate of the finest Venetian glass, Luigi carried the box back to his worktable. As I watched in growing curiosity, he unlatched its narrow door with a flourish.

I peered more closely to see what was within, only to leap back with a gasp when I realized just what it contained.

The box was filled with hair . . . rows of long braids in every shade, from the shiniest black to the palest blond. Each neatly tied hank dangled from a small hook at the top of the box, just as a butcher's wares might be hung.

"Beautiful, aren't they?" Luigi declared with pride.

I laughed a little at my initial reaction, even as I suppressed a shudder. Indeed, the sight called to mind a nest of soft serpents, or perhaps a rather gruesome collection of relics from numerous well-tressed saints. Then my moment of amusement faded as I abruptly recalled Lidia's long, black braid. I wondered in some alarm just where Luigi had harvested this most unusual crop. Surely he did not . . .

When I gingerly questioned him as to their source, however, the tailor wagged a playful finger at me.

"If I told you, you might try to horn in on my business. But you would be surprised at how many poor women are willing to shear their sole claim to beauty for a bit of money." He paused and shot me a keen look. "I trust that when you committed similar butchery upon yourself, you received a pretty sum from some barber or tailor."

"Actually, I burned my hair before I left my house," I admitted in some embarrassment.

Luigi's expression of pain at my admission was not totally feigned. "Foolish girl, you must remember that everything has a value to someone. I do hope if you ever contemplate such a thing again, you come to me instead of tossing good coin into the hearth."

"I promise. But what do you do with so much hair?" I couldn't help but wonder.

The tailor gave me a pitying look. "You have seen the women of the court with their hair bound up, have you not? Surely you did not think that their maids were able to create such elaborate plaiting when most of those women have barely enough locks to cover their scalps? Indeed, their artistry is possible only because of me."

Reaching into the small cabinet, he pulled forth a shiny braid whose color was the rich warm brown of a freshly plowed field. "The most expensive hair comes from young women," he explained, "though I will pay a reasonable bit for a matron's tresses if they have been well kept. Of course, the cheapest hair comes from our equine friends. It is suitable only for elaborate pieces that obviously belong to a costume."

With a snort of disdain, he added, "Or for those with overly tight purse strings who have convinced themselves that no one will notice the difference."

Carefully setting aside the first braid, he reached for a few darker examples. "We are fortunate that your hair, while lovely, is a common shade. I should readily find a match."

Frowning, he held each twisted length against my head, finally deciding upon one. Hanging the remaining hanks of hair back on their hooks, he latched the cabinet shut again and returned it to its position on the shelf.

With an impatient gesture, he bade me sit upon a tall stool near his worktable. I watched from that perch as he carefully untied the braid and smoothed the hair into a single length. Plucking a handful of bone pins from yet another basket, he fastened all but the back portion of my hair atop my head.

"Now, sit still, my girl," he commanded, taking up a needle, which he threaded with a length of dark silk, "and you shall soon be witness to my remedy."

I could not see what he was doing, of course, but I was aware of his needle whipping in and out perilously close to my scalp, much as it had flown through the fabric. The pile of hair upon the table slowly vanished, while I could feel a return of the familiar weight that once tugged at my head. When the braid vanished entirely, he loosened the pins holding the rest of my hair. Finally, he took up a broad comb and gently separated my hair, then began plaiting it into a single heavy braid intertwined with green ribbon. That accomplished, he added a small cap, which he tied beneath my chin.

"Now, you may take a look," he grandly decreed.

I rose from my seat and made my way to the corner mirror, eager to know what it might reflect. It seemed a lifetime since I had last seen myself as a young woman. Indeed, I had grown used to seeing the face of a boy each time I gazed into a bucket of water or caught a glimpse of myself in a bit of glass. Could I ever again resemble the girl I had been before I left my parents' home one final time?

Taking a deep breath, I stepped before that silvery glass and stared.

Looking back at me was a familiar, wide-eyed young woman dressed in a simple yet fashionable gown. She looked thinner than I recalled, yet her face still had the same soft curves and her chin the same hint of stubborn firmness it had known since childhood. Then I twisted to one side and saw her dark hair trailing down her back in a thick braid, the shiny tresses looking as if a knife had never marred their glory.

"Signor Luigi, you have given me back myself," I whispered in awe, embarrassed to realize that tears had risen in my eyes. Quickly swiping them away, I turned to face him. "You are indeed a genius."

"My girl, was there ever any doubt?" he replied in a mock-offended tone. Then, with a shrug, he added, "Of course, your master is the only person who will question your appearance now, so we must make certain to answer any suspicions that are raised."

At my questioning look, he clarified, "As you see, I have given you a high-necked chemise to wear. As there is no flesh on display, this allows me to explain your female figure as nothing more than clever padding. As for the fact that you appear far thinner now, I need only remind your master that a boy's tunic will make one look much broader than will a tightly tied bodice. And, of course, any of my patrons knows that a striped overskirt can slim figures far plumper than yours."

"But, Luigi, you have so thoroughly transformed me," I reminded him with mingled delight and dismay. "What if he takes one look at me and suspects the truth?"

"That, my girl, is the risk you have taken from the first day you pulled on a boy's tunic and cut off your hair," was his sour reply. "Should the truth come out, you have only yourself to blame, whatever the consequences."

A sudden pounding on the door put a quick halt to that debate. "I believe you will soon have your answer," Luigi dryly said, "for that is your master come to fetch you."

9

The Hermit

The quest must be undertaken alone, for the destination lies within.

—Leonardo da Vinci, *The Notebooks of Delfina della Fazia*

As Luigi headed to unlatch the door, I allowed myself a fatalistic sigh. It was too late now to change my mind about either masquerade. I could only pray that the Master would be so intent upon his bold plan that he would credit the tailor with the change he saw, rather than look for a far simpler explanation.

From my position in front of the mirror, I had a reflected view of the shop door where Luigi was now turning the knob. A moment later, Leonardo stepped inside. I saw him glance in my direction before turning to the tailor with a look of dismay.

"Luigi, you know this is a matter of great importance," I heard him say in a low voice, impatience coloring his tone. "I charged you with a task, and yet it seems you are entertaining other customers while you should be attending to my needs. Quickly, send away this new patron of yours and—"

He halted abruptly as he took in Luigi's gleeful look and swung about again to stare at me. Then an answering smile lit his face.

"Dino, this is you?" he exclaimed as I slowly turned to face him. At my nod, he motioned me to the center of the room and slowly circled about me, assessing every detail of my garb as a buyer might examine a horse on market day. Finally, he gave his head an admiring shake and turned to the tailor.

"Signor Luigi, I bow to you as a genius," he exclaimed. "The transformation is indeed remarkable. The clothing is just right, and the hair a work of art. As for the rest"—he grinned a little as he lifted cupped hands in that universally typical male gesture signifying breasts—"let us just say that one would never guess beneath all that padding lies a clever young boy."

Then, to me, he added, "Of course, it is not all the tailor's skill. I see that, even among us, you are taking pains to move with a greater grace and are managing the skirts with a remarkable ease for a boy used to running about in trunk hose. You are to be commended, as well, Dino."

"Thank you, Master," I replied, ducking my head and blushing, though perhaps not for the reason he might expect. And, strangely, I was not sure whether to be relieved at the fact that my boy's masquerade was not undone by my dress or piqued that he could not see the obvious about me.

"But, stay. There is still the matter of your name," he was continuing. "Have you given any thought to what we should call you?"

"I would like to be called Delfina," I declared, drawing the faintest of knowing smiles from Luigi. "It-it is my cousin's name, and close enough to my own that I would easily answer to it."

"Then Delfina it shall be."

Turning to Luigi, he said, "You have performed your task superbly, but time grows short. Let me bring Dino, or rather,

Delfina, to the castle so he may be situated there before dark. I shall return with greatest haste afterwards to settle up with you for the bill."

"I will not be holding my breath for that," Luigi muttered, apparently familiar with the Master's tendency to postpone his debts when possible. To me, the tailor added, "I shall send one of my apprentices around to bring you a change of linen and a few more items to make your wardrobe more complete. And, of course, you will remember how I showed you to put on these garments properly?"

"Yes, signore," I agreed, going along with his pretense. "They are very strange, these clothes, but I shall manage."

While I gathered up my bag of belongings, Leonardo spoke a few minutes longer with the tailor about costumes for the duke's upcoming masquerade.

"I shall bring a few sketches to you," the Master assured him, eliciting a snort of resignation from that man.

To me, the tailor gave a gesture that looked suspiciously like a benediction. "Good luck with your masquerade, my girl . . . er, boy. And, pray, do take good care of your new tresses. They are worth a fair amount of coin, and I should like them back when you are finished with them."

"And so we shall expect a refund of that amount from our good tailor," Leonardo was quick to add as he took me by the arm and escorted me out the door.

"Now, mind your skirts on the streets," he warned me as we headed down the narrow lanes toward the castle gate. "Keep them raised, thusly"—he paused and pantomimed lifting the garment with both hands—"so that they do not drag through the mire."

Suppressing a smile, I did as instructed, making certain that my first attempts were a bit awkward. He gave me an approving nod. "You are a swift student, Dino . . . or as I must now call you, Delfina. Now, pay good heed as I tell you the story that I related to the contessa about your past."

I listened, relieved that the tale he had concocted was

simple enough. I was to be the daughter of a prominent wool merchant with the surname Gullino from the city of Florence. Signor Gullino and the Master had made each other's acquaintance while Leonardo still lived in that city. Unfortunately, my father had run afoul of the wool merchant's guild—"being but a female, you would know no further details"—and subsequently found himself forced to leave his home.

Leonardo went on to explain how my father had settled upon Milan as his family's new home, and that we'd arrived in the city the previous month. By great fortune, Gullino had run across his old friend and was pleased to learn that not only was Leonardo once again living in the same city as he, but that the artist also had as his patron the Duke of Milan. Thus, my father had begged a boon of his old friend to help his daughter find a position at court.

"I told the contessa that her cousin the duke was concerned with the recent loss of her servants, and he asked if I might seek someone to fill one of those roles. Thus, I recommended my friend's daughter as a young woman of good character for one of those posts."

By now, we had reached the castle gates. Not far into the quadrangle, the Master halted and turned to me. "I fear I almost forgot that I have something else for you."

Reaching into his tunic, he pulled forth a small, flat bundle. Even before he unwrapped it, I had guessed what the package contained.

"You will recognize these copies of the contessa's tarocchi cards," he explained unnecessarily, displaying their familiar faces. "I am still convinced that some significance lies in the fact that Bellanca had these particular cards with her at her death."

"Do you wish me to show them to the contessa and gauge her reaction?" I asked in some confusion.

He nodded. "In a manner of speaking, yes. If the opportunity presents itself, you must ask Caterina to read your fortune . . . but, beforehand, you must contrive to slip these copies into her deck. From what Lidia told me of how the game is played, you will be allowed to choose the cards that she reads. And so you must pull these same four from the pile anytime she plays at telling fortunes."

"But how can I know which they are among so many others?" I asked in some concern.

By way of answer, he flipped the cards so that their dark red backs faced upward. Indicating their corners, he said, "If you look closely, you will notice I have scratched small marks onto the backs of each card. Memorize the marks and their corresponding cards; then you will readily be able to distinguish these four cards from all the rest."

Squinting, I could see the faint hash mark in each of their corners. So light were they, however, that they would have escaped my notice had the Master not called them to my attention. Surely, not even the contessa would see them if she was not expecting to find them.

I stowed them in the pouch at my belt. When I glanced up again, however, I saw that the Master's expression had grown suddenly grim.

"My boy, I am having second thoughts as to the prudence of this scheme," he slowly said, stroking his neat beard. "Perhaps it is best if we abandon this folly now and find another way to learn what we must about the contessa's doings.

"Fear not," he added as I opened my mouth to protest. "The good tailor still will be amply rewarded for his efforts."

"But, Master, I wish to play this role!"

I glanced in the direction of the nearby tower at whose foot Lidia had been found dead. The sun was almost beneath the castle walls, and the edifice's lengthening shadow seemed to reach with grim purpose in my direction. Was it beckoning me, I wondered, or simply warning me away?

I set my shoulders, unwilling to give way to superstition. Instead, I proclaimed with unfeigned passion, "If some foul plan has indeed been unleashed upon the court's servants, then it must be stopped. No one else cares that these women have died. Why, even the captain of the guard seemed oddly untouched by his own mother's death!"

When the Master made no answer, I added, "Do you not always tell us apprentices that a great artist is one who embraces new experiences? And that only then can he claim a greater breadth of knowledge, which he can apply to his work? Surely this must count as a new experience."

"Ah, my boy, you use my words against me," Leonardo dryly acknowledged, shaking his head. "Very well. If you are certain you can carry through with the role, we shall proceed. But know that it will go badly for us both should anyone suspect the truth. No matter that you took on this disguise at my bidding, it would be you who would be tossed into the duke's prison should you be found out."

"I am not afraid, Master. Please, let me do this."

He stared at me for a long moment, so that I feared he might indeed put an end to our plan before it was begun. Then, finally, he nodded.

"You have convinced me. Come along, *Delfina*, and I shall bring you to your new mistress."

"Pio, you must sit very still, so that Signor Leonardo can paint you."

At that gentle chiding, Caterina's small hound ceased his game of nibbling upon his tail and settled quietly on her lap. He had folded his ears neatly and stretched his long forelegs, crossing one paw over the other as I had seen him do before, looking every bit the noble beast now. His sleek black-and-white coat stood out to advantage against the gold brocaded robes that his young mistress wore, while his red collar embroidered with gold echoed the hues of her outfit.

As for Caterina, herself, she seemed reluctant to follow her own instructions. Instead, she shifted in the straight chair in which she was seated and finally sighed audibly.

"I fear, signore, that I am no less restless than poor Pio," she complained, though without much apparent rancor. "How much longer must we pose for you today?"

"Not much longer, Contessa," the Master replied. "We will have the light for perhaps a quarter hour more, and then I will be forced to stop for the day."

His attention, however, was not upon her or even upon the rectangular panel propped before him. Rather, he was concentrating upon his paints. He had positioned his easel so that no spectator was privy to his work in process, as was his usual practice. Still, from where I sat at one side of the antechamber with the other maidservants, we all had an unobstructed view of the artist, himself. I noticed that the girls seemed quite content to eye him, instead.

I could not blame them, for he appeared extraordinarily handsome this day. His simple tunic was a rich russet almost the same shade as his flowing mane, that garment trimmed in black and worn over black trunk hose. The sober yet well-cut clothing enhanced his innate air of elegance yet spoke of a high-mindedness that went unanswered in the extravagant garb of most men at court.

Sternly, I reminded myself I was not there to gape but to search for clues. And if none was to be had at the moment, then I would do better to employ my time watching the Master create. Indeed, I was fortunate in the fact that he was employing a new manner of painting with this very portrait.

The technique entailed mixing pigments with oil, rather than with tempera's egg yolk and water. The advantage was that the oil paints dried slowly, allowing the artist to make changes. Moreover, it freed him to form new hues by mixing colors upon a palette, rather than creating them individually in advance. Had the Master been painting with tempera, he would have had to painstakingly overlay the various tints directly onto the panel, eventually yielding the desired color. I knew that was his preferred method even with the oils; however, time did not permit him the luxury of eschewing a palette.

I watched with great interest as, using the thinnest of

weasel hair brushes, he applied a few more deliberate strokes
to the panel. Then, with an impatient look at the window
and the rapidly changing morning sun, he finally set down
his palette and brush and returned his attention to Caterina.

"We have accomplished all that is possible this day," he
said as he covered the panel with a cloth. "I shall see you and
Pio again tomorrow."

"Ah, what a relief," she said with an exaggerated groan
and let Pio jump from her lap. While Caterina rose from her
chair, Pio quickly trotted over to where the Master was
cleaning his brushes and covering his small pots of paint.
Halting before the draped easel, he gave a sharp bark.

Caterina smiled, while the other maidservants and I
smothered giggles. "Master Leonardo, Pio wishes to see how
the painting progresses. Surely you must indulge him."

"I fear I cannot, even for so worthy a hound as he," the
Master replied, although he gave the dog a friendly scratch
behind the ears. "And I warn you ladies not to give way to
curiosity and attempt to lift the cloth. The paint will not
dry for many hours, and you could easily ruin a day's work
with one careless move."

"Fear not, signore, they will leave the painting be," Caterina assured him with a swift stern look in our direction.
"But tell me, how many more sessions must I endure before
you finish the portrait?"

"If you allow me here every day, it will take less than a
fortnight to complete my work."

She considered his reply for a moment and then nodded.
"That is good, for I soon will be busy planning my costume
for the masquerade my cousin will be hosting the week after
this."

I caught Leonardo's eye at this last statement and gave him
the faintest of shake of my head. While word of the scheduled
masquerade was rapidly spreading through the court, Il
Moro's secret remained safe. From what I had overheard thus
far, however, no one—particularly not Caterina—appeared to
know that the festivities were actually meant to be an engage-

ment party for the young contessa and her as-yet-unknown groom.

Giving no indication we'd exchanged anything more than an accidental glance, the Master set down his last brush and wiped his hands upon a rag.

"If you do not have a tailor or seamstress of your own," he addressed the contessa, "might I recommend Signor Luigi to you? He is a master at his craft and would surely create a memorable gown for you. Our young Delfina knows him well and would gladly bring him to you, if you wished. Would you not, Delfina?"

At his gesture, I hurried forward and bobbed a small curtsy. "Certainly, signore, I will be glad to do so if the contessa wishes it."

"I will consider your suggestion, Leonardo," she replied, not bothering to acknowledge my words. Thus dismissed, I ducked my head and swiftly rejoined the other servants while the Master politely took his leave of her and Pio.

My brusque exclusion from that exchange brought smirks from the two golden blond maidservants, Isabella and Rosetta. The willowy girls were twins, and as they made a habit of dressing identically, I was not as yet able to distinguish between them. I already knew, however, that they had been servants to Caterina since she began living at the castle following her father's death a year earlier. I'd also reconciled myself to the fact that the pair likely would never befriend me, given the way they had made it their business since my arrival the day before to lord their seniority over me.

The third servant, Esta—she of the plumper figure and darker blond tresses—was a different story. She had been the one to explain my duties to me and seemed quite willing to gossip with me despite the fact I was a newcomer to the castle. Now she leaned toward me and murmured, "So you really do know Signor Leonardo! My, but he is a handsome gentleman. Tell me, does he have a wife or a woman to care for him?"

"Not a wife," I truthfully whispered back. Then, spurred

by a sudden impulse that I was loath to examine, I added with a little less honesty, "But I believe he does have a woman."

"I should have known," she muttered in disappointment. I felt sure she would have added more, save that Caterina—having waited until the chamber door had closed behind Leonardo—quickly rounded on us.

"Ugh, I find posing tedious," she exclaimed, impatiently kicking the hem of her robe out of her way. "Esta, come with me and help me change into something more comfortable."

Then, as Pio began an insistent whine and looked toward the door, she added, "Isabella, you and Rosetta take Pio to the courtyard for a walk about the grounds."

I waited for my instructions, but Caterina merely whirled in a flounce of gold brocade and started for her private chamber, Esta trotting after her. Rosetta and Isabella exchanged sly smiles and then turned to me.

"You might as well come with us, Delfina," Rosetta—or was it Isabella?—coyly offered. "Pio's rope is on the table in the corner. You may walk the little beast, if you wish, and we'll follow after you."

Since neither girl had yet to make any true overtures of friendship, I suspected some sort of mischief to be forthcoming from the pair. Nevertheless, I retrieved the long gold line, happy for a bit of respite from fetching and carrying and waiting. A bright-eyed Pio was equally excited at the prospect, bounding upon his hind legs in anticipation of the excursion.

At least I have one friend here, I ruefully told myself as I tied the rope to his collar. In return, I received a few dainty licks from his long pink tongue. Cheered by his happy demeanor, I gave the small hound an affectionate hug and then took up his lead.

With the twins following far enough behind me that I could not make out their whispering, I wound my way back through this wing of the castle and slipped out a side door into the quadrangle. Pio followed obediently at my side . . . that was, until his dainty paws touched lawn.

In the next instant, he took off at a dead run, almost jerking my arm from its socket as he reached the rope's end. Fortunately, I'd had the foresight to wrap it securely around my hand so that he did not slip free; still, his sudden burst of speed had taken me by surprise, and I nearly stumbled.

"Pio, bad boy!" I scolded halfheartedly as I attempted to keep pace with him while struggling not to trip over my skirts.

For such a small dog, he had uncommon strength to match his speed, and it took me a moment to rein him back in. Behind me, I could hear the twins' peals of laughter, making me suspect this was not the first time Pio had tried this trick. By the time Pio consented to halt, we were halfway across one portion of the grounds. I knew that, had a rope not confined him, he would have long since reached the main gate and been running around the town square!

My breathing had almost returned to normal—I'd forgotten how exhausting it was to run in long robes—when Rosetta and Isabella strolled up to join me.

"Oh, dear, I'm afraid we forgot to tell you that he only obeys the contessa," one of the pair said with a smirk, confirming my suspicions that they had anticipated such a display and had enjoyed the dog's antics.

Unwilling to let them get the better of me, I summoned a bright smile. "I truly did not mind it. I was finding myself growing quite stiff after sitting all morning, so that I welcomed a bit of exercise. In fact, I think we will run about again in another minute."

The pouting looks the twins exchanged this time reflected disappointment that I'd not reacted as they'd hoped. Still smiling brightly, I set off with Pio again, though this time at a more sedate pace. Muttering between themselves, Isabella and Rosetta once more followed.

We spent the next quarter hour pleasantly walking about the green while Pio happily sniffed at leaves and bugs and pebbles while lifting a leg upon a few select spots. I was content to stroll after him, enjoying my first relaxed moments since the Master left me in Caterina's care the previous morning.

The young contessa had thus far given no hint of being an unduly harsh mistress, though she had a tendency toward careless impatience that was most often directed at us servants. Moreover, her interest in any particular subject wavered as often as did Pio's. It seemed in the short time I'd been in her company that we were constantly jumping up and down at her every change of mind. But my duties—though more tedious—were far lighter as a maidservant than as Leonardo's apprentice.

The greatest relief in all of this was at no longer having to hide my true gender. To be sure, the tightly laced bodice I now wore was as confining as the garment I had worn beneath my boy's tunic, while my skirts were nowhere as comfortable as my trunk hose. And my new braid of hair trailing gloriously down my back did add an undeniable weight to my head. But my lightness of spirit at being freed from this most basic of deceptions outweighed any discomfort I felt at facing the world as a woman once again. Thus, my enjoyment in simply walking about the courtyard with a small hound at my side.

At this time of the day, not long after the midday meal, we had this portion of the quadrangle mostly to ourselves. The contessa had not yet appeared, and I pictured poor Esta being run off her plump feet fetching various gowns and surcoats and slippers while Caterina decided what she preferred to wear. Pio, at least, was content with his collar.

"Delfina, we are tired," a peevish voice belonging either to Rosetta or Isabella called from behind me.

I glanced back to see the pair, cheeks pink with exertion, struggling to keep up with me and my four-legged charge. Doubtless, Pio was shortchanged in his outings when it was not the contessa who took him about. Little wonder that the small hound seemed so pleased to be in my company.

"Isabella and I wish to return to the castle now."

This voice, obviously belonging to Rosetta, was sharper than her sister's. As I looked back again, she added, "The contessa will be waiting on us. Come, bring that wretched dog with you, and let us go back."

Only the fact that the contessa *would* be waiting on us prevented me from pretending temporary deafness at their complaints. With a sigh, I turned Pio about.

"Finally," Isabella huffed with a roll of her blue eyes, linking her arm through her sister's.

By now, I had noted that her features were slightly coarser than Rosetta's, making it a bit easier to tell the two apart. With time, I likely would easily make the distinction, though with luck I would not remain in my role here for more than another few days. I would have to make swift progress, however, for only ten days remained before the duke's masquerade was to be held. While no other of the contessa's servants had met untimely ends of late, I had learned nothing of value in the company of her and her women . . . that was, save for a brief remark I'd heard from Esta the night before.

"You are replacing another girl named Bellanca," she had told me with a small sigh as she directed me to the small cot I would share with her in the servants' quarters not far from Caterina's own chambers. *"She and I were friends, of sorts, even though she was closer to Rosetta and Isabella than to me. She died in a terrible fall only a few days ago. Perhaps you heard what happened?"*

With a silent prayer asking forgiveness for the lie, I had pleaded ignorance of the matter. Esta had sighed again and then plopped herself upon our narrow bed, launching into a dramatic account of events that differed little from what I already knew. But one comment she'd made, almost as an afterthought, had caught my attention.

"She used to carry messages for the contessa, you know," the girl had mused. *"I wonder if she was there at the tower to deliver a note when she fell."*

I had refrained from questioning her about this unexpected bit of information, instead storing it away for future
consideration. I'd also wanted to ask her about Gregorio, the
dashing captain of the guard, and learn if Bellanca's connection to him was common knowledge. But given that I, as a
supposed newcomer to the castle, could know nothing of Bellanca's personal life, I prudently kept my mouth closed on this
matter, as well.

Neither did I dare ask her about Lidia. Like the Master, I
could not believe it was simple coincidence that Lidia's son
might have been carrying on a dalliance with a maidservant
who happened to be well-known to Lidia. Had others—
particularly Bellanca—been aware of the blood relationship
between Lidia and Gregorio? Or had Gregorio's explanation
to Leonardo perhaps been the first public acknowledgment
from either mother or son? I could only hope that, as I
gained Esta's confidence, she would be inclined toward further gossip.

I was still mulling over that conversation when a menacing bark quickly brought me back to the present.

The rough sound had not come from Pio, but it caused his
ears to whip about like small flags as he tried to search out the
source. I glanced about, as well. We were passing by the stables now, and I realized suddenly what that sound meant.

I'd seen on occasion the half dozen curs that lived amid
those outbuildings, though not even the stable master claimed
them as pets. Lean of flank and large of tooth, the sandy colored beasts slunk about the stalls like small wolves. More
than once, I'd watched them gamboling with the horses and
stableboys, as they apparently considered both those dis-
parate species part of their pack. Otherwise, they inevitably
offered a bark—or sometimes worse, a bite—to anyone they
considered an intruder around the stables.

And it seemed that one of them now considered Pio a
threat.

A second bark, more menacing than the first, sounded

a bit closer, though I could not yet see any sign of a dog. I scooped up a now-quivering Pio and protectively hugged him to my chest. Hurrying my steps past the long row of stalls, I chastised myself for not being more aware of my surroundings. A look over my shoulder showed that the twins were even more oblivious than I, lagging farther behind me than before as they laughed and chatted with each other. I shot them a frustrated look, doubting they'd even heard the bark or realized what it meant.

And then Pio gave a small, brave bark of his own.

I whipped back around to see one of the stable curs standing in my path. Hackles raised and teeth bared, he silently challenged me to come closer.

I halted for a few uncertain seconds, feeling a sudden trickle of sweat beneath my bodice, though the day was mild. While I would not dream of calling the dog's bluff and continuing on, neither did I dare turn my back on him and go back the same way I'd come.

With a few whispered words of encouragement in Pio's ear, I casually turned halfway and began walking toward the center of the green. I kept my pace sedate, knowing that any hasty movement could trigger the larger dog to attack. Once I was far enough from the stables for the other dog to lose interest, I could resume my earlier direction. But I'd only managed little more than a dozen paces when I heard a throaty growl behind me.

I glanced over my shoulder in time to see the beast rushing toward us, its white-toothed snarl made all the more fearsome for the swiftness of its pursuit. Valiantly barking in return, Pio struggled in my arms, trying to break free and confront his huge adversary.

"No!" I shrieked, as much to Pio as to the marauding dog, which now was circling about us, seemingly prepared for attack.

I could hear Rosetta and Isabella screaming from somewhere behind me, and I swiftly prayed that one of them had the presence of mind to run for help. Surely there must be someone about in the quadrangle or the stables with a stout stick or a rake to fend off the beast! But help could not come fast enough, I realized in despair as the dog abruptly leaped toward me, jaws opened to snatch Pio from my arms.

Instinctively, I swung about so that, at the last second, the beast missed Pio and instead clamped onto my trailing sleeve. Thus, its long teeth merely grazed my arm instead of sinking directly into either human or canine flesh. And so swiftly was the dog moving that my action sent him off balance, while his own momentum sent him tumbling well past me.

Before he could scramble upright again, I was already running as fast as I could, though I was slowed by the tug of my full skirts and the small weight of Pio in my arms. Still, I kept running, my entire being consumed with the same single-minded terror that my ancient ancestors must have felt as they fled marauding wolves. But even in my fear, I knew the futility of my flight. In a few seconds the dog would again be in pursuit, and with a few powerful bounds he would overtake us.

The thought came to me that I could simply drop Pio, and in doing so perhaps save myself from a mauling. Though the beast would make short work of the tiny hound, he surely would be distracted with his prey long enough for me to make my way to safety. Of course, I dismissed the idea as quickly as it came. I knew I could not abandon the innocent Pio to a horrific death and ever sleep another peaceful night!

In the heartbeat it took me to make that decision, I heard another bark and instinctively turned to look. The dog had regained its feet and was running toward me. My breath was coming in frantic gasps now, sweat dampening my bodice and brow, and I knew I could never outrun the dog. In a final effort to save us both, I abandoned flight and flung myself to the ground, huddling over Pio while protectively wrapping my arms over my head and neck. Maybe if we remained unmoving, I frantically thought, the dog would lose interest before doing us much harm.

I could hear the sound of snarls rapidly approaching and steeled myself for the attack, grateful now for my heavy skirts, which might protect us from the cur's teeth for a few moments. Pio obediently lay unmoving beneath me, the heat of his small body burning through my corset. I knew the valiant little hound would have done battle with his far larger attacker had I abandoned him, but he was clever enough to follow my lead now. I only prayed that, should the dog manage to drag him from my grasp, the end would come quickly for the brave Pio.

And then I heard it . . . a single high-pitched howl that sounded more human than dog. An immense furry weight landed upon my back, all but knocking the breath from me as I struggled not to crush Pio. Eyes squeezed tightly shut, I waited for the clash of teeth upon my neck, only to feel that weight abruptly roll off of me. Then came an odd sound, like something thrashing about on the ground nearby.

I opened my eyes and cautiously turned my head to see the sandy colored cur writhing in the grass beside me, jaws agape and long red tongue lolling. Its pale brown fur now ran with crimson, and I saw the gleaming hilt of a knife protruding from its neck. As I watched in disbelief, its movement slowed to a few twitches and then finally ceased.

Warily, I unhooked my hands from behind my head and rose to my knees, clutching a trembling Pio to me as I waited to see what might come next. A shadow passed over me, and I saw a man's elegant, black-sleeved hand reaching down to pluck the knife from the dead creature and wipe the blade upon its fur.

The sun was now high above, so that I blinked uncertainly as I tried to make out the image of the man standing above me. My first fleeting impression simply was of someone tall and dressed in dark clothing.

The Master?

Then my vision began to adjust, and I swiftly realized

my mistake. True, the man was known to me, but it was not Leonardo who had dispatched the attacking dog with so lethal a weapon. The tall, dark man who had come to my rescue was none other than the dashing Gregorio, captain of Il Moro's guard.

10

The Wheel of Fortune

Where fortune enters, there envy lays siege . . .

—Leonardo da Vinci, *Codex Atlanticus*

"That was a damnably stupid thing to do, walking a dog near the stables like that," Gregorio remarked as he tucked the knife into his boot and then coolly surveyed me from above.

Perhaps it was fright that spurred my improper reaction, for I could only stare back up at him in something akin to wonder. He was wearing the same uniform of black tunic and tightly laced black leather jerkin over parti-colored red and black trunk hose, the severity of his dress offset only by the puffs of white that showed through his slashed sleeves. With his curly dark hair backlit by the sun and a sword at his hip, he resembled nothing so much as one of heaven's fallen. All he lacked were the requisite wings and perhaps a nimbus over his head. As for his handsome dark features, they as easily called to mind an angel as a devil.

And the thought occurred to me that either being would be equally welcome in most women's beds.

"Everyone knows those dogs aren't to be trusted," he was

saying while I indulged in my fancy. "If I hadn't come along, the two of you would have been torn to pieces. You should be whipped for such idiocy."

With those last words of his, indignation flared within me, supplanting my momentary daydreams. I hugged the small hound to me and promptly opened my mouth to protest on my behalf. Of course, I never would have taken Pio in that direction had I realized the danger! I was not as thoughtless as all that.

No words came, however, for my voice seemingly was stilled by the fear that continued to pound in my breast. It did not matter, for he went on. "And you're lucky it was just the one dog, instead of the whole pack. The others must have left with the stableboys to exercise the horses. If all of them had gone after you, it wouldn't have been pretty."

He must have taken my continued silence as assent to my folly, for he did not further chastise me. Instead, with a sudden frown, he asked, "That's Pio, isn't it . . . the contessa's dog?" He reached down and lightly scratched the small hound behind one ear. "He's not hurt, is he?"

"I-I don't think so," I replied, finally managing to find my voice. As for Pio, he whimpered but flicked a quick tongue against the man's hand, seemingly recognizing him.

The captain's stern expression lightened, and he reached out to help me to my feet. "He's a clever little beast," he said, steadying me as I struggled to balance again while juggling the small hound in my arms. "You're lucky he's all right. Anything happens to him, and Caterina would have you flayed alive."

Caterina. Recalling myself to my true mission here at court, I made a mental note of that remark. For surely that was an unduly familiar way for a man of his position to address the young contessa. But I was distracted from my role as the Master's secret eyes and ears when the captain abruptly focused his attention on me.

"What about you, are you hurt? Let me see your arm."

With the air of a man used to taking charge, he plucked

Pio from my grasp—I saw to my surprise that I still had his long gold rope wrapped firmly around one hand—and set him at my feet. Pulling his knife from his boot again, he grasped my same arm that the stable dog had savaged. With cool efficiency, he sliced the laces that tied my outer sleeve to my corset. Then he cut away the torn, bloodied sleeve of my chemise beneath, baring my arm.

Now that my earlier rush of fear was fading, I was aware of a sharp burning from elbow to wrist on my right forearm. Blood still welled from the long gash, and as the morning air washed over it, I gasped in unexpected pain.

"You'll need that attended to, lest it festers," was his curt diagnosis. "Where are Isabella and Rosetta?"

When I gazed at him in surprise—how could he have known my companions?—he merely shrugged. "Since you have Pio with you, I assume you're the contessa's new servant. And her maids usually travel about in a pack, just like the stable dogs."

Dogs! Despite my pain, I bristled a bit at the implication. He must have caught my outraged look, for he responded with a fleeting, lazy grin that made my heart lurch just a little.

"That's not what I meant," he placated me. "But where are they? Or were you wandering here by yourself?"

I gazed about but saw no sign of the blond twins. Unable to suppress a bit of bitterness at this apparent abandonment in a time of dire need, I replied, "They were several paces behind me when the dog first made his attack. Last time I saw them after that, they were screaming and running about. Perhaps they went for help."

"Perhaps."

The single word held a note of scorn. Obviously, his assessment of the pair reflected my own opinion, which cheered me slightly, despite the raw throbbing of my arm.

"Don't worry, I'll take you back to your quarters," he said, the words less an offer than a statement of fact. "Can you walk?"

"Of course," I replied, though in truth my legs suddenly felt wobbly. But I was oddly unwilling to show any weakness before this man, which also meant I must refuse his offer.

I cradled my bleeding arm against me and prayed the smile I summoned did not too closely resemble a grimace. "Thank you, Captain, for all your assistance. Pio and I are both exceedingly grateful that you arrived when you did. I shall be certain to praise you to the contessa. But, truly, we can manage alone."

Addressing the small hound, I urged him, "Come, Pio, back to your mistress," and gave a light tug on his lead. With the tiny dog obediently at my heels, I managed a few defiant steps.

And then, as I feared, my legs gave out from under me.

I would have fallen, save that the captain—or rather, Gregorio, as I now found myself thinking of him—seemingly had anticipated that same outcome. Before I hit the ground, he had swept me up into his arms as easily as I could pick up Pio.

"Don't be foolish," he said, shaking his head in disgust. "You've suffered an injury and a fright. You need a bit of rest, not more exertion."

"B-but I'll get blood on you," I weakly objected, unable—or perhaps unwilling, an inner voice jeered—to think of any better excuse.

He gave a short laugh that held no hint of amusement. "Don't worry, I've had blood on me more times than I can count. Now, give me Pio's rope so I can keep track of you both."

Sensing that any further protest would be futile, I meekly slipped the loop from my wrist and handed it to him. Then, accepting the inevitable, I decided to make the best of the situation and relaxed against his warm, hard chest.

It was not the first time I'd been carried about by a man. Once before, when I was in danger of succumbing to a knife wound I'd suffered at the hands of a murderer, I had similarly collapsed. Then, it had been the Master who had carried me from one of the castle gardens all the way to Signor Luigi's shop. I remembered very little of that event, however, for I had been gravely hurt and senseless most of that time. Moreover, the fact that it had been Leonardo who held me had left me oddly unsettled, so that I could hardly recommend the experience.

But now, I could not help a slightly daring feeling of excitement at being handled in such a fashion. To be sure, his attentions were strictly professional, little more than an extension of his duties in safeguarding the duke's castle. Moreover, both the Master and I had lingering suspicions regarding the man, given his connection to two women who had seemingly died at their own hands within days of each other. Given that, why was I finding it so enjoyable now simply to be in his presence?

Fearful lest I grow a bit too comfortable, I sought refuge in conversation. "It was amazing, the way you were able to kill that dog with only a knife," I ventured. "How did you manage such a feat?"

"Let's just say that I had ample free time as a boy to learn such skills," was his rather cryptic reply. "I'm accurate at quite a fair distance, but I didn't want to risk the attempt until you were on the ground and unlikely to jump in front of my blade by mistake. Otherwise, I would have ended it sooner."

"But what if you'd missed?" I asked in a small voice, once more aware just how close Pio and I had come to a frightful end.

Gregorio had no such doubts about his ability. "I never miss," he simply said. "And if the knife hadn't done the trick, I still had my sword."

Unspoken was the likelihood that, in the time it would have taken him to reach us with that weapon, both Pio and I might have suffered grievous—perhaps even fatal—wounds. I shivered at the thought. Certainly, I would be reliving one version or another of that frantic flight in my future dreams.

Something told me, however, that Gregorio would not endure a similarly restless night.

"I'm surprised we haven't met before," he went on, seemingly unaware of my fears. "You must have just arrived here at the castle. What's your name?"

I told him, giving him a truncated version of the story Leonardo had concocted for me. "So I took my place among the contessa's ladies only yesterday. But how could you be so sure of that? Surely you don't know every woman at court."

"I know all the pretty women . . . and some of them better than the others."

I could practically hear in his voice that same lazy grin he'd turned on me a few minutes earlier. As before, I was torn between being scandalized and feeling an undeniable tremor of excitement at the implication. Ruthlessly tamping down that last emotion, I recalled myself to my proper role. In as innocent a tone as I could muster, I asked, "Did you know Bellanca, the servant whose place I took?"

I could feel a brief and almost imperceptible stiffening of his grip at the question. "I spoke to her a time or two, but that is all."

There was no amusement in his tone this time. I suspected he would answer no further questions about Bellanca but, for the moment, it did not matter. We'd reached the portico that led to the noble family's wing of the castle. Unlike the empty portion of the quadrangle near the stables, here we encountered a steady stream of various servants and tradesmen.

To a man and woman, they stared at the admittedly unusual sight of a young woman being squired about in the arms of the captain of the guard, while a small hound trotted at their side. Most wore expressions of varying levels of disapproval. Only one toothless old woman in a nurse's swaddled white headdress and sober gown clapped her hands together and grinned at me with good-natured envy.

Pio's tiny nails clicked loudly upon the stone floors as he followed us through the dimness of the castle toward Caterina's chambers. I might have wondered how Gregorio knew what direction to go—though surely, as captain of the guard, he was more than familiar with the castle's layout—but for the moment I did not care.

By now, the burning sensation along my forearm felt more like a small raging fire, and I feared the prediction of a festering wound might come true. I could only hope that the contessa's relief when she learned of Pio's safe escape outweighed her likely outrage at me. If so, perhaps she would give me leave to find one of the castle women to tend my injury.

But before we reached Caterina's chambers, the young contessa came rushing toward us with her other three servants trailing behind her. She halted, eyes wide, as her frightened gaze took in the small hound with us.

"Pio!" she cried in relief, dropping to her knees.

Her pet gave an answering bark of joy. Pulling free of the captain's grasp, he scampered toward her, the rope trailing after him like a slim gold serpent. And then, with catlike grace, he bounded into her waiting arms.

"Pio," she cried again, hugging him so tightly to her that he yelped. "I feared you had been murdered most cruelly!"

"He is well, Contessa," Gregorio dryly assured her, "though I cannot say as much for your servant."

She looked up from her dog to gaze up at us, as if only now realizing that we were there, as well. "What is this? What are you doing here, Captain, and why are you carrying my maid about like that?"

"She was injured rescuing Pio from one of the stable dogs. I suggest that you let me bring her to her quarters so that one of your women can attend to her."

"She saved Pio?" Her eyes grew wider still, and she stared at me, seeming to truly notice me for the first time since I had joined her household. Then she saw my bloody arm, and her golden cheeks paled.

"Quickly, bring her to my chambers," she declared, setting down her small hound and leaping to her feet. "I shall attend to her myself."

A few minutes later, I was luxuriously settled upon the softest bed I'd ever known, my injured arm propped tenderly upon a feather-stuffed pillow. At Caterina's direction, Esta had produced a basin of warm water and was gingerly washing the cut. The contessa had also poured me a rather large cup of wine and urged me to drink it down, saying it would help with the pain.

"Wine with a few herbs is what my nurse, Lidia, always prescribed for every ill," she explained.

As for Pio, he sat comfortably upon a pillow beside me, daintily chewing on a sweetmeat while his bright eyes took in every move around him. Gregorio had taken much the same tack as the small hound, lounging lazily against a column while Caterina and her women flitted about. Having reached the point of boredom, he finally straightened and addressed Caterina.

"Your pardon, Contessa, but I must return to my post now," he said, though I suspected that post was a room off the guardhouse, where he and the other soldiers wiled away their time with dice and drink. "If you wish, I shall be glad to give you a full accounting later of what happened. But let me assure you that Delfina did not spare herself in attempting to keep Pio from harm."

He paused and coolly eyed Rosetta and Isabella. The twins were huddled in a corner of the room, their expressions peevish and their postures defensive. With a polite smile that managed to convey deeper meaning, he added, "I fear that is more than I can say for certain other of your servants."

"That's not true!" Rosetta protested, while Isabella vigorously shook her head. "As soon as we saw what was happening, we rushed here to tell the contessa that Pio was in danger—"

"—instead of helping Delfina to save him!" Caterina cut her short, outrage darkening her exotic features. She scooped up her pet again and kissed him tenderly upon his narrow head. "What if the captain had not been near the stables to see what was happening and come to her aid? My poor Pio would have been torn to small pieces, and Delfina, too."

"Please forgive us, Contessa. It is all Isabella's fault. She should have warned Delfina to stay away from the stables," Rosetta meekly replied, her expression one of great innocence as she sadly shook her head at her sister.

Isabella jutted her chin, hands on her hips. "*You* were the one who let her walk Pio in the first place," she accused her twin. "*You* should have told her not to go there."

"It does not matter now," Caterina declared, her delicate brow deeply furrowed. "Go, get out of my sight until I decide I'm not angry with you anymore!"

"Pah, those two bicker like small children," Esta said under her breath while the pouting twins flounced their way from the room. Glancing up at me, she added, "I'm glad you're not like them."

The contessa seemed not to notice this exchange, however, for she was busy dismissing Gregorio. "Captain, you have Pio's and my thanks," she grandly declared, favoring him with a small smile and a regal nod. "I shall see that you are amply rewarded for your heroism."

"Your thanks are all I need, Contessa," he replied with a small bow and a hint of the same lazy grin he'd turned on me. And then, quite to my surprise, he winked at her.

I quickly glanced away, pretending I'd not noticed anything, but not before I saw an answering blush rise on Caterina's cheeks. Oddly enough, she appeared not at all outraged by such familiarity from a man of his station. Instead, her confused yet flattered expression called to mind a woman feeling the sweet pangs of first love.

Could it possibly be that the contessa was one of those women that Gregorio knew better than some of the others?

Recalling Esta's comment the night before that Bellanca had carried messages for Caterina, I was suddenly certain that my guess was correct. After all, it was not unheard of for a noblewoman to have a secret dalliance with a common man, most particularly when that man was as handsome as Gregorio!

Ignoring an unexpected little barb of jealousy that pricked at my heart—had the dashing captain not spared me the same, almost intimate, gesture only minutes earlier?—I managed another furtive look at the pair. Oddly, the two of them did seem well suited with their similar dark beauty and volatile natures, no matter the differences in their ranks. I saw what I fancied was a lingering glance that passed between them before Gregorio bowed again and quit the room.

As soon as the door closed behind him, however, Caterina regained her usual air of flighty superiority.

"Delfina, are you badly hurt?" she demanded, rushing to my side. Not waiting for my answer, she grabbed my uninjured hand and earnestly went on. "I shall never forget that you risked yourself to save my Pio. He is my only family now. I don't know what I would do should anything happen to him!"

Then she turned her attention to Esta, who had finished her ministrations and was wrapping a soft length of linen about my arm. "Did you remember to put on the ointment that Lidia always used? She swore it would heal any wound. Oh, if only she were still here!"

With a muffled sob, Caterina abruptly sat on the edge of the bed and dabbed at her welling eyes with a lacy bit of cloth. Seeing her distress, Pio climbed into her lap and touched his cold nose to her cheek.

"Delfina, you did not know Lidia, but she was a very wise woman," she told me, her lips trembling. "She took care of me when I was a child, for my own mother died soon after I was born. Even after she no longer worked in our household, sometimes we would secretly meet, and she would tell me wonderful stories. I even used to pretend that Lidia was my true mother."

She paused and shook her head. "Yes, I know that was foolish, but it made me happy . . . and her, as well, I think.

I do know she loved me, so that is why I don't know why she took her own life. Killing oneself is a sin, is it not?"

She stared at me entreatingly with that last question, and I realized that she was hoping I might give her an answer other than the one she knew to be true. Inwardly, I groaned at that request. Perhaps if I had another cup of wine, I might feel able to indulge in such philosophical discussions. As it was, I peevishly wished her and Esta away, so that I could weep over my injured arm and my ruined gown in peace.

But since she was, for the moment, my mistress, I was obliged to answer her. I was groping for a kind platitude, when all at once I was reminded of young Vittorio. I recalled the story that Constantin had told me of how the boy's mother had fallen to her death, with some saying that fall had been no accident, at all. What would I have said to Vittorio, had he posed the same question as the contessa had asked?

"The Church does teach that to take one's own life is a mortal sin," I gently agreed, "but only God can know what is in that person's heart at the moment of death. Perhaps as she was breathing her last, Lidia changed her mind and did not want to die, after all. And so then, her death would truly be a mistake, an accident, would it not?"

Caterina's eyes again welled with tears, but now she smiled, suddenly appearing far younger than her years.

"Oh, Delfina, you are as wise as Lidia," she softly cried in relief, grabbing my hand once more. "I am sure you are right, that it *was* an accident. And now my heart feels lighter."

Jumping to her feet, she addressed Esta. "Come, clean up this mess, and let us leave Delfina and Pio to rest after their terrible experience. You shall help me choose one of my gowns for Delfina to wear, as hers is damaged. And later, I shall set Rosetta and Isabella to work repairing her dress so that it is like new again."

"Yes, Contessa, that is a wonderful idea," Esta eagerly agreed. She smiled in my direction, and I knew from the twinkle in her eyes that she would enjoy the look on the twins' faces when they learned of the contessa's plans.

I watched the two of them leave and then settled back upon the stack of pillows with a sigh. Pio gave an answering little whimper and plopped himself comfortably against me, long legs stretched so that he contrived to take up most of the bed, despite his small size.

Fortunately, the cup of wine I had drunk was taking effect now, so that my arm throbbed only slightly. The alcohol also dulled my thoughts of the frightful attack I'd endured and kept me from speculating how it might have ended. Of course, when the Master saw me tomorrow with my arm bandaged, he would demand an explanation of my injury.

The placid fog in which I floated lifted a little as I pictured Leonardo's reaction to this day's events. What if he declared me unfit for the charade I'd taken on and insisted I return to my apprentice's role? The idea sent a small quiver of alarm through me.

But surely that would not happen, I hastened to reassure myself. No doubt the Master would be pleased with what I had thus far learned . . . that, and the fact that my actions in protecting Pio had earned me the contessa's goodwill.

With a fuzzy nod of satisfaction, I let myself drift toward sleep. Later tonight, I would take advantage of that newfound intimacy by suggesting a tranquil round or two of tarocchi while I spent the evening convalescing. Then I could attempt the sleight of hand the Master had instructed me in, and slip the duplicate tarocchi cards into the deck.

In the meantime, I was content to let my drowsy thoughts linger on a certain dashing captain of the guard . . . and to wonder what it might be like to be one of those women that he knew better than the others.

11

Strength

Two weaknesses leaning together create a strength.

—Leonardo da Vinci, *Codex Atlanticus*

Late in the afternoon, Pio and I were awakened from our light slumber by the contessa and Esta. The latter carried a tray. Caterina, after first giving me a few minutes to make myself presentable, brought in with her the court physician.

Any fears I had that the man might recognize me as Leonardo's apprentice were promptly put to rest, as the man barely glanced at me. He did deign to give my injured arm a cursory examination, however, that inspection punctuated by a few barbed remarks concerning women who thought they could practice medicine. Declaring that I would survive, he'd left behind a tonic that smelled and tasted suspiciously like Lidia's herb-tinged wine. He insisted I swallow a good half of it in his presence; then, with curt orders to keep the wound covered lest foul air contaminate it, he took his leave.

"Pah, I think Lidia knew more of healing than that man does," Esta muttered to me while Caterina regally escorted the doctor from the room.

By then, the girl was unwrapping a large platter that overflowed with fare usually reserved for the nobles: slices of beef, a small bird, cheeses, and breads, along with a bowl of sweetmeats. The pain of my arm combined with more wine had left me feeling slightly queasy; thus, I partook gratefully if sparingly of the feast. Pio, however, happily swallowed two large slices of meat and a larger crumb of cheese before plopping back down upon his cushion, his now-bulging belly providing evidence that he was replete.

"Esta, you must help me finish this," I groaned as I sank back on my pillow and gestured to the still-heaping platter. Then, feeling generous, I added, "And give some to Isabella and Rosetta, as well . . . that is, if the contessa will not mind."

"I won't tell her," the girl replied with a puzzled frown, "but why be kind to those two, after all that happened?"

"It was not truly their fault that the dog attacked us. And I cannot blame them for being too frightened to help," I added. "Indeed, I was quite frightened, myself."

"Pah, you have been drinking too much of the surgeon's tonic," was her reply as she took the half-drained cup from me and put it out of my reach. Still, I heard grudging approval in her tone, and I knew she would share the meal.

I rested again briefly. When I awakened once more, it was after dark, for the candles had been lit. Caterina soon returned, accompanied by Esta and the twins. The young contessa surveyed me with a satisfied smile and then sat on the bed beside me.

"You are looking much better, Delfina. How is your arm?"

"I fear it is still sore, Contessa," I admitted, wincing slightly as I raised it, "but I am certain I shall be greatly improved by morning."

Then, recalling where I was, I gave a guilty look about me and struggled into a sitting position. "It is getting late. I must return to my quarters so you can have your bed back."

"Nonsense," Caterina grandly declared. "You may rest here for tonight and return to your own bed tomorrow. Do not worry, Pio and I shall be quite comfortable sleeping upon the sofa in the outer chamber."

Then, with a look at the others, she added, "I'm sure that Delfina must find it tedious lying here in bed. I have an idea. Why don't we tell fortunes . . . just for fun, of course?"

The others responded in eager agreement, so I added my voice to theirs. Caterina hurried to the prettily gilded cabinet at the far side of the room and pulled forth a small rectangular box made from some exotic dark wood. Returning with her prize, she opened its intricately carved lid to reveal the now-familiar deck of tarocchi cards, their painted and gilded faces gleaming in the candlelight.

"If the opportunity presents itself, you must ask Caterina to read your fortune . . . but, beforehand, you must contrive to slip these copies into her deck."

Had I not been slightly dizzy from the wine and the pain, I might have attempted the sleight of hand that the Master had tasked me with trying. But even had I been clearheaded, the four extra cards were still safely in my pouch, which Esta had taken pains to tuck beneath my pillow for safekeeping. I would have to be as accomplished a conjurer as the Master to produce those cards and then slip them among the rest, all without any of the other women noticing my actions.

By now, the other three girls had gathered curiously about the bed while Caterina knelt upon the bed and began a careful shuffling of the thick deck. Obviously, this was a ritual familiar to all of them, I thought with a frown.

The contessa looked up just then and, seeing my wary expression, gave a little laugh.

"Do not look so dismayed, Delfina! This is but a game that Lidia taught me to play. Here, I shall tell Isabella her future first, and you will see it is all harmless fun."

Giving the deck another shuffle, she explained, "You know what a tarocchi deck is, of course. It has four different suits . . . the swords, the coins, the staves, and the cups. Each suit has ten cards plus four court cards. And then, of course, there is the fifth suit of trumps. But did you know that each of the cards has a meaning separate from its place in the game, if only you know how to look for it?"

Stacking the cards together again, Caterina set the deck facedown atop the bedcovers. Then she neatly spread them in a single long line, so that perhaps half of each card's red back was visible.

"First, Isabella must ask a question," she said with a nod to the girl.

A small smirk playing about her lips, Isabella promptly asked, "Will the handsome young gentleman I have my eye on prove faithful to me?"

"An excellent question for the cards," the contessa approved. "Next, she must choose four cards . . . one to represent herself, and one each for her past and present and future."

She waited until the girl carefully pulled four cards and then finished, "Now, Isabella will turn them over so we can determine what lies ahead."

While the others and I watched in interest, the girl revealed her four cards. The contessa nodded at each, frowning ever so slightly as the final one was exposed. Leaning closer, she then stared at the grouping with rapt concentration for several moments.

None of the others seemingly breathed during this silence, their attention now focused on Caterina. Shadows from the candles flickered across her face, adding an even greater veil of mystery to her exotic beauty. And then, quite suddenly, the mood of the room seemed to alter, grow darker.

Whether or not the others noticed this change, I was not certain. Perhaps it was simply my fertile imagination or else a result of the wine I'd swallowed. Whatever the cause, I found myself oddly ready to believe that Caterina might indeed possess some preternatural powers. And, despite myself, I waited with equal breathlessness for her to finally speak.

A moment later, she sat back on her heels and gave Isabella a bright smile. "You have drawn fortunate cards tonight. This is you"—she pointed to the first card, the Page of Swords—"and I fear this means you have a tendency to provoke and react with poor grace."

Then, as Isabella pouted a bit, she added, "But the other cards show that you can overcome your faults in dealing with men. If you are true to him, this gentleman will be constant, as well. But you must be careful to treat him with respect and not try to make him jealous. For if you do, he will find himself another woman, one who appreciates him for himself."

"Like me," Rosetta piped up, earning her sister's glare and a snicker from the rest of us.

That moment of amusement dispelled the dark feeling that had gripped me. What Caterina had offered was nothing more than good advice, I thought in relief. Doubtless she knew her maid's faults and suspected it would be Isabella who was more likely to go astray. If the girl followed this advice disguised as a prediction, chances were the young man in question would reciprocate with equal fidelity, thus proving Caterina right.

"Thank you, Contessa," Isabella meekly replied, though only I saw the sharp pinch she gave her sister that made Rosetta yelp and turn a peevish eye upon her twin.

Caterina gathered up the cards again and smiled at me. "See, it is quite pleasant to have your fortune told. Shall I read the cards for you, as well?"

At my nod, she began shuffling the cards and reminded me, "You must ask a question."

While she carefully stacked the cards and spread them out in a line again, I thought about what question I might pose. Of course, I could not pose the question that was uppermost in my mind regarding Bellanca and Lidia's deaths. Thus, perhaps influenced by the wine, I followed Isabella's lead and blurted, "Will the man who occupies my waking thoughts ever see me for who I truly am?"

Even as the words left my lips, I felt myself blush and wished them back, realizing that I was not even sure which of two men that I meant. Was it Gregorio, the dangerously handsome captain of the guards, who might already be the contessa's lover . . . or else was it Leonardo, my master and the man whom I admired most?

Caterina seemed not to notice my confusion, for she merely smiled. "The question is asked. Now, pick your cards."

Feeling nothing but embarrassment now, I hastily pulled four cards from the deck. Then, at her urging, I turned them up, one by one. It was not until the fourth card lay faceup, however, that I realized which cards were spread before me. To my amazement, I saw four familiar images: the Three of Swords, the Knight of Coins, the Devil, and the fiery Tower.

I blinked, unable to believe that I had randomly chosen the very cards that were tied to Bellanca's death. I schooled my surprise and glanced up at Caterina.

Had I turned up four pictures of Pio, the contessa could not have looked more shocked. Just as swiftly, however, her features reflected nothing more than mild pique, so that I wondered if I had misjudged her reaction, after all.

"I fear my skills have deserted me, for I see nothing in these cards," she declared and gathered them into a pile. "Do not be disappointed, Delfina, for we shall try another time."

Then, with a look at the others, she continued. "Delfina needs her rest, so let the rest of us retire to the other chamber for a simple game of tarocchi. Pio will stay here and keep her company, and Esta will check on her through the night."

A few moments later, the chamber was empty of everyone save Pio and me. I lay back against the pillows once more, listening to the soft sound of laughter from the other chamber as the card game commenced and tricks were taken. Alone now, I wondered how it was that I could have drawn the cards I had, wondered again at the contessa's reaction to them. Was it nothing but odd happenstance, or was something else at work here?

As if sensing my dismay, Pio nudged up against me and softly touched a cold nose to my injured arm in sympathy.

"Ah, Pio, I suspect you could say much if only you could talk," I murmured to him and gave him a hug, grateful for his small company in this large and silent chamber.

I might have spent the time writing in my notebook, which I had sorely neglected of late, save that the candles had begun to gutter. I knew I would soon not have light enough for such a task. With nothing else to distract me, I found myself feeling strangely homesick . . . but for once, not for my family. Instead, it was my fellow apprentices—Constantin, Vittorio, Paolo, Tommaso, Davide, and the rest—whom I missed. I wondered how the Master had explained my absence.

Before my thoughts could slide much further into full-blown self-pity, I recalled just why I was there. I eased from beneath the bedcovers, taking care not to awaken my small slumbering companion. Why was I lying in bed, I scolded myself, when I should be spying upon the contessa and her women?

I snuffed the remaining stubs of candles and made my way to the door. Cautiously, I eased it open just enough to allow a narrow view of the room beyond. I was relieved to find that someone kept the hinges well-oiled, for the door made no sound.

The outer chamber was brightly lit, so that I had no fear of anyone noticing my eye pressed to the crack between door and jamb. From my vantage point, I had a clear view of the small table where the women sat. It appeared they had finished their game, for Caterina was once more gathering up her cards. Her chair faced my doorway, and I could see she was smiling in triumph, as if she'd been the victor in their game.

Esta and the twins had left their respective chairs and

were arranging silk blankets and pillows upon the sofa that would serve as the contessa's makeshift bed this night. I caught murmurs of conversation from the trio, but though I strained my ears, I could make out none of their words. With final curtsies to their mistress, the three young women departed the chamber, leaving Caterina alone.

With the click of the door, the contessa's expression abruptly changed, soft smile fading into a look of hard misery. She sat unmoving at the table for a long moment . . . perhaps waiting lest any of the three return unexpectedly.

A surge of pity welled in me, and I wondered if I should go to her. Something in the hard set of her jaw and stiffness of her pose held me back, however, and I knew with certainty that she would not welcome my overtures. Then, as I watched, she slowly began laying out her cards, one by one.

Unlike the simple four cards that Isabella and I had each chosen, she pulled perhaps five times that number until tarocchi cards were all but covering the small table. Laying down the final one, the contessa sat motionless again, simply staring at the elaborate pattern she had created.

I do not know how long she sat like that, candles slowly guttering around her. I was aware, though, that the flickering light was lulling me into an odd state, somewhere between wakefulness and sleep. Indeed, it might have been minutes or perhaps hours that passed as I stood at my post. One small restless corner of my mind wondered if Caterina was similarly affected, the way she sat with such stillness.

And then, abruptly, her rapt expression transformed into a mask of outrage. With a small cry, she dashed all the cards from the table. The pasteboard rectangles scattered around her like frightened birds, their gilded faces seeming to sparkle as they were caught by the dying candlelight.

I must have gasped in response, for her head snapped up and she stared at the door . . . at me. She could not see me, I was certain; even so, I swiftly padded back to the great bed and climbed beneath the blankets. Draping an arm about Pio, I barely had time to feign sleep before the door softly opened, spilling in a few rays of candlelight. I could feel her standing in the doorway, watching me while I strove to keep my breathing soft and my limbs relaxed. Then, as if satisfied that I indeed slumbered, she slowly closed the door once more.

It took a few minutes for my pounding heartbeat to slow. Even then, I dared not crawl from my bed again to spy upon her. By now, her candles must have died in their own puddles of wax, leaving her in darkness. In my mind's eye I pictured her still sitting in her chair, staring into the shadows. Whatever tormented her, she would hold it to herself.

Fervently wishing I was back with my fellow apprentices, I burrowed more deeply beneath my blankets, eager now for sleep. I knew there was nothing more I would learn from Caterina this night. And, sadly, I suspected there was much I would regret knowing when all was finally revealed.

"I have never known anyone so brave!" Caterina exclaimed with a warm look in my direction. "Signor Leonardo, I am fortunate that you sent Delfina to me!"

With that grand pronouncement, the contessa launched into a dramatic retelling of the vicious attack that Pio and I luckily had survived the previous day.

We were seated in the contessa's outer chamber, as had become the habit each morning as the Master continued work on her portrait. Giving no sign of her previous night's distress, Caterina perched upon the usual chair dressed in her golden robes. Pio, who also seemed none the worse for his adventure, once more posed grandly upon her lap, giving an occasional happy bark to all and sundry.

I joined in listening to her account, alternately blushing as she praised me and shuddering as I recalled again just how close both the small hound and I had come to real harm. While I would have preferred to explain my mishap to the Master privately, I'd not been afforded that luxury. The evidence of my injury had been obvious, for the arm in question was today supported by a sling of delicate lace, which Caterina herself had tied around my neck.

"Of course, Gregorio—that is, the captain of Il Moro's guard—was quite brave, too," the contessa concluded, an almost imperceptible blush coloring her cheeks. "Had he not been nearby and so swift with his knife, I fear I might have been telling you a far different tale."

Leonardo, meanwhile, was listening to her account with what appeared to be nothing more than polite concern as he arranged his paints and brushes. I knew him well enough by now, however, to recognize that he had exercised great restraint in refraining from a flood of questions . . . that was, to a point. True to his nature, he was unable to resist inquiring as to the sort of medical attention I had received for my bite.

"For it is well-known that such wounds, though seemingly minor, can be far more dangerous than even a gash from a blade," he pointed out with a sidelong look at me.

I put a reflexive hand to my ribs, aware of the faint scar that marred that once-smooth flesh. Neither of us had forgotten my near-fatal brush with death at the point of a knife not many weeks earlier.

The contessa waved away his concerns. "Fear not, our Delfina has received only the best of care," she assured him, going on to detail the attention I'd received from her . . . or, rather, from Esta.

"And I made certain that the court surgeon also paid her a visit last night to offer his treatment," she proudly added. "He gave her a special remedy to drink, which he said would ward off any ill humors that might afflict her."

"Let us hope that his nostrum did no more harm than good," the Master muttered, offering his usual biased opinion of the physician's skills.

The remainder of the morning passed quickly. Having told her exciting tale, Caterina seemed content to pose quietly. Isabella and Rosetta sat in the far corner of the chamber. Apparently, my overture the night before had done me little good, for their expressions were mutinous as they muttered between themselves while toiling over my ruined gown. Esta had been put in charge of them, and every so often she smiled over at me with conspiratorial glee.

As for myself, at Caterina's insistence I sat to the other side of her so that I might call upon her should I feel faint or require another potion.

"Though I must beware lest Signor Leonardo add you to my portrait," she'd said with a laugh.

I'd smiled a bit wryly, for the Master was known to do just that, adding subjects to his painting that did not belong at all, simply for his own amusement. But given that the portrait had been commissioned by the duke, himself, I was confident he would not indulge his sense of humor this time.

Thus, I had no duties save to sit comfortably and watch the Master at work. But despite my outer calm, inwardly I was taut with anticipation for my chance to share with the Master not only my version of the attack but also the odd events surrounding the contessa's fortune-telling the night before. That would have to wait until our session was ended, however, and would require my making some excuse to see the Master alone.

Seemingly hours later—though, of course, the sun lagged no more slowly this day than usual—the light changed sufficiently so that the Master called a halt to his work.

"We are making fine progress, Contessa," he assured her as he covered the panel again.

Sighing, Caterina rose from her chair. "That is good news, Signor Leonardo, for it is not many more days until the masquerade. I have already sent your Signor Luigi word that I wish to see him today to consult with him about my costume. Perhaps Delfina will accompany me to his shop this afternoon if she feels well enough."

"I am quite well, Contessa," I assured her, suddenly eager for an escape from the castle. "Indeed, I shall be happy to take you there."

The Master gave me a swift glance and the hint of a nod. "Delfina will prove a fine guide," he said, adding, "And I am pleased, Contessa, that you took my counsel in this matter. Perhaps you will not take it amiss that I took the liberty of sending the good tailor a few sketches for you to choose from for your costume."

Caterina clapped her hands in delight. "How wonderful! I shall have a masquerade gown designed by Leonardo the Florentine, himself! I cannot wait to see what you have done."

"I am certain you shall be pleased. And now, may I ask a boon of you?"

With a smile, Leonardo went on to smoothly offer the excuse I had sought, saying, "If you would be so kind, might Delfina accompany me part of the way back to my workshop? I am sure she has messages she would wish me to convey to her family."

"Certainly," the contessa agreed with a regal nod of her head, gathering Pio into her arms. "But pray do not keep her too long, for I shall be missing her company."

I made Caterina a quick curtsy and followed the Master from her quarters. As we made our way toward the courtyard, I was dismayed to see that his expression had taken on grim purpose. Surely he would not fault me for what had happened before I could give him my own version of events!

He kept his counsel while we crossed the quadrangle. Only when we reached our familiar bench, well out of earshot of any save those who might pass directly by, did he speak.

"This is bad business, my boy," he said with a shake of his head. "First, I must tell you that I already knew of this attack. I happened across the physician and one of his cronies last night, and I overheard him relating the details of his latest case. Of course, he had no idea that it was one of my apprentices who was, in truth, the victim. He claimed you were little worse for wear, so I felt confident that I could wait until this morning to speak with you. But now that I know the captain of the guard was involved . . ."

He paused, his demeanor that of a man who was making an effort to remain calm. Finally, he went on. "Tell me in your own words what happened, that you were so strangely attacked."

My own trepidation growing—though I was not quite sure why—I recounted all that led up to those frightening moments near the stables. I assured him, as well, that my injury pained me but little now and appeared well on its way to healing . . . told him, too, that it had been Gregorio's swift actions that most likely had saved my life.

I was surprised to see that he did not appear comforted by my words; rather, his expression grew grimmer. Still, when I finally ended my tale, I was not prepared for his response.

"This is my fault," he flatly told me. "I should have realized that I would be putting your life at risk by sending you into the castle. We must end this masquerade now, before the next attempt proves fatal."

"Next attempt?" I echoed in a perplexed voice. "Master, what can you mean? What happened was nothing but an accident."

"I fear not, my boy. A strong likelihood exists that the attack on you was deliberately staged."

As I stared at him, my confusion growing, he went on. "I spoke with the stable master this morning regarding the incident. He assured me no such attack from any of his dogs has happened before. A nip or a bite, perhaps, but never such a vicious assault. And then I learned something else."

Glancing about to make sure no one had approached as we spoke, he lowered his voice and went on. "It seems that another of the stable dogs was found dead the same day that Lidia took her life. The stable master showed me where the beast was found, a short distance behind the main stalls."

I nodded, recalling my conversation with the porter the day of Lidia's death and his remark about a foul smell. Doubtless the source of the odor had been that dog of which the stable master had spoken.

"Given that this seemed yet another odd coincidence, I searched the area in hopes of learning why the beast died so unexpectedly," he went on. "To be truthful, I expected to leave empty-handed, but I did not. Behind a stack of wood, I found a small clay jug identical to the one we discovered with Lidia. A bit of liquid remained inside, and it was apparent from the sharp odor it gave off that this wine also had been poisoned."

I frowned. "I confess, Master, that you leave me quite confused. It does seem likely that someone deliberately poisoned the first dog, but what has that to do with the dog that attacked me and Pio?"

"My guess is that the first dog was a test subject, and that the poisoner was attempting to learn how much of his brew was fatal. Too much, and the dog dies. But just a small amount, and perhaps the poison coursing through its system does not kill but merely makes it ill to the point of agitation. And when some manner of disturbance happens, such as another dog passing by, the dog's agitation swiftly becomes frenzy."

Despite myself, I shivered. Had anyone else proposed the possibility of such a fiendish plot, I would have dismissed it as folly. But as the Master explained it, such a plan sounded plausible, even likely. Yet still it made no sense. Why would anyone want to murder me . . . or, rather, the maidservant Delfina?

When I posed the question to Leonardo, he shrugged. "That concerns me, as well. You could not in a single day at court learn something that would sign your death warrant. Thus, the possibility remains that you were not the intended victim."

"But who—"

"Recall that Pio was the catalyst for the attack. No one could guess that it would be you squiring him about that day."

When I stared at him in alarm, comprehension dawning, he nodded and went on. "There is but one person who would be expected to walk Pio about the courtyard, and that is his mistress. And so I fear that the contessa was to have been the victim in this foul scheme."

His pronouncement hung heavily between us for a few long moments as I struggled to make sense of it all. If someone meant to kill Caterina, then why were the other women dead? Perhaps they each had learned something of the scheme and would have warned her, and so had to be silenced? Or maybe they had been part of the plot, and took their own lives out of guilt.

Still, something told me this was not quite right. I could think of no reason someone would want the contessa dead, nor think of anyone who could be the would-be murderer. Indeed, the only person who had raised any suspicion was Gregorio, whose relationship with Caterina seemed far more than simply friendly.

I shook my head. It was as if we were trying to piece together the Master's broken clay model, only to find a few bits of it missing. No matter how we might try, we would never come up with a whole horse until the lost segments were found.

"Forgive me, Master, but I fear I am not yet convinced," I finally said. "There is much that we do not yet know, and you told me once before that it is folly to remain wedded to a theory before having sufficient proof to justify the union."

At my solemn pronouncement, his expression lightened for the first time since we'd sat together.

"Once again, my boy, you use my words against me," he said with a small laugh. "I fear I may have taught you too well. Are you saying that you are willing to continue the masquerade awhile longer?"

"I am," I softly exclaimed with a firm nod. "But there is more still to be told. I did learn something last night that could well be of import."

I explained the contessa's offer to tell fortunes, and how I'd somehow drawn from her deck the same four tarocchi cards that had begun to figure so prominently in this matter . . . this despite having no opportunity to first place the Master's own copies among them. I explained, as well, how the sight of them seemed to startle her, to the point that she called a halt to the amusement without reading the cards for me.

"Her reaction does bear consideration," he agreed when I'd finished, "but as for the cards, themselves, it can be nothing other than coincidence that had you pluck them from the deck. Unless, of course, she had some reason to wish those cards upon you. Could it be that the contessa is cleverer than we think, and she deliberately managed some sleight of hand that caused you to choose them?"

I considered that possibility a moment and then shook my head. "I do not think that is the case, Master. I am certain that my choices were random, and her surprise did not seem feigned. Besides, she could not know that I had ever seen the four cards that Bellanca took away with her the day of her death."

"You must try the experiment again," he declared, "for it seems that this portion of our plan, at least, is yielding results. Perhaps if she continues to see these same cards drawn again and again, she will give you some hint of what they truly mean to her."

I nodded my agreement, relieved because these orders confirmed his agreement that I should continue my role. I went on to explain what had happened later as I'd spied upon the contessa once she was alone again in her chamber.

"This is a greater cause for concern," he replied with a frown, "for she did not know she was being observed, yet she reacted with such emotion. It would seem to indicate that she truly believes what the cards tell her."

"Perhaps she does have some ability that others do not," I tentatively offered, only to have my words met by a small laugh.

"Dino, my boy, you must beware that putting on female skirts does not turn your brain to that of a woman," he lightly scolded. "You have been my apprentice long enough to know that I do not give credence to superstition."

Then, with a wry look at the red silk robes I was wearing, he added, "And speaking of skirts, I fear our good tailor will be most distressed when you arrive in his shop wearing a creation other than his."

"That was not to be helped," came my rueful protest as I self-consciously ran one hand down the sleek fabric. "The contessa insisted I must have one of her gowns to make up for the damage to my own."

Then, recalling that I was supposed to be Dino, I gave an inelegant snort and added, "I confess I did have a moment of fear that I might be found out. Had I not accepted these robes, and gratefully, I fear she and her women would have held me down and stripped my old clothes from me."

"You acted as you should. And you continue to take care to preserve the women's modesty? Good," he replied in approval at my vigorous nod. "Is there anything more I can do to help you keep up your role?"

"Only save that you deafen me," I replied, deliberately putting my hands to my ears in boyish mockery. "Saints' blood, but these women chirp unceasingly, like birds in a bush. I admit I shall be happy to rejoin my fellows again."

He gave me a commiserating smile before assuming a more serious mien. "Just recall that your role is to listen to that chatter. Now, return to your mistress before she has cause to wonder at your long absence."

Giving me a fatherly pat upon the shoulder, he rose from the bench; then, lest we were being watched, he grandly offered a hand and helped me to my feet.

"Be sure you make careful note of the conversation when you visit the good tailor," were his final words of instruction before he took his leave. "You know Luigi's propensity for gossip. Perhaps the contessa will be more forthcoming in his presence and reveal further information of use."

I watched as he headed back across the quadrangle toward the workshop, one part of me wildly wishing that I could return there with him. But I had committed myself to this role, and I would not fail him. Soon enough, I would be

Dino again, temporarily relegated to boiling skins and sweeping floors as I finished out my punishment for that transgression with the plaster that suddenly seemed to have happened a lifetime ago.

Determinedly putting aside all but my firm intention to help the Master resolve this tangled set of affairs, I hurried back to the castle. It was only after I had rejoined Caterina and her women, however, that I realized I had forgotten to tell Leonardo the one other important thing that I had learned the night before.

Or had I deliberately neglected to mention it, simply because I wished to pretend it was not true?

For why else would I have forgotten to tell the Master this most important secret . . . my suspicion that the contessa and the captain of the guard might well be involved in a shockingly illicit affair?

12

The Hanged Man

He who wishes to become rich in a day is hanged in a year.

—Leonardo da Vinci, *Windsor Drawings*

"This is the costume that I wish, Signor Luigi," Caterina declared, pointing to the final of several small sketches upon his worktable. "Quickly, take my measure so you may begin work on it."

The tailor's bushy brows shot up beneath his greasy fringe of black hair. "Er, are you quite certain, Contessa?"

I gave her a questioning look, as well. Before we left from the castle, Caterina had changed her golden robes for a gown of deep brown trimmed in cream, which she wore under a green and cream surcoat. More sober if no less richly made than her usual garb, it gave her the appearance of a matron twice her age . . . that was, until she screwed up her face in an expression of quite girlish pique.

Realizing his error, Luigi swiftly tried for a conciliatory tone. "Rather, might I suggest instead that the Queen of Swords would be an excellent choice for someone of your dark beauty?"

Pulling that sketch from the stack, he went on. "You will

be a vision in white and silver and gold, and you will have a crown and sword to wear, as well. If I may be so bold, that other design is less than appropriate for a young woman of your station. And I do believe that Signor Leonardo intended that other costume for someone else," he added with the faintest of sidelong nods at me.

By way of response, Caterina snatched the first drawing she'd indicated from the table.

"I do not care," she countered, the expression on her pretty face one of pure mutiny. "That is the costume I want!" Then she handed the drawing to me. "Look, Delfina, is it not wonderful? It looks just like the picture of the knave from my tarocchi cards."

I took the paper from her, immediately recognizing the Master's hand in the sketch of an androgynous youth. Labeled *The Knave of Wands*, he—or she—carried the requisite stave in one hand, head bare of any cap or adornment.

Notes alongside the drawing indicated that the figure should be wearing tall red boots etched with gold pulled over red trunk hose. A second set of notes indicated a short tunic of red and gold brocade, its long sleeves ending in wide green cuffs. Over it all, the knave wore a short cloak striped in blue and gold and lavishly trimmed with white and gold fur. And, because it was to be a masquerade, in his free hand the knave held a large gold mask that would easily conceal him from nose to forehead.

I met Luigi's gaze and returned his nod. It was a colorful and dramatic costume well suited to a young boy. A young boy like Dino.

Immediately, I knew the Master's intent. The night of the masquerade, he doubtless meant to costume me as the knave and then slip me in among the noble guests. This way, I could continue to serve as his eyes and his ears on what should prove a most interesting night. Likely it had been only by mischance that he'd not separated this drawing from the rest when he'd handed them to the tailor.

"It is a wonderful costume," I assured her, "but I fear I

must agree with Signor Luigi that the Queen of Swords would be a far better choice. Surely it would be shocking for a contessa to appear costumed in such a manner, wearing boy's trunk hose."

"Pah, you do not understand," she cried in dismay, snatching the drawing back from me. "When else will I ever have a chance for such freedom? It is a masquerade, after all. No one will know my identity until we unmask, and by then I will have fled the hall so that no one would be the wiser."

I opened my mouth to protest, and then promptly shut it.

Of course, Caterina as yet did not know that she was to be a guest of honor at this feast that in truth was a betrothal celebration. What would happen if she did come costumed in so shocking a manner, only to be unmasked before Il Moro and all his court, including the unknown duke who was to be her husband?

My alarm began to grow. Why, the husband-to-be might call off the nuptials . . . might even call off whatever truce Il Moro had brokered with Caterina as the prize. And because he had arranged the masquerade and designed the costumes, Leonardo would be unfairly blamed for this disaster by the duke!

Yet even as such frightful scenarios flashed through my mind, the contessa abruptly relented.

"Very well," she told the tailor, returning the sketch to him and favoring him with a regal smile. "I will follow your counsel. I shall dress as the Queen of Swords . . . but with one condition. You must make up the knave costume for Delfina."

As Luigi and I stared at each other, puzzled at this turn of events, she went on. "I will want her there at the masquerade with me, lest the night prove tedious. As no one will think to find a servant beneath the costume, she may stay until we unmask. And at least she will enjoy a bit of freedom from long skirts for one night."

"Er, yes, that sounds a reasonable request," the tailor replied in an uncertain tone.

While the contessa reached for the sketch of the other costume in question and began studying it in earnest, Luigi once again exchanged glances with me. I gave him a faint shrug and a lift of my brows. Surely this was a fortunate turn of events, in that Caterina's plan would conveniently save the Master a bit of subterfuge. Then I turned to the contessa.

"You do me great honor," I told her in all sincerity. "If you are certain that you wish me there with you, I shall gladly be by your side."

"I knew I could depend upon you. And now, let us quickly let the tailor take our measure, as we have other errands to run this day."

At her insistence, Luigi measured me first, even though by now he doubtless knew each number by heart. Fortunately, I did not have to explain to him my injury, as I had removed my sling before leaving the castle despite the contessa's protests. I saw her disapproving frown when she saw me wince as I raised that arm, however, and I prayed she would not use that as excuse to make me don the cumbersome cloth again.

Caterina patiently watched as he tried a few pieces of cloth upon me, while Pio stared with greater interest at the trilling lark in the willow cage above us. Finishing with me, the tailor then used his knotted cord upon the contessa while remarking, "You are close enough in size to our young Delfina, that I almost need not take your measure."

It seemed that for Caterina's costume, he had already made up in his shop a great variety of elegant white gowns and bodices and sleeves. Upon closer look, I saw that a number of them were from the notorious live chess match, where the human players had all worn either white or black. Idly, I wondered if the contessa had been among those who had played that day. If she had, she made no mention of that fact as the tailor draped her with various snowy lengths of silk and damask.

I assisted Caterina into the bits of costume he cleverly assembled; then, while she was admiring herself in the strip of mirror in the corner, Luigi swiftly took me aside.

"What has happened to that lovely gown I sewed for you?" he demanded in a whisper, gesturing to the dark red silk I wore instead. Before I could answer, he added in resignation, "No, do not tell me—"

"Fear not, signore, it is being repaired as good as new. I will explain all later," I murmured back, more concerned for the moment with keeping a sharp eye on Pio.

The lark in the cage above had seemingly decided that she was safe from this potential predator and so was taunting him with a series of chirps. Pio, meanwhile, refused to believe that she hung out of reach of his small jaws. Thus, he had commenced bouncing up and down on his long hind legs in hopes of snaring his prize.

We remained in the shop but a short while longer. Finally setting aside his cord and pins, Luigi told the contessa, "I will need perhaps two days to complete both costumes, and then I shall send word when they are ready for a final fitting."

"And you are certain, Signor Tailor, that they will be ready in time for the masquerade?" Caterina asked with a frown.

Luigi waved away her concerns. "They shall be ready with time to spare."

Then he glanced down at Pio. The hound had finally conceded defeat and now lay beneath the lark's cage with his nose upon his crossed paws, wearing a sulky look that reminded me of the contessa. "In fact," the tailor added, "I may even have time to sew a fine collar for this handsome boy."

"You are too kind," she exclaimed, her smile returning at the mention of her pet. "Come, Pio," she addressed the small beast, giving a light tug at his rope. "We must leave Signor Luigi to his work."

Outside on the narrow lane waited the small cart driven by one of the duke's own men, which conveyance had carried us the short distance to Luigi's shop. When he would have helped her into her seat, however, she peevishly waved him away.

"I wish to walk," she declared. "You may follow at distance, so that the horse is not breathing upon our heels."

The driver bowed and did as instructed, waiting until Caterina and Pio and I were a short distance ahead of him on the narrow cobbled lane before touching his reins to the sturdy horse's neck. Though of course I had not been consulted, I did not protest this change of plans. So uneven were the streets that, even at a moderate pace, one was always in danger of being jounced right off the cart's hard seat when traveling in such a manner. When going any distance, it was far more comfortable to ride or, failing that, simply to walk.

Caterina, meanwhile, was staring avidly at the townspeople as they went about their day, stopping in at the butcher or apothecary, or pausing at the fountain for a mouthful of water and a moment's rest. Pio and I strolled happily alongside her, enjoying the fine afternoon. After a few moments of this, however, she finally turned to me.

"You don't know how lucky you are, Delfina, to be but the daughter of a merchant," she said with a sigh, reminding me about my fictional family. "You can come here to the city anytime you like, yet I cannot even go to the marketplace alone. And even when I am accompanied by my servants, it would be thought unseemly for me to bargain with the shopkeepers. I must wait with the wagon and send a man to do that for me."

She shook her head and sighed more dramatically. "Indeed, some days, I wish I had been born anything other than a conte's daughter!"

I was debating whether I should remind her that there were hungry enough folks living at the fringes of the city who would gladly trade places with her, when she caught me by the arm and drew me closer.

"Are you not excited, knowing you will be at the masquerade among all the nobles, though you are but a merchant's child?" she asked in delight. At my nod, she went on. "You see, I have done a favor for you, have I not? And now, Delfina, you must do one for me."

"But, of course, Contessa," I automatically agreed, though I suspected from the secretive smile upon her face that this might be no simple request. "What would you have me do?"

"It is but a small task. I need you to deliver a message for me."

Abruptly, I recalled Esta's remark about Bellanca, and how the girl used to deliver messages for the contessa. At the time, I had been certain that if I could but learn what the messages contained and who their recipient was, much would come clearer regarding Bellanca's death.

Careful not to show any undue anticipation at this turn of events, I replied, "Of course, Contessa. To whom shall I carry this message?"

Her expression no longer merry, she glanced behind us to make certain the driver was well out of earshot.

"First, you must swear that you will never tell anyone what I have asked you to do," she urgently whispered. "Nor can you ever reveal the identity of the person to whom you bring the message, lest word reach my cousin the duke. It could prove dangerous for me, for the other person. Now swear, Delfina!"

I hesitated, knowing that I must reveal all to the Master . . . yet knowing, too, that if I gave my word, I could not break it. But perhaps there would be another way I could make certain that the Master would learn the truth without my telling him outright.

Swiftly, I nodded. "I vow that I shall not speak of this to anyone without your leave, Contessa," I softly replied, making the sign of the cross for good measure.

Seemingly satisfied, she released my arm. Then, with her

free hand—Pio on his leash still tugged at the other—she
pulled a folded handkerchief from her bodice. She lightly
put it to her face, as if to pat away an unseemly bit of moisture from her brow.

"There is a message sewn inside this cloth," she murmured. "In a moment, I shall drop it, and you must pick it
up. But do not return the handkerchief to me. Put it in your
sleeve, and I shall tell you what to do with it."

Not waiting for my reply, she leaned away from me as if
to speak to Pio. Then, seemingly unnoticed, the cloth fluttered from her hand. I paused and snatched it from the cob-
bles almost before it landed, tucking it into my sleeve as
she'd instructed.

"Very good," she said with a sidelong glance at me.
"Now, listen to my plan. Before we reach the castle gate, I
shall climb upon the cart again and bid you farewell, as if
you were staying behind in the city. You will wait for several
minutes, until we have had time to pass through the gates.
Do you understand thus far?"

"Yes, Contessa. And then what should I do?"

She lowered her voice so that I had to strain to hear. "Then
you shall go to the gate yourself, but do not pass through. Instead, you must tell the guard there that you have an urgent
missive for his captain."

"For the captain of the guard?" I whispered back. "Do
you mean Gregorio?"

"Yes." Then, looking back once more to assure we were
not overheard, she gave me an eager smile.

"Is it not exciting?" she softly exclaimed. "I always feared
I would never have a chance to know true love. Indeed, I
was certain I would go to my grave having only endured the
touch of whatever dusty duke that my cousin is bound to
force me into marrying one day."

Her smile broadened. "But that changed when Gregorio
arrived at the castle a few months ago. He came to speak to
my cousin on some matter, and I happened to be passing by.
I saw him, and he saw me . . . and we have been secretly

sending messages and even meeting each other, on occasion, ever since."

"But can this be?" I faintly asked. "After all . . ."

"Oh, do not look so shocked, Delfina," she went on, waving away my protests. "It is true we are of different stations, but that makes it all the more romantic. I have fallen in love, and he has sworn devotion, as well. Indeed, he has told me he shall never touch another woman if he cannot have me. Is that not wonderful?"

I summoned a smile in return, hoping she could not see my dismay. While I already suspected that her relationship with the captain might be friendlier than was proper—especially given their respective roles—hearing this admission from her still took me by surprise. Of course, were it but a casual frolic, the relationship might be winked at so long as she kept such dalliances private. But she seemed to believe that she was in love, and to believe that Gregorio returned that sentiment.

Despite myself, I felt a sudden surge of pity for her. Was she the only one who did not know the truth, that he was rather more inconstant than he claimed? I could not help but recall all the whispered stories I'd heard about Gregorio's penchant for pretty women, could not forget his own admission that he knew some better than others.

Neither could I suppress the small jealous voice within that asked why Caterina should have the dashing captain, when she would soon be marrying a duke. Sternly rebuking myself for such unworthy sentiments, I whispered, "But is it safe to bring him such a message? What if it falls into someone else's hands?"

"Do not worry. He always burns my letters upon receiving them, so that no one will ever know they existed."

I would have questioned her further, save that we were nearing the gate. As planned, she scooped up Pio in her arms and then turned to signal her driver.

"I shall ride the rest of the way back," she grandly told him as he halted the cart beside her. To me, she said, "Very

well, Delfina, you may visit with your friend here in the city
for a time. But do not stay too long."

"I shall return soon, Contessa," I replied, playing my
role. Stepping aside, I dropped a small curtsy while the
driver assisted her onto the hard seat.

I watched the cart roll away, Caterina sitting with regal
grace while holding Pio, who seemed to grin at me over her
shoulder. Doubtless, the spoiled beast thought me foolish
for walking rather than riding, I thought in fond amusement. But once I saw the cart maneuver through the smaller
passage cut in the immense gates, I felt my humor fade
again.

"Just take the message to him and be done with it," I
muttered aloud, drawing forth the expensive scrap of lace
that I'd tucked into my sleeve.

Only the faint crackle I could hear as I unfolded the cloth
gave hint that something was hidden between the layers. It
occurred to me that I should try to retrieve the note and read
it first before delivering it, but I did not dare. It was likely
that Gregorio had come to expect the contessa's messages to
arrive sewn into a cloth. He would know that this missive
had been tampered with should it arrive in some other
manner.

I frowned. Of course, I could have Signor Luigi duplicate the stitch, but it would take far too much time to return to his shop. Moreover, the tailor would insist upon
knowing what the note contained, and I would be hard-
pressed to keep him from reading it. My only hope was
that the captain would, in turn, give me a message to carry
back to Caterina, which I could then read before handing it
to her.

*Unless Gregorio took equal trouble to stitch his own missives
into a handkerchief,* I told myself, and then stifled a giggle at
the thought of this dashing soldier wielding a needle instead of a sword.

My good humor somewhat restored, I tucked away the

handkerchief again and made my way to the massive red-brick walls that surrounded the castle grounds. As I approached the heavy wooden gate beneath the imposing clock tower, however, I could not help a sudden surge of nervousness at what I was about to do. And then my nervousness transformed into full-blown dismay when I saw the guards were the same who had accompanied Gregorio a few days earlier, when Lidia's body was found.

Of course, they would never recognize me as the Master's apprentice, I assured myself, even had they spared me a glance amid all the confusion that day. Still I was careful to keep my gaze modestly lowered as I approached them.

"A message to the captain, eh?" the taller of the pair responded to my request.

His words were tinged with an accent, and I recalled the Master's words that many of the mercenaries were foreign born. Blond and square of face, his coarse features reflected an air of brutal dissipation that was not softened by the gap-toothed grin he bestowed on me.

His fellow leered at me with equal loutish humor. "You sure you wouldn't rather give me that message, girl?" he asked suggestively, winking and elbowing the other soldier.

I bit my lip, knowing I would have to placate the pair or risk being sent away. Summoning a small smile, I said, "I fear the message is from someone else, and I have been entrusted to carry it to the captain. Please summon him, if you would, or else tell me where to find him."

The pair exchanged glances again. Finally, the blond mercenary grinned again and thrust a thick thumb over his shoulder, indicating a small door behind him. "You want the captain, you can go through there. The stairway, it goes to the top of the wall. You lucky, you can find the captain up there."

"Yeah, and if you're lucky, he won't be busy," the second one retorted, waggling his eyebrows meaningfully.

Suppressing a distasteful shudder, I thanked them and hurried in the direction he'd indicated. But once I'd closed

the splintered door behind me in a squeal of poorly oiled
hinges, I wondered if this were some sort of foul trick. Only
a few of the sun's fading rays pierced the slit of a window
above, so that I could barely make out the stone stairway before me. Should one of the soldiers follow after me, I would
have no escape other than to continue upward.

I gave myself a moment for my eyes to adjust and then
began the careful climb. No lumbering footsteps echoed behind mine, however, and a few moments later I had reached
the top of the stairs. Here lay a second closed door whose
hinges squealed with equal enthusiasm when I tried the
handle. If the captain *were* busy, as the one soldier had implied, he certainly would be forewarned of my approach.

To my relief, this door opened into the first level of the
clock tower . . . a long room with tall windows on either
side and empty save for a brazier burning in one corner.
Curious despite myself, I cautiously peered through the
battlements toward the glorious sprawl of the town. The
buildings huddled close, many of them bridged by flapping
lines of bright clothing that had been hung to dry that
morning. I could see the marketplace and catch glimpses of
the same stone lanes along which the contessa and I had
walked.

Turning, I had a similar hawk's-eye view of the quadrangle. Its parade grounds and bright gardens and green lawns
stretched in neat order, the people milling about them unaware of my regard. Had I not a mission to complete, I told
myself, I could have spent an hour watching all the small
dramas taking place below.

Recalling why I was there, I glanced uncertainly to either side of me. Open doorways led to the tunnel-like walk-
ways that ran the perimeter of the castle's fortifications.
These were the same steep-roofed battlements where I had
glimpsed the soldiers patrolling countless times before. Walking one way, I would arrive at the same tower at whose foot
Lidia's body had been found. Should I walk in the opposite

direction, I would end up in the very tower from which Bellanca had fallen.

Deciding I did not care to see the spot from which Bellanca had taken her fatal plunge, I turned back toward the other tower . . . and abruptly stumbled into unyielding black leather.

13

Death

Death rather than weariness.

—Leonardo da Vinci, *Windsor Drawings*

"I wondered if we would meet again," a lazy voice murmured as strong hands gripped me about the waist, steadying me.

I looked up to see Gregorio regarding me with a hint of the same dangerous grin that always so unnerved me, though I could not read his eyes for the shadows. Had he been watching my approach and deliberately intercepted me, I wondered, or had I taken him by surprise, as well?

"Captain, you move as silently as Pio!" was the first thought that burst from my lips. Then, feeling myself blush at such foolishness, I promptly added, "That is, I did not expect to stumble over you like this."

"Ah, you wound me, my dear Delfina," he replied, his grin widening just a bit. "I might have hoped that you had deliberately come here to see me, perhaps to thank me again for rescuing you yesterday. Tell me, how is your arm?"

"I do thank you, Captain . . . and my arm continues to improve," I replied, my blush deepening at his banter. "The contessa insisted that I be treated with one of Lidia's potions, which she said should keep the wound from scarring."

"One of Lidia's potions, eh?"

A shadow darkened his expression, and he loosened his grip on me. At his reaction, I silently chastised myself for this error, fearing I might have revealed too much. In the next heartbeat, however, I realized it did not matter. He could not know that I knew Lidia was his mother, or that I had witnessed him at the scene of her death acting oddly unmoved by the event.

Thus, I nodded and innocently replied, "The contessa and her women all say she was very wise. I am sorry that I did not have the chance to know her."

"Yes," was his only reply. Then, with a quirk of one dark brow he asked, "Are you here to see me, after all, or were you waiting for one of my guards to join you up here?"

"One of them?" I squeaked in unfeigned outrage, picturing the two crude soldiers I'd just left. Then, realizing from the amused twist of his lips that he was once again jesting, I allowed myself an answering smile.

"I am here to see you, Captain, but I fear not on my own behalf. I have an important missive for you," I said and pulled the folded cloth from my sleeve. He gave a small nod of recognition and took it from me.

"So you are the contessa's new messenger."

With those wry words, he plucked the knife from his boot, its keen blade glinting in the flickering flames of the brazier. With the same ease with which he'd previously cut my ravaged chemise, he sliced the neat stitches that held the cloth together and pulled forth the note hidden within.

Stepping over to the brazier, he leaned against the stone wall and unfolded the page. He studied it for so long that I wondered if the message within was something quite dire. And then another explanation for his silent concentration abruptly occurred to me.

After all, he was a soldier, a mercenary. What opportunity

would a man of his station have had to learn more than a
cursory bit of reading and writing, just enough for him to
mark his name when he received his pay? Moreover, I had
seen an example of Caterina's hand, with its flowing style as
elaborate as found in any priestly manuscript. Perhaps, un-
lettered as he was, the captain was having difficulty making
out the contessa's words.

"I could read it to you, if you wish," I tentatively suggested, not wishing to embarrass him but feeling it my duty
to make the offer. Besides, how better to find out just what
it was that Caterina's missive said?

He glanced up from the page and slanted an amused look
in my direction. "Your offer is kind, but quite unnecessary.
You may rest assured I have some competency in that area."

Then, as I started to offer a blushing apology, he waved
me to silence, adding, "Of course, you would have been
quite right to assume that I did not spend my boyhood under some priest's tutelage. In fact, I was quite the savage until my sixteenth year. But I was fortunate enough when I
first joined Il Moro's troops to befriend an older man who
had received a true scholar's education. He took me under
his wing and taught me enough of academic matters so that
I might pass as a gentleman."

A slight smile played about his lips. "I proved an apt pupil,
as much to my surprise as to his. Later, on my own, I even
picked up a fair smattering of Latin," he said, momentarily
switching over to that language in demonstration. Then, returning to his native tongue, he added, "I've a bit of Greek, as
well. Would you care to hear a few verses of the *Iliad*?"

"That is not necessary," I assured him, my blush deepening as I realized how badly I had misjudged him.

Here I had worried about embarrassing the man, and yet
it was I who was suffering from mortification; still, that
emotion was tempered by no little admiration. Gregorio
was rather like the Master, I told myself, in that he was a
self-taught man. Indeed, the captain of the guard was a man
of many secrets.

While I struggled with my discomfiture, he must have gleaned what he needed from Caterina's note, for now he tucked the paper into his tunic. I eyed that action in mild alarm, recalling the contessa's assurances that he destroyed all her messages lest they fall into the wrong hands.

"Captain, will you not burn it?" I boldly asked with a nod at the glowing coals.

He shrugged and straightened, walking back toward me with the handkerchief still in hand. The fading sunlight and the red glow of the brazier behind him wrapped him in a fiery mantle that reminded me again of a fallen angel. And, once again, the sight set my heart to beating a bit faster.

"Perhaps later," was his lazy reply. "And you may tell the contessa that my answer is yes."

"Very well, Captain," I replied with a quick curtsy.

He smiled a little and shook his curly dark head as he halted mere inches from me. "My dear Delfina, you need not be so formal. Leave off with your bowing and scraping. And perhaps you will simply call me Gregorio."

With those words, he tucked the scrap of lace into my bodice in a shockingly intimate gesture that made me gasp aloud. I took a reflexive step back, though the shiver that swept through me was not entirely one of alarm.

He favored me with a hint of that grin, at once dangerous and enticing. "I hope you will continue to be Caterina's messenger," he softly said. "Now, shall I walk you back down those stairs, or would you care to stay here a bit longer?"

I knew what it was he offered, and one vain, reckless part of me longed to accept. Then I thought of Caterina, and the Master, and my resolve returned.

"I-I must return to the castle, Captain," came my somewhat breathless reply. "The contessa will be awaiting my return and your answer. And I can manage the stairway alone."

"As you wish."

The lazy grin broadened, and I knew that he knew I had been tempted by his proposal. "Until the next time. And do watch yourself on those stairs, my dear Delfina. They can be a bit treacherous."

Despite his warning, I fled down the stone steps with more haste than was prudent, pausing only when I reached the door below to pluck the handkerchief from my bodice. Returning it to my sleeve, I took a deep breath and stepped outside once more.

To my relief, the two coarse guards were in heated argument with a scrawny old man trying to pass through the gates with an overloaded cart. The blond mercenary merely motioned me through the gate, and I gratefully stepped out into the familiar quadrangle once more.

It was only with the greatest effort that I resisted the impulse to glance up at the tower to see if Gregorio stood there watching me. But as my heartbeat returned to normal, I silently chastised myself for my behavior. The Master had charged me with learning all I could about the contessa, while Caterina had entrusted me with her darkest secret. Yet here I was allowing myself to be tempted by the seductive words of the very man who was the contessa's secret love . . . the same man who might also have had something to do with Bellanca and Lidia's deaths.

Abruptly, I was swept by the urge to rush to Leonardo's workshop and confess all to him. But such a confession would not only break my vow to Caterina, it would force me to reveal my own carefully held secret. I could not do that, at least, not yet.

Taking a deep breath, I deliberately kept a sedate pace as I made my way across the quadrangle and past the wall toward the wing of the castle where Caterina awaited me. I would give her Gregorio's terse reply to her message and then go about my duties. With luck, she would not press me into such service again, I fervently prayed.

For, if she did, I might find it hard to resist the dashing captain's invitation a second time.

* * *

"THE contessa will be dressed as the Queen of Swords," I eagerly told the Master, "and Signor Luigi is making the Knave of Staves costume for me, at her express request. She has decided that I must attend the masquerade with her, though I am not yet certain of her reasons. But as I will be masked, no one will know that I am not one of the invited guests."

It was the next morning, and I was in my familiar seat in the Master's private workshop. Pio, wearing a sober black collar trimmed in silver, sat politely at my side. For once, however, it had not been the Master who had summoned me. Instead, I had been dispatched by Caterina, herself, to tell Leonardo she would not be sitting for her portrait this day.

A slight indisposition, she had claimed. I knew that to be a falsehood, however, for soon after I had overheard her instructing Esta to request that the stable master should saddle her mare. But I could not contradict her, even as she blithely asked me to take charge of her pet for the day, as well.

For the moment, however, Leonardo was more concerned with the masquerade than his progress on the portrait.

"Ah, that makes things much easier," he said with a smile, confirming my guess that he had intended to slip me in among the guests. "Had she not made this offer, I might well have been forced to smuggle you into the hall hidden beneath a platter. And Luigi will be using the sketches I provided?"

We spoke a few moments more of the costumes and the entertainment he planned. Of course, there would be singing and lute playing. And, in keeping with the theme of tarocchi, he also planned a spectacular exhibition of his life-size mechanical lion, which clever creation I had seen once before.

"We shall precede its demonstration with a bit of theater," he explained. "I spoke with our good duke, Ludovico, just this morning, and he has graciously agreed to be garbed to represent the tarocchi card known as Strength. I predict the duke's guests will find this small drama most amusing."

Then, abruptly, the Master's mood grew serious, and he resumed his chair.

"But enough of these plans. We have more important matters to discuss," he said, absently studying the delicate stitches of Caterina's lace handkerchief.

I had struggled all night with the knowledge that I must break my word to the contessa and tell the Master that I was now her messenger, as Bellanca once had been. Leonardo had been swift to assure me that my transgression was outweighed by the dangers afoot. He'd gone on to explain that duty sometimes called for harsh choices that could be construed as cowardly or cruel by those unaware of the true circumstances. And such was the situation I had faced, he assured me.

I had brought the handkerchief with me to demonstrate how she had communicated with Gregorio, much to the Master's interest. He carefully folded the cloth and set it to one side. Then he asked, "Tell me, do you think the contessa's absence this morning was spurred by the message she sent to the captain of the guard, and his reply to her?"

I considered his question for a moment. My tone was more peevish than I'd intended when I finally replied, "From her happy air of anticipation when I gave her the message, I suspect she was riding off this morning to meet the captain somewhere. I wonder how disappointed the contessa will be when she one day discovers that he is less taken with her than she is with him."

"Indeed," Leonardo replied, stroking his neat beard as he keenly surveyed me. "And it bears consideration, his reason for pursuing the relationship, other than the obvious. He must know that the duke eventually intends her as bride to another noble, and he would be risking his career should Ludovico learn of his dalliance with his young cousin."

Even as I nodded my agreement to this last, he abruptly

added, "But there is more. I cannot help but think your words regarding the contessa hide an unseemly jealousy. Tell me, are you in love?"

The unexpected question hit me like a blow. Had I not done all in my power to preserve my masquerade, only to be undone now by a moment of weakness? I dared not answer but could only stare miserably in return. Surely, he had not guessed . . .

"I do not fault you, my dear Dino," he went on, seeing my consternation. "Caterina is a beautiful young woman, and it is not surprising that a sensitive boy such as you would easily fall under her spell. Knowing that she loves someone other than you must bring your heart great pain. But surely you must know that what you wish for can never be."

"I-I do understand that, Master," I answered, hanging my head and blushing, while Pio touched a consoling nose to my hand. My relief that my secret remained safe was tempered by the fact that Leonardo had rightly gleaned the truth of my emotions. Little did it matter that he had logically assumed it was Caterina who was the object of those unseemly feelings.

"It is all right," he gently added when I remained silent. "You must never be ashamed to love someone. That emotion is a great gift, both in its giving and its acceptance. Though, of course," he added with the hint of a smile, "I must warn you that the physical expression of such feelings is far more farcical than sublime, if one takes into account the various appendages that such an act requires."

His momentary lapse into humor faded, however, and he once more took on a serious tone.

"You will soon discover that romantic love has a cruel tendency to lead to heartbreak rather than happiness," he said with a shake of his russet mane. "And that pain only deepens when the object of your love is someone who cannot—or who will not—return that same emotion. So try to put this from you, if you can. For the moment, your duty requires the greater use of your head, rather than your heart."

"I will do as you ask, Master," I agreed with a sigh, though I suspected it would not be as easy as he made it sound to dismiss my emotions.

He nodded in approval. "Good boy. Now, let me tell you what else I have learned in the past day that will distract you from your unpleasant thoughts."

He reached for a stack of papers upon his table. I recognized the sketches of Caterina he had earlier done, as well as a few other drawings that appeared to be costumes similar to those he had provided to the tailor. The one that he withdrew from the pile, however, was not his creation.

"You will recall this sketch, I am certain."

I nodded, immediately recognizing the small rendition I had done a few days earlier at Leonardo's request. It was of the young page who, along with the tipsy porter, I had seen at Bellanca's graveside.

Studying the thin features surrounded by a halo of neatly waxed brown hair, I frowned. "Yes, I recall the young man's face, though I fear I was never able to find him again."

"Ah, but I did."

With a look of triumph, he took the sketch from me.

"Your drawing was remarkably accurate," he went on in a tone of approval that warmed me. "When I left the duke's chambers following my discussion with him, I practically stumbled across this young man in one of the outer halls and immediately recognized him from your sketch. When I explained to him that Il Moro wished his cooperation in this matter, he readily told me what he knew."

While I listened in wonder, the Master related the page's memory of his last conversation with Bellanca. He and Bellanca had spoken on many occasions, though he admitted that their relationship had gone no further than friendship. Still, he was disturbed when, for the first time since he'd known her, the brash maidservant had seemed frightened.

Soon enough, she had confessed the cause for her distress,

though it had struck the young man as foolish. She had allowed the contessa to read her fortune, only to be told that she was doomed to be betrayed by a man and suffer some sinister consequences, as a result. She had then told him of her relief that another of the contessa's servants claimed she could break the seeming curse that was to be visited upon her. First, however, Bellanca had been instructed to steal the fateful cards from the contessa, which she had done.

"Our page said this was the last conversation he had with Bellanca. Apparently, she went off to meet this unknown servant, though he had no idea what happened next. He said that it was not much later that Bellanca took her fateful plunge from the tower."

While I sat silently, digesting this new information, Leonardo set aside the drawing again.

"It would seem that the contessa's pastime is not as benign as I thought," he observed with a frown, "given that it resulted in a woman's death. As to the identity of the servant who claimed she could break the curse, I suspect we can both guess that name."

"Lidia," I exclaimed, earning a nod from him. "And this may explain why you found the tarocchi cards in the tower."

"Yes, for keep in mind that Lidia's son is captain of the guard; thus, it is plausible that she would have access to the fortifications."

Recalling how ready the two guards were to allow me access to the clock tower, I did not doubt this. Still, I was not quite convinced.

"But surely you do not think that Lidia was somehow responsible for Bellanca's death?" I asked in dismay, recalling the woman's seemingly genuine grief at the humble service.

This time, he shrugged. "It is possible. Unfortunately for our investigation, she is no longer here to question her as to her actions. Still, I confess I cannot conceive of a reason why she would wish the younger woman any harm."

"Perhaps Bellanca's death was indeed a suicide, and Lidia was a witness," I suggested. "It could be that she took her own life out of guilt that she could not prevent her from jumping."

"An interesting theory, my boy, and not without merit. There is, of course, the possibility that the death Lidia witnessed was actually a murder, and she had to be silenced lest she told what she knew."

"But is not poisoning a method usually reserved for the nobles?" I made haste to point out, only to realize in the next moment what that could mean. With a gasp, I added, "Surely the contessa could not be the one responsible for Lidia's death . . . or Bellanca's, either?"

"Recall that it was Caterina who predicted harm for Bellanca," the Master reminded me with a wry lift of one brow. "Moreover, it is telling that Bellanca once served in the same messenger role between the contessa and Gregorio that you now hold. Perhaps Bellanca was carrying on her own dalliance with the handsome captain, and Caterina learned of her betrayal."

"Perhaps," I echoed, a bit uncomfortably as I recalled my own rather traitorous thoughts.

Leonardo did not seem to notice my discomfiture, for he had taken up another sheet and was idly sketching yet another face upon one of his earlier drawings of Caterina.

"Dino, my boy," he said with a weary sigh, "we have far too many suspects in this matter, and little time left in which to solve the mystery. Once Il Moro's treaty is in place, and the contessa's betrothal is announced, there can be no further incidents. Thus, we have but four days remaining to put this business to rest."

I sighed, as well, wondering how we would ever untangle these various threads. That soft sound was echoed by Pio as he leaned quite woefully against my knee, seemingly distraught over his mistress's abandonment of him. I gave him a fond pat and then addressed the Master.

"I must leave now, lest anyone question my long absence. What more would you have me do?"

"Attempt another session with the tarocchi cards," was

his absent reply, his attention on the sketch he was embellishing. "I am still convinced that they hold a part of the answer to this mystery."

"I shall try this night," I obediently agreed, taking up Pio's leash as I rose from my seat. Then another thought occurred to me, and I paused.

"Master, the portrait," I said in some apprehension. "Will it be finished in time?"

"On that account, my dear boy, you need have no concern. The duke shall have his portrait of the lady in hand by the night of the masquerade."

Somewhat reassured, I took my leave. My mood continued pensive, however, as Pio and I—giving the stables wide berth—started back across the quadrangle. It seemed from my conversation with the Master that far more questions had been raised now than we'd yet answered. Despite myself, I could not help but fear we might fail in our quest for the truth . . . and that our failure could prove the end of Leonardo's tenure here at court.

A few moments later, I had again passed through the far wall of the quadrangle and reached the elegant portico that ran along the wing that housed the nobles. I paused to sit upon one of the stone benches sheltered beneath it, staring pensively out at the small courtyard there. I had given my prolonged absence as an excuse to take my leave of the Master, yet I found I was in no mood to return to the contessa's chambers and listen to the twins' sly jibes or even Esta's friendly gossip.

But as I settled against the cool stone, I reluctantly acknowledged the truth. It was not the other women I wished to avoid, I realized; rather, I could not bear to encounter Caterina returning from her clandestine morning ride and see her face aglow with the same excitement that had lit her features when she left.

Perhaps sensing my mood, even Pio seemed out of sorts. He pranced from foot to foot and refused to settle on the bench beside me.

"Saints' blood, is there nothing to make you happy?" I finally complained as he whined and tugged at his leash.

But barely had the words left my lips than a lazy voice whispered in my ear, "There is one thing that might make me happy . . . and that is you."

14

Temperance

Moderate your passions lest they prove your undoing.

—Leonardo da Vinci, *The Notebooks of Delfina della Fazia*

Of course, I did not need to glance over to know who had come up behind me and settled upon the stone bench beside me. Had he not slipped into the church pew beside me in the same silent manner, and later stealthily accosted me when I thought myself alone in the clock tower?

Feigning disapproval, though my heartbeat had quickened with sudden excitement, I turned and gave him a stern look. "Really, Captain, must you make it a habit of sneaking up on me like this?"

"My dear Delfina, you make it sound so . . . unsavory," Gregorio replied with a hint of the lazy grin I'd come to know. Stretching his long legs before him—he was seated facing the castle walls, while I still looked toward the quadrangle—he added, "Besides, I did not come in search of you. It is only by the greatest coincidence that I happened to rest here upon the same bench."

"I fear I do not believe in coincidence, Captain," I replied, trying with but little success to suppress my own answering smile.

Then, abruptly recalling just why I sat there, my amusement faded, and I glanced about to see if we were being watched. Reassured that no one was staring our way, I said with soft urgency, "But you should not be here. That is, I thought that you and the contessa . . . that you were . . ."

"The duke summoned me first thing this morning to discuss a few matters of security regarding his masquerade," he said with a shrug. "He will have a special guest in attendance, and that person's presence will require more precautions than normal for such a gathering. Unfortunately, I was unable to send Caterina word in time of this change in plans."

I pictured the contessa waiting impatiently somewhere for her lover, only to realize finally that he was not putting in an appearance, after all. Knowing her volatile nature, I was certain that she would return to the castle in a fury.

"But you still must tell her what happened," I insisted. "What if someone sees you here talking to me and tells her, and she thinks the worst?"

"I imagine she is thinking the worst, already," he replied with a grin that belied any such concern. "As to the matter of anyone seeing you and me together, that is why I am talking to you . . . to give you a message for her."

"And what is that, Captain?" I asked in sudden suspicion.

He leaned a bit closer, so that I could feel the heat radiating from his body. "My message is that you should let her know what happened and give her my apologies," he softly said, idly tracing a leather-gloved finger down my arm. "And now that I've given you my message, I await a message from you."

"F-from me?" I echoed, his touch sending a shiver through me. For some reason, I found myself suddenly powerless to pull away from him . . . could not force myself to leap to my feet in protest, as surely I should at this intimate gesture.

"Perhaps I can help you with that message," he replied, his words now but a whisper of breath upon my neck. "Tell me that you will make an excuse to slip away from the castle tomorrow and meet me at the cathedral."

"But I cannot," I started to protest, only to realize with a stir of excitement that perhaps I could.

For the contessa and I had yet one more visit to Signor Luigi's shop so that the tailor could fit our costumes for the masquerade. Why could I not suggest to the contessa that I take on this task for her? That way, she could pose for the Master longer than usual to make up for missing this day's session with him.

Hardly believing my own daring, I swiftly explained my plan to Gregorio, adding, "The cathedral is not far from the tailor's shop, so if the contessa gives me leave to visit him, I can meet you there once the noon Angelus is rung. But why—"

He raised a playful finger to my lips to stop my words. "You ask too many questions, my dear Delfina," he said with his usual lazy smile. "Come to the cathedral tomorrow, and you will learn all you need to know."

He abruptly stood, sword lightly swinging at his hip. "I fear I must take my leave of your charming company, as I have arrangements to make for Il Moro. I count upon you to give the contessa my message."

At my nod, he added, "And when you visit the cathedral, look to the stained glass windows along the far aisle. The one that depicts Saint Michael has always been my particular favorite."

With those rather cryptic words and a lightly sketched bow, he strode off through the small courtyard and out the gated wall. I must admit that I stared after him, admiring the way his trunk hose showed his muscular legs to advantage, and how his tightly laced jerkin emphasized his wide shoulders. It was no small wonder that he had known more than his share of the castle's women.

That last thought caused me to groan softly and bury my

face in my hands. I would meet him tomorrow at the cathedral . . . he knew it, as well as I. And so, had I just bargained my soul away to the devil, or had I set myself upon the path to heavenly delight?

"VERY well. Now it is Delfina's turn," the contessa declared with a smile. "I shall shuffle the cards once more, and let us see what her fortune will be."

Once again, the tarocchi cards were spread upon the small table in the contessa's outer chamber. We four servants all crowded around it, while Caterina sat at its head. Candles at either of her elbows spilled gold light and black shadow across her exotic features as she let the cards flow fluidly from one hand to the other. Watching her, I thought back to earlier in the day.

As I had feared, the contessa had returned to the castle not long after Gregorio left me. She'd been thoroughly out of sorts at being forgotten, though swift explanation had mollified her somewhat. *"Indeed, he cursed his duty and swore he would be with you soon,"* I had exclaimed as I made his excuses, while I deliberately put from my mind the image of his lazy grin and his shrug of indifference.

Fortunately, such dramatic words had been what Caterina had hoped to hear, so that she had sulked but for a short time. Soon enough, Pio's antics and her servants' attention had roused her from her displeasure. We spent a pleasant enough afternoon, and I had later broached the subject of my visit to the tailor's shop. Though I had feared with every word that she would read the truth in my eyes, to my surprise she agreed wholeheartedly with my plan.

"That is a sensible idea, Delfina," she had said in warm approval. *"Signor Luigi can as easily fit my costume to you as he can to me. And by the time I finish posing for Master Leonardo, you will have returned from the tailor's shop."*

But seated before her now, I began to have small regrets. Secretly meeting with the captain could easily be seen as a betrayal, I thought with no little guilt. But, on the other hand, the Master had charged me with learning all I could about those around the contessa. Surely what I planned was nothing more than what he expected of me.

And Dino would do it, would he not?

Clinging to that bit of righteous justification with the same fervor that a drowning man clutched a tossed rope, I managed to meet Caterina's dark gaze with outer equanimity. Far simpler than this deception had been my task of secretly adding the Master's tarocchi cards to her deck.

Pio had proved my unwitting accomplice. I had waited until he stretched his long neck to snatch a bit of sweetmeat I had deliberately left on the table's edge. Then, while the others were distracted by laughter as Caterina halfheartedly attempted to wrestle the treat back from him, I'd swiftly caught up the cards I'd earlier hidden in my lap and added them to the ones Pio had scattered.

"You must ask a question," Rosetta now reminded me as the contessa neatly stacked the deck before spreading the cards in a long line before me.

I pretended to consider my question while, with a sharp gaze, I searched for the four duplicates I had placed among them. Fortunately, the Master had marked those cards' every corner, so that it did not matter how they lay. Even so, in the dim light it took a few moments to discover them all.

"I have my question," I finally said, while Isabella gave an exasperated puff of breath at my delay. "Which should I concern myself with, love or duty?"

"Pah, I can answer that," Rosetta muttered with a smirk. Her sister and Esta merely shook their heads in dismay at what was, to their minds, a waste of the cards' powers.

Caterina, however, smiled. "That is a wonderful question. Quickly, choose your cards, and you shall have your answer."

Pretending to select at random, I chose the four marked cards, carefully keeping them facedown until all were before me. Then, at her nod, I slowly turned them up, one by one.

I was not sure what reaction I expected from the contessa this time. A scream? Perhaps a swoon? When I finally glanced up, however, I saw that her dark gaze was fixed not on the cards but upon me. Her expression was not that of a girl playing at fortunes but of a woman who had seen beyond the veil and had been granted knowledge beyond the rest of our grasp.

"You know the answer to this question already," she said, her features now an unreadable mask. "You will always choose duty over love, but not always for the right reasons. Indeed, you are often led astray by those you think you can trust. Still, you and your duty both will prevail, though at the cost of your heart . . . and, perhaps one day, your life."

Then she fell silent and shut her eyes as if to block any further insights. As the echo of her words faded, I turned my gaze on the other women, searching out their reactions.

Rosetta was no longer smirking but wore an expression of uncertainty. As for Esta and Isabella, they had linked hands and slid their chairs back from the table, their features reflecting cautious fear.

A moment later, Caterina had opened her eyes and appeared herself once more. Her smile was gone, however, replaced now by a sigh and a tired shake of her head.

"I fear it has been a long day, so I shall retire to my chamber now. No, Esta," she added as that young woman hurried to her feet, "I do not need you to attend me tonight. You and the others may stay and play a hand of tarocchi, if you wish."

With a signal to her pet, she rose and swept toward the doorway beyond, leaving her cards upon the table. Pio gave a final look back at us, as if hoping for another treat, and then placidly trotted after her.

Barely had the door closed after her than Rosetta jumped up from her seat, almost overturning the table in her haste. Indeed, half the cards cascaded to the floor in a flutter of bright colors. With a swift move, I rescued the four copies before they were mixed with the rest, hiding them in my lap once more.

Rosetta, however, seemed hardly to realize what she'd done, let alone notice my crude sleight of hand.

"You heard what the contessa said about death! I vow I shall never touch those cards again, not even to play tarocchi," she softly exclaimed, while her sister nodded in agreement. "Remember what happened to Bellanca?"

"Pah, that is nonsense," Esta replied, though her worried frown as she began gathering the cards from the floor seemed to belie her words. "Do not listen to her, Delfina. It is but a foolish game we play. This talk of death means nothing."

"I'm not worried," I assured her, even as I knew my words for a lie.

Yet my concern was not for myself, I realized, as I hid away my four cards in my pouch and then helped Esta collect the scattered pasteboards. It was Caterina's safety that I feared for, instead. With all that had happened of late, I could not help but think she had unwittingly unleashed a spate of ill luck . . . not just on her servants but upon herself. The Master would scorn such a theory, I knew, but something told me I was right.

And if we did not manage to protect her, it would be Caterina who would join those other two women in death.

"Now, Delfina, remind Signor Luigi that he must find me a sword for my costume as well as a crown," Caterina decreed the next morning as Esta and I helped her into her golden robes. "And it must be a true sword, not a wooden imitation."

Grinning girlishly, she added, "I know Cousin Ludovico will never lend me one of his blades, and I cannot pass up this one opportunity to wield such a weapon!"

"I shall make certain to tell him," I agreed with a small smile that I prayed concealed my unsettled emotions.

The Master had not yet arrived to continue work on the portrait, for which small mercy I gave thanks. Indeed, I dreaded crossing paths with him this day lest he guess from my guilty countenance that I had greater plans than simply paying the tailor a visit. For I had made my decision to go through with my secret meeting with Gregorio this day.

Yet, was it truly an assignation that he had in mind? After yesterday's first flush of excitement, I had regained my usual rational frame of mind. Later that night, once the cards had been put away and we servants had taken to our beds, I had fought sleep's embrace to instead search the darkness for answers. Just before slumber finally proved the victor, the possibility presented itself that the captain's interest in me might be spurred by something other than romance. Perhaps his feelings for the contessa were sincere, after all, and he thought to divert attention from their forbidden love by pretending to woo me.

Or perhaps his motives were far more sinister. Maybe he had sensed my suspicions of him, and this was but a pretense of interest simply to lull me into complacency.

Under any other circumstances, I would not have struggled alone but would have sought the Master's counsel. He would not be swayed by unseemly emotion or forbidden longings. He, of all people, would best know what I should do. But talking to him this time would not help me, after all. He could not guess the true nature of my unsettled state, I realized, simply because he thought of me as a boy.

Esta and I finished helping the contessa with her robes; then, while Esta arranged her hair, I busied myself fastening Pio's red and gold collar about his long neck and then burnishing his sleek fur with a soft cloth. That accomplished, I took my leave of the contessa encumbered by only the smallest bit of guilt.

"Remember the sword, Delfina," she gaily called after me, this time earning my genuine smile. I wondered what Luigi would say about this particular bit of verisimilitude. Indeed, I would have to ask Luigi about a stave for my costume, as well.

This day, however, brought little opportunity for banter with the tailor. With the masquerade but two days away, he and his young apprentices had spent the past week stitching their fingers bloody on costumes for perhaps half the court. I found myself impatiently waiting in his shop behind a minor, gray-haired barone and a conte's stern manservant until I could finally take my turn with the tailor.

"It's not that I don't mind the florins," Luigi sourly acknowledged sometime later. Eying my borrowed red gown peevishly—I'd deliberately worn the more elegant garb this day, rather than the mended green—he fitted me first into Caterina's costume, and then my own. "It is simply that I cannot trust these two boys with anything more complicated than a hem," he complained. "Thus, all the work falls upon me."

I gave him a sympathetic nod but could not quite smother my smile. I knew as well as he that, as a result of his strict training, his apprentices were skilled far beyond their years. Indeed, their cleverness with a needle almost matched his, even if they lacked his sheer artistry with cloth. Luigi might be keeping busy with his needle, but likely the two youths were carrying the bulk of the burden.

The final modifications to both costumes took longer than I had hoped. My farewells, therefore, were uncharacteristically brief when I finally took my leave and hurried in the direction of the cathedral.

Despite my earlier remonstrations to myself, a reckless sense of excitement swept me as I saw the church tower in the distance. Feeling suddenly as fleet of foot as Pio, I quickened my pace. But barely had I reached the public square before it, when the first Angelus bells sounded from its tower.

As always whenever I heard them ring, I promptly dropped to my knees upon the rough stones and bowed my head. Joining the others kneeling there in the square, I made my three Aves at each pause of the bells. For once, however, the familiar words of Our Lady's prayer seemed to catch upon my lips, rather than spilling forth with the usual ritualistic ease.

Was it a sign, I wondered . . . or simply a bit of guilty nervousness at what I was about to do?

The final peal had not yet faded when I was on my feet again headed toward the cathedral. Now my fear was that I would be late, that he would not wait for me. I quickened my pace a bit more, so that I was breathing rather more swiftly than usual by the time I crossed the square and reached the cathedral's towering white marble facade.

Standing there dwarfed by the building's tall shadow, I realized I could still change my mind. Should he ever question me, I could simply tell Gregorio that the contessa had not allowed me my freedom. He could hardly question such an excuse, being all too aware of his own subjugation to a higher rank.

Then I shook my head. Too many bits of this broader puzzle seemed to bear Gregorio's lazy mark. I pictured the Master's shattered model of the horse, the pieces so small that they were unrecognizable until they were fitted to larger sections of the damaged clay. Now I had the opportunity to learn how another, more important group of pieces might fit together. And if I dared not take this chance, then perhaps I should put on my boy's tunic again and simply cease this masquerade!

Thus steeled, I gripped the curved metal handle with the same grim resolve I might have used in grabbing at hell's outer gates. Pulling open the heavy door, I abandoned sunlight and stepped inside.

Cool dimness washed over me like an ocean's wave, the sudden change from light to darkness as sharp as a blow. I gasped reflexively, taking in a deep breath of air heavy with incense and sin and redemption. That soft sound did little to disturb the silence, for I was not alone here in the dark. Around me, I could hear the echoed murmurs of prayers, the rhythmic click of beads, and the soft tap of footsteps from the many clergy and pilgrims wandering about.

I made a quick genuflection and paused to let my eyes grow used to the darkness. I had never been inside Milan's grand cathedral before, having always attended Mass each Sunday at the chapel outside the churchyard near the castle.

Still, I had heard many testimonies as to its grandeur, and just as many jests regarding its design. For the cathedral already was almost one hundred years old, and yet still the workmen toiled upon it. Wags claimed that it might be another hundred years before the cathedral was deemed finished . . . or maybe two hundred more years, given that work had not yet begun upon its facade!

Though my artist's eye noted several flaws with its plan, I still stared curiously about me. How could one not be awed, I wondered, by this white marble edifice larger than a dozen chapels and built in the shape of an immense, blunt cross? Niches filled with standing and recumbent stone figures lined the outermost walls. Most of them were merely devotional images, though some served as top pieces for the sepulchers in which noble personages and clergy were interred.

Unfortunately, it was difficult to make out any great detail of the surrounding works. Other than the flickering glow of candles arranged before the various statues, the only light was that which spilled through the stained glass windows that lined either length of the building. Those jewellike colors puddled like tempera upon the elaborate mosaic of stone that made up the floor, adding an almost festive air to the solemn interior. But those narrow casements were too few and too low to fully illuminate such a vast space.

Thus, the already-encroaching shadows gave way to an even greater darkness above that filled the cathedral's immense arched dome. That vaulted ceiling ran the entire length of the nave—the wide center aisle—which stretched from entry to altar. Narrower aisles, two on each side, ran parallel to the nave. These aisles, in turn, were delineated by four long rows of marble columns that extended past the transepts, the two lateral arms of the building that formed the crosspiece of the cathedral's cruciform floor plan.

There were perhaps half a hundred columns in total, I saw in amazement. Each one was so large that five or six people linking hands would barely be able to encircle it. With their richly carved capitals, which broadened at the

top, the columns resembled nothing so much as a frozen for-
est of stone growing in neat formation in the darkness.

By now, I was used to the dim light and so could not put
off my mission any longer. Recalling Gregorio's reference to
the stained glass image of Saint Michael, I began making
my way down the farthermost aisle, carefully searching the
colored images for the warrior angel.

I found that heavenly avenger with his flaming sword
tucked behind one of the columns just before the transept.
The colors of this smaller glass were somber, with the only
bright note the gleam of his golden sword. Had I not been
looking for it, I might have passed it by, so well did it fade
into the shadows.

As I admired the work, I realized it was less the artistry of
the glass than it was the angel's handsome dark face that held
my attention. The glass figure, with his sensuous lips and
look of cold pride that somehow befitted his Godly mission,
reminded me of Gregorio. Little wonder that the captain had
claimed this as his favorite, I wryly told myself. Likely he,
too, saw something of himself reflected in that image.

But where was he? Why had he not yet appeared behind
me, silent as any of these shadows, as was his habit?

Barely had I time to ponder those questions when something stirred within the darkness of a broad niche beside
that very window. A chill swept me, and my first supersti-
tious thought was that the statue within it had come to life.
I had raised one hand in the reflexive gesture to cross myself
as protection against that spirit, when I realized in relief
that the figure I had seen was indeed quite human.

Yet as Gregorio stepped from the shadows, I reminded
myself that perhaps I should be as wary of him as of any unknown being. I could not help but recall he was the man
who might know more than he should about two women's
deaths . . . might even have been the one to set the stable
dog upon me. What was I thinking, to meet him here alone,
having told no one of my plans?

Then, with a lazy grin, he grasped my hand and pulled

me toward him, the warm flesh against mine reassuring me. Leaning toward me, so that his lips brushed my ear, he softly said, "I've been anxiously awaiting this moment since yesterday. When the Angelus rang, and you were not here, I feared you had chosen not to come, after all."

"I hurried as quickly as I could," I whispered back, uncommonly cheered by his admission. "But Signor Luigi was busy, so I had to wait for him to finish with the barone, and then there was the conte's man, and then—"

His soft laugh stopped me short. "You need not give me a litany of your day, my dear Delfina. All that matters is that you are here now."

He paused to glance about us, and then shook his head. "I fear there are too many devout pilgrims wandering about for us to speak without risk of being overheard. Come with me; I know a private spot here."

15

The Devil

He who neglects to punish evil sanctions the doing thereof.

—Leonardo da Vinci, *Manuscript H*

Before I could protest, Gregorio led me past the column and into the transept, where a few marble steps led to an elaborate side altar set against the far wall. Candles in golden cups lined its edges, their flickering light illuminating the white altar cloths embroidered in gold and throwing shadows onto the small crucifix mounted above. I wondered what he was about, for the transept—though offset from the nave—still opened toward the main cathedral so that passing worshippers could be seen. And then Gregorio nodded toward the broad niche along the side wall.

Wrapped as it was in shadows, the void behind the forbidding black iron gate seemed but an empty mouth. Peering more deeply into it, I made out the rough-hewn edges of a sepulcher. The stone representation of its occupant lay in stiff repose upon its lid. Puzzled, I glanced at Gregorio again, only to see that he had opened the latch that held the elaborate gate closed.

It swung open with but the faintest of creaks. Still grasping my hand, he led me inside the dark chamber and then pulled the gate shut behind us.

My first thought was one of surprise to find that the niche was no shallow hollow. Instead, a single flickering candle high upon the wall behind that vault gave just enough light to reveal it was a small room, narrow but almost as long as the transept. My second reaction was one of reflexive panic as I recalled being locked in another tomb once before. I stiffened, barely suppressing the impulse to cling to the bars and cry out.

But the lock on this tomb was not fastened, I hurriedly reminded myself, nor was the crypt beneath the ground. With a shout, I could readily summon help to free myself should I somehow become trapped behind its bars.

Misinterpreting my distress, Gregorio led me away from the gate to the foot of the sepulcher, where the figure's stone slippers pointed heavenward. I heard the amusement in his voice as he whispered in my ear, "Do not worry, no one will see us here, and our friend the bishop does not mind company."

At my questioning look, he added, "Rumor is that, in life, he was not opposed to pleasures of the flesh and indulged himself with numerous ladies who came to make their confessions. I daresay he won't object to others doing the same."

A moment too late, I understood what it was he meant. Almost before I knew what had happened, I found myself backed against the rough wall, far from the faint glimmer of that single candle. More troubling still was the fact that my every curve suddenly seemed molded to the hard planes of Gregorio's body as he pressed against me. His arms were like iron bars locking me in place, and yet I realized with a small thrill that I did not truly wish to escape him.

Somehow in the darkness, his lips found mine, his mouth taking me with an urgency that I but vaguely understood . . . at least, at first. After my small gasp of shock, however, I was kissing him back. By then, it hardly mattered that the cold stone behind me was pressing uncomfortably through my gown, or that the chill from the marble floors had turned my feet to ice. I was aware only that my heart was beating so swiftly that I feared I might swoon.

And then, all too soon, he pulled away.

The sudden loss of his touch was as keen as if I'd been cleft in two. Despite myself, I could not suppress a small cry of disappointment. I heard his soft laugh in return; then, unexpectedly, he caught me by the waist and lifted me about, setting me down again atop the sepulcher so that I was seated on its edge in front of the dead bishop's stone feet.

Now our gazes were on a level, and I could make out his handsome features in the shadows. A sudden wash of feminine power filled me, and I instinctively reached a hand to his face. At my touch, his amusement faded, replaced by an urgency that I knew could not be denied.

He kissed me again . . . roughly this time, though I did not protest the assault. Neither did I cry out when I felt him sliding my skirts above my knees and spreading my legs apart so that he could press with shocking intimacy against me. Vaguely, it occurred to me that something sinful was about to happen between us, but suddenly I did not seem to care.

A heavy metallic clang that was the iron gate falling back upon itself abruptly jarred me from my lustful reverie. My soft, startled cry was echoed by a strangled gasp as a voice behind us choked out, "How dare you desecrate the Lord's house like this!"

With a guilty glance over my shoulder, I saw the speaker was an ancient, brown-robed priest whose raised fist shook with outrage and palsy. He stood just outside the gate, not so close that he could identify us in the shadows but near enough to be quite sure what we were about.

Swept by sudden shame, I would have scrambled from my unseemly perch, save that Gregorio had not released me. And when I turned back to him with a beseeching word ready on my lips, what I saw made me shudder . . . this time, with fright.

The expression in his dark eyes as he stared back at the priest was one of cold fury, the look of a man who could kill another in the space of a heartbeat, and without remorse. And I knew that if ever that look was turned upon me, I could only pray that my feet were swifter than his blade.

Just as this fearsome thought flashed through my mind, I saw the familiar lazy look of amusement in his eyes and gladly dismissed the other as but a trick of the flickering candlelight. With a murmured, "I fear that we have been discovered, after all," he easily lifted me from the sepulcher and set me down beside him.

"Our apologies, good Father," he addressed the frail clergyman as he took my hand and swiftly led me past the gate. "I fear we took the Lord's admonition to go forth and multiply a bit too literally."

"You shall burn for such a sacrilege," was the old man's muttered threat in return, though, at the sight of Gregorio's sword at his hip, he prudently stood back to let us pass.

Gregorio merely shrugged. "I have no doubt I'll burn, but it shall be for much worse than this, I assure you."

By now, the whispered confrontation had attracted a few worshippers who had paused in their prayers to stare in open interest. I could feel my cheeks turning crimson and gave thanks that the dim light shielded us from greater scrutiny.

To my dismay, Gregorio did not lead us with modest haste down the farthermost aisle, where we would attract the least attention as we made our escape. Rather, with an elaborate genuflection toward the main altar, he grasped my hand and casually strode down the broad center nave toward the rear of the cathedral. I had no choice but to stumble after him, head lowered in shame and all too aware that the outraged priest had followed us to the nave and stood shaking his fist after us.

Never had I been so grateful for the blinding glare of sunlight as I was when we finally stood outside in the square once more. I would have run as fast as I could in the opposite direction, save that Gregorio still had hold of my hand and did not seem inclined to let me go.

"What is your haste?" he asked me with a grin, looking quite boyish with his disheveled hair and air of sly glee. "I assure you, now that he's chased us from his cathedral, the good father will be content to let us go. Though I must admit I'm surprised he did not wait to banish us until after we were finished. That way, he could have indulged himself in the sins of envy and lust, as well as wrath."

"How can you say such things?" I choked out, half fearing that such blasphemy would cause us both to be struck down here in the square.

My appalled tone seemed merely to amuse him further. He reached a hand as if to brush against my cheek, then drew back in mock concern.

"I fear I might burn myself should I brush my fingers against your face, it flames with such glorious color," he said with a soft laugh. "Perhaps I should toss you into the water to quench your ardor."

He nodded in the direction of the immense fountain in the square's center. A stream of water splashed from a stone maiden's vase down a series of progressively larger basins, ending in a white marble circle the size of a small pool. My eyes widened in alarm at the prospect.

Then, realizing he merely jested, I allowed myself a grudging smile, even as I muttered, "It is embarrassment and not ardor that colors my face. I can only thank the saints that the priest did nothing worse than cast us out."

"Rather like Adam and Eve from the garden . . . though fortunately we were wearing far more clothes at our moment of expulsion than were they."

"Fortunately," I agreed, though my earlier shame was now tempered by a bit of reluctant amusement at the way Gregorio had so casually met the priest's outrage. I could think of no other man save one who would so readily flout both God and man in such a manner.

Somewhat appeased, I followed him back across the square, where we paused again beside a small shop. A length of blue cloth tied to the wall and supported by two wooden sticks overhung us, providing a bit of shade. This time, he did not hesitate as he reached a hand to touch my face.

"Ardor quite suits you, my dear Delfina," he said, stroking my cheek in a manner that was comforting and yet far too intimate for so public a setting. "We should make certain that the next time we meet, it will be in a more secluded spot."

Had the circumstances been different, I would have eagerly agreed with him. But now, standing here in the light, I realized the folly of what had happened in the shadows of the cathedral. Saints' blood, I thought in dismay, what if that priest had not interrupted us when he had? My betrayal would not only have been to myself but to Caterina.

Hanging my head, I softly said, "I do not understand, Gregorio. You attempt to seduce me, and yet I thought that you and the contessa . . . that is, it seemed that the two of you . . ."

I trailed off miserably, not able to finish my thought, though knowing he must understand what I meant. I waited for his response, expecting him to laugh, or perhaps to answer with some soothing words that he would think would excuse his inconstancy. When I ventured a glance up at him, however, I was surprised to see a spark of anger in his dark eyes.

Once again, the emotion was so fleeting that, had I not been looking for some sort of response, I might not have recognized it. And yet, it was not a return of the cold fury that I thought I had seen him turn upon the priest. Rather, it was a heated emotion, one tinged with pain and despair, the sort of raw anger that could drive a person to desperate acts. And I realized that I was glimpsing a bit of the true man who lurked beneath the outer guise of the lazily sensual lover, or even that of the coldly remorseless soldier.

"You are forgetting that Caterina is a contessa, and I am but the captain of the guard," he replied, that anger spilling out with every word, though I could see he strove to hold it back. "As a child, she knew only wealth, and fine clothes, and lavish meals. When I was a boy, I thought a florin was a grand fortune. I wore the stableboy's cast-off rags and slept with an empty belly more nights than I care to remember. An entire world separated us then . . . separates us, still. And, one day soon, Caterina shall learn just how fortunate she truly was in her birth."

It was an odd sort of declaration, even had he been a lover scorned. My puzzlement at his words must have shown, for he abruptly shook his head, as if he'd just climbed out from a dunking in the fountain. A hint of his lazy grin returned, though when he spoke, his tone had a hard edge to it still.

"I would have you forget all I just said," he went on with a dismissive snort, "but as I know you cannot, I shall confess all. Beware, though, that you will surely think even worse of me when I am finished."

"Please, do speak freely," I urged with a nod. "I shall make no judgments."

"Ah, but if you do not, I will be forced to judge myself," he declared with a wry lift of his brow. "While it is true that I have affection for the contessa, I am no fool to think this is more than a temporary amusement on her part. And now that I find myself desiring another woman"—he gave me a telling look that made me blush again—"I find myself eager to put an end to the charade."

Any hint of a grin faded as he went on. "Unfortunately, I find myself in an uncomfortable situation. Should I attempt to end my liaison with Caterina, she might be angered enough to tell all to her cousin the duke . . . and, as a result, I would be lucky should I lose only my commission. On the other hand, should I continue on with her, and the duke learns of our relationship through some other means, I still risk my post."

"So what will you do?" I asked, feeling a rush of sympathy as one who understood what it was like to live a charade.

He shrugged. "For the moment, nothing. I can only hope that she soon tires of me and finds someone else more to her liking. Unless, of course, you have a suggestion?"

I bit my lip, wishing I could tell him of the duke's plans for the contessa's marriage, yet bound to hold my peace. Thus, I simply shook my head.

"I fear I can be of no help in that, though I am certain it all will be resolved soon." Then, reluctantly, I added, "And perhaps, until that time, I should ask the contessa to find someone else to be her messenger."

"Do that, my dear Delfina, and you shall break my heart," he flatly replied.

His words sent a rush of happiness through me, so that I could not hold back a smile. "Very well. I shall continue that role," I declared in satisfaction. Then, abruptly recalling that I was indeed on Caterina's business now, I gasped.

"I must return to the castle," I said in alarm. "I've been gone far too long, and the contessa will be wondering what has become of me."

"Then you should know there are some advantages to being the captain of the guard's woman," he replied, beckoning me to follow him. "One of them is that I usually have a horse somewhere about."

And indeed, down the narrow passage next to where we had stood, a sleepy young boy stood grasping the reins of tall black stallion.

We made swift progress back toward the castle. And though I cared little for riding, I felt oddly secure perched before Gregorio upon that sleek steed. All too soon, we had reached the main gate. Easily dismounting, he reached up and lifted me from atop the stallion, his hands lingering at my waist as he steadied me.

Aware that the same two crude guards were watching us with ill-concealed interest, I reluctantly eased from his grasp. "Perhaps the contessa will have another message for me to carry tomorrow," I hopefully suggested.

He shrugged, looking faintly amused at my sudden enthusiasm. "Perhaps," he agreed. "And, if not, I will scribe a message for you to carry that will certainly require a reply."

The gate was open for me already, and with a final look

back at him, I hurried into the quadrangle. I had spared a glance at the clock tower and saw in surprise that less time had passed since I left the castle than I'd feared had gone by. The Master would likely have just finished his work for the day, and by the time I reached the chamber, the women would be helping the contessa from her robes. With luck, Caterina would not comment on my absence, other than to ask how the fitting had gone. And she would be pleased to hear that Signor Luigi had agreed to procure her a sword for her costume, so that she would have the weapon she desired.

The remainder of the day proceeded uneventfully, save that Isabella sourly remarked that I seemed far more cheerful than usual. "If I didn't know better," was her snide assessment of the perceived change, "I would say that Delfina has found herself a man."

And as I'd predicted, Caterina was pleased with Signor Luigi's cleverness in finding her the requisite sword, rather than a wooden representation.

"But he will have the costumes completed by tomorrow, will he not?" she anxiously wanted to know. "After all, the masquerade is the day after."

I assured her that the tailor had confirmed that one of his apprentices would bring our finished garb to the castle by tomorrow night.

"And you're sure my gown is quite beautiful? I cannot wait for *everyone* to see me in it," she declared with a satisfied smile that told me she wished for one person, in particular, to see her in her glory. I wondered if she would be quite so anxious once she learned of the duke's marriage plans for her.

I sighed now as I climbed into my bed for the night, thinking back upon that conversation. No word yet had come of the duke's planned alliance, so that I wondered if it would still come to pass. And, if it did, perhaps the warring duke who had come to terms would be as dashing as a certain captain of the guard, so that Caterina would be satisfied with her lot.

And with the contessa safely settled away, I could then decide what I wished to do . . . return to my role as the boy apprentice Dino, or else remain as Delfina and become the captain of the guard's woman. The latter choice would mean giving up my painting, at least for a time, but I suddenly realized that was a sacrifice I was willing to make.

It was just as I had finally shut my eyes to sleep that I abruptly recalled Bellanca. Some had referred to her as the captain of the guard's woman. But surely she'd been only the messenger between him and the contessa. Gregorio could not have thought of her in that way. If he'd had any affection for her, he could not have so easily forgotten her and turned his attention to me. Only somewhat reassured by my own arguments, I boldly decided I would ask him as much the next time we met.

But what I refused to do alone in the darkness was recall the fortune that Caterina had read for me, the bleak fortune that claimed I might be led astray by a man and thus lose my heart . . . and perhaps my life.

16

The Tower

Fire destroys all sophistry . . . and maintains truth alone . . .

—Leonardo da Vinci, *Windsor Drawings*

Leonardo set down his brush and wiped his hands upon a paint-streaked cloth, careful not to smear any upon the yellow tunic he wore over parti-colored red and black trunk hose. Then, stepping away from the panel propped upon its easel, he swept off his puffed red cap and bowed toward the contessa.

"You have honored me, my lady, by posing for what I believe will be considered one of my finer works," he said without any pretense at false modesty. "Now I declare your portrait to be complete, and with a day to spare."

"At last!"

With that cry of relief, Caterina nimbly rose from her chair. Setting the hound Pio upon the floor, she spread her arms wide, pretending to stretch the stiffness from her young bones. I smiled as Pio promptly followed his mistress's example, sliding his long legs forward, so that his narrow rump pointed skyward and his long whip of a tail curved over his back. He, however, added a yawn that exposed a long pink tongue and a set of small but formidable teeth.

"I do not think I could have borne sitting in that chair one day longer," Caterina went on with an answering smile for the Master. "Indeed, I fear I must appear far older now than I did when the panel was first begun, it has been so long."

Then, clasping her hands in a gesture of mock beseeching, she added, "And now, Master Leonardo, will you finally allow me to look upon this grand painting?"

"I will allow all of you ladies to view it," he gallantly agreed as he replaced his cap, his words drawing excited cries from Esta and the twins. "But you must first give your word that none of you will admit to having seen it before the duke himself reveals the painting at tomorrow night's masquerade."

"We all swear," Caterina promptly spoke for us, though we each gave our solemn nod. "Now, may we look?"

"You may," Leonardo said, gesturing us forward.

All of us rushed to join him, I as eagerly as the rest. Knowing something of the Master's technique by now, I was curious to see how he had portrayed the young woman . . . whether he had painted her against the simple background where she sat or if he'd added some imaginary landscape to the scene. I would want to examine how he had represented the drape and flow of her beautiful gold gown and the cascade of her raven hair. And, of course, I could not wait to see if he had depicted Pio as an elegant companion or a lanky little clown.

Caterina took the first look, and her smile abruptly faded. She stared fixedly at the portrait for a long moment, unspeaking, so that the rest of us hesitated to join her there behind the easel. Sensing trouble, Pio stilled his wagging tail and stared at his mistress in concern. Even Leonardo's proud smile faltered as the expected effusive praise did not come.

Just when I feared that the contessa might flee the room

in distress, she abruptly looked up again. Though her eyes were filled with tears, her smile returned as she softly cried, "Oh, signore, it is so beautiful!"

At her words, the rest of us rushed to join her. Isabella and Rosetta added their own enthusiastic approval, as did Esta. For myself, I could only stare, much as Caterina had done.

The portrait was a study in blacks and golds, and yet one could not call it somber. *Mysterious* was a better description, I thought after pondering the painting for a moment. Though the subject was that of a young woman and her pet, Leonardo had somehow imbued what could have been a banal scene with a sense of drama. Wrapped in her golden robes, with her raven hair spilling about her, Caterina appeared less a young contessa than a priestess of old. He had easily captured the faintly exotic beauty of her features, lighting them with the reflected glow from her golden robes. Though her rounded cheeks were that of a girl, her dark eyes reflected the arcane knowledge of a woman far older. But rather than the stern expression one might have expected Leonardo to paint, her full lips hinted at the faintest of secretive smiles.

I found more to admire, the closer that I examined the portrait. He had not depicted her sitting against a wall; rather, Leonardo had painted her perched amid a background of jagged wet rocks and three twisted black trees, with a few fallen red leaves scattered at the foot of the largest of the trio. The setting recalled the sort of hidden grotto where those who questioned life sought knowledge. As for the sky above her, it was almost as dark as the trees, though flashes of gold from a half-hidden sun echoed the metallic hue of her gown.

The only bright spot was the sleek hound lying upon Caterina's lap. In something of a whimsical touch, the painted version of Pio showed his crossed paws resting atop his mistress's knee, the pose echoing the similar fold of her hands atop his narrow back. And, if one looked closely enough, the painted hound seemed to wear a matching expression of faint amusement upon his canine features.

"And what do you think of the portrait, Delfina?" I heard the Master ask me.

Reluctantly pulling my gaze from the panel, I could only shake my head in amazement. "It is beautiful. You are indeed a genius, Signor Leonardo."

Looking pleased at the praise he had garnered, the Master carefully covered the panel with a cloth. "If you have no objection, Contessa, I will leave the painting here until tomorrow evening. And now, might I beg Delfina's assistance in carrying a few of my brushes for me?" he asked as he began gathering together his paints.

A few minutes later, I was following him from the chamber carrying more than a few brushes. In fact, we were both quite laden. He had brought with him this day in addition to his usual gear a long wrapped bundle and an oversized folio. Tucking one beneath each arm, he nodded for me to follow with the pot of brushes precariously balanced atop the box of paints.

But our destination was not his workshop, as I quickly discovered. Instead, he brought me to the same immense hall where, not many weeks earlier, I had disguised myself as a porter and served wine during one of Il Moro's banquets.

Then, the room had been filled with sufficient rows of tables so that numerous visiting dignitaries and guests could dine along with the duke and his family. Now, only a few of those trestles topped with their elegantly carved planks remained, and they had been lined along the walls. Their accompanying chairs and benches served a different purpose, as well, arranged in several rows facing a new addition to the hall.

For, along the rear wall where the duke usually took his meals, a round wooden platform had replaced his long marble table. What that large stage might hold, I could not guess, for it was shielded by moss green velvet curtains supported by a series of golden ropes hanging from the high ceiling above.

More green curtains softened the room's columns, creating

what appeared to be small glades. There, musicians might be discreetly hidden, or guests desiring a bit of privacy could steal away. As for the frescoed walls, they seemed to have come to life. Broad twists of greenery interlaced by immense flowers in every hue adorned the doorways and windows, seeming to sprout from the painted landscapes. But lest anyone forget the theme of the masquerade, gilded cutouts of the four tarocchi suits—coins, staves, cups, and swords—dangled like fantastical stars from above.

Leonardo set his folio and bundle upon one of the tables and motioned me to do likewise, and then directed me toward the platform.

"More work remains to be done," he explained, "but you can see that all is almost ready for Il Moro's masquerade tomorrow evening. And now, if you like, I shall give you a demonstration of what I have planned for our entertainment."

At my eager nod, he reached for a tasseled gold rope dangling from the line of curtains and gave it a firm tug. Abruptly released, the luxurious green fabric puddled in a broad semicircle around the stage, revealing a most marvelous sight.

In the center of the raised platform—but which now with its wrap of green velvet appeared as a small hill—rose a gold metal sun twice as tall and broad as a man. To the rear edge of the platform hung still more curtains, these in red velvet, so that the sun appeared to be rising with the dawn.

"Constantin, Paolo, and Davide will be with me, concealed behind that curtain, where we shall operate the scenery," the Master explained. "You will note that the sun is made of two pieces, front and back. Between them are a series of cogs and gears which will allow us to spin our man-made sun in place like a wheel. But that is only the beginning."

He led me to the other side of the platform so that I could see that the sun hid an even greater secret: the metal lion! Almost as tall as I, the figure sat quite placidly there. Once again I marveled at the wonderful detail of the burnished beast, from the lethal-looking claws set into its metal paws, to the wire whiskers that sprouted from its muzzle.

"Another set of gears controls the center of the platform," he explained, and from my angle I could glimpse the mechanism in question. "That portion of the stage will rotate the sun about to reveal our beast lying in wait."

Leaving me where I stood, he leaped gracefully atop the platform. "As I've already told you, Il Moro himself will portray the tarocchi triumph of Strength. At a predetermined moment, he will bound onto the stage, thusly, to confront the lion. It will roar in response and raise its limbs when I tug upon the appropriate levers . . . I, of course, being well screened behind the sun," he added.

He pointed to a cleverly concealed panel upon the lion's chest. "As the duke pretends to subdue the beast with his club, I will cause this small hatch to spring open, and a shower of crimson blooms to pour forth, representing its lifeblood spilling upon the earth. And then our victorious duke will take his bows."

His explanation finished, he gave the lion a fond pat upon its metallic mane. "So, my dear boy, do you approve?"

"Even Il Moro should be astounded," I declared with an admiring smile. "I cannot wait to watch this marvelous show."

"You must pay close attention," he agreed, "since I will be hidden behind the scenery at the climactic moment. I shall want you to give me a full accounting of the guests' reactions."

Looking pleased by my compliments, he lightly stepped back onto the ground again. With a few more tugs of the gold rope, he had reanchored his curtains back into place, once more concealing the lion and sun from view.

"Speaking of your presence at the festivities, how fares work upon the costumes for you and the contessa? Shall Luigi's apprentice deliver them today?"

When I confirmed that the final fitting had gone well, he nodded in satisfaction. "Good."

Then, with a wry lift of his brow, he added, "I vow this is

most disconcerting. You are costumed as a girl, and so cleverly that I find myself forgetting at times that you are Dino beneath those skirts. And now our good Luigi is to dress you as a young man again. I will have to guard my tongue when I next see you lest I call you by the wrong name."

"I find things most confusing, as well," I admitted with a rueful smile. "Indeed, I shall be glad to dress as my old self again." *Though, which self is that,* I found myself silently wondering, *Dino or Delfina?*

But the Master was already moving on to a new subject. "Now, tell me what new information you have learned since we last spoke. Were you able to make use of the tarocchi cards? And have you carried any further messages between Caterina and the captain?"

I addressed the matter of the cards first, telling him of my success in stacking the deck. From there, I repeated the contessa's prediction, and the reaction from the other servants, who seemed to see a connection between those cards and Bellanca's death.

Then, recalling my role as Dino, I added, "I will admit, Master, that I am not comfortable with the gloomy fate she has seen for me, even though it was posed to me as if I were a girl."

"Fear not, my boy. Soothsayers make a habit of predicting death and misfortune." He dismissed my concerns with an impatient flick of his fingers, though he frowned just a little as he said it.

He nodded thoughtfully as I went on to explain how the planned meeting between the contessa and the captain had not come to pass, after all. I told him of the explanation Gregorio had given for his absence, and the contessa's reaction to it. Of course, I said nothing of my own private meeting with Gregorio at the cathedral the day after, though I feared the sudden color in my face as I recalled those tantalizing moments would betray my guilt over the matter.

To my relief, however, his attention seemed firmly fixed upon the duke's conversation with the captain.

"This must mean that Il Moro has finally selected his future cousin and ally," Leonardo muttered, stroking his beard as he considered my words, "else why would he arrange with his captain of the guard for increased security? And there is also a good chance that the captain knows not only that man's identity but also his other reason for being the duke's honored guest at the masquerade. I wonder that he did not warn the contessa of her cousin's plans."

Glancing up at me again, he asked, "Have you been charged yet with delivering another message between them?"

Though Gregorio had promised that, one way or another, I would have a missive to carry, I had not seen him this day. Neither had the contessa entrusted me with another message tidily sewn into a handkerchief. Thus, I shook my head.

"It makes little sense," he replied, though from his preoccupied air I suspected he was speaking of some entirely different subject now. "And yet, on the other hand, it is a possibility."

Then, abruptly, he seemed to recall my presence. "But this was not the reason I brought you here," he went on. "I wish to show you something which may have some bearing on these mysteries that we have so far been unable to resolve."

With me at his heels, he returned to the table where he'd left his bundle and folio. I joined him, watching as he thumbed through the folio's leaves overflowing with all manner of notes and sketches. Finally, he paused at one particular page.

"Take a look at this, my boy, and tell me what you think."

The drawing appeared at first glance to be simply a study of a nude woman, heavily shadowed, though all he had sketched was her thin upper torso and one slender arm. I studied the page for a moment, and then shook my head. "It is quite interesting," I admitted, "but I am not certain what it is about the drawing that you wish me to see."

"That will become quite clear momentarily."

While I was deliberating over the drawing, he had begun unwrapping the mysterious long bundle. Now he withdrew from that length of tied burlap a familiar object, though one I had not expected to see.

For, strangely, what he'd brought was one of the clay models we used in the workshop. This particular piece represented a female arm and hand, its lightly curled fingers seeming to beckon me as Leonardo twisted it about in his grasp.

I glanced again at the sketch, and understanding began to dawn. What I had mistaken for shadowing now seemed to form a pattern that I realized was not meant to represent shadows, at all, but bruises.

"This is the sketch you made of Bellanca's body in the surgery," I softly exclaimed. "But I still don't understand—"

"If you will allow me to use you as a subject," he cut me short with a stern look, "you shall see what I mean. Keep in mind that you are still but half-grown, my boy; thus, your limbs retain the slenderness of youth and sufficiently resemble those of a woman for the purpose of my demonstration."

Setting down the clay arm, he reached into the box of paints and pulled out a jar of lampblack. Carefully, he untied the cloth that served as its cover and then reached for a brush whose bristles were as thick as his thumb. He dipped its tip into the soft soot and then looked at me expectantly.

"Your hand," he clarified when I remained puzzled. I obediently held it out, and then opened my eyes wide as he began dusting the black powder on my palm and fingers.

"There," he proclaimed in a satisfied tone once the soot covered the entire surface of my inner hand. Setting down the brush again, he picked up the clay model and held it toward me as if it were his own limb.

"Now, for our experiment. Dino, I want you to reach with your blackened hand and grasp this arm around its wrist."

Once I'd done so, he twisted the arm about so that I

could see the black imprint left behind that matched where my soot-covered flesh had contacted clay. He set down the model once more and, while I busied myself wiping the worst of the black away with a cloth, he similarly dusted his own far larger hand with powdered ocher.

"It is my turn. Hold the clay arm as I did," he instructed, "and mind you do not smudge your handprint. Now, I shall grasp it in the same way."

A moment later, the clay arm bore a second handprint, this one in red and covering quite a bit more surface than did the much smaller black mark.

Leonardo wiped the red dust from his hand and then took the model from me, studying it from all angles. Finally, he nodded.

"Our demonstration has made my point quite plainly," he said in satisfaction. "You will notice that the fingers of the black handprint are not spread so widely as the red, nor do they completely span the distance around this clay wrist. As for the red print, not only is it far broader, but the fingers and thumb significantly overlap one another as they wrap around the wrist."

Then he indicated his sketch. "Look again at the bruises on the shoulders and wrist of our victim. Though the sketch itself is hardly a quarter of the page in size, you can still readily see that the marks upon her flesh seem to fit the smaller pattern of the black handprint."

At my nod, he flipped the page to the next in the folio.

"As my original sketch was to scale, it was an easy matter to redraw a portion to its true dimensions," he went on, indicating a life-size sketch of a woman's hand and wrist, complete with bruises. As I stared at the drawing in growing comprehension, he set the clay arm upon the folio page next to that sketch.

The similarity between the bruises and the black hand mark was now inescapable.

"So the bruises that Bellanca suffered were made by a

woman," I softly exclaimed, unable to escape the surge of relief that swept me at what seemed proof that Gregorio had no involvement with the servant's death.

"I would say that was a logical assumption," the Master agreed. "And given certain other information we've gleaned, I believe we have enough facts to make an educated assumption as to this woman's identity. Thus, I have concluded that her fellow servant Lidia was the one who caused her death."

Carefully wrapping the clay arm again so as not to smudge the handprints on it, he set it in the box along with the paints and then closed the folio once more.

"You see, Lidia's seeming suicide was troubling simply because she seemed to have no motive for taking her own life," he continued. "And this brings us to the matter of the wine."

He handed me the folio, then gathered up the box containing the rest of his supplies. Starting off toward the door again, with me alongside him, he continued. "Lidia died as a result of drinking poisoned wine. While I have given strong consideration to the possibility that someone else gave her the fatal drink, I have concluded that is unlikely. If you'll recall, she had rather extensive knowledge of healing. She would certainly recognize the distinctive odor of the poison used, derived as it was from fruit pits and seeds."

"And she used wine herself to create healing potions," I eagerly added, recalling the strong brew of Lidia's that Caterina had forced upon me following my attack by the stable dog. Between that and Lidia's salve, the gash on my arm had all but faded away now and was only the slightest bit tender.

Leonardo nodded his agreement. "Then we have the two stable dogs. One almost certainly died from lapping a large quantity of poisoned wine, while the other that attacked you and Pio quite likely was suffering from the nonlethal yet permanent effects of a smaller amount. Of course, they did not drink the poison without urging. Rather, I suspect that Lidia used the dogs to determine how swiftly the poison took effect, and how much was a fatal dose, before she swallowed it down, herself."

"So she murdered Bellanca and then took her own life in remorse?" I asked, shaking my head. "But what could have been her reason for wanting Bellanca dead?"

"That still remains a mystery we must solve, my boy," he grimly replied, "but if my suspicions are correct, tomorrow night's masquerade may shed some light on that final question."

17

The Star

He who fixes his course by a star changes not.

—Leonardo da Vinci, *Windsor Drawings*

The gown of the Queen of Swords lay neatly arranged atop the Contessa di Sasina's bed. The silver skirts trimmed in white fur were neatly spread in the shape of a bell, while gold slippers peeked from beneath its hem. The attached silver and gold brocaded sleeves—puffed from shoulder to elbow, and tight from elbow to wrist—had been inserted into short silver gauntlets, and then neatly crossed over the gown's silver brocade bodice. A silver-tipped gold crown lay atop the pillow, while alongside the gown was the promised sword sheathed in silver and gold, which hung from a tasseled gold cord.

Looking at Signor Luigi's beautiful creation, however, I was reminded of an elegant corpse laid upon a bier.

Perhaps it was Caterina's stony expression as she stared down at her costume that had inspired so unsettling an image in my mind. She had called me to her private chamber first thing this morning, having summarily dismissed her other three servants and bidden them to make themselves scarce for the remainder of the day.

They had swiftly obeyed. From the pitying look Esta had sent my way as she closed the door behind them, the trio counted themselves fortunate to be spared the contessa's displeasure. Even Pio had sensed his mistress's unhappiness and had prudently crept over to his pillow in the room's corner, where he now snoozed quite happily.

I suspected I knew the cause of her distress, for she had just returned from an unexpected summons from her cousin the duke. Tonight would be the long-awaited masquerade . . . and with it, the announcement of Caterina's betrothal. I wondered if Il Moro had decided to warn her of his plans, after all. Perhaps he had been concerned that she might disrupt the festivities with unseemly tears and wailing should she be taken by surprise with the news.

Finally, the young contessa turned to look at me, and her stony expression dissolved into one of abject misery as she confirmed my guess. "It has happened," she softly cried. "Cousin Ludovico told me that he has decided I must wed, and that I am to meet my future husband this night when we all unmask at the end of the evening."

She paused and shook her head in disgust. "Pah, I have never even heard of the man before . . . this Duke of Pontalba. His is some minor province, a mere speck upon the map, which Ludovico is at war with. Now this duke agreed to a peace in return for a well-dowered wife. Oh, Delfina, what shall I do?"

Not waiting for my reply, she sank onto the edge of her bed—heedless of the fact that she crumpled her marvelous costume—and buried her face in her hands. I hesitated a moment, knowing too well how she must feel. Had it not been the prospect of arranged marriage of my own that had first set me upon my boyish masquerade and journey to Milan?

Sighing, I knelt on the floor beside her, so that we were on a level with each other.

"Do not weep, Contessa," I consoled her, "for perhaps it is not the tragedy it seems. I am certain your cousin would not see you unhappy. Maybe this Duke of Pontalba is a kind and handsome man and will make a wonderful husband."

She raised her damp gaze to meet mine and shook her head. "It matters not, don't you understand? I don't want a duke . . . I only want Gregorio."

Her tearful wail sent a sharp dart into my heart. Why could she not be content with a duke, I bitterly wondered, and leave Gregorio for me? But, then, even if she protested the marriage, Il Moro would never let her forgo her duty. And while a humble young woman could easily vanish into another, equally humble life, it would be far harder—indeed, if not impossible—for a contessa raised with every luxury and used to servants rushing to do her bidding to turn her back on all she was, even if it was for love.

Thus, I was able to manage genuine sympathy for her as I asked, "Would you have me take a message to the captain to let him know what is to happen?"

"Yes, you must do that, and quickly."

Dashing the tears from her cheeks, she reached into her bodice and pulled forth a folded square of delicate linen.

"I have already written the message," she said, handing me the embroidered cloth that faintly crackled from the scrap of paper neatly sewn within it. "Give it to him, and also tell him what I have just told you. But you must hurry, before Gregorio leaves with his men. They are to ride out to meet the Duke of Pontalba some distance from the city and then safely escort him back to the castle."

I nodded and swiftly stood. "I shall make haste," I promised, tucking the cloth into my sleeve.

She smiled a little and grasped my hand. "You are my trusted servant, Delfina. I shall always be grateful that Signor Leonardo sent you my way."

I bobbed a small curtsy and managed a smile, even as guilt suddenly wrapped me in its shameful blanket. I could only pray that she never learned how she had been deceived . . .

first as a spy in her household, and then as a secret rival for the dashing captain's affections.

The morning was early enough that dew dampened my slippers as I hurried across the quadrangle toward the castle's main gate. I could see perhaps two dozen steeds being readied at the stables, their gleaming hides covered with brilliant parti-colored blankets beneath elaborate saddles and harnesses. Of course, Il Moro would wish his former enemy to be met by a richly appointed contingent of soldiers representing Milan's glorious army, no matter that both sides supposedly had declared peace between them.

I saw in some relief that the gate was manned by two soldiers I'd not encountered before, rather than the same two loutish mercenaries who now knew me by sight. My request to speak with their captain was met with a shrug from the stockier of the pair.

"You'll find him in his quarters, if you hurry," came his bored response.

With a stubby finger, he pointed at one of several vaulted openings along the wall apparently leading to where the duke's soldiers were housed. The archway he'd indicated turned out to be the shallow passage to a heavy, iron-braced wood door. Praying I was not about to wander into a barracks full of soldiers, I gave a hesitant knock.

A muffled voice bade me to enter; even so, my hand paused on the latch as I momentarily considered the propriety of what I was doing. Of course, I had been alone with the Master in his quarters before, but that had been in my guise as Dino. I suspected that being alone with Gregorio in his quarters would be a slightly different matter. But I was here on the contessa's business, I sternly reminded myself, and thus should conduct myself accordingly.

I must have hesitated outside the door a bit too long, for abruptly the latch turned beneath my hand. Before I could step back, the door had swung inward. I all but stumbled into the room and right into Gregorio's arms.

"Well, this is a pleasant surprise," he said with a lazy grin as he steadied me. "I was expecting one of my men, not a lovely young woman. What brings you here so early in the day?"

I would have made some proper answer, but my earlier moment of resolve had faded when I realized he was standing before me wearing his trunk hose and high boots and nothing else. It did not help my good intentions when he deliberately pulled me closer and then shut the door behind me.

"I-I have a message from the contessa," I finally managed, not daring to meet his gaze. Thus, my only other option was to stare in fascination at his bare torso.

His golden skin, taut over well-defined muscle, was almost flawless, save for an angry red scar that sliced several inches down his right side and an oddly shaped dark birthmark just above his heart. The scar, I guessed, was what remained of the wound that had brought him home from the fighting several months earlier. As for the birthmark, it appeared less a random mark on his flesh than it did a deliberate shape. *A sun,* I thought in surprise, resisting the urge to brush my fingers over it.

For I knew that if I gave in to that one seemingly innocent temptation, I might well succumb to far more dangerous desires.

"The message can wait, at least for another moment," he softly said, drawing me closer, so that I was now firmly in the circle of his sleekly muscled arms. As he spoke, his lips brushed my ear in a way that made me shiver, and the warmth of his flesh seemed to melt my resistance.

The sudden sound of a heavy fist pounding upon wood broke the spell that held me.

"Captain, you said to advise you when the men were assembled," a rough voice called through the door.

Gregorio's muttered curse held equal parts frustration and amusement as he lightly released me from his grasp. "I sense a familiar pattern here," he said with a shake of his head, his smile for me rueful. To his man, he called back, "Have them mount. I shall be there shortly."

His lazy manner slipped away, replaced by purposeful haste as he gestured me into the room.

"I am afraid my quarters are not as elegant as the contessa's," he wryly said, "but you might as well sit while I finish dressing. You have your choice of the bench or the bed. Both are equally uncomfortable."

I prudently settled myself upon the hard wooden bench next to a simple wooden table while he strode over to a large cabinet and began pulling forth various garments. Lest I focus too closely upon that most interesting sight of his half-naked form, I gazed about the room instead.

Gregorio's quarters were a far cry from the Master's well-lit chamber littered with papers and books and all manner of oddities. Rather, his was an austere space lit only by a single torch and a series of high, narrow windows, so that the room would be in a perpetual state of gloom. The dark bricked walls were unrelieved by any tapestry, though a collection of swords, shields, and light armor hung on the wall beside the cabinet.

That large carved piece, along with the ones I'd already noted—the bed, neatly wrapped in a brown wool blanket, and the simple table and bench—were the only furnishings. One shelf on the wall held a cup, plate, and bowl. Anything else he might own must be tucked away inside the cabinet.

Indeed, it seemed a chamber befitting a soldier never in one place for long . . . or, save for the weaponry, one belonging to a monk.

By now, he had pulled on a clean white shirt and a long, parti-colored red and gold doublet and was finishing tying his black trunk hose to the latter. The upper and lower halves of his sleeves were already tied on, and he carefully puffed the fabric of his shirt through their gaps. Satisfied, he turned to me.

"I'd best have that message now."

I nodded and pulled the folded handkerchief from my sleeve, feeling somewhat more composed now that he was completely dressed. He took the bit of cloth, once more using his boot knife to slice the stitches. His expression as he read the few lines was thoughtful.

"The contessa also bade me tell you that Il Moro will make an announcement at this night's masquerade," I added. "The Duke of Pontalba, whom you and your men are escorting here, is to be her husband. They are to wed as part of the peace treaty between the two dukes."

"So I have heard."

His reply was absent, his attention still fixed upon the note. His words confirmed Leonardo's guess that Il Moro would have shared with him this bit of information. Recalling our conversation in the cathedral square, I was not surprised to see that, unlike Caterina's distress at the news, Gregorio's reaction seemed to reflect satisfaction.

Carefully, he folded both note and handkerchief and tucked them into his tunic and then turned his attention to me.

"Surely you did not expect me to weep at the news," he said with the hint of an ironic smile. "You know that I have been eagerly awaiting this announcement. And now that it has come to pass, we must make our plans, for time is short."

Slowly, he circled around me, like a sleek, dark panther lazily stalking his prey. "First, return and tell the contessa that I agree to her request and will be awaiting her in the tower approximately an hour before midnight tonight. It seems that she wishes her final farewell to be, shall we say, of a physical nature."

I felt myself blush a little at that explanation but managed a nod. Whether or not he noticed my reaction, I was not certain, for he went on. "It would be unkind of me to refuse her this last wish, do you not think? And as chances are that Il Moro will push for the wedding to take place immediately, tonight likely will be our final opportunity for such a meeting."

He paused directly behind me and laid his hands upon my shoulders, then murmured in my ear, "And now, my dear Delfina, I must know where your loyalties lie . . . with Caterina, or with me."

"I-I don't understand," I truthfully whispered.

His grip upon me tightened.

"It is quite simple," he replied, his words taking on a tone of seductive urgency. "I have a plan in mind that can make me a wealthy man, far wealthier than I shall ever be from the paltry wages of Il Moro and his like. Choose me, choose to be the captain of the guard's woman, and I shall share that wealth with you. I'll give you a life that you would never know in your current position."

He paused just long enough for me to consider that possibility and then flatly finished, "Choose Caterina, and you shall remain a maidservant the rest of your life."

Abruptly, I pulled from his grasp and turned toward him. "And if I choose you," I asked, searching his face for some sign of what lay behind his words, "what part do I play in these plans of yours?"

"Your role will be quite simple. All you need do is make certain she is able to meet me in the tower as planned . . . and you must be there, as well, to secretly watch all that happens between us."

My expression must have betrayed my surprise and dismay at such a request, for he softly laughed.

"My dear Delfina, do not look so shocked," he replied, though I heard the hard edge beneath the humor and knew this was no jest. "Believe me that I am not asking this of you simply for my own twisted amusement. I will need a witness to what occurred, or my plan will come to naught."

"So you intend to blackmail the contessa?" I asked as understanding dawned. Then I shook my head. "But I still don't understand. It is well-known that many ladies of the court take their pleasure with men other than their husbands. Why would she care that you threaten to reveal such a thing? How could such a story truly hurt her?"

"Let us just say that there is more between me and the contessa than you—or even Caterina—know about," he replied with a small shrug. "But I can assure you that once she is aware of what I could reveal, she will pay any price for my silence."

The sound of more pounding upon the door abruptly forestalled further conversation. "Begging your pardon, Captain," came a hesitant voice through the door again, "but the men are mounted and ready."

"I am on my way," he called back and strode over to the far wall.

Pulling a few pieces from the collection there, he swiftly buckled on a shiny silver breastplate and two swords: one a long ceremonial blade, and the other a short sword as the nobles customarily carried about the town. Finally, he fastened on a knee-length black cloak and grabbed up a sleek silver helmet with a short crest of black feathers and a pair of silver gauntlets. Tucking gloves and helmet beneath one arm, he made his way back to me.

"Time grows short. I must have your answer now, Delfina. Will your loyalties lie with me or with the contessa?"

I had used the few moments as he finished dressing to frantically consider my options. If I did not agree to join him, then the Master and I would lose this final chance to perhaps learn the truth behind Bellanca and Lidia's deaths . . . assuming that they even had any connection to what Gregorio now proposed. But if I took Gregorio's side, I might learn all this, and more. It might come too late to save the contessa from his scheme, but at least the Master would be involved and would surely know what to do.

And, thus, my decision was simple.

"My loyalties are with you, Gregorio," I softly declared, earning a cool smile of approval from him.

Lightly, he stroked a warm hand down my cheek and nodded. "I hoped you would make that choice," he said. "I have found myself quite taken with you and would regret if we had to part ways. It is not often one finds a woman who is beautiful and clever as well as loyal."

I blushed a little at that last, though the compliment was blunted by his next words, as he softly added, "But keep in mind, my dear Delfina, that you have made your choice. Should you change your mind afterward and think to betray me, know that you would suffer the consequences, as surely as will I."

"I won't change my mind. My loyalty is to you," I declared again, steadily meeting his dark gaze.

He nodded and leaned forward to brush his lips against mine. "Then remember, the east tower tonight, at half past ten. And now, I must be off to bring Caterina her bridegroom."

He pulled open the door again and gestured me to precede him. Just inside the gate, the other soldiers were assembled on horseback. With their colorful garb and their horses' bright blankets, along with their multihued flags carried on tall staffs, they made a most dramatic sight. Surely the Duke of Pontalba could not help but be impressed!

I remained in the alcove's shadow while Gregorio strode toward the soldier who held the reins of the same black stallion we'd ridden from the cathedral. By now, he had pulled on his helmet and gauntlets, looking every inch the warrior as he lightly mounted his steed and whirled the beast about. Despite myself, I could not help a small sigh at the handsome figure he cut and wondered if it had been that dashing image alone that had earned him his post.

In unison, the other soldiers pulled about their horses, as well, and the contingent smartly trotted toward the open gate. I watched them go, somewhat disappointed when the only backward glance for me came not from Gregorio, but from the familiar loutish mercenary. His blond mustaches twitched with the gap-toothed leer he sent me over his shoulder, and I suppressed a grimace. Once I was officially the captain of the guard's woman, I told myself in some pique, the first thing I would do was request that Gregorio demote the man . . . that, or send him out for a beating.

Then I gave myself a mental shake, reminding myself that this was but a role I was playing. Once this business was over with, Delfina would surely vanish again, and Dino take her place. What would happen with Gregorio, I dared not guess.

And I shouldn't care, I stoutly told myself. Despite his handsome and dashing façade, had he not shown himself to be but a mercenary, himself, coolly clever and prepared to do anything or use anyone who could advance his personal cause? I would be a fool to believe that he truly cared for me, no matter the seductive kisses and sweet words he bestowed upon me.

And it was only when the gate had closed after the men that it occurred to me to wonder what he would have done had I not agreed to his plan.

The thought nagged uncomfortably at me as I made my way across the quadrangle. Perhaps that was what had happened with Bellanca, I found myself speculating with no little alarm. Perhaps she had agreed to a similar plot and then changed her mind. And then, rather than handling the matter, himself, Gregorio had charged Lidia with making sure that Bellanca would not betray him to the contessa.

My steps slowed, even as my thoughts raced. Or perhaps Lidia had taken it upon herself to deal with Bellanca, and Gregorio had learned of her actions only after the fact. Recalling his chill presence at Bellanca's burial, and Lidia's overt demonstrations of grief, I told myself that this scenario made equal sense.

Indeed, I could picture how it must have happened. Fierce as any mother when her child was threatened, Lidia had sought to protect her son by whatever means was at her disposal. Perhaps the fall had been an accident, and Lidia had simply meant to frighten Bellanca into silence. Or maybe that swift push from the tower window had been a coldly deliberate act. Either way, it seemed that the woman had come to regret what she had done.

Then I shook my head. The Master had implied the day before that he knew the truth of the matter, though he had refused to speculate any further about it in my presence. Perhaps, as he said, all would come clear this night. All I could do was take my place in the tower at the appointed hour and pray that any secrets I learned would break only the contessa's heart and not my own.

18

The Moon

The moon has every month a winter and a summer.

—Leonardo da Vinci, *Codex Atlanticus*

"No, Constantin, place it there," the Master softly called over the sweet strains of music drifting to us from behind the concealing lengths of green velvet curtains.

I was standing behind the platform at the far end of the great hall. There, Leonardo and the apprentices made the final adjustments to the great sun and the mechanical lion that would figure so prominently in the night's entertainment. He was indicating what appeared to be a pile of boulders, but what was instead a stage prop made from painted canvas stretched over a wooden frame. Constantin moved it as directed to a spot behind the lion, hiding any trace of those pipes and pulleys extending from the metal beast to the opposite side of the sun. There the Master, out of view of the audience, would operate those controls to cause the lion's movement. For now, however, those lines and rods were concealed by a half circle of green velvet laid atop the otherwise empty side of the platform that would first face the audience.

I had found Leonardo earlier that day there in the hall directing the workmen who were hanging the remaining ornamentation and rearranging the benches and chairs yet another time. He had listened to my account of this last meeting with Gregorio with keen interest, alternately frowning and nodding. I had blushed as I revealed what the contessa's intention was, to lay with a man not her husband on the night of her betrothal to another. To my surprise, however, he had not appeared shocked as much as worried by my words.

Harder still was explaining the way Gregorio had made me choose between him and Caterina, knowing the issue must be addressed. For surely, had I truly been a boy under such circumstances, the captain would have long since deduced my true gender. Thus, I could give but an abbreviated account of what actually had passed between us, making it seem that florins and not seduction had been the crux of the matter.

Assuming Dino's bravado, I had bragged, "I must have played my role quite cleverly, for he readily took me for a girl easily enticed by promises of wealth."

"Yes, quite clever," he had absently agreed. Then, his frown deepening, he bade me return to the contessa's quarters.

"I must ponder this awhile longer and settle upon a solution," he had decreed. "Proceed the rest of the day as if we had not spoken, but keep a close eye on the contessa lest she suddenly decide to deviate from her own plan. Once you both arrive at the masquerade, you can slip away and find me at the lion's platform. I will give you your final instructions then."

The remainder of the day had passed with agonizing slowness, though I suspected for the contessa nighttime could not come fast enough. Her cheeks burning with color, she had paced about her room alternately laughing and sobbing. Once, she had mockingly pulled the sword from its jeweled scabbard and pressed its sharp tip to her breast.

"I might as well thrust this blade into me now," she dramatically declared, "for tonight my heart will be pierced with equal pain. I will know the joy of lying with the man I love and at the same time know that I will never experience such bliss again. I should die right now and end my sorrow."

"Please, Contessa, you alarm poor Pio," I hurriedly protested, seeking to distract her. I raced to the corner and snatched the sleeping hound from his pillow, and then carried him to her. "See his frightened face. Should anything happen to you, he would be bereft, as would I."

Pio chose that moment to give a lazy yawn, seemingly unconcerned by his mistress's actions. Despite herself, Caterina laughed at the sight. Setting down the sword, she took him into her arms and fondly cradled him.

"Very well, Delfina, you are right, and I am being foolish." Then her smile faded as she softly cried, "But what if my new husband refuses to allow Pio to accompany me? I could never allow that!"

"Do not worry, Contessa," I once more hastened to reassure her. "Most noble gentlemen are fond of hounds, and I am certain he will welcome Pio. But if not, be assured that Master Leonardo will make certain he is well cared for."

"Do you promise?" Her dark gaze burned fiercely, abruptly reminding me of Gregorio. "He has been my loyal companion, and I could not bear him to want for anything."

"I swear, Contessa," I replied, firmly meeting her gaze. "But do not worry about that now. You must rest awhile, as it shall be a long night."

"And, of course, I would not wish to appear before my new husband with a sagging countenance and dark circles beneath my eyes," she replied with a tone of scorn, though she obediently took herself to her bed, Pio curled at her side.

But barely had she closed her eyes than she sat up again to address me.

"I almost forgot to tell you that I laid out the tarocchi cards a final time for myself this morning. Once more, I drew those same four cards that have been haunting us since Bellanca's death. But I think I know what they mean now."

She lay back down again, gaze fixed upon the ceiling above her. "I fear that, for me, they predicted Ludovico's betrayal, bartering me away like a mare to some man I do not know, and thus foretold an end to my happy life. But I accept that this is how it must be, for the cards have never lied before."

She had closed her eyes then, and I'd crept away to the outer chamber, grateful for the return of Isabella and the others. News of the contessa's impending betrothal had already trickled down to the castle's servants, so that the trio was eagerly speculating as to what Caterina's new role would mean for them. I listened but did not contribute to the discussion, unable for the moment to look beyond the night to come.

To my surprise, Caterina had been quite cheerful when she awakened again, seeming almost excited while Esta and Rosetta helped her into her elaborate gown. Once Esta had set the crown upon her head and stepped back for a final look, all four of us had gasped in wonder at the image that Caterina presented.

"You will be the most beautiful woman there, Contessa," Isabella had cried with unfeigned enthusiasm, clapping her hands together. The rest of us eagerly agreed and carried over the narrow mirror from the corner for her to see her reflection.

Caterina had done well to follow Luigi's advice in the matter, I thought in approval. The white, silver, and gold costume showed off her golden coloring and dark hair to an advantage. Moreover, the tucks from the tailor's clever needle emphasized her curves, so that in this gown she looked more a woman than a girl.

But Esta's talents were not to be diminished. Rather than hide her hair beneath the crown, Esta had arranged the contessa's raven locks into loose plaits, which were softly gathered at the nape of her neck and flowed down her back. The effect was one of beauty and grace, as befitted her costume of a warrior queen.

While the other women poked and prodded at the gown, making last-minute adjustments, I hurried to the servants' quarters and donned my own clothes for the night.

Signor Luigi had done equal justice to this costume, I thought in satisfaction as I pulled on red trunk hose and matching red boots and then the short tunic of red and gold brocade. Just as in Leonardo's sketch, the tunic's long sleeves ended in wide green cuffs, which I rakishly flipped back. The short cloak striped in blue and gold also matched Leonardo's notes, though of course the white and gold fur that trimmed it was nowhere as lavish as the white fur hem of Caterina's gown.

To give the costume a more boyish look, I pinned my long false braid around my head like a victor's wreath. And though I did not resort to my old corset that I wore in my guise as Dino, I did wear a tightly laced bodice beneath my tunic so that I was left with a more boyish figure. The result was comfortably familiar, no matter that I had enjoyed wearing women's clothes once again this past fortnight.

Finally, I picked up the stave that finished my costume. The simple wooden wand was almost as tall as I, with elaborate finials attached to either end, all of which were painted gold. Grinning, I gave a few mock thrusts of the weapon as if I were beating back an attacker; then, tying the long threads of my mask loosely enough so that it dangled down upon my chest, I rejoined the other maids in the contessa's outer chamber.

My new appearance had caused something of a stir among the three. Esta merely grinned, though Rosetta declared to her sister, "I think that Delfina makes a fine boy, don't you?"

"Pah, she could fool me."

The snide note in Isabella's reply matched her smirk, though that smug expression promptly dissolved into a frown at Esta's single murmured word, "Jealous?"

For both the twins had spent the past few days soundly protesting—out of the contessa's hearing, of course—the fact that one of them and not I should have been the one to accompany Caterina to the masquerade. Fortunately, their barbs subsided as Caterina made her way to the outer chamber, sword dangling from her waist and mask in one hand, ready for the masquerade.

It was a fine night out, and we could hear the sounds of gaiety from the hall long before we arrived. Caterina's mood, however, had once more sunk into one of despair. I glanced over at her a time or two, thinking to make light conversation, but the misery in her young face forestalled me. Still, once we arrived at the hall and stopped to tie on our masks, I reached out a comforting hand to her.

She grabbed my fingers tightly in response, and I was consumed with the sudden urge to whisk her away from the castle and what was to come. We could crop her hair and disguise her like a boy, I eagerly thought; perhaps let her join the Master's workshop as another apprentice. Of course, I would have to confess my deception to him, but that would be a small price to preserve Caterina's happiness.

Yet even as I realized the folly of such a plan, Caterina let go of my hand and straightened her slim shoulders.

"Why are we so glum?" she demanded, her lips curling into a chill smile beneath her mask. "After all, it's not as if I were going off to my death. Come, let us enjoy this night."

While she mingled with the other nobles, I quickly drifted back into the growing crowd and went in search of the Master. The evening could already be judged a success for Leonardo, for the sounds of merriment all but drowned out the musicians as they played in one corner. He had arranged the lighting in such a way that the hall seemed caught in those final moments of dusk, when the rosy sky added its special glow to the earth. That magical blush gave life to the greenery and added sparkle to the costumes, some grand in their opulence and others titillating in their lack of fabric.

I was certain Il Moro would be well satisfied with his master of pageantry this night . . . that was, assuming the announcement of the new treaty and of Caterina's betrothal went as planned.

Now, having found Leonardo at the lion's platform, I waited for him to notice me and take me aside. Luckily, I had no fear of discovery by the apprentices, even though I was dressed in boyish garb once more. I knew that the gold mask I wore sufficiently concealed my features.

Leonardo was not masked but was in costume, as well, I saw with some interest. Though the clothing was vaguely familiar, it took me a moment to recognize what he represented with his long, white-trimmed red robe worn over a green tunic, red trunk hose, and short red boots. For a hat, he wore a broad, soft cap of red velvet trimmed in white fur, which was perched atop what appeared to be a green turban that he'd wrapped around his head.

"The magician," I declared aloud, as I finally recalled the first of the tarocchi triumphs.

Hearing me, he turned; then, obviously recognizing his design in my costume, he smiled and hurried toward me.

"Dino, my boy, is that you beneath that mask?" he softly asked. I nodded, lifting the pasteboard creation just enough so that he could glimpse my features before letting it fall once more. Satisfied, he took me by the arm and walked me out of earshot of the other apprentices.

"It is good to see you in young man's clothing again," he said in approval. "And I see that Luigi made a tolerable attempt at my design. Did he do as well with the contessa's costume?"

"She looks beautiful," I assured him, earning a satisfied smile from him. Then, glancing either way to make sure we were not overheard, he assumed a more serious mien.

"I believe I have discovered what the captain's blackmail plan entails," he said. "It is both evil and cunning in its simplicity, and it cannot fail unless we stop him before he meets with the contessa this night."

"But what is it?" I asked with a combination of eagerness and dread. "And did he have anything to do with Bellanca's and Lidia's deaths?"

To my relief, Leonardo shook his head. "I believe him innocent of murder, though I am certain he knows why both women died. As for his plot against Caterina, I would prefer to wait until we confront him before exposing his plan to you, lest by some small chance I am wrong."

He gripped my arm and leaned closer. "But, no matter what else happens, it is crucial that the contessa not go to the tower tonight, as that will surely be her downfall. So long as she avoids his bed and remains ignorant of the secret he holds, she need have no fear that he will use it against her."

He reached into his robe and pulled forth the same handkerchief of Caterina's that I had left with him earlier.

"I've stitched a message inside this cloth, which you must take to her, telling her that it is from the captain. The note instructs her that there has been a change of plans, and he cannot meet her this night, after all. Give it to her as soon as you leave me."

I took the cloth and tucked it into my own tunic, nodding. "But what of me? You said that we would confront Gregorio in the tower."

"You shall be at the tower," he said. "But it will be me, rather than the contessa, who arrives there at the appointed hour. My hope is to convince him to confess all. At the very least, we shall have prevented the contessa from committing an act she would surely regret. How we proceed from there shall be up to the captain."

"And once this night is over, will I go back to my role as Dino?" I softly asked.

He patted my arm reassuringly. "I am certain that, once this night is over, all will be resolved . . . so, yes, you shall return as Dino again tomorrow."

"That is well," I said with a sigh that was not feigned, "for I have grown weary of this role."

"You have done well, my boy," he replied with a smile. "I

am proud of you. And, though she will never know it, the contessa will always be grateful to you, as well. Now, be off with you."

With those words, he hurried back to the platform, where Constantin, Davide, and Paolo were now lighting the inner lamps that would set the artificial sun aglow. "Be careful with the oil and brazier," he softly exclaimed, "lest you set the entire hall on fire."

Leaving them to their tasks, I slipped back around the curtained area. The long marble table where Il Moro normally took his meals had been moved to one side of the hall and was filled with costumed guests. Standing behind it in the center was the duke, himself, recognizable despite his gold mask by his stocky figure and thick cap of black hair. He carried a club and wore the short blue tunic over a red shirt that was his costume as the triumph of Strength.

I stared a bit longer, thinking I recognized a few other members of the family. To the far side sat the ancient Marchesa d'Este, wearing her usual all black, with a small slip of a white mask covering her eyes as her only concession to the masquerade. Another uncle and male cousin, costumed as the King and Knight of Cups, sat on either side of a young girl dressed as the Lady Fortune, whom I guessed to be one of the duke's mistresses.

To the duke's immediate right stood a man I had never before seen at court. His tall, thin body was wrapped in gold trunk hose and a short gold tunic opened to expose much of his sunken chest. Gold wings sprouted from his thin shoulders, and he carried a matching gold pitchfork. Even had his horned mask with its carved leather leer not given him a recognizable face, something about him immediately called to mind the Devil.

This must be Caterina's husband-to-be, I thought in dismay, even as I reproved myself for judging the man solely upon his costume. As I watched, he and Il Moro exchanged seemingly friendly words as they both drank deeply from their respective wine cups. I noticed a seat beside the Duke of Pontalba that was empty. No doubt it was waiting for Caterina.

Leonardo had installed a large clock near the stage so that the guests could know exactly when midnight arrived, and the unmasking—and, of course, the betrothal announcement—would commence. Thus, I could see that I still had time to find the contessa and give her the message before I slipped away to the tower. But where was she?

Swiftly, I scanned the hall, looking for the glorious silver gown. Surely she had not taken one look at her future husband and fled the hall, I thought in no little concern. I wondered, as well, if Gregorio was somewhere among the guests. Though he'd not be part of the festivities, perhaps the duke would have him ensconced somewhere among the shadows lest trouble brew with the duke's former enemy as guest.

Why had I not thought to ask this question of him this morning? I had not seen him and his contingent when they'd returned to the castle earlier in the day, though surely he had returned safely with his men. Perhaps he put aside his dashing uniform and had donned a costume. Maybe he was somewhere in the hall watching Caterina and me, maybe even watching Leonardo.

Suddenly unnerved, I put my efforts back into searching out the contessa, but to no avail. I was just about to return to her chambers, when I spotted a flash of silver behind one of the green-draped columns. I ducked behind it and saw to my relief that the contessa was alone in the corner, seated upon one of the small benches. Her mask lay at her feet, and her face was buried in her hands, her crown askew.

"Contessa," I softly called, pulling off my own mask and kneeling beside her.

She glanced up with a start, seeming not to recognize me for a moment. Once she did, however, she dropped her face into her hands again, softly wailing, "Delfina, I cannot bear it. Did you see him, the Duke of Pontalba?"

"I did, but it was only a glimpse. He was in costume, so I could not be sure what he looked like."

"I am sure," she bitterly replied, raising her damp gaze to meet mine. "He's old and ugly and looks quite cruel. How could Ludovico do this to me?"

"Can you simply not tell your cousin that you will not marry this man?" I asked, though I knew the answer to this question as well as she.

She merely shook her head, not bothering to reply. Watching her despair, I steeled myself, for I knew I was about to add to her grief. "Contessa, I bring a message to you from the captain," I said and handed her the kerchief.

She took it eagerly, though uncertainty furrowed her young brow. "Why would he send me a message," she wondered aloud as she anxiously tugged at the stitches, "unless—"

She scanned the slip of paper, and a look of bewilderment replaced that uncertainty. In a small voice, she said, "He sends word that he cannot meet me, after all. He says that Ludovico requires his presence at the masquerade the entire night, and he dare not risk disobeying those orders."

"I-I'm sure he is as distressed as you at this turn of events," I promptly assured her, ruthlessly suppressing any twinges of guilt. "Surely you can manage to see him another day before this marriage takes place."

"No! I must see him tonight." She jumped from her seat, and a large cup that would have once held wine tumbled to the floor. "I will go find him. Tell me, what was he wearing when he gave you the message?"

"Wearing?" I asked in confusion. "He did not—that is, I did not see him, Contessa. He merely whispered in my ear and handed me the handkerchief. When I turned around, he was gone."

"It does not matter, I will find him," she insisted, stumbling a little now as she tried to straighten her skirts, which somehow had gotten entangled between her legs.

I stared at her in some concern, wondering how much

wine she had already imbibed this night. For her own sake, I dared not let her go in search of Gregorio lest she say or do the wrong thing in front of the rest of the guests.

"Contessa, do not vex yourself," I pleaded. "I will find him and tell him you must speak with him. You must remain here and pretend that nothing is wrong, so that you raise no suspicions. Besides, if you go wandering about looking for the captain, you will miss Master Leonardo's grand display. He would be so disappointed if you did not see it."

She blinked a few times, and then finally nodded, proudly lifting her chin. "You are right, Delfina, as usual. I shall let you find Gregorio for me. In the meantime, I shall be seated next to my future husband."

Then she smiled, her lips trembling and her eyes welling, as she added, "Perhaps after a few more cups of wine, he will seem less repulsive to me."

She tied on her mask a bit crookedly and then gracefully stumbled back in the direction of her cousin's table. I watched her go, giving a fervent prayer that she would have the good sense to stay there quietly.

A glance at the clock told me I would soon have to leave for the tower. My earlier trepidation, which I had forgotten with my concern for Caterina, returned. But surely the Master was right, I told myself, and once this night was over, all would be well again.

Not quite believing that this could be true, I tied my own mask on again and slipped back among the crowd.

19

The Sun

Nothing is hidden beneath the sun.

—Leonardo da Vinci, *Windsor Drawings*

"**G**ood nobles and ladies, might I have your attention!"

Standing upon a small box near the curtained platform, Leonardo waved the crowd to silence. When the only sound remaining was the muffled clank of wine cups, he turned to the table where Il Moro sat and made a sweeping bow.

"Before we begin this night's entertainment, let us offer a round of thanks to our great Excellency, Ludovico Sforza, who is responsible for this glorious masquerade," he said, bowing again as the crowd gave a boisterous cheer.

The duke grinned heartily and nodded, accepting the accolades. Then, graciously, he raised his wine cup and proclaimed, "Of course, I must acknowledge my master of pageantry, Leonardo the Florentine, who has turned this dull hall into a thing of beauty and promises us marvels to come."

The applause for Leonardo was equal, and he smiled slightly as he dipped his head in recognition of their praise.

Then, raising his hand once more for silence, he went on. "And now, I am here as your humble magician to entertain you. Feast your eyes upon sights not seen outside of Milan."

He tugged the gold cord, which released the curtains surrounding the platform. An appreciative gasp rose from the crowd as they saw the immense golden sun. From my spot at the rear of the hall, I gasped a bit, myself. Now lights flickered in each of its metal rays, the reflected glare almost as blinding as the true sun, itself.

Then the sun began to spin like a wheel, moving faster and faster until each light seem to merge into the other, and the entire sun seemed surrounded by a ring of fire. Just when it seemed that the swirling light might leap from the platform of its own volition, Leonardo raised a hand. The light promptly quenched, leaving the room in half darkness again.

More applause followed, but the Master was not finished. With another wave of his hand, small flames burst into life all along the platform's edge, drawing another gasp. Now the musicians began to play again, their strings and drums beating out a martial tune as the sun began to slowly turn. Leonardo, meanwhile, had vanished, though I knew he was now hidden behind the platform waiting for the sun to make its full rotation.

A moment later the grand mechanical lion came into view, seeming almost alive amid the flickering lights. The beast opened its mouth and let out a roar—that sound, I knew, created by Davide blowing across a series of pipes—drawing excited cries from the ladies and appreciative calls from the men.

Then came Leonardo's voice from behind the curtain, his words amplified by one of his talking devices.

"Nobles and ladies," he said again, "behold the beast, which is War that threatens our great city. And see our glorious regent in the person of Strength slay that beast and bring peace to the land."

At that, a rather tipsy Ludovico jumped upon the stage,

narrowly missing one of the flaming pots. Grinning, he lifted his club to the mechanical lion. In response, the lion raised one paw, and then the other, as if clawing at the duke. Ludovico jumped back a bit in surprise and then grinned more broadly as he began swinging his club.

Fortunately for the Master's creation, he managed to miss with every blow, or else the lion would have been sorely dented. As the battle raged, several women cried out in alarm, while the men cheered him on, and the musicians beat their drums with growing enthusiasm.

The Master's voice rose once again over the crowd, saying, "And now, the lion goes down to defeat at our ruler's hand."

At that cue, the duke lightly tapped the mechanical beast upon the chest. The lion's paws abruptly dropped, and his mouth snapped shut. In the next moment, his metallic chest sprang open to spill a seeming garden's worth of red blooms like blood upon the platform.

The resulting applause would have gratified a man with twice the Master's sense of self-worth. Il Moro, meanwhile, shook his fist in triumph and then began tossing the blooms, one by one, into the audience. Something of a brawl began to break out as the ladies fought over the flowers, but I saw no more. By then I had slipped from my spot at the rear of the hall and was hurrying from the castle into the night.

At least the contessa was safely out of the matter, I thought in relief. When I'd left the hall, I'd spotted her seated between the two dukes and appearing slightly the worse for her wine, though her mask made it hard to tell for certain. But as she'd seemed agreeable enough to let me continue as her messenger, I would worry tomorrow what the Master and I should tell her of what happened tonight.

My steps slowed as I wondered with no little apprehension about what would be the outcome of this secret meeting. I suspected things would turn ugly, though I knew the Master was clever enough to resolve almost any unpleasant matter. But would my presence there in the tower be enough to forestall the threat of violence? I shivered a little, recalling that wall of armament in Gregorio's chamber. Such items did not belong to a man who was not well versed in their uses.

But far worse was the realization that, by joining the Master in confronting Gregorio, I would destroy the tentative bond that seemingly had grown between us . . . a bond that, in my secret dreams, I had eagerly pictured blossoming into something greater. Though, of course, I bitterly reminded myself, how could I care for a man who had planned to betray the contessa using the cruel weapon of her heart? And what would stop him from doing the same thing to me, one day, when he finally tired of our relationship?

I drew my cloak more snugly about me, but even its soft warmth offered no comfort for the sudden anguish that pierced me. When this was over, I fiercely vowed, I would return to my boy's disguise and never again play a woman's role. It was a life far too painful to endure and fraught with far too many sorrows to bear.

By now, the deeper shadow of the tower lay across my already darkened path. Pulling off my mask, I squinted up at it and fancied I saw a flicker of light there. Gregorio must be waiting, I dully told myself, letting the mask drop from my fingers onto the grass. I could delay this no longer but must join him there and play my appointed role.

The narrow tower door was unlatched. Glancing about to see if I were being spied upon—though, certainly, I'd not be able to spot anyone lurking in the shadows—I slipped past that wooden entry and let it quietly close behind me. I had not taken this path up to the tower's peak before, and the sight of the dark stone staircase spiraling far up above me made me blink dizzily for a moment. At least the darkness would make the view midway through the climb seem less frightening, I tried to reassure myself as I set my foot upon that first rough stair.

My nervousness at what was to come already had my heart beating faster. By the time I reached the top step—having long since lost count of how many I'd climbed to reach that summit—I was certain that organ's pounding was loud enough to be heard back at the great hall. I paused for several moments at the closed door leading into the tower room to regain my composure, along with my breath; then, steeling myself, I cautiously turned the latch and stepped inside.

From far below, the tower appeared immense, seeming half as wide around as it was tall. The circular room in which I now stood was every bit as large as it appeared from without, with open windows wrapping about it so that the night spilled in from every side. Had the space been empty, a small battle could have been fought within its confines. As it was, large sections of the tower had been given over to storage, for boxes and crates piled atop one another and threatened to tumble should one step too close.

I moved cautiously through the shadows, hearing the dried reeds that had been spread to muffle the chill crackling beneath my feet. The sound loudly announced my presence, so I knew that Gregorio must know I was there. Even so, I hesitated to call out but continued my cautious approach.

A few steps farther, and the stacks gave way to a broad open space with a clear view of the windows. It had been through one of these that the luckless Bellanca had fallen to her death, and I shivered despite myself. The shadows here were far less dense, not only because the moonlight streamed in uninhibited but because to one side a low brazier glowed with welcome heat and light.

A muffled sound came from the shadows I'd just left, and I whirled about again. "Gregorio?" I softly called. Then, realizing my boyish dress might too well disguise me, I added, "It is I, Delfina."

A dark form emerged from the shadows, and then a stray thread of moonlight threw the figure into sharp relief.

"I vow I almost did not recognize you, so cleverly are you dressed."

I could hear the faint amusement in Gregorio's voice.

The flickering light of the brazier as he drew closer revealed the familiar hint of a lazy grin. He halted before me and ran a possessive hand along my cheek as he added, "But you do call to mind someone else in that page's garb, my dear Delfina, though I cannot think for the moment who it might be."

I thought to make some glib reply. Instead, I could only stare in silence, taking in what might be my last sight of him before the firestorm of the Master's plan surely turned to cinders whatever was between us.

He had put aside his earlier gaily colored uniform and was dressed all in black, save for the silver glint of the sword at his hip. He was dressed as a man familiar with the shadows, a man with much practice stalking the night.

And, tonight more than ever before, his darkly handsome features seemed to call to mind God's fallen, rather than those golden angels who had prudently stayed to His right side.

I could not help myself. A sudden sob escaped me, for all that I tried to hold it back. I knew that, after this night, never again would I see his seductive grin turned upon me or feel his touch upon my warm flesh. Never again would he tempt me with his kisses or with the promise of something that burned within his eyes.

And never again would his voice say my name aloud, save as a curse.

He frowned at this sudden lapse into emotion, though his tone sounded deliberately light as he said, "I cannot recall the sight of me ever bringing a woman to tears before. Tell me what is wrong."

"It's nothing," I insisted, doing my best to summon a smile even as I sought a quick lie. "It's just that I'm afraid at what might happen tonight. What if the contessa learns that I was here? Can't you tell me what this is about, and put my mind more at ease?"

He slowly shook his head, giving me a keen look. "Surely you're not having second thoughts this late in the game, are you?" he softly asked.

The hand that had brushed my face had slid to my shoulder, and now his grip on me tightened almost imperceptibly. His other hand lightly caught my other arm . . . perhaps to hold me so that I could not escape, I wondered in faint alarm, or maybe simply to pull me closer?

I lifted my chin and determinedly met his dark gaze. "I've not changed my mind," I assured him. "Tell me what you wish of me, and I shall gladly do it."

He gave a satisfied nod and released his hold on me.

"As I told you before, yours is a simple task. All you must do is be silent and watch, and do not step forward unless I give you leave to do so." With a wry look about the room, he added, "As you can see, there are plenty of places where one might conceal oneself. But come to the fire for a few moments to warm yourself. We have a bit of time yet before I send you off into the shadows."

Gratefully, I followed him to where the glowing brazier hunkered close to the ground. I spread my hands as close as I could to the red coals, enjoying a bit of welcome heat here in this room that felt strangely chilled though it was a mild night. Gregorio settled down in the rushes on the opposite side of the open metal pan, but unlike me he did not stretch his hands to the warmth.

"Aren't you cold?" I curiously asked.

He shook his head. "Remember, I'm a soldier. I don't feel the cold or the heat."

Then, with a soft, ironic laugh, he went on. "And I don't feel hunger, or thirst, or even pain, most times. And fear . . . I never feel fear."

"But what about——"

Abruptly, I caught myself. *But what about love?* I had almost asked, before I realized I did not want an answer to that question. Instead, I lamely finished, "That is, surely you must feel something, sometime?"

He was quiet for a long moment, staring off into the shadows, so that I thought he would not reply. And then, his tone oddly flat, he said, "Emptiness. That is something I feel. And anger . . . I do feel anger."

Barely had he uttered those words than he gave a soft, harsh laugh and shook his head. He gracefully rose again, and his tone sounded rueful now as he muttered, "I don't know why it is, but you somehow manage to make me say things I do not intend to say."

Reaching a hand down toward me, he lightly pulled me up to stand before him again just as the clock in the tower rang three quarters past the hour. He glanced out in the direction of the courtyard below, and I wondered if he had watched me make my way across it not many moments before.

"You'd best find your hiding place now, lest impatience bring our contessa here early," he said in a soft voice and lightly brushed his lips against my temple.

It was only with the greatest effort that I was able to release his hand and turn away. Picking my way carefully in the darkness, I settled behind a short stack of heavy crates. I made sure I had a place to sit and prudently cleared a small space in the rushes so that that they would not crackle beneath my feet should I move about.

My heart heavy, I also made sure that the spot I chose was not so tightly packed that a path of sorts did not lead back to the door. I knew that I dared not be trapped in my small perch should things go badly when the Master confronted Gregorio. A gap the size of my hand between two of the boxes gave me a clear view of the open space between the brazier and the tower door. This way, I could be witness to all that happened . . . though not quite in the way that Gregorio had intended.

When I'd left him, he had settled against the wall to wait. I could see him faintly among the shadows, his stillness absolute like a panther awaiting his prey. A small stab of fear struck me as I thought of the Master confronting him. Though Leonardo would have the element of surprise, his only other weapon would be whatever knowledge he had about what it was that Gregorio planned. And, even then, Gregorio had but to deny it all and walk away.

But what if Gregorio was not content to leave? What then?

The tower clock abruptly began chiming again. Hands tightly clenched, I silently counted off each hour until the clock had struck eleven times. And then, as the final chime died away, I heard the soft squeal of hinges as the tower door swung inward.

I knew that Gregorio must have heard it, too, but his shadow did not shift in the darkness. Surely just as he had with me, he would make certain that whoever had entered was indeed the contessa before he made himself known.

But as a figure emerged from the doorway, I frowned in sudden confusion. In shape and height, it vaguely appeared to be a woman, but it did not move as a person; neither did its footsteps lightly crackle through the dry rushes, as mine had done. Instead, it seemed to drift lightly toward the center of the tower room, a pale wisp of a form barely visible in the shadows and hardly more substantial than a shadow, itself.

The flesh on my arms began to prickle, and I was suddenly grateful that I was well hidden behind my small fortress of crates. The figure was not that of Caterina, I was sure. Neither was it the Master disguised in women's robes . . . not unless he possessed the ability to drift with cloudlike silence above the ground. But who—or what—could it be?

Bellanca?

My eyes opened wide, and another shiver chilled me. Of course, I did not believe in spirits, I tried to remind myself, but to little avail. For surely what had joined us here in the tower room was not of the natural world.

Now I could see the almost imperceptible shift of the shadows where Gregorio had been standing. I realized he'd left his post, moving with much the same silence as the drifting figure, though now he was quite visible in the half-light. This phantom being was headed toward him, I saw in dread, and despite my shaking legs, I readied myself to rush to his aid should something happen.

Then I heard it, the faintest whisper of steel. Almost before I realized what that sound meant, moonlight flashed upon the blade of his sword as it sliced with lethal swiftness through the darkness. An instant later, the white figure before him had collapsed soundlessly at his feet.

"Very clever," Gregorio said, his tone sharpened to a knife's edge with barely held anger.

With the point of his sword, he caught up the long length of gauzy white fabric puddled on the floor before him. Now I realized in chagrin mingled with no little relief that this was all that the phantom had been. With a sound of contempt, he flung the flowing cloth back in the direction of the door.

"Who is this trickster who plays such childish games in the dark?" he demanded in the same icy tone. "Step forth from the shadows, so I may see you."

A soft footstep crackled somewhere nearby, and I stiffened. Now that I knew the true nature of the ghostly figure, I had no doubt as to who was responsible for its uncanny performance.

Leonardo would have made his way to the tower earlier in the day, I realized, entering unseen through the secret door he'd claimed to have found. Much as he'd hung the curtains around the lion's platform, he must have arranged a series of ropes and pulleys along the ceiling of the tower room. By this means, he could have pulled a few cords and caused the cloth to drift about as he wished.

But to what purpose?

Even as that question flashed through my mind, I heard the Master's voice mildly answer, "My apologies, Captain. I thought you might enjoy a bit of entertainment tonight, since you were unable to witness my earlier performance at the masquerade."

As he spoke, he uncovered the boxlike lamp he was carrying. Abruptly, its cleverly reflected series of flames banished the shadows around him, illuminating a portion of the tower room almost bright as day.

"You!" Gregorio spat the word as if it were a swallow of sour wine. "I should have guessed you were the one responsible for such foolery, Florentine."

He slowly circled to one side, so that with a few steps he had moved to the center of the room. Then, with the faintest of sneers, he added, "But what else should I expect of a man who has performed the greatest illusion of all . . . making Ludovico Sforza believe himself to be a man of culture simply because you are his court artist."

"And are you not a man of equal illusion?" Leonardo evenly countered. Setting his lamp upon a nearby barrel, he advanced on Gregorio with equal purpose. "With but a few words you can make a woman believe whatever you wish her to believe, no matter if she be a maidservant . . . or if she be a contessa."

"That is not your concern."

"Ah, but it is."

The Master halted before him, his expression one of stern purpose. Gregorio's dark gaze narrowed, and his sword abruptly flashed upward, its tip catching Leonardo just below the chin.

"Where is she, Florentine?" he demanded in a soft voice. "Where is Caterina?"

"She's not coming, Captain. Not tonight or any night after, for she now knows that you are not to be trusted. And running me through with your blade will not change that fact."

"Perhaps not," Gregorio agreed with a hint of a smile, raising the hilt of his sword higher, "but spilling your blood will give me great satisfaction, nonetheless."

20

Judgment

Experience is not at fault; it is only our judgment that is in error . . .

—Leonardo da Vinci, *Codex Atlanticus*

"No!" My cry was reflexive, as was my leap to my feet. Heedless now of the instructions either man had given me, I fled my hiding spot and rushed to where the pair stood, one at either end of a sword. Neither had expected to see me step forth, I knew, and I prayed that this distraction might be enough to stop any bloodshed.

Halting beside Gregorio, I caught his arm and gave him a beseeching look. "Please, do not do this, I beg you. I'm sure the Master . . . that is, Leonardo . . . only wishes to speak with you."

"You were told to keep yourself hidden," came his chill reply. Not taking his gaze from the other man, he dislodged my grip with the slightest movement of his arm, the swift gesture sending me stumbling back several paces. "And what is your concern with this artist?"

"I-I know him. He is a friend of my family."

I was not sure whether or not he believed me, but to my relief he lowered the blade sufficiently so that Leonardo could take a step back. Then he shot me a sidelong look, and I shivered a little at the way his features had so easily set into the ruthless mask of a man accustomed to unquestioned command. I knew that, had I been one of his men, I would have suffered mightily for my interference. "I suggest, my dear Delfina, that you keep in mind that I am the one—"

He broke off abruptly, and his gaze narrowed as he studied me a moment longer. Suddenly self-conscious in my boy's garb, I wondered why he stared at me with such concentration. Then he shook his head, and I saw the recognition in his eyes.

"That was you, the young page in the churchyard, hiding behind the gravestone."

His words held no uncertainty, so that I knew there was no use in trying to deny his claim. Tentatively, I nodded.

His cold gaze flicked over to Leonardo and then back to me again. "So tell me, Delfina, how long have you and the Florentine been plotting together? And who was it that you sought to bring down . . . me, or Caterina?"

"It was not a plot, Gregorio," I miserably protested. "We sought only to learn—"

"Silence, Dino!"

Leonardo's words cracked whiplike through the tower room, so that I abruptly held my peace. His anger was not for me, however, as he sternly met the other man's gaze.

"Whatever you wish to know, you shall ask it of me," he went on, seemingly unconcerned that Gregorio's blade still lingered but inches from his heart. "I am the one who our good duke has charged with unraveling the mystery behind these recent unpleasant deaths here at court."

He paused and nodded toward me. "This person you know as Delfina is in fact my young apprentice Dino. He has loyally served as my eyes and ears by playing a girl's role in the contessa's household this past fortnight. Whatever he has done, it has been at my command . . . and thus, he answers only to me."

A flicker of incredulity flashed over Gregorio's features, and he glanced back at me again. Wide-eyed, I stared back, wanting nothing more than to deny the Master's words and yet knowing that I must not. But would Gregorio accept Leonardo's claim? Would he believe what the Master thought was fact . . . that I was truly the boy Dino?

Or was the captain of the guard a far keener student of such matters than the Master ever was?

Then I saw the faintest of ironic smiles play about his lips, and I realized that Gregorio knew the truth. Even as one small part of me rejoiced, I hung my head and waited in dread for him to tell Leonardo just how thoroughly he had been deceived by me these past months.

To my surprise, however, he instead lowered his sword and laughingly shook his head.

"Very well, Florentine, you promised me entertainment, and you have provided it," he said, sounding genuinely amused as he sheathed his sword and purposefully walked toward me.

He caught me by the chin, forcing me to look up again. His touch was light, yet I found myself flinching beneath his burning gaze.

"And as for your apprentice," he softly added, "I congratulate him on a most convincing performance."

Abruptly, he released me and strode over to the nearest stack of crates. Pulling one down, he settled himself upon it, long legs stretched before him and arms crossed over his chest as he leaned against the remaining boxes. Then, flashing a lazy grin, he addressed Leonardo.

"The stage is now yours, Florentine. I await the next act."

"And I await answers, Captain," the Master sharply replied, his manner making evident he refused to pretend this was but a game. "To start with, I want to know the connection between the death of Bellanca and that of your mother, Lidia."

Gregorio gave him a considering look and then nodded.

"Very well," he replied with a shrug. "I have nothing to hide on that account. Bellanca and I had a business arrangement, much as I attempted with your so-called apprentice," he added with a cool glance at me.

"Unfortunately for her, Bellanca was more greedy than clever," he continued. "She was not content to follow my orders but thought to try her own hand at blackmail, unaware she could see but a very small part of a much larger picture. Her mistake was confiding in Lidia, not knowing that our contessa held a special place in my mother's heart."

Those last words were laced with a bitterness that surprised me, but before I could wonder over it, he went on. "Later, Lidia confessed to me what happened. I truly believe she meant only to frighten Bellanca. She used those cards of hers to make the girl believe that some evil would befall her if she carried through with her plans. Odd how, in the end, it was only Lidia that she had to fear."

He abruptly rose again and began pacing, seeming to stalk his thoughts through the shadows as he left the circle of light and moved toward the windows once more.

"She lured the girl up here on some pretense, hoping to settle the matter with talk. But when Bellanca refused to give up her plan, Lidia did what she had to do to safeguard Caterina. One moment they were struggling, and the next, our fair Bellanca had fallen from the tower."

He halted at one of the windows, perhaps the very one from which the young woman tumbled to her death, and gazed into the night. For myself, I could not help but shudder at this dispassionate account . . . shudder at the memory of discovering Bellanca's broken body.

Leonardo, however, merely nodded.

"That fits with my theory," he agreed. "But we both know there is far more to the matter of Lidia's death. The threat of Bellanca had been eliminated, but that did not mean you would not proceed with the same plan with another partner. I cannot believe that Lidia would choose to kill herself while you still held the secret you could use against Caterina."

"In that, you are correct, Florentine," Gregorio replied, turning from the window to face him again. "And that is why, before she took her own life, she first tried to murder me."

Even Leonardo appeared momentarily stunned at those last words, while I gasped outright. As for Gregorio, he gave a soft, humorless laugh.

"Ah, yes, what an unnatural mother, to slay her own son. Of course, I was suspecting such an attempt, though I admit I was a bit disappointed in the crude manner she chose. She brought it to me with her own hand, claiming it was a peace offering for the bitter words that had passed between us."

A hint of an ironic smile twisted his lips. "Poisoned wine . . . hardly an original tactic, would you not say?"

"That would explain the dogs," the Master thoughtfully answered. "You suspected the wine she gave you was tainted and fed it to them."

Gregorio shrugged. "I will admit that I wasn't really convinced she could do it, up until the moment I saw the one dog lying dead at my feet and the other howling in pain."

"The same dog that later attacked Dino and Pio," the Master interjected, earning another nod from the captain.

"I did not anticipate such a result, else I would have dispatched the second dog on the spot." He glanced at me then, his expression unreadable in the flickering light. "It was fortunate that I happened to be near the stables attending my horse when it happened. Otherwise, I fear the great painter might have found himself missing a clever young apprentice."

Leonardo eyed him sharply but merely said, "So Lidia must have waited until enough time would have passed for you to drink the wine, and then swallowed her own dose to join you in death."

Silence fell for a moment between them, and despite

myself I could not help feeling an ache in my heart for what he had endured. I knew too well my own small hurt that my mother seemed to care less for me than my brothers. Soldier or not, how painful it must have been for him to realize that his mother loved her noble mistress far better than her own son . . . and that she would kill him rather than see the girl come to any harm.

Then Gregorio gave his curly head a slight shake, like a sleeper awakening from an unwelcome dream. Briskly, he rubbed his hands together as if brushing away that dream's remnants, and then focused on Leonardo again.

"Very well, Florentine, I believe you now have the answers you sought," he said as he started toward the Master again. "And because I am a reasonable man, I am willing to let you and your apprentice walk out of here with no blood spilled. All I want is your word that you will not interfere with my business a second time . . . for, another night, I might be far less reasonable."

"That is a generous offer, Captain," Leonardo replied in a calm voice as Gregorio halted several feet from him, waiting. "Another night, I might have been willing to accept it. But there remains the matter of the secret you hold over Caterina. I cannot leave here with it left untold."

I saw it in Gregorio's obsidian eyes, then . . . the same look of rage I had seen him turn upon the priest that day in the cathedral. But this time, he did not bother to check that emotion, and I feared for the Master's life in a way that I never had before.

"I gave you your chance, Florentine," he said in a tone of soft menace. "You have ceased now to be amusing, so I am going to put an end to this. Delfina"—he flicked an emotionless look in my direction—"when we are done, I shall give you a final chance to decide whose side you wish to take. But do not attempt to flee this tower while you think me distracted with your master. You will recall what I told you that day at the stables."

I bit my lip and nodded. I had little doubt that, should I try to run for help, the last thing I would know would be the sharp pain of his knife between my shoulder blades. Even before I reached the door, I would be as dead as the crazed stable dog.

As he spoke, Gregorio had pulled on the black leather gauntlets he'd had tucked in his belt. Now he began to circle the Master, hand on the hilt of his sword though he'd not yet drawn it. Leonardo was unarmed, I knew . . . always was, preferring to rely upon his physical strength rather than a sword or knife.

Far too late, I thought of the stave that was part of my costume, which I realized I'd left behind in the great hall. But, even if I'd had it upon me, the thin club would prove a puny weapon against a blade.

Leonardo was not waiting quietly for him, however. With the same swordsman's grace with which Gregorio stalked him, he was staying carefully out of reach. His tone still preternaturally calm, he said, "You may kill me, but first know that I have discovered your secret. I had hoped to hear it from your own lips, but it seems it must come from mine."

"Speak all the secrets you wish," Gregorio retorted. "There is no one else save your apprentice to hear them."

"You are wrong, Gregorio," came a clear, light voice from within the shadows near the door. "I shall hear them, as well."

At that unexpected reply, he halted and swung about. A flicker of surprise momentarily dimmed the rage in his eyes, and he frowned. "Caterina?"

I had recognized the voice, as well. The young contessa, still in her glorious white and gold gown, though having abandoned her crown, stepped out of the darkness and into the inner circle of light. Her features were set in lines of disbelieving misery, so that I knew she must have heard all that had been said thus far.

And surely this had been the reason for Leonardo's trick

with the ghostly image that was but a bit of cloth, I now realized. While we'd been distracted by the seemingly otherworldly sight, not only had he but also the contessa slipped into the tower room. But why had he lied to me and claimed she would be safely away this night?

He caught my accusing look and gently shook his head. "I knew the contessa would not believe the truth from me, and so I brought her to the tower to hear it from the captain, himself." To Caterina, he softly said, "Contessa, you should have stayed hidden as I asked."

"I will not stay hidden and listen to cruel accusations," she told him with a proud lift of her chin, though I could see her lips quivering. Turning to the captain, she said more softly, "Gregorio, I do not understand. Please tell me what this is about. What secret do you hide from me, save the fact that you seemingly care naught for me, after all?"

Those last words trembled on a sob, but her proud gaze never left his. By now, his rage had faded, that expression replaced now by contempt as he returned his attention to Leonardo. "Go ahead, Florentine," he said with a shrug. "Tell her, if you know . . . if you dare."

At those words of challenge, I saw a look of sorrow cross the Master's face, and I knew he regretted that things had come to this pass.

"There is much to the story, Contessa," he grimly began, "but I shall make it brief so as not to prolong your pain. You now know that your servant Lidia was the captain's mother. But, long before that, you knew from her the story of your earliest days, when she was your nurse. She would have told you how your mother died soon after you were born, and that your good father could spare little thought for you, so caught up was he in his loss."

Caterina gave an uncertain nod. "That is what Lidia always told me."

"And she must have told you, as well, that she'd had a daughter of her own born not long before you, but who died quite tragically when she was but a few weeks old."

Again, Caterina nodded, though now impatience had begun to supplant her dismay. "Yes, Signor Leonardo, all of this is familiar to me. Pray tell me something I do not know."

"What you do not know, Contessa, is that the babe who died was not Lidia's daughter. Instead, it was the Conte di Sasina's child who tragically did not awaken from sleep one morning."

His sad gaze flicked from Caterina to me, while both of us stared back at him, wide-eyed. Gregorio, meanwhile, seemed quite untouched by the Master's words, though I sensed a taut air about him that belied his apparent indifference.

"Of course, Lidia would have been frantic when she saw the conte's daughter dead in her crib," Leonardo went on. "Not only would she have mourned the girl, but she would have feared for herself. Who else would the already grieving father blame but the wet nurse, when no other cause for the child's death would have been apparent?"

He paused and took a deep breath. Then, with a sigh, he finished, "And so Lidia conceived a daring plan born of her own terror. With the rest of the household in mourning for the late contessa, Lidia was the only one to have any contact with the motherless child . . . and, for the moment, the only one to know of her death. That was why she knew she could carry out her plan, with no one the wiser."

Caterina's pinched features were almost as white as her gown, her eyes wide as cruel truth began to shatter all she'd ever known. I knew as well as Caterina what this meant; still, I did not allow myself to believe it until he turned his grim gaze on Gregorio.

"No one, not even the child's own father, ever guessed that Lidia had substituted her healthy daughter for the dead child. No one ever questioned her claim that it was her own babe who had so cruelly died. And, as the years passed, no one else besides Lidia ever knew that the girl called Caterina di Sasina was in truth the wet nurse's daughter."

"No one else, that is, save for her brother."

The silence that followed his words was such that I could

hear the faint crackle of the lantern flames, could hear the soft rustle of rushes as a whisper of breeze drifted through the tower room. Caterina stood as motionless as one of the Master's clay models, so still that she seemed not to breathe. Then, very slowly, she turned to face Gregorio.

"It can't be true," she said in a flat voice that was little more than a whisper. "There is no proof of what he says. Tell me that he is lying, Gregorio."

He held her stark gaze for a moment, but when he spoke, his words were for Leonardo. "How could you know?" he softly demanded, his tone as emotionless as Caterina's.

The Master shook his head.

"I knew that something darker lay beneath the ties that bound the three of you," he explained, "but it was not until I began painting Caterina that it came to me. You see, I have a habit of sketching faces that interest me. It was only a few days ago that, quite by accident, I put your features to paper alongside one of the drawings I had made of the contessa. I was immediately struck by the similarities between your features, a similarity too pronounced for mere coincidence. From there, it was but a matter of piecing together the rest of the puzzle."

To me, he added, "And I had the good fortune to return a bit of linen to a washerwoman who had known Lidia from those days and had always wondered at her seeming lack of grief over her own child's death. She also knew of Lidia's odd obsession with the young contessa and how she contrived to see the child on occasion despite being dismissed from the conte's household."

I barely heard this last, staring as I was from Gregorio to Caterina and seeing now the similarities of which the Master spoke. I remembered in dismay how, the first time I had seen the pair together, I had thought them oddly well suited. But now I realized it was the blood tie between them that I had unknowingly recognized.

Caterina, meanwhile, was shaking her head in frenzied

protest. "You lie, Leonardo!" she sobbed in mingled pain and anger. "You cannot make me believe so vile a thing. Gregorio is not my brother."

The sound of a cold laugh cut short her cries. Gregorio had broken from the stillness that held him and was regarding her with ironic amusement. "Ah, Caterina, you've always had a gift for self-delusion. So let me disabuse you of your fantasies, once and for all. There is a very simple way to prove what the Florentine says."

He slowly circled around her, much as he'd stalked the Master. "You have a mark upon you," he said, "one that is quite unusual. At first glance, one might dismiss it as a small discoloration of the skin, but on closer look it has a distinctive shape."

He paused behind her and laid his hands upon her shoulders, the possessive gesture causing her to shudder. Leaning closer to her, he spoke so softly that I could barely hear him.

"The mark is in the shape of a sun, just about the size of a florin." He slid one hand down the silky white fabric of her gown, pausing at the small of her back. "And it is right there, is it not?"

She jerked from his grasp as if burned and whirled to face him. "You could have learned of my mark from Lidia, from any of my servants," she cried. "It has always been there . . . it signifies nothing."

"Indeed?" was his ironic reply. "And I suppose that this signifies nothing, as well?"

With those words, he swiftly unlaced the black leather jerkin he wore so that it hung open. I knew what must happen next; even so, I could not help but gasp when, with both hands, he grasped the collar of the black shirt he wore beneath and swiftly rent it, revealing his bare chest.

Even in the flickering light, we could see the dark blemish the size of a coin upon his golden skin, just above his heart. It was the same mark I'd seen close up the day before as he stood before me, half-dressed.

Just as I'd been tempted to do, Caterina reached trembling fingers to touch the small black image in the shape of a sun.

"It-it is the same," she whispered. Then, as if that sun had seared her flesh, she jerked back her hand and raised her gaze to meet Gregorio's.

21

The World

The senses are of the earth, the reason stands apart from them in contemplation.

—Leonardo da Vinci, *Codex Trivulziano*

"You knew," Caterina softly exclaimed, her tone one of mingled despair and disbelief. "You knew all along that I was your true sister, and yet you sought to seduce me . . . to lie with me. How could you?"

Eyes wide, she reached into her bodice and pulled forth four red bits of pasteboard that I immediately recognized as tarocchi cards. I did not need to see their faces to know which ones they must be. She stared at them in silence for a moment and then slowly shook her head.

"These same cards have been predicting a most evil betrayal by a man I trusted. I thought all along that they meant Ludovico, but now I know that it is you who has stabbed me to the heart!"

With a cry of disgust, she flung the cards at her brother and whirled about, rushing toward the tower's broad windows. For a single frantic moment, I thought she might fling herself from one of them. The Master must have feared the same, for a look of alarm crossed his face as he rushed after her.

But as he drew near, she abruptly halted and crumpled to her knees in a small cloud of white silk, face buried in her hands to muffle her anguished sobs. His face reflecting similar sorrow, Leonardo knelt beside her and wrapped his arms about her. At first, she made as if to pull away, perhaps thinking it was her brother who cradled her. Then, realizing it was Leonardo and not Gregorio, she allowed his embrace, though her doleful sobs continued unabated.

Dashing a tear from my own eye, I dared to look upon Gregorio again. His flat gaze fixed on his sister, he appeared quite untouched by her show of pain.

"Go ahead, Caterina, weep," he told her. "But I can assure you that I have shed far many more tears than you ever will over all that happened."

Then his words took on a softer tone as he said, "I was there when Lidia . . . when our mother . . . put that mark upon you. It was the day after she had buried the child everyone believed to have been hers. She took a needle and some lampblack, and drew that small sun upon your back."

He paused, and something of a rueful smile played upon his lips. "You never once cried, though it took a long while for her to finish. When she put the same mark on me, I dared not shed a tear because you had not, no matter that it hurt mightily with every stab."

Abruptly, his expression hardened again, as if he were once more caught up in that day.

"And as she drew upon my flesh, she made me swear I would never tell what had happened. I must always act as if it were my sister buried in the churchyard. I was only seven years old, and I didn't understand the reasons why. All I knew was that I loved you with that unblemished love that only a child can give . . . and yet she took you away from me."

He fleetingly put his own fingers to the sun on his chest, and I wondered with an unexpected pang how often he'd done so over the years. But when I heard no softness in his next words, I knew the gesture held something other than tender sentiment.

"When she was finished making that mark upon me," he went on, "she said that this way we would always know each other, no matter how many years passed. But, of course, I could never see you again, save at a distance when the conte brought you out for some feast day or another. Eventually, enough time went by that I should have forgotten I ever had a sister, at all. But every time I pulled off my tunic and glanced down to see that mark of the sun upon my chest, I had no choice but to think of you."

As he spoke, Caterina's sobs had begun to subside. Now, still wrapped in the Master's arms, she raised a tearful face to her brother.

"You never could have loved me," she cried in soft despair, "else how could you do what you've done to me?"

His short laugh in response held a bitter note. "Oh, I did love you . . . then."

As she stared at him uncertainly, he explained, "You see, my dear Caterina, your true father was a mercenary. He came home every few years, most times just long enough to leave Lidia big with another child, before going off to fight again. But he never came back after you were born. Later on, we learned he'd been killed in some battle or another, his body but one of many left behind on an unknown field."

He shrugged, but despite his air of nonchalance I could see something in his face of the long-ago hurt of a small boy.

"The few florins he'd sent our way over the years ceased, of course. Even worse, by then Lidia had been sent away from the conte's household."

An ironic smile momentarily twisted his lips. "It seems that some of the other servants had been frightened by her habit of divining the future using playing cards. No one else would take her in for many months after that, and I was still too young to earn more than a few soldi on occasion. Most nights, I went to bed hungry . . . but it was not the kind of hunger that people like you know."

Any trace of humor had faded from his face and his voice as he regarded her.

"My hunger was not the sort that came from rising too late in the morning, so that I had to wait for the midday meal to break my fast. It came from living day to day on nothing more than a crust of bread and a crumb of cheese. Once in a while, we would find a shriveled vegetable to boil in a pot and call it a fine soup. I've never forgotten that feeling of hunger . . . that unceasing pain in my belly, like some living thing shredding me from the inside out with its teeth and claws."

With a sound of contempt, he abruptly spun about, as if he could bear to look upon her no more. "And all the while, you were living in the conte's castle, growing plump and satisfied from the choice delicacies that filled his table. That's all I thought of, those nights that I lay crying in hunger . . . and that is when I first started to hate you."

While Gregorio spoke, Leonardo was helping Caterina to her feet. She gave him a grateful look but pulled away to stand proudly on her own. Her tears dried now, her tone held a similar note of contempt as Gregorio's when she addressed him.

"How can you blame me for that? And surely you cannot think that you were the only one to suffer from our mother's choice. The conte had no love for me. From the first day that I can remember, he blamed me for my mother's"—she paused and bit her lip, then corrected herself—"for the contessa's death. I should have preferred to know a true mother and brother who loved me, no matter that we were hungry, to the coldness of the conte's castle."

He shook his head as he turned back again to meet her gaze. Once again, his soft, harsh laugh held no humor.

"You say that now, my dear Caterina, but I daresay that after a time you would gladly have traded both mother and brother for a full belly. I know that I would have done so, and gladly. In fact, I am quite certain I would have joined my so-called sister in the churchyard within a few months of her death, had I not found a small blade that some unlucky traveler had lost upon the road.

"I practiced with that knife for hours each day, until finally I had the skill to bring down any small bird or beast that came within my sight. After that, we had food . . . not much, but enough to put a bit of flesh upon my bones. But I could never stop thinking about you in your fine castle, not even when I was finally old enough to join Il Moro's army and journey far from here. For I vowed that one day I would return to take what was yours . . . and that you would know the reason why."

He abruptly fell silent and briefly lowered his head, scrubbing his hand over his face as if to banish the emotions that his words had allowed to take rein. Hardly daring now to breathe, I glanced at the Master, still standing protectively at Caterina's side. His features set in stern lines, he quietly addressed her.

"I fear your brother's plan was quite simple. He knew that you had the conte's title and lands and the wealth that went with it. And he also knew that, sooner or later, the duke would marry you off to an ally . . . or, in this case, to an enemy."

His frown deepened. "Once you had willingly come to his bed, he had only to prove to you the truth of your relationship. He would have guessed—and rightly so, I am certain—that you would have paid him any amount to keep silent lest the truth reach Il Moro's ears before your marriage day."

"Florentine, you are far cleverer than I thought."

Gregorio's harsh words cut the air more sharply than his sword, which I saw in sudden fear he had drawn from its scabbard. The momentary weakness I had seen in him was gone, his purpose now as unyielding as his blade.

With a telling look at Leonardo, he added, "I wonder which would have distressed the great Ludovico more, knowing that his lovely young cousin had lain with her brother, or that she was not truly of noble blood. But I suppose it no longer matters."

Holding the sword low, he gave a few swift slashes as if testing its worthiness and smiled tightly in satisfaction.

"And now, unfortunately, your cleverness will cost you your life," he went on. "You've seen to it that too many people now know the secret that should have properly stayed between my sister and me. But, just so there are fewer questions, we shall have a fair fight before I run you through."

"You know that I have no weapon, Captain," Leonardo calmly replied, lifting his arms slightly to demonstrate that truth.

Gregorio quirked a brow. "So I see. But it is fortunate for you that my sister thought to come to our tryst armed." With a nod at her, he said, "Give the Florentine your sword."

"No!"

Eyes wide but chin stubborn, she shook her head. "I will not allow you to do this, Gregorio. Kill me, if you wish, but you may not harm Leonardo or Delfina."

He'd not expected her refusal, I knew. The look he turned upon her was the same one he'd earlier turned on Leonardo . . . a look of godless rage that should have struck her down where she stood. And yet his words, though they cracked like a whip through the tower room, were oddly calm.

"Give him the sword, Caterina, or by all that is holy I shall butcher him where he stands and then make you bathe in his blood."

She knew as well as I that this was no idle threat; thus, she made no further protest. Silent tears slipping down her cheeks, she untied the scabbard from her belt and silently handed it to the Master.

He gave her a small smile of reassurance and then stepped toward the center of the room, where Gregorio waited. The younger man stood motionless, with only the slight twitching of his sword blade—like the reflexive movement of a great cat's tail as it waited to pounce—betraying his impatience.

Swiftly crossing herself as if asking absolution for her part in this duel, Caterina rushed to where I stood and grasped my chilled hand in hers. We exchanged frantic glances, both of us knowing the futility of trying to flee the room. Even should one of us escape the winged death that was Gregorio's knife, one man or the other likely would be dead before either of us could return with help. We had no choice now but to helplessly watch the battle that was about to unfold.

Leonardo, meanwhile, had shrugged off his cloak and plucked off his turbaned hat, tossing both aside. Now, awkwardly, he pulled the sword from its jeweled scabbard and examined the blade as if he'd never seen such a weapon before. Then, sounding remarkably unruffled under the circumstances, he addressed the other man.

"What of my apprentice, Captain? Given the likelihood that you will best me in this contest, I would have your word that Dino will be allowed to walk free when I am dead."

For the first time in some minutes, Gregorio spared me a look. I stared back, unable to forget the feelings I'd had for him these past days, knowing I could never forgive him should Leonardo come to harm. But from his implacable gaze, I feared I would be next to feel his steel should Gregorio defeat Leonardo.

The possibility made my stomach clench in fear; still, I refused to look away. And the thought flashed through my mind that, should he show mercy and spare me the blade, I would not rest until I one day avenged the Master.

He must have read something of my emotions in my face, for a hint of approval flickered in his eyes. "I've not yet decided what I shall do about my sister and your apprentice," he replied. "But if it eases you, you have my word that I will give your request some thought."

Slowly, he began to circle Leonardo, his black clothing making him look part of the shadows. "And now, we shall see if you are as skilled with a blade as you are with a brush," Gregorio softly said, sword at the ready. "Take your guard, for the fight commences."

So swift was his first attack that Leonardo had barely time to lift his weapon before Gregorio's blade lashed like a steel serpent toward him.

I gasped. A man with normal reflexes would have been impaled on that first strike, but Leonardo was no normal man. Moving with the swift grace of his namesake lion, he twisted out of the way in time to deflect Gregorio's blade with his own.

An instant later the two stood apart again, and Gregorio gave him a mocking salute. "Very good, Florentine. I see you have some small skill, after all. That will make running my sword through you all the more enjoyable."

His next attack was just as swift, but this time Leonardo was ready for him. Though still on the defensive, he avoided each thrust with a quick parry, the clang of steel upon steel ringing through the room.

Again they parted, the reeds beneath their feet scattered now so that the stone floor in the center of the room lay bare. Any hint of amusement had left Gregorio's face, and his expression was now the coldly implacable look of a man prepared to dispatch his enemy with no further delay. The swift bursts of motion had not taxed him at all, it seemed, but I saw in concern that Leonardo appeared to be breathing more heavily now.

The fear that I had managed for a few moments to keep at bay gripped me even more tightly now. *How can Leonardo hope to best a professional soldier?* I wildly wondered, recalling how Gregorio's men practiced their skills for hours at a time upon the quadrangle's parade grounds. I could only pray that the fact that the Master fought with his left hand might give him some small advantage, in that Gregorio must surely modify his technique in response.

Again, it was Gregorio who struck first, the fury of his attack frightening to behold. This time Leonardo's parries were slower, less graceful, though he valiantly met every thrust . . . that was, until the last one.

I cried out as Gregorio's blade abruptly found its target, slicing through the heavy fabric of the Master's tunic and into his sword arm.

Save for the swift flash of pain that washed over his face,

Leonardo gave no sign that he'd been hurt. But I could see the look of cool triumph on Gregorio's face and knew in dread that the next onslaught would be meant to end the match. They stood several sword lengths apart, Gregorio with his back to the windows and the Master against the wall of barrels and crates. If Leonardo could not swiftly break free of the blockade that was behind him, he would surely be unable to escape the other man's sword!

This time, Leonardo did not wait for Gregorio to make the first move. Instead, with a burst of speed far greater than any he'd yet displayed, he launched his own swift attack that took him away from the wooden barrier. But Gregorio seemingly had expected such a ploy, for already he was countering with his own blade. Effectively blocking Leonardo's path, he forced him back against the crates again and aimed a killing thrust.

How Leonardo escaped the point of that sword, I do not know, for I had hidden my face in my hands. An instant later I heard a harsh oath, followed by the crash of wood upon stone, and I looked up again in disbelief. Boxes and barrels lay scattered upon the floor, the scattering of dry rushes eagerly soaking up oil that slowly spilled from one small cask.

The Master had escaped him!

Yet even as I gave a gasp of relief, I saw that he was rapidly succumbing to his injury. The sleeve of his green tunic was soaked with blood from shoulder to wrist, and he stumbled a bit as he warily circled his opponent. He'd not yet managed to land a blow upon the other man; even so, his face reflected unwavering purpose.

As for Gregorio, never had he looked more like a fallen angel, dressed all in black with his shirt torn open. His earlier expression of triumph was gone, however, replaced by a hotter anger now that he'd been momentarily bested by his less skilled rival. He, too, had begun to breathe a bit heavily, and I held out a faint hope that his anger along with his slowing pace might cause him to make an error in judgment.

But anger seemingly served only to narrow his purpose. A terrible stillness settled over his dark features, and I knew this must be how he looked just before the moment of battle, before hell on earth erupted and the ground ran red with blood. Leonardo, meanwhile, had switched his sword to his right hand, and his stillness now matched Gregorio's.

Then, like a panther springing, Gregorio was upon him again, and I knew with dread certainty the Master could not defend against this onslaught. This time, however, though I willed my eyes to close, I could not seem to look away as Gregorio drove him back toward the center of the room, toward the spill of wooden boxes.

And then, a slash from Gregorio's sword across his thigh dropped Leonardo to the ground.

In the moment of silence that followed, I could hear the sound of both men's rasping breath and the gasping little cries of Caterina beside me. As Gregorio stood over Leonardo, his sword poised to pierce the other man's heart, the clock tower began to toll midnight.

Numbly, I counted each strike. Back in the great hall, the duke's exuberant guests now would be busy unmasking, their tipsy laughter ringing out into the night.

Here in the tower, the trump of Death would soon be doing his own gleeful dance as blood spilled upon the tower room's cold stone floor.

I could not see either man's face; Gregorio stood with his back to me now, and his dark form blocked the Master from my view. At least I would be spared seeing his final moments of suffering, I thought as I waited with fatalistic calm for it to be over with.

"Gregorio, no!"

Pulling from my grasp, Caterina rushed toward her brother like a small fury set upon an unsuspecting world. What she intended to do, I could not guess . . . wrest the sword from him, or perhaps take the blade into her own breast. But before she could reach him, he switched the sword to his other hand and, barely sparing her a glance, caught her with his free arm. He held her in this parody of an embrace for an instant before carelessly flinging her away from him again.

Neither man saw what happened next, as Leonardo was crouched upon the floor, and Gregorio was once more poised to strike his final blow. But the horror of those next few moments would stay always in my mind. Much later, when I could think more clearly about that night, I would wonder what might have happened if I had been the first to react . . . if events would have turned out far differently.

In my heart, however, I would always know that they would not have changed, that perhaps this tragic end had been destined from the very start.

As Caterina tumbled backward, she fell against the same barrel upon which the Master had set his clever reflecting lantern. The light teetered for an instant upon the barrel's edge. Before I could cry out a warning, it had tumbled to the stone floor, landing softly amid the same rushes that had lapped up the spilled lamp oil from the broken cask.

The lantern's small flames abruptly roared to life. Like ravening beasts, they surrounded Caterina and licked at the hem of her gown as she struggled to regain her feet. For a moment, she did not realize what had happened; then, as the first searing flames touched her flesh, she started to scream.

The high-pitched keen, like the cry of a wounded small animal, made my blood turn to ice and abruptly stilled Gregorio's hand.

He whipped about to see his sister enveloped in flames. Her scream was now a single ceaseless cry of agony as she spun like an unholy parody of the Master's glorious metal sun toward the tower's windows in an attempt to escape the hellish fire.

And that fire burned with a fury I could not believe, blinding in its brilliance, as if Lucifer himself had wrapped the young woman in his brimstone embrace. By now, the flames had raced up her gown and were consuming her glorious raven braids. The delicate gold sleeves Luigi had so carefully stitched had already burned away, revealing the blackened flesh of her bared arms.

"Caterina!"

The single hoarse cry rang with fear and hopelessness and despair. His sword clattering unheeded from his hand, Gregorio rushed toward her. In the space of a few moments, her screams had faded to anguished moans, and I bit back my own cries as I realized in horror that, for her, it was too late.

"Caterina," he shouted again as, heedless of the flames, he caught her in his embrace.

They spun about once, like dancers wrapped in hell's fury, and I caught a final glimpse of Gregorio's face. His gaze locked with mine for less than a heartbeat, just long enough for me to see the sorrow and regret and longing in his eyes. An instant later, brother and sister were tumbling through the tower's window and into the night.

Strangely, the screams never ceased, though one small portion of my mind realized that the cries of horror were mine now, and not Caterina's. I realized, as well, that the remaining flames had begun to spread, feeding upon the dried wood of the crates and racing along the carpet of rushes that covered most of the stone floor. Smoke began to fill the room in earnest, so that with every anguished cry I choked upon its acrid tendrils.

Yet I was fixed where I stood, staring in disbelief at the empty space where Gregorio and Caterina had been but an instant before. *Surely this has not happened,* the small voice in my head cried out. Maybe if I closed my eyes, I would wake up in my bed in the workshop surrounded by the other apprentices, both Caterina and Gregorio alive and perhaps never destined to meet in this way, after all.

Then a rough hand grasped my shoulder and shook me, so that I was forced to open my eyes before I was quite ready.

"Dino!" the Master was shouting. "Cease your lamentations and come with me. We must flee before the smoke overtakes us, or we will suffer Caterina's same fate."

Those last words, more than anything, spurred me back

to awareness. "Yes," I agreed and then started coughing as smoke filled my lungs.

"Quickly, Dino, drop to the floor," he shouted, his words almost drowned now by the crackling fire as he fell to his knees and pulled me down beside him. "The smoke is less dense here, and we will be able to breathe a bit longer."

"But surely we are trapped," I managed to gasp in fear, seeing now that the fire blocked our way to the tower door. "We cannot walk through the flames!"

"We need not risk the fire. Stay low and follow me," he sternly ordered. "The hidden door that will be our way out is but a few feet from us."

We made our escape, not through some secret opening in the wall, but instead by means of a small trapdoor in the floor. Barely large enough to accommodate a man the Master's size, it opened down onto what appeared to be a narrow railed platform.

"Take the greatest care," he said, gripping my arm a moment to make certain I understood his words before he lowered me through that opening in the floor. "The platform leads a few steps to the wall. There, you will find a series of iron rungs set into the stone. You must make your way down them, until you reach the bottom of the tower. It is a dangerous descent—one misstep, and you will surely plunge to your death—but it is our only chance."

"I can do it," I stoutly assured him; then, recalling his injuries, I stared at him in fear. "But what about you, Master? You are hurt, and—"

"I shall manage," he said with a brisk nod, though I could see that his skin beneath a faint layer of soot was pinched and white. "Now, quickly, my boy . . . we must close the door after us to keep the smoke out as long as possible."

How long the descent took, I do not know. All I recall is hot and dizzying darkness relieved only by an occasional bit of light where a chink between stones allowed in the moonlight beyond. Above me, I could hear the rhythmic metallic clang of boots upon iron as the Master made his own way down. His labored breathing was punctuated by an occasional muffled grunt of pain, so that I feared the exertion might be too much for him in his wounded state; still, as he'd said, we had no choice but to make our escape this way.

Finally, my foot touched stone. With a sigh of relief, I let go of the last rung and stepped aside as I waited for Leonardo to join me. Across from me, I could make out a faint rectangular outline of light that must be the hidden door. In my disoriented state I could not guess if it led out to the courtyard or somewhere inside the fortifications.

A moment later, the shadowy figure of the Master had joined me, his own reflexive sigh of relief at safely reaching the bottom sounding even more heartfelt than mine. He swayed a little, and I caught his uninjured arm to steady him.

"Thank you, my boy," he murmured. "Now, come, we must be out of here."

Leaning his hand upon my shoulder as much to support himself as to guide me, he led us to the same faint rectangle of illumination that I'd spotted. He paused there, and I could see that he was running his hand down the rough bricks.

"It must be here somewhere," he muttered just before I heard the distinctive click of a latch giving way. The section of stone slid outward like a door, opening into the tall covered alcove at the tower's foot. Beyond was the grassy lawn of the quadrangle, from which frantic cries of alarm and shouts from the soldiers were already sounding as the fire in the tower above raged on.

I should have been prepared for the sight that met me as we stepped from the alcove, yet I was not. Just beyond us in the tower's fearsome shadow sprawled two motionless figures. A few tiny flames still gently danced upon what remained of Caterina's glorious gown, though mercifully she was long past knowing any pain. Gregorio lay a few feet from her, facedown as if he were but sleeping upon the soft grass. One arm was stretched toward his sister in a final gesture of yearning so tender that the sight of it abruptly broke what was left of my heart.

With a cry of anguish, I fell to my knees and buried my face in my hands. I could hear the voices around me now, hear the Master's halting explanation of a terrible accident. One voice, oddly familiar in its rough accent, simply cried out, "God, why?"

Then I felt the Master's arms as he gently pulled me to my feet. His voice full of sadness, I heard him say, "This is no sight for a boy. Please, take him to the tailor Luigi so he may look upon this horror no more."

I was aware of strong arms lifting me as if I were no heavier than a child, and then carrying me off into the night. Listlessly, I opened my eyes for a moment to see which poor soul the Master had commandeered for this thankless task. Through my tears I saw above me a familiar coarse face and a sweeping blond mustache. No genial leer twisted the mercenary's face this time. Instead, his features were set in an attitude of stony misery unexpected for a man who dealt in battle and death.

I closed my eyes again, only to feel a single small drop that was not my own tear splash down upon my cheek. *So I am not the only one who grieves him,* I thought with a sigh and gave myself up to darkness for a time.

I roused myself again when I heard the sharp pounding of a fist upon wood, and the harsh cry, "Tailor, open your door."

Blearily, I opened my eyes to see that we stood upon Luigi's step. Through the window of his workshop, I could see a small lamp begin to glow. The door opened a moment later, and the sputtering tailor, dressed only in his long shirt, stuck his head out.

"Who is breaking the peace?" he demanded, only to stop short, mouth agape, as he recognized me beneath the layer of soot. "Wh-what has happened?" he weakly asked as the soldier unceremoniously set me onto the ground again.

The man shook his head, his mustaches quivering, though

his words were brusque. "A very bad thing, it happen at the castle. The Master Leonardo, he tell me to bring you this boy."

He spun about on his heel and marched off into the night, leaving me to stare mutely at the tailor. His expression one of alarm, he grasped me by the arm and pulled me into his shop before shutting the door behind us.

"Delfina, what has happened this night?"

His voice was soft, and his small dark eyes were filled with concern as he took in my disheveled appearance and the unmistakable acrid stench that clung to me.

I stared back at him a long moment, searching for my voice. Finally, the words thick with smoke and tears, I cried, "Oh, Luigi, he is dead!" and flung myself into the tailor's arms.

EPILOGUE

The Fool

Folly is the buckler of shame . . .

—Leonardo da Vinci, *Codex Trivulziano*

I did not attend Caterina's funeral, though later Luigi told me that it had been a magnificent spectacle. Her ravaged body carefully wrapped in the finest of linens and covered in blooms and greenery, she was laid in a grand crypt alongside the Conte di Sasina and the rest of his family. Whether she might have preferred to lie in a simple grave alongside her true mother, I could not guess. But because she had lived her life as a conte's daughter, she would be buried as a contessa and not the child of a wet nurse.

Her death, though tragic, did not change Il Moro's plans. He had other wards and cousins from which to choose a bride to seal the alliance with the Duke of Pontalba. As for that man, he had been little concerned by the fact that one would-be wife had been unceremoniously replaced with another. He still received the lands and dowry originally promised him and was satisfied with his bargain.

I never knew what became of Gregorio afterward . . . if he was buried among the court's fallen soldiers or if he was put alongside Lidia and the infant girl who would have been the true contessa had she grown to womanhood. Indeed, I did not want to know where his grave lay.

If I did, I feared I might make my way there and lie upon it until Death claimed me, as well.

For I had realized in that last instant as I gazed into his anguished eyes that I had truly loved him, no matter what he had done, no matter what he had intended to do. Later that terrible night, I had confessed all to Luigi, telling him between sobs of the secret meetings between me and Gregorio, and his offer—truly meant or not—to make me his woman.

The usually acerbic tailor had listened with unexpected sympathy to my painful admission. I did not know if he indulged me because he somehow understood the emotions of which I spoke. Perhaps he'd given me his ear simply out of kindness, aware there was no other person to whom I could tell such things.

"Why did Gregorio do it?" I'd demanded of Luigi through my sobs once I had related all leading up to this night's tragic events. "Surely Caterina's death was sacrifice enough. He didn't have to die with her."

"Perhaps he did," the tailor had muttered. "In cutting short her final agony that way, perhaps he bought himself a bit of redemption for all that had happened before."

But rather than bring me comfort, his words had only made me weep with greater passion. Finally, when I'd been too exhausted to shed another tear, he had made me up a pallet on which to sleep and assured me I could remain with him as long as I wished.

It was only as I lay alone in the dark, with daylight but scant hours away, that I recalled I'd not told him of Leonardo's wounds. It occurred to me in that moment, as well, that I did not care if Leonardo now lay feverish in his bed from his injuries, with no one to bind them or to see to his comfort.

For, sometime during that hot storm of my tears, the small, shattered bits that remained of my heart had hardened toward him. After all, it had been by his design that Caterina had come to the tower, when he'd sworn she would not. Had he not changed his mind, none of this would have happened.

Had he not interfered, Gregorio would still be alive.

The next day, I borrowed a simple gown from Luigi's collection and set off for the castle. Esta, Isabella, and Rosetta were gathered in the contessa's outer chamber weeping when I slipped past the door. They greeted me with cries of relief, for they had feared from my absence that I might have perished in the fire, as well. Though the tower was constructed in such a way that the raging flames had never made it beyond the one large room, everything within had been consumed.

I had waved off their questions, too exhausted in body and spirit to concoct a tale to explain all. Instead, I gathered my few belongings and then bade them farewell.

"I must return to my family," I had told them. *"I cannot bear to remain here at the castle, now that the contessa is gone."* They nodded their understanding and did not try to stop me, for which I was grateful. But as I started toward the door, a small tug upon my skirt had made me pause.

I looked down to see Pio. He wore no embroidered collar now, and his whip of a tail, which usually wagged with joy, was tucked low between his long legs. His liquid dark eyes gazed up at me, worried and puzzled.

"He knows something is wrong," Esta had said with a small sob. *"He waits for her, not knowing she will never return."* I had nodded; then, recalling my promise to Caterina, I'd softly called for him to follow me.

Pio padding despondently at my heels, I returned to Luigi's shop. He made no mention of my small companion but merely sat me at his worktable and with his sharp scissors began my transformation back to Dino.

Later, when my hair was once more boyishly cropped and I had resumed my apprentice's brown tunic and green trunk hose, he sternly addressed me.

"Your master came looking for you this morning, though

he had no business wandering about. He has been gravely injured, though he managed to stitch himself together again with fair skill and should keep full use of both limbs. Why did you not tell me of this?"

"Leonardo can take care of himself," I coolly replied, feeding Pio a small sliver of meat I had begged from the kitchen as I left the castle.

Luigi's frown deepened. "Ungrateful child, do you not care that your master has suffered harm? You should have returned to his workshop to care for him. At the very least, you should have gone there to let him know you are well."

But I am not well, a frightened voice inside me cried. *And I fear I might never be well again.*

Aloud, I simply said, "You are right, Luigi. I will go talk to him and see how he progresses."

Pio at my heels, I made my way back to the castle a second time this day, keeping my gaze low so that I would not have to look upon those fearsome towers that had been the site of such evil. This time as I passed the gates, I saw the square-faced mercenary with the blond mustaches addressing another man.

He was dressed differently, his black leather jerkin and parti-colored red and black trunk hose similar to the garb that Gregorio had always worn. I wondered without much interest if he'd earned a promotion in the wake of what had happened.

I was relieved to find the main workshop empty, with the apprentices likely off at work upon the fresco. Had they been about, I would have been peppered with their many questions, to which I knew I would have no answers.

The door to Leonardo's personal workshop was open. I could see him seated at his table, bent over yet another sketch. I noted dispassionately that his face appeared pale, while hot color burned high upon either cheek. His wounds must have caused him a fever; indeed, he should be resting in his bed and attended to by one of his apprentices.

But not by me. Let Constantin or one of the others minister to him, for I surely will not.

Those unworthy thoughts held me a moment in the doorway, uncertain now of what I wanted to say to him. Pio had no such doubts, however, but gave a gleeful little yelp as he bounded inside and jumped into Leonardo's lap.

His leg where Gregorio's sword had cut him was neatly bandaged, and I saw his grimace as the small hound inadvertently stepped upon tender flesh. Just as quickly, he grinned, seemingly well pleased by this unexpected visitor.

"Pio," he softly exclaimed, scratching the hound behind his sleek ears. "I had wondered how you fared." Then, realizing that the dog would not have come to him unaccompanied, he looked up to meet my cool gaze.

"Dino," he said in equal delight, stiffly rising from his chair and setting Pio upon his nearby cot.

Limping toward me, he went on. "Did Luigi tell you I came looking for you earlier this day? I knew you would be safe in his care, but I did not wish to abandon you for long, given these tragic events. It is well you have returned, for there is much we need discuss."

He must have seen some of my thoughts in my expression, for he trailed off abruptly and stared at me in some concern. "Come, my boy," he urged. "Seat yourself with me."

"I cannot."

He surveyed me in silence for a moment and then slowly nodded. "Very well, if that is your preference," he replied. "Though perhaps you will not object if I take my chair again. I fear that standing is still somewhat painful."

Far less painful than death, I hotly thought, though I managed to control my tongue and not say such scathing things aloud. But my resolve lasted only a moment. Barely had he seated himself again than I burst out, "Why did you do it? Why did you allow Caterina to come to the tower, after you said you would not?"

"It is as I said then," he replied with a sorrowful look at

me. "I knew she would not believe the truth unless she heard it from the captain himself. I could not know that matters would resolve themselves in so tragic a manner. I merely thought that was the best course of action."

"Yes, you always think you know what is best, Leonardo!"

My words ringing through the small chamber, I met his gaze with my own look of condemnation. He stared back at me with as much surprise as if I had slapped him across the face.

Even I was momentarily nonplussed by my retort, but now the flood was unleashed. Unable to stop the words from spilling out, I cried, "I have always believed you to know all, and you have never disabused me of that thought. Indeed, you take pains to let everyone know that the great Leonardo is far cleverer than any other man in Milan, perhaps in the whole world. But the truth is that you know nothing more than the rest of us mere mortals . . . and sometimes, you know far less!"

"I have already told you that I erred in this matter," he replied, his frown puzzled. "I would undo those last moments if I could . . . do you not think I would? Believe me that I mourn Caterina as deeply as do you."

"How can you?" I asked with a contemptuous shake of my head. "To mourn, you must first know how to love. Indeed, I do not think you can do either."

Anger flashed over his face now, and he half rose in his chair. "Mind your words, Dino," he warned, "for I shall have no such disrespect. You are still my apprentice, and—"

"I am not your apprentice any longer!"

Swiftly, I stripped off my brown tunic, so that I stood only in my shirt and trunk hose. Tossing the garment at his feet, I cried, "Find another apprentice to do your bidding, to spy for you and follow you about in the night. I cannot bear to look upon you ever again."

Not waiting for his reply, I swiftly called to Pio, "Come." Then, when the small hound remained unmoving upon his soft perch, I cried, "Fine! Stay with him, you traitorous hound, for I shall not!"

Half-blinded by my tears, I fled his workshop, running across the courtyard to the main gate. Pausing but an instant there for the guards to let me by, I did not stop running again until I had reached Luigi's shop.

The tailor looked up from his workbench in surprise, his small dark eyes promptly taking in my half-dressed state. Dashing the remaining tears from my eyes, I told him, "I am no longer apprentice to Leonardo the Florentine."

Luigi sighed and slowly nodded. Then, awkwardly getting to his feet he said, "I have been considering taking on another apprentice. The position is yours, should you wish it."

Not trusting myself to speak, I simply nodded. He sighed again and walked over to his shelves, pulling down a small blue tunic similar to what his other apprentices wore. "I believe this should fit you," he said and handed it to me. "Put it on, and I shall make your formal introduction to my other two boys."

I settled into life at Luigi's workshop with greater ease than I'd hoped. Of course, I knew nothing of tailoring, but I could sweep a floor. Luigi taught me a few simple stitches and allowed me to practice upon worn clothing, making them over as if new. In this, my artist's eye proved an advantage, for I found I had a talent for selecting trims and colors to create a stylish robe or doublet. The other two apprentices, Giovanni and Batto, remembered me from my past visits with Leonardo and welcomed me with true pleasure. Thus, the days passed quickly.

It was only the nights that proved hard to endure. Lying in my narrow bed to the far side of the storeroom—Luigi had managed some excuse to give me a private spot behind a curtain—I would stare up into the darkness and recall what had been. And every morning I would awaken with my cheeks still damp from the tears I had shed.

By the end of my fourth week in his employ, Luigi charged me with an errand. "Here are a few florins," he said, spilling the coins into my palm along with a short list. "Go to the main square by the cathedral. Behind the fountain there is a shopkeeper who sells fine lace. Procure what is written here, and do not tarry."

"Of course, signore," I replied, ruthlessly shoving aside my memories of that particular cathedral. "I shall be back as soon as I can."

I made my way through the narrow streets, glad despite my destination for a small respite from the shop. I had not left its four walls since I arrived there, save to empty my piss pot into the street. The day was mild, and the sky above a brilliant blue unmarred by any cloud, so that for the first time since that terrible night I felt my pain ease just a bit.

Upon reaching the broad square that stretched before the cathedral, I readily spied the fountain of which Luigi spoke. It was the same marble pool into which Gregorio once had jestingly threatened to toss me, and my heart twisted just a little. But though I set my feet in its direction, somehow I found myself instead walking toward the immense cathedral, which dominated the far side of the square.

The feel of the handle beneath my hand was familiar, as was the rush of cool darkness and the sweet odor of incense that swept over me. As I had once before, I stood inside the door for a long moment to let my eyes adjust to the dimness. Then, my footsteps sounding loud in the silence, I slowly made my way up the far aisle toward the small stained glass window where Saint Michael held sway in the shadows.

Perhaps it was simply the angle of the sun, but this day the window glowed with a beauty that made my breath catch in my throat. But something else had changed about the image. Before, I had been captured by his sensual beauty and his air of ruthless determination as he wielded his sword high. Now, I saw in that beautiful glass face an air of sadness beneath the victory, as if some small part of him regretted he must serve as God's instrument of destruction.

"Ah, Saint Michael, God's own avenger," a whispery voice beside me said.

I glanced beside me to see the same ancient priest who, seemingly a lifetime ago, had discovered Gregorio and me hidden in the alcove off the transept. For a single panicked instant, I feared he recognized me . . . but of course, he did not.

And this time, no anger darkened the softly crumpled skin of his face. Instead, he was smiling slightly, his pale lips seeming to hide a secret but quite gentle amusement. Something about his smile abruptly reminded me of Leonardo. It occurred to me that he might look like this one day, soft humor on his face and sad wisdom in his eyes.

I could only nod in reply, but it seemed the priest did not expect an answer. In the same quavering voice, he went on. "Many a time I have asked for the archangel's intercession when I have seen a wrong that needed righting. He has never yet failed me."

"Then perhaps he will not fail me, either," I could not help but bitterly reply.

The priest shook his head. "My child, you must remember that Saint Michael's anger is never on his own behalf. His is a righteous fury untainted by pain and affront. Such is the only anger that can ever be justified in this life."

"But then what shall I do, Father?" I softly cried. "The anger in my heart burns so hotly that I fear it will never die."

"There is but one way to quench anger's flames, and that is with forgiveness."

He paused and put his frail hand upon my head in a gesture of benediction. "Find it in your heart to forgive," he gently said, "and you will be free of the pain that so grieves you."

I closed my eyes against the sudden tears that threatened.

When I opened them again, the priest was gone. As for the stained glass image of the archangel, its light had dulled again, so that all that gleamed was his golden sword.

A sob escaped me, and then another. And then I was running down the aisle toward cathedral's door again, each step bringing a bit more lightness to my heart.

Once out in the square again, I dashed the tears from my face and rushed to the small shop that had been my destination. Impatiently, I waited for the merchant to cut the lace. The bundle he gave me in return for my coin was heavy, but I hardly felt its weight as I ran with it back across the square and down the narrow streets until I reached Luigi's shop.

I burst through the door and, as the tailor stared at me openmouthed, I dropped the package upon his table.

"I'm sorry, signore," I said, panting with my exertions, "but I fear I must go out again."

"Indeed," he dryly replied, his thick brows shooting up into the greasy fringe of his black hair. "And may I ask where you are going in such a hurry?"

"To the castle," I gasped out. "I must talk to Leonardo."

"Then go," he said with a wave of his hand.

But I was already out the door again, running with a greater urgency than I had ever known. I did not know if the Master would even see me, let alone listen to my sincere words of contrition. And maybe it did not matter. What was important was that I had found it in my heart to forgive him . . . and perhaps, in doing so, to forgive myself.

The door to his workshop was open again, but he was not at his table. Instead, he'd set up an easel and small panel and was painting. So fixed was his attention that he did not notice me until Pio, comfortably stretched upon the Master's bed, awoke from his afternoon nap and gave a happy bark.

Leonardo glanced up, and a look of surprise flashed over his face. "Dino?" he asked, as if not quite believing what he saw before him.

I nodded, taking a moment to catch my breath. "My

apologies for disturbing you, Master," I gasped out, "but I hoped I might speak to you for a moment."

"But, of course."

Stepping from behind his easel, he started toward me. I saw in relief that his leg was no longer bandaged and that he walked with only the slightest stiffness. Neither was his arm wrapped, and the fact that he was again painting with it reassured me it, too, was healing.

Concern coloring his tone, he halted before me and asked, "What is wrong, to send you rushing here like this? Surely our friend Luigi is not—"

"Signor Luigi is fine," I hastened to assure him, earning a nod of relief from him. I hesitated, biting my lip, and then said in a rush, "I simply want to talk."

"You may sit if you wish," he said.

Once more, I shook my head at his offer, but this time it was respect and not anger that caused my refusal.

"I dare not sit before you, Master, not until I have said what I must."

When he gave me an inquiring look, I took a deep breath and went on. "I am here to offer my humble apologies for the things I said to you before we last parted. I was wrong to question you, to pretend your sorrow was less pure than mine. I cannot take back my words, and I do not expect your forgiveness, but I must still beg your pardon and tell you that I hold no anger toward you in my heart."

The words spoken, I dropped my gaze, waiting for him to curse me or at least banish me from his sight. Instead, I heard his soft sigh.

"Ah, Dino, my boy, I have long since forgiven you for what was said in the heat of anger and grief," he replied. "And I fear I was the cause of much of my own anger, for you only spoke the truth."

"No!" I protested, gazing up at him again. "Your wisdom far surpasses mine, and you do nothing without good cause."

"But I am as prone as any man to be wrong in my judgment, and sometimes I am too eager to forget that." He smiled gently and reached a hand toward me, lightly placing it upon my head in the same gesture as had the old priest. "You are young, but you have a wisdom of your own that I ignore at my peril."

"Dino!"

The cry from the door was a familiar one. I turned to see Vittorio standing at the threshold, his face aglow. Before I could say anything, he rushed toward me and hugged me in a fierce embrace that almost took me from my feet.

"Dino," he cried again, "I feared I would never see you again. I have missed you so, as have all the other apprentices. It is not the same here without you. You must tell me that you are back again for good!"

I glanced back at the Master, who beamed and nodded. Turning again to the boy, I felt the first smile I had known since that terrible night slowly flicker across my face.

"Yes, Vittorio," I firmly said. "I am back for good."

His resulting cheer sent Pio springing from his bed to prance in happy circles. "I knew it! Now I must go tell the others," he cried.

Grinning broadly, the boy rushed from the room again. Still smiling, I turned again to Leonardo, only to see that he was rummaging in a small chest beside the bed. A moment later, he had pulled forth a familiar brown tunic, which he tossed to me. "I believe this is yours, my boy. I only trust that the good tailor Luigi will not be too angry that I have stolen away his new apprentice."

Then, seeing that my gaze had turned toward the easel, he added, "Would you care to see my latest painting?"

I started to nod, only to feel my smile slip. "It-it's not of Caterina?" I asked, knowing it would be some time before I could bear to look upon that portrait of her.

Leonardo shook his head. "The painting I did for Ludovico is hanging in some back hall along with countless other portraits of his various relatives."

At my questioning look, he confirmed, "As far as Il Moro

or anyone else knows, Caterina was the conte's true daughter, and the fire in the tower but an accident. As for the captain of the guard, he died in a valiant yet failed attempt to save her from the fire."

I swallowed against the sudden lump in my throat, grateful that the reputation of both had been spared yet wanting to know no more. Instead, I nodded in the direction of the easel. "Yes, please, may I see it?"

With a small smile, he grandly gestured me to step behind the panel for a look. I needed but a single glance before I gasped and stared back at him. "Why, it is a portrait of me . . . or, rather, of Delfina."

For the face staring back at me from the half-finished portrait could be none other than my own. Yet in some ways it was not a face I recognized. Surely that strong yet pensive gaze that my painted self turned toward the viewer was not mine. The gown, however, was familiar . . . the deep red gown that had once been Caterina's and which she had insisted I wear when my own gown had been ruined.

Leonardo shrugged a little. "The day that you sat beside the contessa as I painted, I could not help but be struck by some expression in your eyes that struck a strange chord in my heart. I made a few sketches and put them aside. Then, a few days ago, I came across them again and decided you would make a fine subject for me."

"But what if someone recognizes me in this woman?" I asked in some alarm.

"Fear not, my boy," he said with a small laugh. "As you can see, I have changed her eyes to amber instead of green, and her hair is lighter than yours. I shall simply call it *Portrait of a Lady*, and no one will ever be the wiser."

I nodded, and then gave a sigh. "Well, I should return to Signor Luigi and break the news of my departure," I said with a small smile. "I am sure he will be glad to see the back of me, as he claims I cannot sew a straight stitch."

"Send the good tailor my apologies," he said with an

answering grin. "And hurry back. If I recall correctly, you have three weeks ahead of you stirring the gesso pot before you will be allowed to pick up a brush again."

But Luigi appeared less distressed by my departure than I had feared . . . or hoped. "Bah, you are Leonardo's problem again," he said, waving me away, though I heard no rancor in his voice. And he did not protest when I gave him a grateful hug before setting aside my blue tunic and picking up my sack with all my worldly belongings.

The main workshop was still empty when I returned, giving me a small respite before my reunion with my fellows. Soon enough, they would be returning for the late-afternoon meal. In the meantime, I had some time to myself as I unpacked my sack and stowed away my few clothes and goods in the chest at the foot of my old bed.

The last item I pulled forth was my notebook. I could barely remember the last time I had written in it; neither could I yet bear to read its pages, filled as they were with memories still too fragile to examine. But as I went to tuck it away, four large cards fluttered from the book's pages, their gilded faces catching the light.

Closing the chest upon my notebook, I carried the pasteboard cards with me into the main workshop and knelt before the small fire burning in the hearth. The originals had been consumed in that terrible fire, leaving Caterina's deck incomplete. Perhaps I should find a way to reunite the copies with the remaining cards, so that set was whole once more.

Staring down at the small works of art, I made my decision. The original four cards had left nothing but tragedy in their wake. Just as fire had taken them, so should fire take the ones that would replace them.

One by one, I tossed the cards upon the fire, watching as each was consumed in a colorful flare of light. I lingered a moment over the last card . . . the triumph of Fire, with its ruined tower and falling men. Had it been but a coincidence, I wondered, or had the cards known what was to come and had tried to warn us all?

Sadly, it no longer mattered.

I closed my eyes for a moment against the memories and then slowly opened them again. One last tear for Caterina and Gregorio trickled hotly down my cheek . . . one last tear for all that had been and for all that never would be. Then, with a sigh, I tossed the final card into the flames.

AUTHOR'S NOTE

One defining characteristic of the species human is our pre-occupation with the future. Not content to accept things as they happen, we crave a glimpse of what is to be, lest we are caught unawares when danger, illness, or other misfortune comes to call. But seeing beyond the moment requires that fabled sixth sense that most of us lack; thus we've assigned certain inanimate objects with the power to look into the future for us. And so it is by the toss of common objects such as stones or sticks or bones that we attempt to acquire knowledge that otherwise would have been beyond our reach.

Tarot cards are one such popular tool of divination, though most scholars of the mystical arts now agree they were not originally meant for fortune-telling. Instead, the first decks, which may have made an appearance as early as the fourteenth century, were used to play the Italian card game known as trionfi (triumphs) and, later, as tarocchi. Similar to modern trick-taking games like hearts or spades, tarocchi employed a deck that was the precursor of our tra-ditional playing cards, though with four slightly different suits: swords, staves, coins, and cups. Around Leonardo's time, a fifth suit of twenty-two separate triumphs, or trump cards, was added to the mix.

Each triumph was different, and they included such

representations as the Magician, the Chariot, and Temperance. Those figures were firmly based in religious and classical symbolism, and represented a hero's journey of sorts . . . a popular motif that would have been quite familiar to the people of the time. But by the mid–sixteenth century, the triumphs had morphed into something a bit more esoteric. No longer were they the iconic images of the Church past; instead, they had begun to take on more modern—and slightly darker—meanings. And by the eighteenth century, the tarot deck had become a common tool of those who walked the arcane path, its devotees interpreting random cards' symbolism in order to divine the hidden present or else to speak of things to come.

It was while I was doing research for *The Queen's Gambit* that I stumbled across the mention of a particular tarocchi deck from the mid-fifteenth century. It was painted by then court artist Bonifacio Bembo for the noble Visconti and Sforza families of Milan, and it has survived (though sadly tattered) into modern times. Unfortunately, the deck is not complete. Four cards are missing from it: the Three of Swords, the Knight of Pentacles, the Devil, and the Tower.

What happened to those four cards, no one knows. It is suggested that the two missing triumphs, the Devil and the Tower, were not even part of the original deck . . . that those two particular images were added much later. But the small mystery of the four vanished cards made for an interesting bit of speculation, and it was the jumping-off point for this book. For, if anyone could learn what became of those cards, I was certain that it would be Leonardo and Dino!

Further notes and disclaimers. While I've tried to remain as true as possible to Leonardo's time period, I have once again taken a bit of artistic license here and there with people and places for the purpose of my story. So if you visit Ludovico's magnificent castle—in particular, its battlements and towers—and the glorious cathedral that is the Duomo, don't expect to find the same hidden passages and darkened alcoves that Dino stumbles across. Just like most of Leonardo's grand inventions, they exist only upon paper.